PENGUIN BOOKS

T0359164

The Secret Years

A former English teacher, Barbara Hannay is a city-bred girl with a yen for country life. Many of her forty-plus books are set in rural and outback Australia and have been enjoyed by readers around the world. She has won the RITA, awarded by Romance Writers of America, and has twice won the Romantic Book of the Year award in Australia. In her own version of life imitating art, Barbara and her husband currently live on a misty hillside in beautiful Far North Queensland where they keep heritage pigs and chickens and an untidy but productive garden.

barbarahannay.com

PRAISE FOR BARBARA HANNAY'S BESTSELLERS

'It's a pleasure to follow an author who gets better
with every book. Barbara Hannay delights with this
cross-generational love story, which is terrifically
romantic and full of surprises.'
APPLE IBOOKS, 'BEST BOOKS OF THE MONTH'

'Barbara Hannay has delivered another wonderful
book . . . For me no one does emotional punch
quite like Barbara Hannay.'
HELENE YOUNG

'Gripping tale of outback romance . . . Her
most epic novel to date.'
QUEENSLAND COUNTRY LIFE

'Lovers of romance will enjoy this feel-good
read. Hannay captures the romantic spirit of
the outback perfectly.'
TOWNSVILLE BULLETIN

'Get your hands on a copy of this book
and you will not be disappointed.'
WEEKLY TIMES

BARBARA HANNAY

The Secret Years

PENGUIN BOOKS

PENGUIN BOOKS

UK | USA | Canada | Ireland | Australia
India | New Zealand | South Africa | China

Penguin Books is part of the Penguin Random House group of companies
whose addresses can be found at global.penguinrandomhouse.com.

Penguin
Random House
Australia

First published by Penguin Group (Australia), 2015
This edition published by Penguin Random House Australia Pty Ltd, 2016

10 9 8 7 6 5 4 3 2 1

Cover design by Debra Billson and Grace West © Penguin Group (Australia)
Text design by Grace West © Penguin Group (Australia)
Cover photographs: Girl by Jessica Truscott/Trevillion Images
Sunset by Megan R. Hoover/Shutterstock
Typeset in Sabon by Penguin Group (Australia)
Colour separation by Splitting Image Colour Studio, Clayton, Victoria
Printed and bound in Australia by Griffin Press, an accredited ISO AS/NZS
14001 Environmental Management Systems printer

National Library of Australia
Cataloguing-in-Publication data:

Hannay, Barbara, author.
The secret years / Barbara Hannay.
9780143573203 (paperback)
Family secrets—Australia—Fiction.
Love stories, Australian.

A823.3

penguin.com.au

MIX
Paper from
responsible sources
FSC® C009448

For my special writing friends,
thanks for your wisdom and your cheerfulness
and for always understanding

PROLOGUE

North Queensland, 1963

The Englishwoman arrived at Kalkadoon on a hot and sultry summer's afternoon when even the crows were silent and the creaky old windmill was deathly still.

Rosie was hanging upside down from her favourite branch in a shady bottlebrush tree, but it was Dougie, beside her, who first saw the cloud of dust on the horizon.

'Car comin',' he remarked with a resigned lack of interest.

They both knew that visitors who ventured out to Kalkadoon Station only ever came to see Rosie's father, the Boss.

Hanging there together, their skinny knees gripping the tree branch, the children stared through the thin fringe of leaves, out across the shimmering stretch of flat dry paddocks, watching with idle curiosity as the dust cloud grew gradually bigger.

'Wonder who it is?' Rosie mused, although she knew it had to be a neighbour or someone bringing supplies from Cloncurry.

Then Shirleen's voice cut the lazy afternoon stillness. '*Rosieee!*' she yelled from the homestead. 'Come here, quick!'

'You better go,' Dougie said.

Rosie pouted. Why did she have to go? Visitors never came to see her.

'Come on. Hurry up,' called Shirleen. 'You got a visitor and your dad'll skin me alive if I don't get you ready.'

Rosie might not have moved if she hadn't also heard horses' hooves drumming across the hard ground. That would be her father riding back to the homestead. Maybe he'd seen the dust, too. Maybe these visitors were important after all.

'Don't make me come out there and get you, Missy.'

Reluctantly, Rosie wriggled her knees free from the branch and swung down. It had taken her ages to learn how to do this as easily as Dougie could, but she was quite the little acrobat now. Letting go with her hands, she dropped the last bit to the ground, her bare feet landing in dust softened by many similar landings.

Dougie was still hanging like a fruit bat, his white teeth grinning in his dark face. Even though Shirleen was his mum, not Rosie's, he didn't have to stop playing because of visitors. As far as Rosie knew, he never had to bother about getting tidy.

'See ya,' he said sympathetically.

Rosie shrugged. 'See ya.'

Shirleen met her at the foot of the homestead steps and grabbed her arm. 'Come on.' Her tone was urgent, but not unkind. 'No dragging your feet today.'

A glance beyond the homestead showed Rosie's father, riding his horse hard.

'Who's coming?' Rosie wanted to know.

Shirleen bustled her inside and dragged her T-shirt over her head. 'Don't pester me with questions. Just get here.' Already she was yanking Rosie's shorts down. 'I shoulda called you in earlier. Come on, quick, get these off. Then we got to get your shoes on.'

'But my feet are dirty.'

'Too bad. There's no time for gettin' clean.' Shirleen was already kneeling beside Rosie, pushing her dusty feet into clean white socks and then into her best black patent leather shoes. The shoes were newish but Rosie hadn't worn them for a while, and when Shirleen did up the buckles, they already felt too tight.

Shirleen sprang to her feet again and reached for Rosie's best dress, hanging on the back of a kitchen chair.

'I can't wear that!' the little girl cried. 'Not without having a bath.'

The dress had come all the way from a store in Townsville and was a lovely pale-lemon voile with white daisies on the collar and a full skirt that was held out by a stiff net petticoat. She hadn't worn it since Christmas.

Now, without comment, Shirleen lowered the dress over Rosie's head. It felt uncomfortably clean and crisp against her hot, sticky skin.

'Now, hold still. I gotta do up your sash, then brush your hair.'

Rosie winced. 'Can you wet my hair first?' It was long and curly and she hated having it brushed.

'I told you. We don't have time.'

'Ouch,' the child wailed as the brush was dragged mercilessly through the knots.

'Sorry, darlin'.' Shirleen sounded sympathetic, but she didn't slow down.

Rosie might have yelped louder, but she heard her father's voice outside.

'Shirleen,' he called. 'That damn woman's come early. She's bloody well almost here. Where's Rosie?'

'Up here, Boss. Almost ready.'

'Who's coming?' Rosie demanded again. Then she heard her father's boots on the steps. 'Who's the visitor?'

'Someone from England,' Shirleen muttered between dragging strokes of the brush.

England? But that was where the Queen lived, far away on the other side of the world. At Christmas, Rosie had received a parcel from England, a lovely storybook about Christopher Robin and Winnie-the-Pooh, and her father had read it to her so many times she almost knew every word by heart.

Someone in England – Rosie couldn't remember her name – had also sent a jigsaw puzzle with a picture of a girl and boy riding ponies. The first time Rosie had done the puzzle, Shirleen had helped her to find the bits that fitted together, but now she could do it on her own, sitting at the kitchen table with all the pieces spread out. She never tired of seeing the images emerge of the rosy-cheeked pair on their beautiful, shiny horses. Shirleen had told her their names were Prince Charles and Princess Anne.

But Rosie was just fascinated by the grass where the children played. So lush and green, not the colour of pale biscuits like Kalkadoon's grass – and it was soft looking, like the velvet inside the jewellery box that had once belonged to Rosie's mother.

The intricately woven metal box was precious, the only thing of her mother's that she owned, and she loved it fiercely.

Now the growl of a motor in the distance signalled that the car was almost here. A shadow fell as Rosie's father stepped into the kitchen. Without a word, he flipped his broadbrimmed hat onto a hook by the door, took one sharp glance in Rosie's direction, gave a curt nod of approval, then strode straight to the sink to wash his hands and face.

That done, he flicked his damp dark hair out of his eyes, then crossed the room to Rosie. He was tall and big and the kitchen always felt smaller when he came inside. Smaller but somehow safer.

Shirleen retreated to the stove to check on a pot of simmering corned beef. 'I'll go now, Boss?' Her dark eyes were big and round, as if she was worried.

Rosie's father nodded. 'Thank you.'

Rosie didn't understand the sudden tension that had descended, but now that she and her father were alone, she could feel it growing stronger, filling the kitchen in the same way the room had once filled with smoke when Shirleen burned their dinner. The rumble of the car's engine drew closer and her father took her hand.

She loved the feel of his strong hand wrapped warmly around hers and she wanted to ask questions, but the stern look on his handsome face silenced her.

'Don't worry,' he said, his hand tightening around hers. 'I'll deal with this. Everything will be all right.'

Completely bewildered, Rosie stood very still beside him, trying to ignore the way her dress itched against her sweaty skin. Through the open front doorway, she could see the car that had come all the way from England and was now bumping up the track to the homestead.

Her father's grip was so tight now, he was almost hurting her. When the car came to a stop at the bottom of the front steps, Rosie saw the stern profile of a man at the wheel. Two ladies sat in the back and the man got out and opened a back door for them.

Still sensing her father's tension, Rosie held her breath as the first lady emerged. She was wearing a black hat, a silly hat that didn't shade her face and would be of no use to her at all here at Kalkadoon. It was more like an upside-down flowerpot, but it did look smart. The lady's jacket and skirt were smart, too – pink and tight-fitting with a black trim and buttons – so different from the faded, loose cotton shifts that Shirleen wore.

Their visitor stood very stiffly with no hint of a smile on her painted lips. She was wearing dark sunglasses that didn't quite hide the pale prettiness of her face and she wore gloves, too, black gloves that reached up to her elbows. Her shoes had very high heels. Rosie had never seen anyone quite like her.

'It's okay, Rosie,' her father said now in the gentle, soothing way she'd heard him use with a frightened horse. But even though his voice was soft and calm, he was watching the Englishwoman with a face as hard as stone and he gripped Rosie so fiercely that she almost cried out.

'It's okay,' he said again. 'You're not going anywhere. She can't have you. I won't let her. You're staying here, safe with me.'

1

The plane dipped to the right, offering a view of Magnetic Island, dark green and hilly as it floated in an unwrinkled silver sea. Then Townsville came into view and Lucy felt a familiar pang when she saw Castle Hill's craggy profile and the ever-growing cluster of city buildings at its base.

Home. A crosshatching of sun-bleached streets splashed with the brilliant red and green of poincianas, heralds of summer and Christmas time in the north.

And yet this time, coming home was different.

To begin with, there would be no return to Afghanistan and Lucy still hadn't totally wrapped her head around the fact that her deployment was finally over. The monotony of her old desk job in Townsville loomed.

Worse, her beloved grandfather was seriously ill. Harry-pa she'd called him when she first learned to talk, although as an adult she'd shortened it to Harry – and now he'd been diagnosed with kidney failure. At ninety plus, he'd been told he was too old for transplants or dialysis and after several weeks in hospital, he'd been sent home to his little worker's cottage, half-hidden behind ancient frangipani trees in Railway Estate, where the Blue Care nurses would call daily.

Lucy was disappointed that her mother hadn't taken Harry home to Mango Avenue, although there'd always been tensions between her mother and her grandfather – maddening tensions that she'd never properly understood – and she had to admit Harry loved his independence.

She wondered how much time he had, but it was a question that brought her close to tears as the plane touched down and went into rapid deceleration. This was no time to be maudlin, not when seat-belts were snapping and her fellow soldiers were scrambling to their feet and exchanging happy grins. An air of excitement filled the cabin now. Just a few metres away, inside the terminal, their loved ones were waiting to welcome them.

Lucy was safely home at last – for good – and getting married to Sam.

A sweet little diamond sparkled on her finger and her thoughts were all about Sam as she collected her slouch hat and small back-pack from the overhead locker. Beside her, Kaz, her best friend, was reading a message on her phone and her face broke into a huge, blushing grin.

'Idiot,' Kaz told the phone with a laughing roll of her eyes, and Lucy knew she was grinning over a risqué message from her boyfriend.

She totally understood how Kaz felt. She'd experienced that drunken state of besottedness herself.

'You'll have the best Christmas,' she told Kaz as they impatiently filed down the plane's narrow aisle.

'Yeah, I know.' Kaz shot Lucy a mock scowl. 'But I still haven't forgiven you for pulling out of our London trip.'

The girls had been planning to spend Christmas in England, but that was before Sam had surprised Lucy by popping the question out of the blue.

She hastily checked her phone, hoping to find a message from Sam. There wasn't one, but it was silly to feel disappointed. She knew he was waiting inside the terminal. She could picture him standing in the expectant crowd or, perhaps, just a little to one side. He wasn't especially tall or rugged, but he was totally gorgeous with his sparkling blue eyes and suntan, his light brown hair cut short and spiky. As soon as he saw her, his face would light up and he'd send her that special grin of his. He would hurry towards her, no doubt knocking her hat sideways when he swept her off her feet.

In the arrivals lounge, the crowd was even bigger than usual and there were cameras flashing as, one by one, Lucy's comrades were enveloped in welcoming arms. Laughter and excitement bubbled and echoed all around her. A television cameraman zoomed in as a couple hugged, and zoomed again as children squealed, 'Hey, Dad! Daddy! Look, Mummy, there he is!'

A battle-hardened sergeant, who'd been christened the Ice Man in Tarin Kowt, had glistening damp eyes when a round-faced woman presented him with a chubby, bouncing baby boy.

Lucy kept her happy smile tightly in place as she scanned the crowd. Sam would be here somewhere. Any second now she would catch sight of him. She just had to be patient.

'Lucy, darling!'

Spinning towards the familiar voice, Lucy was astonished to see her mum, auburn-tinted curls damp from the heat, and wearing a rather youthful white, cinch-waisted cotton dress with an off-the-shoulder frill. Her mother looked plump and flushed and just a little self-conscious as she held out her bare arms.

'Mum, what a lovely surprise.' They kissed cheeks and hugged.

'I'm so glad I made it on time.' Her mother sounded a tad breathless and her smile was almost awkward. 'You know me, always running late, but by some miracle the lights were on my side and I had a good run.'

'That's wonderful. It's so good to see you.' Lucy meant it. She was truly touched that her normally scatter-brained mum had not only remembered the date and the time of her arrival, but had got herself organised to be here. 'How are you?'

'Fine, Luce.' She fanned herself with her hand, making her silver bracelets rattle. 'Apart from these damned hot flushes. How are *you*?'

'Great. How's Harry?'

'Oh, he seems fine to me.'

Lucy didn't miss the slight tightening of her mother's jaw, a sure sign that her tensions with Harry hadn't eased. Damn, surely those two could make up now, when the poor old guy was in danger of dying?

She switched her focus to scan the sea of people. 'Have you seen Sam?'

'Ah, no.' Her mum said this quickly, almost nervously. 'But he phoned me. He was *really* sorry that he couldn't be here, love.'

Not here? Lucy's insides plummeted the way they had the first time she'd gone down the fast-rope.

'He said he had a terribly important commitment and he just couldn't get away.'

'Oh?' Lucy struggled to squash her disappointment. Of course, it was possible that Sam had a more important call on his time. His army PR job kept him busy: escorting VIPs, writing speeches for the brigadier and other senior officers, organising open days at the base, liaising with the council for welcome home parades. And those tasks came on top of his routine job of promoting or defending the army's image in the press.

Lucy loved that Sam's work was very different and yet closely connected to hers. The combo was just about perfect as far as she was concerned, but she'd been dreaming of his welcome, of having his arms around her at last. His hungry lips on hers. Her beautiful charmer would look so damn hot in his dress uniform she would no doubt want to jump him then and there.

'Did he say when he'll be free?'

Her mum frowned, looked guilty. 'Sorry, love. I'm not sure if I asked him that.'

Swallowing a need to sigh, Lucy lifted her shoulders in a deliberately casual shrug. 'Oh, well.' She checked her phone again, just to make sure she hadn't missed a message. 'I dare say he'll ring soon.'

Kaz and Callum had already disappeared and the others were now absorbed into happy family groups. Lucy collected her gear and went out into the blinding tropical sunshine where she crammed everything into the boot of her mum's tiny, bright-purple Hyundai. To her surprise, when they left the airport they headed through Belgian Gardens, which was the wrong direction, surely.

She might have said something but her phone pinged, making her heart leap. A message from Sam at last.

Welcome home! So sorry I couldn't make it. C U tonight?!!! xxx

It was a huge relief to hear from him, but somehow his message didn't cheer Lucy quite as much as she would have liked. Silly, because she knew that she was never completely relaxed about Sam until she actually saw him again, until she looked into his eyes and they talked and touched and made love. And she knew that despite the wonders of email and the internet, most defence-force couples had similar experiences after being separated for months. Readjustment always took a little time and patience.

She sent him a reply. *Can't wait to see you. Love you. xxx*

Actually, it was probably a good thing that Sam couldn't meet her now. It gave her a chance to change out of her army gear, to wash her hair and get into something feminine and sexy before their reunion.

For a moment or two Lucy mused over what she might wear and by the time she looked up from the phone, she realised that her mother had driven through Belgian Gardens and North Ward and was about to head over the crest of Denham Street into the city.

It was rather a roundabout way home, but she didn't comment until they reached the lights and her mum steered into a centre lane.

'Shouldn't you turn right here?' she suggested gently, not wanting to sound like a back-seat driver.

This was met by a surprisingly coy smile. 'Wait and see.'

'What do you mean?'

With an almost giggly shrug, her mum drove on, over the bridge that crossed Ross Creek and into South Townsville. When she turned down Palmer Street, the city's restaurant strip, Lucy frowned. 'It's a bit early for lunch, isn't it?'

'Hang on.' Her mum was grinning broadly. 'Not far to go now.'

The penny dropped, making Lucy gasp. 'You haven't bought an apartment?'

But already they were turning into a car park with tall gates that rolled open in response to her mother's swipe tag, and then they were driving beneath a massive concrete apartment block. 'Wow, Mum, why didn't you tell me?'

'I only moved in last week and I thought it would be a nice surprise.'

Lucy gulped as she absorbed this new shock. 'Does this mean you've sold Mango Avenue?'

'Yes, love, but you wait till you see this place. You'll understand why I fell in love with it.'

Lucy might have worried about how her mum had funded the move if she hadn't been concerned with her own sense of loss. She knew that a woman who'd been away on active service and was now on the brink of marriage should not hanker after the home of her girlhood, but she felt a wash of sentimental yearning.

She was remembering the bedroom she'd known all her life with floor-to-ceiling shelves crammed with her favourite books, green shag-pile rugs on the scratched timber floor, and a view out the window into the shady branches of an enormous African rain tree.

Now – the house might as well have been destroyed by a bomb. It felt weird that she would never see inside it again.

At least her army training had taught her to adapt and, anyway, she would soon be living with Sam. Flashing a smile to match her mother's, Lucy hefted her weighty pack from the boot and they headed for the lift. She could sense her mum's barely contained excitement and she kept the smile in place as the lift rose to the eighth floor.

For one crazy moment, as her mother hurried ahead down a blue-tiled corridor, sorting through keys, Lucy wondered if this was something she and Sam had cooked up between them. Would he actually be waiting inside the apartment?

Her mother, unlocking the door of No. 67, sent a beaming smile back to her. 'Come and see.'

Sam was not inside. Well, Lucy hadn't really expected it, had she? But the apartment was indeed stunning. Very white, very new and gleaming, and very spacious, with sleek, pale granite benchtops in the kitchen and sliding shutters in the living room that revealed stunning views down the sweep of the river, right to its mouth and out to the sparkling sea.

'Wow!' Lucy couldn't help but be impressed, although she felt rather out of place in her battle dress and heavy boots amidst all the pristine newness. She wasn't sure if she should set her dusty pack on the floor and she looked back to make sure she hadn't left dirty marks on the shining white tiles. 'So all the furniture's brand new, too,' she couldn't help commenting as she looked around her at pale green leather lounges, a glass dining table with stylishly slim white chairs.

'The old stuff would have looked too shabby here.'

'I guess . . . but have you saved anything from home?'

'Not any of the furniture, love. It's all gone to St Vinnies and that second hand place at Rising Sun.' Her mother looked worried. 'Why? Did you want something?'

Lucy shrugged. *A bit late to ask that now, Mother dearest.*

'Well, hello, there,' boomed a masculine voice and Lucy whirled round to find a strange man coming out of what looked like the main bedroom. Beefy, red-faced, with faded ginger hair turning white, the man wore a navy and green striped polo shirt and chinos. He looked super-relaxed and at home and he smiled extravagantly as he extended a solid, freckled hand to Lucy.

Oh, Mum, not another one.

Lucy almost groaned aloud. This was one surprise too many. Damn it, how many men was it now? Four? No, this must be the fifth guy who'd moved in with her mother since she'd divorced Lucy's dad when Lucy was in preschool.

'Lucy, this is Keith Hayes,' her mother said almost defensively, and she gave his elbow a proprietary pat.

'Hey, there. Pleased to meet you.' Keith pumped Lucy's hand vigorously. 'Ro's told me so much about you —' He glanced quickly at the pips on Lucy's shoulder. 'Captain Hunter,' he added and he gave her a playful salute.

'Hi, Keith.' *I've heard zilch about you.*

For her mum's sake, Lucy tried to crack a warmish smile. She knew how desperate her mother was to have a solid, lasting relationship. All they had left of Lucy's father was his surname, and she was unhappily familiar with the pattern of her mum's repeated failures. Things usually started off well with each new man, sometimes *really* well. Lucy could remember some fabulous holidays in the early months of her mum's new romances, but eventually the new man became a huge disappointment. When it came to relationships, her mother seemed to have a knack for making bad choices, but Lucy had never really pinned down why.

'I'll put the kettle on,' her mum said now, her hands fluttering nervously. 'And I've bought scones. Date scones from Woolies, Luce, your favourite. I'll just pop them in the microwave. We can have them on the balcony and enjoy the view.'

'Sure, sounds great. Where should I stow my gear?'

'Oh, sorry, love. Your room's through here.'

Lucy crossed to the doorway indicated and found a room with off-white walls and thick beige carpet, plain beige vertical blinds on the windows, and a wall of sliding mirrored doors. The double bed was covered by a quilted bedspread in champagne and cream.

It was all so . . . tasteful and *bland*. So different from the bright tropical corals and teals and the cheerful yellows of their old place on Mango Avenue, and a world away from the four-to-a-room shipping container that had been Lucy's 'private' space in Tarin Kowt.

She saw her reflection in the mirror – her heavy pack, her long dark hair scraped back from her face and pulled tightly into a bun, her camouflage-patterned combat gear and boots. Mere days ago, her world had been grey desert and dry wind, the rattle of helicopters and regular bursts of distant gunfire. Today, white-and-cream-carpeted luxury, mirrored glass and views of an aquamarine sea.

Tentatively, she set down her pack in a carpeted corner and slid open one of the wardrobe doors. The space was filled with piles of cardboard cartons and on the sides were labels scrawled in marker pen: *Lucy's books, Lucy's CDs, Lucy's winter clothes, Lucy's photo albums*.

Her whole life had been put into boxes. Yet another weird experience. So far, nothing about her homecoming had lived up to her expectations.

She felt suddenly exhausted. Her deployment had been a long six months of hard, hard work with sixteen to eighteen hour days and no time off. Now, all she wanted was to drag off her boots and belt, hurl herself onto the immaculate bedspread and sleep till it was night-time, till she could go to Sam.

'Coffee and scones are ready.' Her mum was in the doorway, watching her with an anxious smile. 'I didn't think there was much point in unpacking your gear, love. I mean, you're getting married, so I wasn't sure —'

'No, no, that's fine. You're right. It probably wouldn't be worth it.'

Lucy had agreed with Sam that it was sensible to wait till the end of her deployment before setting a date for their wedding. They hadn't moved in together yet, but that would be the next step. No doubt Sam would want to discuss it tonight. 'I'll just wash my hands and join you,' she said.

'You have your own bathroom.' Her mum pointed to another doorway.

'Oh, lovely, thanks.' Lucy was sliding the wardrobe door closed, when she noticed a smaller carton on a shelf with the word *Dad* scrawled on the side. She frowned. 'What's this, Mum?'

'Oh.' Her mum gave a dismissive wave of her hand. 'Just some of your grandfather's things. From his war days, I think.'

'Medals?'

'I guess. Medals, photos, a couple of letters. He went into a flap when he had to go into hospital and he wanted me to keep them safe for him. I've been so busy with the move I haven't got around to taking them back to his place yet.'

'I can do that. I want to see him as soon as I can. Maybe I should give him a call?'

'Sure, but not now, Lucy. Come on. We don't want the scones to go cold.'

2

Afternoon shadows stretched across the room. Lucy had slept for a couple of hours and then soaked in the bath, washed her hair and shaved her legs. She'd applied lotions to her skin, adding extra layers of balm to her lips, since they'd become quite chapped in the unforgiving Afghan winter.

Now, changed into a pair of hip-hugging floral jeans and a pale-pink sleeveless top, with her dark brown hair clean and bouncing around her shoulders, she found a very different reflection in the mirror. It was weird to be back in civilian clothes after all this time, and she was pleased that she hadn't seen Sam yet. She imagined him peeling these clothes off her almost as soon as she arrived at his flat and a delicious shiver ran through her. Tonight's reunion was going to be special.

Right from the start, the chemistry with Sam had been damn near explosive, despite the French girlfriend who'd been with him when he first arrived in Townsville. He'd met Camille in Europe when he was working as the marketing and PR guy for a Formula One team. Camille had come back to Australia with Sam, first to the ACT where he'd worked on the *Canberra Times*, until the ADF had headhunted him and sent him to Queensland.

From day one in the Townsville barracks, Sam had flirted with Lucy. She had tried to ignore his so obviously cute blue eyes and beautiful smile, but he'd pursued her with a flattering doggedness – had charmed, beguiled and eventually won her – and when they finally got together, the chemistry had been breathtaking. Incendiary.

By the time she'd learned about Camille, Sam had already broken it off, assuring Lucy that she wasn't the cause. He and Camille had been heading for the rocks . . .

Since then, Sam and Lucy had come a long way. Yes, his proposal had come out of the blue, but Lucy hadn't hesitated to say yes. She'd quickly changed her plans to travel to England with Kaz during their leave. She was going to be far too busy househunting, making wedding plans, making love . . .

At times it almost seemed too good to be true, especially now, when she'd been away for so long.

Lucy shook off a niggling worry. Everything would be fine. She knew from past experience that her worries always evaporated as soon as she saw her gorgeous guy again.

Still, she had a bit of time to fill in now, and she wasn't inclined to head for the living room where Keith was watching the cricket while her mum fussed in her new, atypically tidy kitchen. She'd already rung her grandfather, so perhaps this was a good time to ring Anna Duncan. Anna would know their unit was back in town, so it was best to make contact without delay.

Lucy took a moment to compose herself. Communicating by email with the widow of one of her fellow soldiers was one thing. Actually speaking on the phone was trickier. Anna would be feeling especially low today, knowing that all Mitch's mates were safely home.

Deliberately blotting out her memory of the day Mitch had been killed, Lucy dialled.

'Hello?' piped a childish voice.

Crikey. Lucy couldn't be sure if it was male or female. 'Is that Jack?' she guessed.

'No, I'm Maddie.'

'Oh, Maddie, sorry. I didn't recognise you. You're sounding so grown up.'

'I'm free.'

'Three? Wow.'

In the background Lucy heard Anna's voice asking for the phone.

'I'm talking to a lady, Mummy.'

A beat later, Anna was on the phone. 'Hello?' she asked cautiously.

'Anna, it's Lucy Hunter.'

'Oh, Lucy, how lovely.' Her voice was instantly warmer. 'It's so good of you to call. You must have only just got in.'

'I wanted to say hello, to see how you're faring.'

'Thanks, that's thoughtful.'

It was the least she could do, Lucy thought. She was alive, after all.

'I'm keeping my head above water,' said Anna. 'And I'm so relieved that all of Mitch's mates have made it home safe and sound.'

Such a brave thing to say, but there was a shake in Anna's voice.

'We miss Mitch,' said Lucy gently, and then, because Anna didn't or couldn't respond, she went on brightly, 'Maddie's sounding very grown up.'

'Tell me about it. Little Miss Independent.'

'And how's Jack?'

'Growing faster than buffalo grass in the wet season. He's in primary school now and he's started playing soccer.'

'Fantastic! I used to be mad about junior soccer. I must come and watch him play.'

'He'd love a cheer squad. Why don't you come over for coffee some time? I'd love to see you, Lucy.'

'That would be great. I'm on leave, of course, so I'm free any time. Name the day.'

'Tuesday? Come for afternoon tea around four, after I pick up Jack from school.'

'Wonderful. See you then.'

After Lucy hung up, she considered throwing a few clothes in the wash, but she wasn't in the mood for housework. Then she remembered the box in the wardrobe with her grandfather's things.

Harry had hardly ever talked about his war experiences, not even after she'd joined the army. She'd often wondered how many of his mates had died and how he'd been affected by it.

Curious, she crossed the room and slid open the wardrobe door. The carton wasn't very big and it wasn't sealed. She lifted a flap and saw an old Arnott's biscuit tin inside.

That was all – just a black, rectangular tin with a picture of a green and red parrot holding a cracker in its claw and *Arnott's Famous Biscuits* printed in white block capitals. The tin was old and battered with a few rust spots. Lucy ran her hand over it, feeling the scratches. She was pretty sure she could remember seeing it in the past, on a shelf at the back of her grandfather's pantry.

For a moment she was back in Harry's kitchen, sitting at the old scrubbed pine table, drinking sugary tea and eating thickly sliced bread with butter and golden syrup. She could see his wrinkled, angular face and soft, white hair, the gentle love in his faded grey eyes.

Oh, Harry-pa.

It was hard to think that he might leave them soon.

Memories burned, making her throat ache. She remembered the many times as an adult when she'd sat with Harry to watch a Cowboys game on TV, munching hot chicken wings from the dodgy shop around the corner and drinking rum and coke from ancient scarred tumblers. She would have to make time to be with him now, in spite of her new life with Sam. The next few months would be precious.

Besides, she needed to debrief with Harry. No one else, not even Sam, was as keenly interested in her job in Afghanistan as her grandfather was. When she'd first joined the army, Harry had been upset, claiming he'd seen enough of war to last him ten lifetimes. But he hadn't said she was crazy, the way her mum had, and in the end he'd supported her career choice, had even told her he was proud of her.

Lucy genuinely appreciated the way the old guy gently probed her with tactful questions, and then listened, apparently engrossed by her answers, nodding with that understanding, doting smile of his. It didn't seem right that she knew nothing about his time in the army.

Emboldened by this thought, she lifted the tin out of the box, testing its weight. It wasn't heavy and when she gave it a shake, she heard the soft shuffle of paper and a metallic clink.

What sorts of things had been important enough to her grandfather that he'd wanted them, above all else, kept safe?

The hinges squeaked a little as she lifted the lid. There seemed to be quite a few army medals, medals that she would have investigated had she not been completely distracted by a photograph lying on the very top.

The photo was old, a black-and-white portrait, slightly battered and dog-eared, of a beautiful, glamorous woman.

Lucy stared at her, entranced. She must have been no more than twenty and she was as lovely as any of the famous movie stars from the thirties or forties. Her face was oval, beautifully shaped, her chin neat but determined, while her complexion had the flawless alabaster quality that was so perfectly captured in black-and-white.

It was hard to guess the colour of her hair, but it was fair, possibly light brown, swept back from her forehead and styled in elegant waves. She wasn't smiling, yet a lively, almost challenging impishness shone in her eyes.

Her grooming was faultless, her eyebrows elegantly arched, her lovely eyes and lips made up to perfection. The shot was only of her head and shoulders, but she was wearing a beautiful fur and pearls and there was a tantalising glimpse of her evening dress, which looked very sophisticated with dark leaves embroidered dramatically onto a sheer background.

'Wow,' Lucy whispered, deeply fascinated. 'Who are you?'

She could feel her heart beating faster as she turned the photo over, hoping to find a clue on the back. A message was handwritten in black ink.

> To Dearest Harry,
> Remember me, won't you?
> Love,
> George

3

The procession of motor vehicles crept at a snail's pace down the Mall towards Buckingham Palace. Impatiently, the Honourable Georgina Lenton sat stiffly beside her aunt in the back of her father's Rolls Royce and desperately tried to ignore the curious crowds lining the footpath.

The onlookers were all in good spirits, peering in through the windows, waving and blowing kisses, but despite their goodwill, Georgina didn't enjoy being stared at. She just wished she could reach the palace gates quickly and have the ordeal of being presented at court over and done with.

For weeks she'd been standing around, going blue with cold, while fussy dressmakers fiddled with pins. She'd also suffered dance classes, learning how to do the dreaded curtsey with a curtain fastened to her shoulders in lieu of the train she wore now.

'Left foot behind and keep your back perfectly straight,' Miss Betty of the Vacani School of Dancing had instructed, over and over. 'Now sink and rise in one smooth and fluid motion.'

Georgina had borne the classes stoically, and she had to admit she rather liked the results of her dressmaker's efforts, especially this evening's gown – an off-the-shoulder, fairytale affair in white silk with a full skirt and a sweet little black net rose sewn at the waist. Now, however, Georgina faced not only this evening's trial of making her appearance before the King and Queen, which brought the immediate fear of wobbling in the curtsey or tripping on her train, but also the whole frenetic, bothersome season that stretched out in front of her.

The long summer months would be filled with night after night of parties and balls, a prospect that might have been enjoyable if the primary objective of these parties hadn't been 'meeting the right people'. Decoded, this meant that Georgina's parents expected her to charm as many eligible and preferably titled young gentlemen as possible, and to bag one of them as her husband.

The pressure started as soon as her family arrived in London and moved into their house in Mayfair. Her mother, Lady Lavinia Lenton, had set to work immediately, giving and attending luncheons with the express purpose of exchanging lists of marriageable candidates with the other debutantes' mothers.

Georgina found the whole business embarrassing and tedious, not all that different from a livestock sale, although in this case, the stock in question comprised a mob of pretty girls with fashionably arched brows, languid eyes and bee-stung lips.

Unfortunately, her parents had never asked her if she wanted to do the season. They'd more or less assumed that she was dying to enter society and they would have been appalled if she'd told them she would prefer to stay quietly on her father's country estate in Cornwall, spending her days in comfortable kilts and jerseys, or her riding habit.

'Chin up, my darling,' said Georgina's aunt, Lady Cora Harlow. Looking utterly splendid in a glittering diamond tiara and earrings, she turned to Georgina and gave her an encouraging smile. 'It won't be long before we're in the forecourt and away from these crowds.

Then we can have a sandwich and a cup of soup from the thermos.'

Georgina shivered, cold, despite her fur wrap and the hot water bottle she was hugging under her lap rug. This year, the presentation of debutantes had been shifted from May to chilly March to accommodate the King and Queen's plans to travel to America. This March night was freezing and she would be grateful for something hot to drink.

'You look as miserable as I was for my coming out,' her aunt said next and Georgina stared at her in surprise. Then she dropped her gaze, embarrassed that her negative feelings had been so easy to read, but also a little shocked that Lady Cora would say such a thing.

Georgina had been brought up to keep her emotions well hidden. A stiff upper lip was expected in her family's circles, and no matter how much she disliked this evening's ordeal, she would never dream of complaining. Besides, she couldn't possibly complain after all the money Mummy had spent on her.

She knew she should be grateful. Her sister, Alice, had been the perfect daughter when she'd come out last year. While Georgina was being 'finished' in Paris, living with a family who had helped her to polish up her French, Alice had adored every minute of the season, especially her own coming out dance, and she'd collected a string of impressive beaus.

The beaus were impressive on paper, at least, with pots of money and a pleasing array of titles, but Georgina had met most of these chaps and she thought they were rather lacklustre in the flesh. Rather pale and unexciting and dull. Nevertheless, Alice had dutifully fallen in love and there was soon to be an engagement announcement. Their mother was incredibly pleased.

Now, Georgina was expected to follow her sister's excellent example.

'You weren't really miserable, were you?' she asked her aunt.

Lady Cora couldn't have had a miserable season. With her sparkling dark eyes and glossy brown hair, she always looked lovely, and so elegant and poised, with an air of serene enjoyment. And she never had any problem with making polite or interesting conversation.

It was for these very reasons that Lady Lenton had asked Cora to stand in as Georgina's sponsor, given that the rules wouldn't allow the same sponsor to appear in court two years in a row.

Admittedly, Georgina didn't know her aunt particularly well, even though she was her father's sister. Cora had married Lord Harlow's son, Edward, and the two of them had taken off soon after their wedding to run a plantation in the South Pacific. Even though Uncle Edward had recently inherited his father's title and estate, he and Cora still spent most of their time on the other side of the world.

So, although her aunt was charming and an appropriately respectable, titled Englishwoman, she also carried a slight aura of mystique and, for Georgina, an air of the exotic.

Watching Georgina now, Lady Cora smiled again. 'I don't suppose I was miserable exactly, but I was certainly bored. Like you, I was brought up in the country and that's such a different lifestyle, isn't it?'

'Completely,' Georgina agreed. 'And so much more fun.'

'Your father and I had so much freedom when we were young,' Cora added warmly. 'We practically ran wild, riding our ponies everywhere and climbing enormous pine trees, exploring the riverbanks, making friends with the shepherds.'

'Oh, yes.' Georgina knew exactly what her aunt meant. Her childhood had been very similar. In fact, until she was ten, her very best friend had been their gamekeeper's son and she'd adored him. His name was Rob and Georgina had convinced him to call her George. Together they'd had so many adventures. Rob had taught her how to tickle trout and find a badger's sett.

'When I came to London,' Lady Cora went on, 'I was bored to death – until I met Teddy, of course.'

'So you met Uncle Edward during the season? At a party?'

Cora smiled, looking past the crowds into the distance, as if she was captured by a very pleasant memory. 'Teddy wasn't really making much of an effort on the party circuit. He certainly wasn't dancing. It hadn't been long since he'd lost his arm.'

It had happened in the war, Georgina remembered. 'In Belgium, wasn't it?'

Lady Cora nodded. 'Yes, at the Somme.' With a little shudder, she pulled the collar of her ermine coat higher under her chin till there was only a hint of the peacock blue satin gown beneath. 'Dear heaven,' she said. 'I'm so disappointed in Neville Chamberlain telling us now that his appeasement hasn't worked. I'm still praying that we're not about to have another despicable war.'

Georgina fervently hoped so, too, although Monsieur Reynard, the father of the family she'd stayed with in Paris, was convinced that another war with Germany was imminent.

'Anyway, I met Teddy at Cynthia Kingsley's dance in Belgravia,' Lady Cora said, continuing her story. 'I wandered outside to get some fresh air and more or less bumped into him lurking in the shadows. He was hiding behind a Corinthian column, trying to light a cigarette, but the poor boy was still getting used to only having one arm and he was in all sorts of bother dealing with the match.'

'So you lit his cigarette for him,' supplied Georgina, leaning forward and smiling broadly at the thought. 'How jolly romantic.'

She could so easily imagine it. There was still something strikingly attractive about Uncle Teddy. He wasn't merely tall and slim and suntanned, he was also confident, charming and gracious. There was usually a hint of amusement in his eyes, too, as if he regularly saw the funny side of life and, despite his missing arm, or perhaps because of it, he carried an added air of adventure about him.

'Meeting Teddy was *very* romantic, actually.' Lady Cora's dark eyes shone. 'Straight out of a fairytale. One of those moments when you look into a man's eyes and just know —' She stopped as the Rolls Royce suddenly turned. 'Oh, good, we're going in at last.'

Georgina swallowed and sat up straighter as they drove through the tall iron gates and into the forecourt of Buckingham Palace. And now, for the first time since the procession had begun, she felt nervous. She glanced again at her aunt, who looked so beautiful and glamorous and relaxed, not fussing or frowning the way her mother would have been.

I want to be like you.

The thought was a mere impulse, but almost immediately Georgina reached a decision. She would not let this season wear her down and she would not end it with an engagement ring on her finger – *unless* she found a man who completely swept her away.

Yes, she was prepared to flirt with the young men and to 'play the game' through the summer, but she was not going to marry simply to please her parents.

She supposed it was foolishly romantic, but she wanted an experience like Cora and Teddy's. She wanted to look into a man's eyes and to *know.*

4

Another hour crawled by while the debutantes and their sponsors stood around, chatting and waiting in the forecourt. Fortunately, the tedium didn't quite quell the buzz of excitement among the girls, most of whom Georgina had met at the dancing school and at various afternoon teas hosted by their mothers.

The debutantes looked beautiful, like exotic moths, with their fur wraps over white, cream or palest pink gowns and teamed with elbow-length gloves of the finest white kid. Each girl also held a floral bouquet, and wore the requisite headdress made from three white ostrich feathers while keeping her train carefully looped over her left arm.

Georgina's train had been made from her mother's wedding veil and her sister Alice had worn it the year before.

'Let's hope it brings you good luck, just as it did for Alice and me,' her mother had said as she'd watched Hettie, Georgina's maid, carefully pin the train in place and then hide the pins beneath a pretty pearl headband.

Georgina had smiled dutifully at this not-so-subtle reminder that she was expected to secure a rich husband by the end of the summer.

Looking around now at the other girls, she wondered if they felt burdened by the same weight of maternal expectation. They didn't seem bothered. Most of them looked as if they just wanted to have a jolly good time.

And yet . . . there was a competitive undertone to the evening that was hard to ignore and Georgina was relieved to see her oldest and best friend, Primrose Cavendish, finally arrive in the courtyard. The Cavendish and Lenton families both owned estates in Cornwall. In fact they were practically neighbours and the girls had shared a governess for several years.

This evening, however, Primrose was almost unrecognisable.

'My goodness, you look so grown up and glamorous,' Georgina told her as they kissed.

Primrose's hair, normally a mass of wild, glossy brown curls, had been magically tamed for the evening into the latest style of smooth, dramatic waves.

Primrose merely laughed and rolled her eyes. 'It's all thanks to tons and tons of hair lacquer. I only hope it holds till I'm out of the Throne Room.'

'Oh, I'm sure it will. You look wonderful.'

'Are you nervous?' asked Primrose.

'A bit. What about you?'

'Not really. I can't afford to be.' Primrose shot a glance back at the Bentley she'd arrived in. 'My mother's being nervous for both of us.'

'Oh.' Georgina gave her friend a smile of sympathy and thought again how lucky she was to have the calming company of Lady Cora.

It was ages before a court official arrived to invite them inside. Then there was an excited fluttering of debutantes as they once again paired with their mothers and sponsors.

'So, here we go,' said Lady Cora, with an encouraging wink. 'Not too long now before it's all over and you can enjoy a well-earned supper and some fun.'

Georgina had never been inside the palace, so she couldn't hold back a gasp of surprise when she saw the grandeur. She was used to stately homes and to glamorous London hotels, but the red and gold sumptuousness was far grander than anything she'd ever seen before.

The proportions were impressive. The carpets and gilt-framed paintings were positively enormous, the ornate ceiling so very, very high, and the chandeliers huge and glittering. Ahead of the girls, a red-carpeted staircase, lined by Yeomen of the Guard, led to the next gallery and, somewhere beyond, the Throne Room. All of it was breathtakingly beautiful and splendid.

The scent of lilies and carnations drifted on the night air as a footman in a white powdered wig stepped forward to receive their wraps. From above floated the strains of music from a military band. Every detail combined into an atmosphere so dazzling, it was impossible to resist its spell.

Georgina sent up a silent prayer. *Please don't let me trip or make a fool of myself.*

The debutantes ascended the stairs with due pomp and ceremony and were seated in the White Drawing Room, the last staging post before the Throne Room.

Excitement was building, building . . .

Until Primrose Cavendish let out a cry of pure panic.

'Oh, good heavens, no, I can't find my card. I – Oh, help. I've lost it.'

There was a collective gasp of horror from the girls and sponsors seated near her. The Card of Command was absolutely vital for admittance to the Throne Room. One simply couldn't enter without it.

Poor Primrose's mother let out an agonised moan. 'You can't be presented if you've lost it,' she wailed.

'I know, I *know*, but it's not here! It's gone.' Primrose had scrambled to her feet. Her big brown eyes were already filling with tears as she frantically searched under the gold chair where she'd been seated, then in the posy she carried, in the folds of her train. 'It's not here,' she cried again, her voice high-pitched and desperate with panic. 'It's not anywhere. It's simply vanished.'

Georgina's stomach was hollow. This was most debutantes' worst nightmare. So much importance was placed on this upper-class rite of passage, and they'd endured such a huge build-up to this night with all the fuss about gowns and all the planning of parties and balls. To miss out on the presentation at this point was unthinkable.

Primrose's mother, the Honourable Hermione Cavendish, a nervy woman at the best of times, now gave another moan and looked deathly pale, as if she was on the very verge of fainting.

'Did you definitely bring the card with you?' Georgina asked Primrose.

'Yes, yes, I know I had it with me when we were out in the forecourt.'

'Then you must have dropped it. Perhaps it slipped from your hand when you were taking off your wrap.'

Primrose gave her a grateful, if watery, smile. 'Yes, that might be what happened. But gosh, how can I possibly get it back now?'

'We'll ask one of the staff to search for it,' said Lady Cora calmly, while Hermione Cavendish sobbed and whimpered into a lace handkerchief.

Georgina looked at the empty rows at the front of the room. The chairs' occupants had already been presented. Now that the official ceremony had actually begun, matters were proceeding rather swiftly and smoothly, and the staff appeared to be occupied elsewhere, or were busy at the door to the Throne Room.

As Georgina had been with Primrose for most of the evening, she felt a measure of responsibility.

There was no time to spare.

'It will probably be quicker if I slip downstairs,' she said. After all, Primrose was too shaken to think straight and her mother was in no state to do anything but cry.

Already on her feet, Georgina set her own card and bouquet of pink and cream roses on her chair. 'I'll be back in a blink.'

'Georgina, darling, I don't think —' her Aunt Cora began, but Georgina didn't stay to hear the rest. Ignoring the shocked stares of the other debutantes and their mothers, she hurried out of the drawing room and, holding her train in one hand, her skirt in the other, she rushed unceremoniously down the long, grand staircase.

When a yeoman stepped forward with a forbidding frown, she told him quickly, 'Primrose Cavendish has lost her card, and we've got to find it.' With that, she hurried past him, praying that she didn't trip and break her neck.

'Have you seen a card?' she called to the footmen as she reached the bottom of the staircase. 'A Card of Command for Primrose Cavendish?' But her heart sank as the men looked at her with puzzled frowns and shook their heads.

Slightly breathless from her downstairs dash, she scanned the red and gold carpets covering most of the reception hall's floor area. Surely a pink card would stand out if it had fallen?

At least one footman seemed to understand. 'I'll check in the cloakroom,' he said.

'Thank you.' Gratefully, she hurried after him, trying not to worry about what might be happening upstairs. How many girls had passed through to the Throne Room since she'd left? She knew there was a strict order of precedence. The list was planned based on the lineage of each debutante's sponsor. Duchesses were received first by His Majesty and then marchionesses and countesses preceded ladies. Primrose's mother was an Honourable, and so Lady Cora – and Georgina – were ahead of her in the line.

Time was running out.

Georgina felt dizzy and slightly sick. Her heart seemed to be roaring in her ears as she suddenly realised how very reckless she'd been to set off on this wild goose chase. Did she really think she would find a card that no one else had seen fall?

Why on earth had she been so foolish? It was like waking up inside a nightmare. Poor Aunt Cora would be in a terrible state.

Too late, she realised that her impetuous action could very easily spoil the entire evening's proceedings.

She had no choice but to admit defeat and to race back up the stairs, hoping against hope that something dire hadn't happened.

'Excuse me, m'lady?'

Georgina was at the foot of the staircase when she heard a voice behind her.

'Is this what you're looking for?'

Spinning around, she met a very young footman holding out a pink card. She saw Hermione and Primrose's names in a copperplate script, and nearly fainted with relief.

'Thank you,' she said breathlessly, and without wasting valuable time asking where the footman had found it, she grabbed the card and dashed up the grand staircase again with as much unseemly haste as her long skirts would allow.

Panting, she arrived in the White Drawing Room and saw, to her horror, that all the seats ahead of her were empty. Her Aunt Cora was standing, holding her card and bouquet, looking more anxious and put out than Georgina had ever seen her.

'I've got it!' Georgina called, waving the card high and then thrusting it at Primrose, before hurrying to her aunt. 'Am I too late?'

'Of course you're too late,' Lady Cora told her coldly.

No. Georgina was instantly jealous of women who could faint at the drop of a hat. She didn't want to be here at this moment. She would do anything to escape this ghastly humiliation.

Her aunt said stiffly, 'We're on the brink of being struck off the list.'

On the brink?

Was there still a glimmer of hope?

There was certainly no time for apologies, and Georgina very much doubted that her aunt was in any mood to hear an apology if she'd tried to offer one. Without another word, Lady Cora handed her the bouquet and prodded her to move forward towards the doorway where the court usher stood stiffly in full regalia, his steely gaze signalling his severe disapproval.

How long had he been waiting for her?

How long had the King and Queen been kept waiting?

The usher stepped closer and ran a stern eye over Georgina, checking her appearance. She prayed that she didn't look too flushed, that her headpiece hadn't slipped sideways, that a curl hadn't come unpinned.

The usher showed no sign that he approved of her, but he took her train and began to arrange it behind her.

A faint wave of relief washed over her as he completed this task and Lady Cora, at her most regal, handed him her card. 'Lady Cora Harlow presenting the Honourable Georgina Lenton.'

Turning back to the doorway, the usher presented the card to another powdered footman, who carried it with great ceremony to the Lord Chamberlain.

Through the open doorway, Georgina could just see the Lord Chamberlain looking splendid in a black uniform embroidered with gold leaves as he frowned at the card and then announced in a deep booming baritone: 'Lady Cora Harlow presenting the Honourable Georgina Lenton.'

So, here it was – happening at last. And now she simply mustn't put another foot wrong.

Desperately trying to remember everything she'd been taught, Georgina proceeded smoothly forward into the Throne Room that was, predictably, even more magnificent than any of the preceding rooms.

The cavernous space was filled with nobility dressed in glittering uniforms and gowns. The King and Queen were seated on gold chairs on a red-carpeted stage at one distant end. Brilliant chandeliers were reflected in mirrors. Georgina fancied the Queen was smiling, but the King looked rather serious.

She was aware of a buzz of talk in the room and, again, she wondered how long Their Majesties had been kept waiting for her. Somewhere out there in the throng of tiaras and medals were her parents, but she concentrated on the small golden crown woven into the carpet, which marked the spot where she had to come to a halt and to curtsey.

Now, she was grateful for the tedious lessons at the dancing school and all those hours of learning how to keep her back straight as she bent her knee. To her relief she didn't wobble as she bowed her head in the deepest part of the curtsey, and she remembered to smile at the King as she rose again.

For a moment, she imagined that he was going to speak to her – possibly reprimand her – but she was either mistaken or he changed his mind.

Then it was a matter of taking three careful steps to the right without stepping on her train, before going through the same deep curtsey again for Queen Elizabeth. The Queen looked especially lovely this evening in cream and gold, with a diamond tiara and diamonds at her ears, throat and wrists. She remained smiling warmly throughout.

And suddenly, it was all over and Georgina was walking away, remembering to hold her bouquet low in front of her and to not turn her back on the royal couple.

After all the fuss and bother, it was done in a flash. Already, behind her, the Lord Chamberlain was announcing: 'The Honourable Hermione Cavendish presenting Miss Primrose Cavendish.'

The fuss and bother resumed, however, just as soon as Georgina was cornered by her mother in the nearby chamber where the champagne supper was held.

There was no kiss or hug. Not a word of congratulations. Her mother, appearing especially elegant in a soft dove-grey gown and rubies, looked as upset as Hermione Cavendish had such a short time earlier. 'What on earth happened?'

In self-defence, Georgina chose to misunderstand. 'Happened? What do you mean?'

'For heaven's sake, Georgina. You held up the entire presentation. There was such a gap after Lady Sarah Courtbridge presented Lucinda. *Everyone's* talking about it. Such a terrible scandal. What happened?' Her voice was shrill and shaking. 'Did you faint? Were you ill?'

Georgina shot a quick glance to Lady Cora, hoping for her support, but her aunt remained silent and her usually eloquent face was, for once, hard to read.

So Georgina explained as gently as she could. 'Primrose lost her card, so I went back to look for it.'

'*You* went back?'

'Poor Primrose was in such a state, Mummy, and her mother was having kittens. I knew the card had to be somewhere downstairs.'

'So you rushed off without a thought for the embarrassment you'd cause me and your father.'

'I'm afraid I was thinking of Primrose and her mother's embarrassment.'

Lady Lenton sniffed. 'Hermione and Primrose are fine. As far as the court is concerned, *they* weren't the ones who held up the proceedings.' She shot an angry glance at her sister-in-law. 'Couldn't you have stopped her, Cora?'

Cora sighed. 'Not without making an unpleasant scene. And perhaps you should think about that now, Lavinia. We don't want to attract any *more* attention.'

Georgina's mother ignored this and gave an exasperated shake of her head. 'The Lord Chamberlain's staff would have made out a new card for the Cavendishes.'

'Would they? Really?' Georgina swallowed guiltily. 'I didn't think of that. No one mentioned it. I thought Primrose would have to miss out on being presented.'

'Oh, for heaven's sake.' Her mother gave a helpless roll of her eyes. 'If you hadn't been so impetuous, someone might have had a chance to explain. As it is, I'm going to be pestered all night with questions. And heaven knows what scandalous comment will show up in *The Times* tomorrow morning.'

Oh, help. Georgina hadn't given a thought to *The Times*, but she knew there would be a full-page report of the evening at court. Forlornly, she remembered her mother's great joy last year when the details of Alice's gown had been lovingly reported. Alice had been described as 'one of the most beautiful debutantes of the season'.

Instead of pride, Mummy will only feel shame because of me.

But before she could sink to the very depths of despair, her father came up to their group, looking handsome in his full dress uniform and, without hesitation, he gave Georgina a kiss and a loving smile.

'Well done, my darling,' he said warmly. 'My only sadness tonight is that my little companion, George, has become a woman. We'll probably never see you now, you'll be so in demand.'

Georgina's heart swelled with gratitude and love. Her father had called her George from when she was little, mainly, she'd imagined, because she loved to be outdoors, playing with the boys whenever possible. Of course, as she'd grown older, she'd come to realise that her father would have loved a son, so a tomboy daughter was probably the next best thing. For whatever reason, she and her father had always enjoyed a special bond, while Alice had always been her mother's 'dream daughter'.

And now Primrose rushed up, her big brown eyes glowing with excitement. 'Thank you,' she cried, squeezing Georgina in a breath-robbing hug. 'You saved my life. Or my head.' Primrose laughed. 'You certainly saved my face.'

Georgina's mother sniffed loudly.

Georgina tried to enjoy the supper. After all, it was very grand and grown up to be surrounded by so many bejewelled duchesses and decorated generals – and in such a beautiful room, with huge mirrors reflecting the enormous flower arrangements that had, apparently, been specially ordered by the Queen and must have taken weeks to create.

There were powdered footmen to serve champagne at long damask-covered tables, and guests were eating delicate sandwiches and daintily filled pastry cases on small white plates decorated with a rim of gold crowns. Georgina might have enjoyed herself if she hadn't been so aware of the muttering and whispers behind ostrich-feather fans, but she kept her distance from the whisperers. She didn't want to know what the mothers and sponsors were saying.

To her relief, Aunt Cora eventually approached her with a sympathetic smile. 'Oh, dear. If I hear your mother try to apologise for you one more time, I think I might scream.'

'But I thought you were upset with me, too.'

'Oh, darling, I was: for ten minutes, which was more time than was warranted. I've told your mother as much, but I'm afraid she's intent on making everything worse by fretting so publicly. She's practically handfeeding the gossip to *The Times*.'

Georgina's sense of guilt tightened like a crushing band around her chest.

Her aunt, watching her with concern, said more gently, 'I was being facetious. Don't worry about it, my dear.' She waved a gloved hand at a nearby table. 'Have you tried one of these delightful fruit jellies?'

The jellies were indeed delicious, but her mother's anxiety hovered over Georgina like a dark cloud and the pressure didn't ease until they finally left the palace for Lucinda Courtbridge's presentation party at the Savoy.

Such a relief it was then to unhook her train at last and to leave it in the hotel cloakroom along with her veil and feathers and posy. Now, while a jazz band played swing tunes like 'One Day When We Were Young', Georgina could finally dance – first with her father and with Uncle Teddy, and then with Primrose's brother James, with her rather dishy cousin Gus Harlow and eventually with a succession of young men she barely knew.

The formalities were over, the band was lively, and the young men looked dashing in their tail coats and white ties. Georgina had fun, swinging to jazz tunes and literally kicking up her heels.

It was well after midnight when her parents eventually took her home. By then, her mother had mellowed at last and all was pretty much back to normal.

Georgina woke when Hettie came in with breakfast on a tray.

'Sorry to disturb you,' she said softly. 'Her Ladyship sent me to wake you.'

Georgina stared at her blankly for a moment and then sat up with a start. 'Oh, no.' Already she was flinging the bedclothes aside. 'What time is it?'

'Eleven o'clock, Miss Georgina.'

'My mother must have read *The Times*. Oh, Hettie, is she in a terrible state?'

Hettie frowned. 'I'm not sure, Miss.'

'So you haven't heard anything about the report in *The Times*, about last night's presentation?'

'No.'

'There hasn't been talk in the kitchen?' Georgina knew that Groves, the butler, always read *The Times*.

Hettie shook her head. 'No news about your coming out. I'm afraid they were all buzzing about Germany.'

Georgina still didn't find this very reassuring. Of course there was news about Germany. It was in the papers every day. But she needed to know her own fate. Ignoring the tray Hettie had set beside her bed, she pulled on her embroidered-silk dressing-gown and thrust her feet into slippers.

'I'll have to go and speak to my mother. I can't eat until I know the worst.'

Leaving a gaping-mouthed maid – she didn't even bother to wash her face or brush her hair – she hurried out of her room and down the carpeted corridor to her parents' rooms, where she knocked.

'Who is it?' called her mother.

'It's just me. Georgina.'

'Come in, dear.'

Cautiously, Georgina opened the door to find her mother sitting up in bed, propped by pillows, with a pink crocheted bed jacket around her shoulders and a cup of tea in her hand. Her father, wrapped in an emerald satin dressing-gown, was sitting on the edge of the bed, holding a copy of *The Times*.

Her mother looked pale and not exactly happy.

Still clutching the door handle, Georgina wished she'd had the forethought to take a fortifying sip of tea before she'd rushed here. Her knees were shaking, but she tried to sound calm. 'What does

The Times have to say?' she asked softly.

With a weary sigh, her mother set her teacup in its saucer. 'There's not a word,' she said, her eyes signalling shock.

Georgina almost sagged against the doorframe with relief. 'That is good news.'

'It's astonishing,' said her mother. 'It's such a snub.'

'But surely you didn't want them to —' Georgina began, but her mother interrupted.

'Georgina, there's nothing at *all* about last night's court.' She almost knocked her teacup as she flung an arm dramatically wide. 'The entire newspaper has been taken over by this dreadful business in Europe.'

'What's happened now?'

Her father turned to her and waved the paper's front page. 'Germany's invaded Czechoslovakia,' he said gravely. 'Last night, while you and Cora were waiting in the forecourt, Adolf Hitler's troops were marching into Prague.'

5

It was close to dusk when Lucy drove her mum's car to Sam's place, but the blazing tropical sun was still bright in the western sky and she needed to adjust the visor to block the glare. Zipping through the familiar suburbs, she passed her old primary school, the sports oval where she'd played junior soccer, and the busy corner on Bayswater Road where she'd come off her bike and broken her collarbone.

She found it strange, after living in a country where every sight was alien or dangerous or challenging, to once again see familiar, predictable landmarks at every turn. A heady luxury, too, to be able to stop at a bottle shop – Lucy felt almost reckless walking into a store where she could buy any alcoholic drink that took her fancy. She settled on a sixpack of Sam's favourite Japanese beer, a chilled bottle of champagne and a good quality red. After all, she would probably end up staying at Sam's place for the whole weekend.

As she approached his street, knots tightened in her stomach but she told herself they were caused by excitement, not nerves. Just the same, she held her breath as she rounded the corner, only letting it out when she saw Sam's Volkswagen Golf parked in the driveway.

He was home, waiting for her. She gave a happy sigh and felt her body relax. Everything was okay. Of course it was.

As soon as she pulled up, Sam's front door opened and there he stood, with his special brand of hot and sexy, and his heartbreaking smile. Lucy's breath caught in her throat and her skin tingled and tightened.

She had it bad for this guy. It was how she'd been from their first date and she still considered it a miracle that he'd chased her.

Now, too excited to be sedate, she leaped from the car, slammed the door behind her and rushed up the driveway.

Then everything happened just as she'd hoped. She was in Sam's arms and they were kissing, hugging, their bodies pressing close as they breathlessly stumbled inside. Wrapped in Sam's arms, Lucy pushed the door closed with her foot, dropped her car keys onto a hall table and they headed straight for Sam's bed.

'Hello,' she whispered, much later, as they lay together in the darkness, spent and languid in the afterglow.

Sam gave a soft chuckle. 'Yeah . . . hello.'

'That was some welcome home.' Lucy pressed a kiss to his warm, bare shoulder. 'Thank you. I've missed you. So much.'

'Me too.'

Of course they'd talked about missing each other before this, in emails and phone calls while she was away, but now, as Lucy nestled closer, she felt compelled to state the obvious. 'At last I'm home for good. No more deployments on the horizon.'

When Sam made no comment she held up her left hand. In the soft shimmer of light coming down the hallway from the kitchen, she caught a tiny wink of sparkle from her engagement ring. 'I'm really looking forward to making proper plans, about where we're going to live and . . . and everything.'

Had she imagined she felt a sudden tension in him?

Her stomach knotted unpleasantly as she waited for him to

reassure her that his plans to marry her hadn't changed. She willed herself to stay calm.

I won't be like my mum.

Her mother had never trusted any of her relationships to work.

I trust Sam. I know we're okay. He's never given me any reason to doubt.

After all, Sam had coughed up the suggestion of marriage without any special prompting.

'I bought Thai takeaway for dinner,' he said now. 'But I guess it's probably gone cold.'

Lucy let out a small huff of relief. Here she was fretting over their relationship status while Sam – typical man – only had thoughts for his stomach.

'Well, I bought beer and champagne, but they've probably gone hot. They're still in the car.' She rolled onto her back and stretched luxuriously, then smiled towards him through the dim light. 'A microwave and a freezer can soon fix both our problems.'

'Of course.' There was a weird note in Sam's voice and he sighed heavily.

Lucy wished she could see his face clearly. Leaning in, she tentatively touched her lips to his shoulder again and then to the grainy rough skin on his jaw. 'You okay, mate?'

'Yeah, sure.' Turning, he dropped a hasty kiss on the tip of her nose. 'Just hungry.' A beat later, he sat up and snapped on the bedside lamp.

Blinking in the sudden brightness, Lucy squinted at the tangled bed sheets and their discarded clothing littering the floor. She told herself this was pretty clear evidence that everything was fine.

Just the same, she tried to check Sam's expression as he pulled on jocks and jeans but he had his back to her, so she couldn't see his face, couldn't completely shut off another niggle of disquiet.

Annoyed with herself for potentially spoiling a perfect evening, she followed his lead and hunted for her knickers and bra. By the time she was dressed and had visited the bathroom, Sam had brought the drinks from her car and their dinner was circling in the microwave.

Sam didn't look particularly tense, but then he didn't look over-the-top happy either. Perhaps it was the absence of any definable emotion that bothered Lucy most.

Or perhaps I'm being totally neurotic.

'What would you like to drink?' he asked as he opened the fridge. 'There's a sav blanc here.' He flashed Lucy a quick smile. 'You usually like white with Thai, don't you?'

'Yeah, thanks.' They could save the champagne for a proper celebration. She found two glasses in an overhead cupboard, set them on the counter and watched Sam's cute frown of concentration as he poured.

'So what's it like to be back?' he asked.

'Fan-bloody-tastic.' Lucy grinned.

'But does it also feel weird, to no longer be in a war zone?'

'A bit, yeah. I miss having my pistol.'

He shot her a sharp frown. 'Really?'

'We had to carry a weapon all the time – couldn't go anywhere without it – or we were charged. So yes, it feels strange to not have it with me now. Makes me feel a bit anxious, to be honest, but I'm sure I'll get used to it.'

The pained expression on his face sent a chill down her spine. Had she said something terribly wrong?

'So what's been happening lately?' she asked, quickly changing the subject. 'Anything exciting?'

'Nothing out of the ordinary.' He shrugged. 'Just the usual media circus.'

His job involved plenty of interaction with the local media, including drinks with journos and with advertising agencies and TV crews. He partied with them, too, and it seemed to pay off. Most of the local coverage of the army was positive.

Now he touched his glass to Lucy's. 'Cheers.'

'Here's to us,' she said brightly.

'Welcome home.' Sam's gaze didn't quite meet hers, but she refrained from asking yet again whether everything was okay. At least she'd learned something from her mother's mistakes. Guys hated to be pestered, and she would have hated to spoil their first meal together after six long months.

When the microwave pinged, she and Sam gathered plates, cutlery and mats to put beneath the heated food. He'd ordered her favourites – seafood curry and steamed fish in an exotic coconut and chilli sauce. Sensational aromas filled the flat as they lifted the lids on the containers.

'I suppose you've heard that my mum's moved into a new apartment on Palmer Street?' Lucy said as she helped herself to a heaped spoonful of steaming jasmine rice.

'She mentioned it when I phoned her this morning. So what do you think of it?'

'The apartment? It's —' Lucy shrugged. 'It's beautiful, I guess, but it takes a bit of getting used to.' She added a helping of the seafood curry to her plate. 'Mum has a new man as well. He's already moved in with her.'

Sam's eyebrows rose. 'Anyone we know?'

'I'd never met him before. His name's Keith, um . . . Keith Hayes. Have you heard of him?'

'I've heard the name.' Although Sam had only been in Townsville for two years, he'd developed masses of contacts and he seemed to know most of the movers and shakers around town. 'I'm pretty sure he's in business – Chamber of Commerce and the like, so he's probably reasonably successful.'

'Well, that would make a nice change,' Lucy couldn't help

commenting. And then, against her better judgement, 'It would be even better if he actually stayed with Mum for more than a few months.'

This time there was no missing Sam's reaction, and at the sight of his frowning, narrow-eyed tension, a chill ran through Lucy. A lump in her throat made it hard to swallow and she took a quick sip of wine.

As she set the glass down she felt compelled to say something. 'You seem very on edge, Sam.'

'Do I?' His expression went blank, a sure sign that he was desperately trying to look innocent.

Lucy couldn't hold back a moment longer. 'What's the matter? If there's anything wrong, I'd rather you told me, before I start imagining things.' Of course, she was already imagining the worst – another woman. Nevertheless, she forced herself to broach this. 'If there's someone else, I'd rather you just spit it out now.'

His blue eyes blazed with unexpected fire. 'Of course there's no one else.' He gave an angry shake of his head. 'I swear there's no one. Jeez, Luce, you sure know how to spoil a good meal.'

She dropped her gaze to her plate where the brightly coloured curry was piled over snowy white, perfect rice. Sam was right about spoiling it. Already, she'd lost her appetite. But she wasn't prepared to apologise. Not yet. 'So you're saying that everything's fine? With us, I mean. There's no change to our plans?'

Sam grimaced and stared at his plate and Lucy's chest and stomach tightened uncomfortably.

Then he gave a fed-up kind of sigh as he set his fork down and lifted his hands in surrender. 'I didn't want to bring it up the minute you walked in the door.'

'You didn't,' Lucy said crisply and their gazes met again, this time in silent, bristling acknowledgement of *exactly* what had happened the minute she'd walked in the door.

Sam had the grace to look embarrassed and he swallowed. 'It's just . . . I'm just not sure we should hurry into, you know, the next step.'

The tendril of fear that had first sprung to life at the airport this morning took off now, exploding through Lucy's veins.

'So you don't want me to move in with you?' She was surprised that she managed to sound so calm.

Sam gave a helpless shrug, as if this was all completely beyond his control. 'I think we should give ourselves a little time to adjust. I'm not just saying this for my own benefit. I reckon you need time, too, to get used to being back here.'

'Sounds to me like you're getting cold feet.'

'That's not how I'd describe it.' Sam's handsome jaw squared as he grimaced. 'Hell, I don't know. Maybe. It's kinda hitting me now that you're back here fulltime and with no plans to leave the army. I'm just not sure that I'm comfortable with the balance.'

'What balance?' she asked quietly, trying to be reasonable, despite the sick churning in her stomach.

'It's not easy to explain.'

'Sorry, but you're going to have to try.'

His smile was more a scowl and he shifted in his seat. 'Now that you're here all the time, we're going . . . Ah, it's going to be more like an office affair, isn't it?'

'I guess, but plenty of people have office affairs. Office *romances*,' Lucy amended with deliberate emphasis.

Another shrug. 'I know this probably sounds sexist, but usually the guy in the relationship is, you know, senior, the boss.'

This time Lucy almost laughed. With shock. Sam couldn't be serious, surely? Had he time travelled back to the fifties? 'I'm not exactly a brigadier, Sam.' Anyway, he'd been commissioned as soon as he joined the army. 'We're both the same rank.'

'Yeah, well, I guess it's purely an ego thing then.'

'But I still don't get it. What's the problem?'

With a small, self-conscious smile, Sam tapped the centre of his chest. 'I might wear a uniform. I might work my arse off to present the best possible image of the army to the public, but I've never had to carry a weapon to work, never heard a shot fired in anger.'

'So?'

He held up a hand, as if now that he'd started, he was keen to keep going. 'I'll be writing articles – "Training in the High Range" or something similar – but you'll actually be up there, *doing* the training.' He lifted both hands in another gesture of helplessness. 'You'll be Action Woman, while I'll be nothing more than a fucking desk jockey.'

Wow.

Lucy drew a stunned breath. She was back in a war zone. *Incoming direct fire.*

'I guess,' Sam went on, 'I'm not very good at dealing with the fact that you'll always be the real thing while I'm just the reporter, the reflector.'

'I had no idea it bothered you.'

This had certainly never bothered Lucy. If she'd wanted a tough, hard-eyed combat soldier for a boyfriend, she could have had one. There'd been plenty of opportunities, plenty of soldiers who'd felt compelled to make a pass at her and then expected her to be flattered. She'd given them short shrift, and she'd chosen her gorgeous, charming Sam. Yet now, the scary thing was that she believed Sam. She could understand where he was coming from.

Even though he'd never voiced this concern before and even though his arguments would be dismissed by most as outdated, sexist crap, to Lucy his backflip suddenly made a crazy kind of sense.

Sam had always been into speed and he loved a hint of danger. In Europe he'd worked with a Formula One team. When he was in Canberra, he'd raced in two Sydney to Hobart yacht races. In north Queensland he'd taken up skindiving on the reef. So yes, working in a desk job while living with a female partner who was a fully trained soldier and had served in a war zone could quite possibly put a major dent in his masculine ego. Even if she was never in the frontline.

Just the same, there were plenty of other things Lucy didn't understand. Like, Sam's lousy sense of timing. 'Why did you wait to tell me this *now*? Couldn't you have raised it before I was deployed?' *Instead of dangling an engagement ring under my nose?*

'It . . . it was complicated. And I don't think it really hit me till you were on your way home.' He had the bad grace to scowl at her. 'Be reasonable, Luce. I haven't been unfaithful. If you must know, I've knocked back offers.'

'Oh, how bloody heroic!' Lucy was so suddenly furious she jumped to her feet. 'And I guess I'm supposed to be grateful.'

It was pathetic that he'd had to tell her about the offers, to protect his stupid ego, his wounded masculine pride.

Stuff him.

Lucy wanted to howl, to thump the table, to scrape the chair noisily over the tiles. Thump Sam.

But there'd been too many times when she'd seen her mother lose her dignity over romantic disappointments and she knew that tears, pleas and fury only made things uglier. So she managed to keep quiet and just stood there, not uttering a word, but trembling inside.

'Lucy, you do understand, don't you? Can't we take things slowly, play it by ear?'

'But nothing's going to change. I'm not going to give up being a soldier.'

'You never know, you might.'

'Is that what you're hoping? That I'll leave the army?' It was impossible to ask this calmly.

'Hey, don't lose it.' Sam looked nervous now. 'I just thought a resignation might be on the cards. You've worked your way up the ranks. You've had your deployment to Afghanistan. What do you want now? To grow old in the forces?'

'Possibly,' she said tightly, although if she was honest, she'd been wondering about her future career. One thing was definite, though. She would only leave the army when she was good and ready and not as a salve for her boyfriend's fragile ego. 'I'm certainly not happy that you've just assumed I'll give it up.'

'I'm sorry,' Sam said, but he didn't look particularly sorry. There was hardness in his eyes, a lack of sympathy that scared Lucy.

With an angry grimace, he picked up his fork and poked at the food on his plate, then dropped the fork again with a frustrated sigh. 'I told you I didn't want to talk about this now. I knew you'd take it the wrong way.'

Was there a right way to react to his bombshell?

Perhaps if he'd come to her at that moment, put his arms around her and told her he still loved her, she might have weakened. Actually, it was pretty much a given that she would have caved and agreed to take things more slowly, to talk it all through. She might even have been prepared to work out some kind of compromise.

But Sam made no move to come to her. He simply sat there, looking stubborn and petulant, rather like a teenager who considered himself hard done by.

Watching him, the small kernel of sympathy inside Lucy shrivelled. She glanced to where he'd left her car keys, and then to her dismay, her vision blurred and she was frantically blinking back tears as she hurried across the room.

'You're not leaving?'

With her back to him, she widened her eyes, keeping them hard open until the threat of tears passed. Finally, she turned. 'I'm sorry I've spoiled your dinner, but I'm not hungry, and I'm actually pretty tired. Jet lag's catching up with me.'

Then she picked up the keys and walked out, closing the front door quietly behind her.

6

Ro Hunter couldn't decide which of the views from her new apartment she liked better, the daytime vista of the river and the distant sea, or the scene at night-time when the city lights shone in silver-and-gold splashes on the black silky water. The best thing was, she could enjoy any of these views from her beautiful new kitchen, which offered a perfect line of sight across the living room and the balcony to the water.

Even now, as the dishwasher hummed gently and Keith retired to their bedroom to read, Ro was able to give her gleaming granite benches a final wipe down and still keep an eye on the lights of a yacht as it slipped silently downstream and out to sea. She absolutely adored living here.

Even without the views, the apartment was lovely and it was wonderfully easy to look after. Ro had never been motivated to keep her living space especially neat and tidy and she was revelling in her transformation into domestic goddess. Now that she was retired, she had enough time to keep the apartment looking like a photograph in *Home Beautiful*.

The word *retired* had such a wonderful ring to it, Ro thought, especially as her working life had been haphazard at best. There'd been times when she'd really struggled to keep a roof over her and Lucy's heads. Her boyfriends had always been such bloody no-hopers.

She had a talent for attracting classic problem partners. It started with Lucy's father, who'd had a gambling addiction. By the time he left them, her money was gone, except for a few grand in an old account he couldn't access.

All of the men in her life had been tarred with a similar brush – deadset charming at first, but with major flaws that were only revealed after they'd shacked up with her. Not one of them had been a breadwinner's toenail.

Just thinking about them sent a nervous shudder through her. She'd plugged away at all kinds of jobs, trying valiantly to make ends meet, starting with secretarial work, then a job in real estate for a few years – before the boom, of course – and she'd sold ads for the *Townsville Bulletin*. Finally, she'd managed a boutique shoe store in the Mall, but it had struggled to compete with all the big shoe barns and outlet stores.

So her new retired life with Keith was a huge relief. Damn near perfect, in fact. The apartment's location was amazingly convenient. She could wander with Keith down Palmer Street to the restaurant of their choice, and they could enjoy a few drinks and then amble home again without having to worry about a designated driver.

At other times, if she was feeling energetic, she could even walk to the shops in the city centre, or she could accompany Keith to his office.

Then there was the unexpected joy of a balcony garden. Ro had brought only the showiest of her pot plants from Mango Avenue. If she was honest, she'd been relieved to leave behind the rest of the tropical jungle she'd called a garden, which had become wilder and more overgrown with each passing wet season.

Since she left the old place, she'd driven past just once and she'd noted with interest that the new owners had already begun to heavily prune the duranta hedge, a task that Ro had never quite got around to tackling.

So yes, this new lifestyle really suited her.

The only disappointment for Ro, so far, had been Lucy's lukewarm reaction to the apartment. Her daughter's distinct lack of enthusiasm had stung, but when Ro shared this disappointment with Keith, he'd merely slipped an arm around her shoulders.

'Lucy doesn't have to like it,' he'd said as he gave Ro a hug. 'She won't be living here. All that matters is that you like the place, that we both like living here.'

Keith was right, of course. He usually was and Ro hoped fervently, hoped *desperately,* actually, that their new life together worked out. Keith was a good man, a widower with two grown daughters. When they'd pooled their resources to buy this unit, Ro felt as if she'd finally got her act together. She wanted like crazy to be able to trust in the future. She couldn't bear to have another failure.

It had been important for her to be an equal partner in the purchase of the unit, so she hadn't felt guilty about selling the old place without telling Lucy.

At the time of the sale, she'd assured herself that Lucy wouldn't want to be burdened with the news, not when she was already under pressure in Afghanistan. But Ro had to admit that her daughter was always surprisingly sentimental about her childhood home. Ro got that, actually – she'd once felt deeply emotional about Kalkadoon Station, way in the outback, where she'd spent most of her childhood.

Okay. Ro still felt deeply emotional about Kalkadoon. Some nights she dreamed that she was still Rosie Kemp, back out there, racing on horseback beside her good mate Dougie over silvery grassed paddocks, or sitting by a campfire on the riverbank with her dad, drinking hot chocolate from a chipped enamel mug and look-ing up at the huge ceiling of the night sky with its dazzle of stars.

Unfortunately, Ro's emotions about Kalkadoon were also fraught and confused and dark, whereas Lucy's feelings for Mango Avenue had always been surprisingly rosy and warm, as if *please God* her daughter had glossed over their troubled times.

Ro gave a little shake in a deliberate effort to cast off memories she needed to put behind her, once and for all. And she reassured herself that she needn't feel guilty about Lucy. Despite her daugh-ter's rebellious streak, she'd turned out just fine and she had her own life to lead now with Sam.

It was more than likely that the two of them would settle on their wedding date this evening or at some point over the weekend. Ro hoped they didn't want to be married too quickly. These days, weddings seemed to require a fearful lot of planning. Modern brides wanted every tiny detail nailed down and made absolutely perfect. Perfect dress, perfect reception venue, perfect flowers and menu selections . . .

On the other hand, Ro quite liked contemplating the frock she might wear as mother-of-the-bride. She'd decided that jacaranda would suit her quite well, although her hairdresser would probably need to take her hair to a darker shade of auburn. She was ponder-ing this pleasant prospect and giving a final polishing flick to the kitchen bench, when she heard the sound of a key in the lock. Then the front door opened.

Goodness. Could this be Lucy and Sam rushing back to share their happy news? Hastily, Ro wrung out the dishcloth and placed it, neatly folded, beside the sink. It was only as she stepped back and admired her gleaming benches that she realised there was only one set of footsteps coming down the hall.

'Lucy!' Despite her daughter's pale face, Ro managed to stop herself from blurting, 'What's happened? What's the matter?'

Instead, she said a little too nervously, 'You're . . . home early.'

'Yeah, I'm tired.'

It was nonsense, of course. They both knew Lucy usually stayed at Sam's all night. Ro had half-expected her to be gone for the entire weekend. Now she stared at her daughter with a sinking heart. There could be no doubt that something had gone wrong, almost certainly with Sam. Ro wasn't sure she could bear it.

She knew how besotted Lucy was and she had hoped, with a kind of churning desperation, that her daughter might escape the romantic bad luck that had marred her own life.

Now, as Lucy stood there, just beyond the kitchen, her hands resting lightly on her hips and her long silky dark hair framing her too-pale, oval face, a thousand questions raced through Ro's head. Her daughter looked so much younger and more feminine out of her army uniform, but more fragile, too. Tonight there were shadows beneath her grey eyes. Actually, Ro thought Lucy's eyes were a bit pink, as if she'd been crying.

The evidence was damning, and Ro was gripped by a strong urge to rush to Lucy, to give her a lovely big motherly hug. But she was quelled by a forbidding tightness about her daughter's mouth. She'd always been a strong, self-sufficient little thing. And Ro had never been a confident mum.

In the end Ro simply stood, twisting her hands nervously, not brave enough to follow her instincts.

'Where's Keith?' Lucy asked, looking about her.

'He's already in bed. Reading.'

Lucy's eyes widened, as if she found this hard to believe, and Ro couldn't really blame her. None of her previous boyfriends had been readers and they would never have tackled the great, thick novels that Keith enjoyed. But if Lucy wanted to talk, Keith's absence was probably opportune now.

Problem was, Ro had no idea how to invite her daughter's

confidence. She'd coped so poorly with her own failed relationships, coming close to a nervous breakdown on a couple of occasions, and she felt terribly inadequate at this moment.

'Would – would you like a cup of tea?' she asked lamely.

'Tea?' Lucy shook her head and sent Ro a rather cynical smile. 'No, thanks.'

Helpless, Ro pointed to the fridge. 'There's always wine.'

Lucy waved this aside, too, then headed for the hallway that led to her bedroom. 'No need to fuss, Mum. I'm fine. Just tired.'

'Okay,' Ro called after her, reaching for the kettle anyway. 'But if you change your mind, feel free to help yourself to anything from the kitchen.'

Perhaps it was the right thing to say, for Lucy stopped and turned back. For a moment she stood in the hallway, frowning. 'Are you making tea for yourself?'

'Yes, dear. And for Keith. And it's dead easy to throw another teabag in a mug.'

'Then I would like one, actually,' her daughter said, and this time her tired smile held a hint of apology.

'I could bring it to you in bed, if you like.'

'That would be awesome, Mum. Thanks. You're a champion.'

At the unexpected praise, Ro's cheeks heated with pleasure.

———

Lucy felt no better after she'd scrubbed her face and changed into light summer pyjamas. She checked her phone, fearing it was pointless, but needing to know if Sam had tried to make contact.

She didn't expect him to beg her to come back, but she'd thought there might have been an apology. An opening, something to build on.

But there was nothing from Sam, which in itself was actually a pretty clear message, and Lucy felt as if she was drowning in her wretched disappointment. A heavy weight pressed against her chest as she sunk onto the bed, making it hard to breathe, and her entire body felt leaden and aching as if she'd just finished a twenty-kilo-metre march with weapons and webbing.

Her mum appeared in the doorway. 'Here's your cuppa, love.' Coming almost shyly into the room, her mother set a delicate mug patterned with violets on the bedside table. 'And I made a little snack, just in case you were hungry.'

The plate her mum offered held two slices of toast covered with grilled cheese, all melting and browned and smelling divine. It had been Lucy's favourite comfort food, when she was little.

'No worries if you don't feel like it,' her mum said gently.

But Lucy had barely eaten a mouthful of Thai and she now real-ised she was starving. 'Oh, that's perfect,' she said. 'Exactly what I need.' She felt a rush of gratitude. Her mother was trying so hard. 'Thanks so much, Mum.'

Looking bashfully pleased, Ro set the plate beside the mug. 'I'll leave you to enjoy it, then.'

Straightening, she stood looking down at Lucy and her mouth opened as if she wanted to say something else, but then she looked worried, almost scared, and she shut it again with an uncertain smile.

Of course, her mother must be wondering what had happened, but Lucy was very grateful for the silence. She couldn't possibly talk about Sam now – her mum would be so upset she'd only make things worse – so she gave her best attempt at a smile. 'Night, Mum.'

'Night-night, love. You know how to adjust the aircon, don't you?'

'Yep, I'll be fine, thanks.'

'Night, then. Hope you sleep well.'

Not much chance of that, Lucy thought as her mother disap-peared and she took her first appreciative sip of the hot, slightly too sweet tea.

7

Lucy was wrong about not sleeping. By the time she finished her tea and toast, she felt distinctly drowsy and was too mentally and emotionally exhausted to drag herself through the miserable muddle of thoughts that had plagued her since she left Sam's place. She fell asleep quickly and slept soundly, only to wake early, her body clock still not adjusted to the shift in time zones.

Only the thinnest pre-dawn light trickled through the tiny slits in the vertical blinds, and Lucy knew her mother never roused before seven-thirty, but from force of habit she sat up, ready to meet the day. Then she remembered Sam and the way they'd parted last night.

Oh God.

A fresh slug of despair caught her mid chest and she reached quickly for her phone to check for new messages.

Still nothing from Sam. Just a message from her friend Kaz.

Hope your first night home was fabulous. Catch up soon? K xx

Lucy flinched. Just as well she hadn't already asked Kaz to be her bridesmaid.

With a groan, she sank back into the bed and drew the covers over her head as she tried to shut off a new tidal wave of misery.

Once again her mind reeled with questions, with arguments, with rationalisations.

It's not me, it's him. He has the problem.

I did the right thing when I walked out. If I'd stayed, we would have had a huge fight.

Why should I get a discharge just to please his ego?

Round and round Lucy's thoughts chased each other. Somewhere in the middle of her angst over Sam, she realised that she had another problem. If Sam made no attempt at a reconciliation, she had no idea where she would live now. And what the hell was she going to do with the lovely long weeks of leave that she'd earned?

She certainly couldn't moon around this apartment for a month with her mother and Keith, and no way was she going to move into Lavarack Barracks. Would she have to start hunting for a flat?

In a burst of frustration, she threw back the sheets again, then stared morosely at the wardrobe containing the boxes that held all her worldly possessions. When she tried to imagine setting up a place of her own, her brain refused to come to the party. She didn't want to set up house on her own. That wasn't the way she'd planned it, and it certainly wasn't what she'd been looking forward to all the time she'd been away. She simply couldn't imagine it.

To her dismay, tears filled her eyes and then spilled. *Damn Sam.* She couldn't lie in bed weeping. Summoning new reserves of willpower, she jumped up and slid the wardrobe door open.

The first thing that caught her eye was the tin with her grandfather's things.

If only I could talk to you, Harry.

But it was too early to charge over to his place and anyway, his failed kidneys were enough for him to deal with. He didn't need a lovesick granddaughter spilling her guts.

Lucy might have given in to a tear or two, but she was afraid the tears might turn into sobs that reached the other bedroom and bring her mum rushing to her aid in her pyjamas.

With a shuddering sigh, she forced herself to focus on the tin holding Harry's cherished bits and pieces. Yesterday afternoon she'd been so sidetracked by the photo of the beautiful woman called George that she hadn't paid much attention to the old letters and military medals that were also in there. It would probably be ages till the others got up and she needed something that would take her mind off Sam.

Settling on the bed again, she opened the tin and set the photo aside. There was a swag of Harry's medals. Clearly he'd had a *big* war. There were letters, too.

It was puzzling that she knew so very little about her grandfather as a soldier. Sure, he'd admitted to serving in the Middle East and New Guinea but when she'd tried several times to quiz him, she'd gleaned very few details.

She could only suppose his reluctance to talk meant he'd had a grim time of it. He certainly hadn't been thrilled when she'd wanted to join the army, and she might have listened to his reasoning if her mum hadn't thrown such a tantrum. Ro's frenzied yelling that Lucy was crazy and that the army was a man's world had roused Lucy's stubborn rebellious streak.

It was an echo of an earlier stubbornness that had begun in her childhood when the boys next door had refused to let her join in their backyard war games. They'd even put up a sign on the fence that bordered her place. *Gerls not aloud.*

Lucy had heckled. 'Drop-kicks, you can't even spell.' Then she'd swallowed her pride and pleaded with them and when that hadn't worked, she'd pelted the boys with fallen rotting mangoes.

The high point of her childhood had been the day they'd eventually given in and had grudgingly agreed she could join them. She hadn't minded that her rifle was only a long stick and not one of the realistic plastic rifles the boys had received for their birthdays. She'd adored stalking with them through tall patches of heliconias, and painting her face with dirt before wriggling on her stomach through the dangling roots of a huge banyan tree.

That had been the start of her interest in soldiering but, growing up in Townsville, it was impossible to miss seeing real soldiers as part of everyday life. In their exciting camouflage-print uniforms and boots, soldiers were everywhere – in shopping centres, at the airport, in convoy on the roads, or turning out in force to help with clean-ups after cyclones.

To Lucy they had always looked impressively fit and ready for action, so perhaps it was inevitable that she'd viewed an army career as an exciting and adventurous challenge.

Of course, when she'd joined up, she'd soon learned that the army had its downside. Suddenly, there were countless decisions imposed on her by others in which she had absolutely no say. Given her headstrong and independent spirit, she'd found this hard to stomach at first.

She smiled now, as she sorted through Harry's tin, remembering how those early months had rankled, but her musings came to an abrupt halt when she turned over a medal that was totally different from all the others.

'Hello, what's this?'

The medal was roughly made, with none of the traditional ribbons attached, and the metal badge itself was triangular rather than round. In the centre of the triangle, a rat had been cut from brass.

A rat?

Surely that could only mean one thing. This medal was from Tobruk. Harry had been a Rat of Tobruk.

A sharp little thrill ran through Lucy. The Rats of Tobruk were so famous . . . part of the Australian legend . . . in the tradition of the Anzacs . . .

She read the inscription: *Presented by Lord Haw-Haw to the Tobruk Rats 1941.*

Wow.

Minutes earlier she'd been sunk in despair and heartache, but now, as she rubbed the thin metal between her thumb and two fingers, excitement rushed over her skin. She tried to picture her grandfather as a young soldier at Tobruk and wondered who Lord Haw-Haw was. She wondered also about the story behind this medal. It definitely wasn't regular army issue.

She looked again at the tin and the folded sheets of letter paper, wondering if they held a clue. Setting the medals to one side, she carefully lifted the letters and, as she did so, another photo fell out – a small black-and-white snapshot of two young soldiers, clearly in the desert, on the peak of a bare, gritty ridge.

They were dressed for the heat in baggy shorts and khaki shirts with their sleeves rolled back. One man was sitting beside a pile of tent poles, his face shaded by the brim of his round metal helmet. The other was squatting nearby and his head was bare, so Lucy could see his face more clearly.

Surely he looked familiar? She held the photo into the morning light now streaming through the blinds and studied this fellow more closely. His eyes were squinted against the desert glare, but with that thick, slightly curly dark hair and that longish, handsome face, he *had* to be Harry. Yes, there was no mistaking that long firm jaw, with a cleft in the chin. It was definitely her grandfather, but my God, he looked so young.

Glancing up, Lucy caught her own reflection in the mirrored wardrobe doors. She'd never realised how much she looked like Harry – same dark hair with a tendency to curl, same longish face and cleft chin.

A painful lump filled her throat as the bonds that had always tied her to her grandfather tightened another notch. The photo had quite possibly been taken near Tobruk. She didn't have extensive knowledge of that famous siege set between the sands of the Sahara and the waters of the Mediterranean, but she knew the Aussie forces had hunkered down in trenches and caves – hence their nickname of Rats – and, under appalling conditions, they'd held their position for months and months.

But I never realised you were there, Harry.

What else didn't she know about her dear old grandfather? Harry had moved from his outback cattle property to Townsville before Lucy was born, and during the unsettling procession of her mum's boyfriends, he had become Lucy's father figure, her rock. She'd spent most of her weekends at his place and it was Harry who'd taken her to swimming lessons and to junior soccer, cheering her on with embarrassingly noisy enthusiasm from the sidelines.

He'd told her wonderful stories about growing up on Kalkadoon with his older brother, Jack, who'd been killed during the Second World War. But now, looking back, she couldn't believe she'd spent so much time with him without asking more of the really important questions.

And now it was almost too late.

Lucy's emotions were unravelling again as she set the photo on her pillow, next to the other picture of the glamorous and mysterious George. She opened the top sheet of creased and yellowed paper.

Box Street
Ashgrove
Brisbane
20 November 1939

Dear Harry,
Well, mate, it's all happening down here now. The 2/9th Battalion was formed a week ago at Redbank and I'm now

wearing the King's uniform, with my slouch hat at such a rakish angle the girls reckon I look pretty swish.

Mum is less impressed, of course, but I think my old man (despite all his usual forebodings) is quietly chuffed that I'll be part of the 18th Brigade, which was his unit in the last war.

With Poland gone and Jerry threatening France, there's a good chance that I'll be off to merry England before Christmas. Someone has to give this jumped-up former German corporal a bloody nose and it needs to be done quickly.

So, the reason for this letter is twofold. First, to give you the good news that I'm no longer in the ranks of the unemployed. I can now shout a round of beers or place more than two bob on a sure thing at Eagle Farm. Second is to entreat you to also come and join your old mates.

Naturally, it's up to you, Harry, but I wouldn't have written this letter if I didn't think you'd be up for it. If you are thinking about joining up, for God's sake don't enlist in some unit with total strangers. Where's the fun in that?

Rollo and Ted have also signed up and we're in the barracks, trying our best to make life miserable for the sergeant major. 'Snotty' Williams, who put in a couple of years playing soldiers in the militia, has scored a commission, would you believe? Naturally, we're already giving him a hard time.

I know you couldn't wait to get back to the bush after you finished at boarding school, but it doesn't seem right for Rollo, Ted and me to be part of all this without Harry the Hard Man. Just to spur you on, Rollo is under the delusion that he's actually a better shot than you were and he reckons he'll be the first one of us to get his crossed rifles.

Hope to see you soon.

Your mate,

Stu

'Good morning, love.'

Lucy was deeply engrossed in yet another letter – her third or fourth, she'd lost count – when she heard her mum's voice at the doorway.

'Oh, hi,' she said, somewhat startled. 'You're up early.'

Her mother was looking surprisingly elegant in a long, white cotton summer dressing-gown with deep pockets delicately embroidered in white on white. She'd left the gown open over a soft, floral cotton nightie and Lucy thought she looked so pretty, she could almost pose for a Mother's Day photo shoot.

'Early?' her mum said, surprised. 'It's a quarter past seven.'

'Is it really? Already?' Lucy gave a dazed shake of her head. She'd been so absorbed she'd completely lost track of time.

Cautiously curious, her mother folded her arms and propped a shoulder against the doorframe. 'What are you doing?' She frowned at the scattering of medals and letters on the bed. 'Are you going through Dad's things?'

'Yes. I hope he won't mind. It's all pretty amazing, Mum. Did you know he was a Rat of Tobruk?'

'Um . . .' Her mum looked a little flustered now and perhaps a little guilty as she gave a shrug. 'I don't think he ever mentioned it.'

'That's what I thought. He never said anything to me, either, and yet he wasn't just any old Rat.' Lucy picked up the rat medal. 'He was awarded a special badge. I checked it on Google and this is quite something – one of the unofficial badges that the men actually made while they were there in the desert.'

'Oh?'

Lucy held the badge out for her mother's inspection. 'Apparently, there were only about twenty of these given out, and the men who received them were highly valued by their fellow soldiers.'

'Oh,' her mother said again, rather flatly, and she didn't look happy as she turned the triangle of metal over in her palm.

Her reaction troubled Lucy. She'd never understood the tension between her mother and her grandfather. Harry was such a dear old thing. It had never made sense. 'They made these medals right there on the battlefield,' she said again, hoping her mum would grasp the significance. 'From shell casings and parts of a downed German plane.'

'Who's Lord Haw-Haw?' her mother asked, squinting at the inscription.

'He was part of the German propaganda. He used to broadcast on the radio and he was the first person to call the Diggers rats. It was supposed to demoralise them.' Lucy couldn't help smiling. 'But the Aussies soon turned that around. The rat nickname became a badge of honour.'

Her mum nodded as if she found this vaguely interesting and then she handed the medal back to Lucy. 'Would you like a cup of tea?'

Disappointed by this clear dismissal of Harry's achievements, Lucy nodded. 'Yes, sure.'

But her mother didn't leave for the kitchen immediately. She hovered uncertainly in the doorway, her long cotton dressing-gown floating about her ankles as she rubbed one bare foot nervously against the other. Lucy noticed that her toenails were painted deep claret and looked rather glamorous. She thought, irrelevantly, that her mum must have had a pedicure. Seemed her lifestyle had improved since she'd taken up with Keith.

'So, how's Sam?' her mum asked.

Oh God. *Whoosh.* Talk about having the rug pulled from under her. Now it was Lucy's turn to say, 'Oh.' But although her mum had asked the question carefully, there was a baleful look in her eyes that suggested she wouldn't be fobbed off.

'I – I'm not sure,' Lucy admitted. 'I mean, Sam's okay. He's perfectly fine, but —' She swallowed and avoided her mother's gaze. 'Actually, no, he's not. He's a dickhead and there might not be a wedding after all. In fact, I'm pretty sure there won't be.'

'Oh, darling.'

Lucy half-expected to be wrapped in a huge hug, but when this didn't happen, she shot her mum a forced smile that felt horribly out of shape. 'Don't quiz me about it just now, okay? I'm still pretty fragile.'

'But are you —?'

'Mum,' Lucy interjected, a warning note in her voice.

'Okay, okay, sorry. So what else did you find in that old tin?'

Grateful to return her attention to the assortment of Harry's belongings, Lucy touched the jumble on her bed. 'There are all sorts of medals. Some from New Guinea that I want to check out. And letters.' She looked up. 'Nearly all this stuff is from around the war-time, which is intriguing. There are a couple of letters from Harry's mates and one from his parents when he was in Tobruk —'

Lucy hesitated. 'But there's another letter here that was written quite a while after the war – in the early sixties, I think. It's about you.'

To Lucy's surprise her mum went bright red. 'A letter from England?' This was asked with a surly curl of her lip.

'Yes. It's pretty weird. It was sent to Harry, practically demanding that he send you to live in England.'

Actually, it was an incredibly emotional outpouring from some Englishwoman from Cornwall. Judging by her comments, she was Harry's sister-in-law, but the corner where she'd signed the letter was gone, the edges brown and nibbled looking, as if someone had once started to burn the letter and then changed their mind.

Looking up, she saw that her mother's face was still florid and her lips were trembling. Had she made a terrible gaffe by mentioning this?

'Give it here,' her mother said tightly, lunging forward and almost snatching the pages from Lucy's hand. Her lips were compressed and her eyes fierce as she scanned the first page.

'Bitch!' She spat the word out before she'd even finished, then her fist closed around the paper, scrunching the letter into a tightly crumpled ball.

'Mum!' Lucy couldn't hold back her cry.

'I'm throwing it out,' her mother snapped. 'I won't have it in my house.'

'Okay, okay.' Lucy used her most appeasing tone, although she wasn't sure her mother had the right to dispose of the letter. She began to feel guilty about opening the tin.

Her mum shoved the paper into the pocket of her dressing-gown and scowled at the rest of the letters and medals scattered on the bed. 'So, what else have you got there?' She sounded angry and suspicious now, as if she was almost accusing Lucy of assembling these things just to upset her.

'Well, there are a couple of photos.' Surely photos were safe? Lucy handed over the snap of the soldiers in the desert. 'I reckon the guy on the left must be Harry.'

Eyes still fierce, her mother accepted the photo, and, as she studied it, her expression gentled a tad. 'Yeah, that's him,' she said softly, and her mouth tilted in a sad little smile. 'He looks so young, doesn't he?'

'Incredibly young,' Lucy agreed, and now that her mum's mood was a little calmer, she *had* to ask. 'Mum, what happened when Harry got that letter from England? Did he send you over there to her? You did spend some time in England, didn't you?'

'He promised he wouldn't send me.' Her mother said this so quietly it was little more than a whisper. Her lips trembled again and she twisted the dangling sash of her dressing-gown with nervous fingers. 'Leave it, Luce. All that's best forgotten.'

Really? Seeing her mum's obvious distress, Lucy felt compelled to protest. Had Harry broken a promise? 'But you haven't forgotten,' she said. 'It still upsets you.'

For all she knew, this demanding letter might have been the source of her mum's ongoing tension with Harry. It might even have been at the root of some of her mother's other issues, like her general lack of self-confidence. Perhaps it had something to do with why her mother at times seemed more like a troubled girlfriend or sister than a parent.

But Lucy knew next to nothing about psychology, so there was little to be gained by trying to press the matter then and there.

Ro turned her attention to the other photograph of the beautiful woman called George, who so perfectly epitomised the glamour and elegance of the forties. Her hazel eyes widened with sudden interest. 'I – I wonder if this is . . .' She swallowed, clearly overcome by a new emotion. 'Do you know who that is?' she asked.

'Her name's George,' Lucy said. 'At least that's what she calls herself on the back of the photo. She's written a message to Harry.' She held the portrait out.

'Of course,' her mum whispered as she took it and her eyes visibly misted as she stared at the picture, not with bitterness this time, but with something close to reverence. 'I haven't seen this for years – not since I was a very little girl.'

It was quite a while before she turned the photo over and read the words on the back. 'George,' she said with a fond smile. 'Her proper name was Georgina.'

'Your mother?' Lucy whispered, completely entranced by this sudden switch from hard anger to a gentle, almost childlike devotion. 'She was English, wasn't she?'

It seemed her mum didn't hear her. Her thoughts were apparently miles away.

'She's so glamorous and beautiful,' Lucy said.

'Yes, she was,' her mum said at last.

'She looks posh, though. Well, no, maybe posh isn't the right word.'

'Well, her father was a baronet. Sir Richard Lenton.'

'Wow. So we're descended from aristocrats?'

'Believe me, it's not a big deal, Luce.'

'I think it is.' To Lucy it was a huge deal. For the first time she had a chance to discover more about her family's past. 'Have you any other photos of her?'

'No. All I have is her little jewellery box.'

'The one you keep on your dressing table for your rings?'

'Yes.'

'But Harry must have photos, surely?'

'I guess,' her mum said softly, still gazing at the picture in her hand, touching it with the tip of her finger with a kind of reverent awe.

A little thrill sang through Lucy. 'I wonder how on earth she met Harry.'

8

Georgina woke with a start as the Underground train jerked to a standstill and the carriage doors rattled open. She'd been so exhausted she'd fallen asleep and now, to her embarrassed surprise, she found her head on the shoulder of a soldier, her nose burrowed against his warm neck. She sat up quickly, blushing at her forwardness.

'Sorry,' she told the soldier as she rubbed at the stiffness in her neck.

'No worries, Miss.' His voice was deep and drawling with an accent she couldn't quite place. 'My pleasure.'

He had thick dark hair, cut short at the back and sides to military regulations, and his light-grey eyes sparkled with intelligent humour. His face was longish, handsome and suntanned, with the kind of ingrained tan that came from a life in the outdoors rather than a few weeks holidaying in the south of France. Georgina wondered how she'd missed seeing him earlier. Perhaps he'd boarded the train after she'd fallen asleep.

She might have taken a longer look at him, if she hadn't glanced through the carriage window and realised that they'd reached

Victoria already. This was her station. She had no choice but to fight her weariness and launch to her feet. Automatically, she smoothed the khaki skirt of her Auxiliary Territorial Service uniform and she was about to hurry away, but on an impulse that was completely out of character she looked back at the handsome soldier and smiled again. 'Thanks for letting me borrow your shoulder.'

Then she dashed for the door, her heart thrashing madly, for she *knew* that she'd just experienced a *moment*.

Hardly more than a split second, an electrifying heartbeat in time, and yet she was sure it would stay with her for ages, possibly forever. The soldier was a complete stranger, but Georgina Lenton had found something in his face, in his eyes and his voice, that was astonishingly, *frighteningly* attractive.

Flushed and slightly breathless, she stepped onto the platform, which was already crowded with people who used the Underground as an air-raid shelter. The station smelled of train smoke and hot metal. From behind her came the sound of heavy wooden doors slamming shut. The guard blew his whistle. But her thoughts were still with the soldier and she felt quite deflated as the train wheezed and began to chug forward. With deliberate effort, she straightened her shoulders.

Buck up, George.

It was time to hurry home to a hasty supper and bed, but she couldn't help turning back, just once, to watch the train pull away.

Her heart leaped when she saw the soldier right there on the platform.

'Oh, hello.' Her voice was high-pitched with surprise.

He smiled. 'G'day.'

There it was again – that deep, sun-drenched, lazy voice – and now, looking more closely, Georgina could see that his uniform wasn't British. Along with the kit bag slung over his shoulder, he carried a slouch hat.

'You're an Australian?'

'I am, indeed.'

It was time to remember her upbringing. After all, she could tell by the crown on his epaulette that he was only a warrant officer. She should give him a curt nod and swiftly ignore him. Turn and leave immediately.

But Georgina was tired of being sensible. This darned war demanded so much – long hours at work, blackouts, rations, living with the nightly fear of the ongoing Blitz. She said, 'I've never met an Australian before. I wondered about your accent.'

Another slow smile transformed his face. 'Well, I've never met a girl with such a plummy Pommy accent.'

'Plummy?'

'A very pretty shade of plum. Musical and silvery.'

Good grief. Now he was flirting with her and she'd more or less invited it, hadn't she? She was mad. And yet . . . Georgina found it so hard to ignore the compelling glow inside her, the sparks that flared when she looked into this man's light-grey eyes.

'Are you in London on leave?' She knew from her own job with the Royal Army Service Corps that Australian troops were based on the Salisbury Plain.

'I was sent up here to liaise with your mob. I have a meeting in the morning.'

Georgina knew better than to press for details.

'But I'll be free in the afternoon,' he added. 'And this is my first time in London, so I thought I'd take a look around, catch a few of the famous sights.'

'I'm afraid the city's not looking her best at the moment.'

'I dare say, but it's too good a chance to miss.' He smiled again, his eyes as sparkling as stars. 'I don't suppose you'd be free to act as a tour guide tomorrow?'

The cheek of him. Georgina opened her mouth to send him

marching, just as her mother would have done, but the necessary words of dismissal refused to emerge. She was too aware of the delicious warmth spreading through her.

It was such an unexpected thing to happen in the middle of this beastly war. Every day, often including weekends, Georgina worked hard and for long hours in the Royal Army Service Corps office in Dulwich, and each night she dragged herself back to her lonely digs. For long, dreary months, she and her fellow Londoners had lived under a permanent cloud, first with the threat of invasion and now with the terror of air raids, only to wake each morning to toppled buildings, hideous bonfires and news of fresh heartbreak.

In the midst of so much grimness, meeting this attractive man from a distant shore felt no more bizarre or dangerous than anything else that was happening. Besides, there was a steadiness in his eyes, a quiet strength about his manner that invited her to trust her deeper instincts.

'Actually,' she found herself saying, 'we had an emergency at work last weekend and I worked right through, so I do happen to have a day off tomorrow in lieu.'

The soldier covered his surprise with a charming grin. 'How's that for luck?'

It did feel surprisingly lucky.

He held out his hand. 'The name's Harry. Harry Kemp.'

'Mine's George. George Lenton.'

'George?' His eyebrows rose and his smile tilted with obvious amusement. 'I've never met a girl called George before.'

'Well, now you have.' Her father's private nickname for her had been widely adopted during last year's debutante season. Shortening girls' names to their masculine form had been quite the rage, and somehow George had stuck.

Looking back on that giddy time twelve months ago, she found it hard to believe that she'd ever been so carefree and careless. So many times at the height of the season, she'd come home from a party or a dance in the early hours of the morning, blithely stepping out of her clothes and leaving them to lie on the floor as she crawled into bed. It would have been hours later that she was woken by Hettie, who had picked up the evening clothes and taken them away to launder or mend before delivering breakfast on a tray.

The arrival of war had brought that lifestyle crashing to a halt. In a matter of weeks, *everything* had changed.

Now, Georgina led the way out of the Underground and up the broad stone steps. Outside, it was already dark, especially dark now that black curtains were drawn across everyone's windows and the headlights of vehicles were covered with hoods so they showed only the dimmest beam.

High above, the stars were shining, though, and the half-moon shone silver-white. Unfortunately, a cloudless sky with a bright moon was exactly what the German bombers wanted. There'd be an air raid tonight for sure.

'Have you arranged somewhere to stay?' she asked Harry Kemp.

'I was planning to look around for a hotel.'

'I'm not sure you'll have much luck around here. The hotels are all jolly crowded. Many people have moved into them after their houses were bombed.'

'That's an expensive option.'

Georgina shrugged. Most residents of Belgravia had pots of money.

'I can always swag down in the Underground,' he said.

'Oh, you don't want to do that. You won't get a wink of sleep. You'd better come with me, but we should probably hurry. The sirens will be starting soon.'

'Where are we going?'

'My place is just around the corner.'

Again, Harry looked momentarily surprised, but he seemed to

quickly recover. Georgina, on the other hand, was more than a little shocked by the temerity of her invitation. Despite the endless parties of last year's debutante season, her behaviour had been heavily supervised. All the debutantes' mothers had seen to that – watching from the benches with eagle eyes to make sure their darling daughters weren't dancing too close or for too long with the same young man.

Since Georgina had joined the army, she'd met a very different class of girl – girls who scorned any airs and graces and who drank and smoked as avidly as the men. These girls were also fun in a down-to-earth way that she rather liked, even though many of them considered their night out wasted if they didn't pick up a chap for a bit of slap and tickle.

Georgina had been rather stunned by their loose behaviour and now she wondered what Harry Kemp must think of her. What would he expect?

She might have worried about this, but as they turned the corner into Wilton Street, the sirens began to wail. At any moment they'd hear the grinding engines of the first German planes, the whistle of falling bombs, followed by shuddering explosions. There was no time to analyse her rashness.

'Do you have a shelter to go to?' Harry asked, keeping step with her.

She shook her head. 'I tried, but I couldn't bear it down there with all the old men coughing and snoring and babies crying. I decided I'd rather take a gamble on staying in our basement.' At this, Georgina paused, realising how presumptuous she'd been, coaxing him away from the safety of the Underground. 'Perhaps you'd rather not risk our basement though.'

Harry grinned. 'If it's good enough for you, it's good enough for me.'

'Right.' She was sure she shouldn't feel so pleased. 'Here we are.'

Grabbing the keys from her pocket, she mounted three steps and thrust a key into the brass door-lock.

Inside, she dropped the keys onto the hallstand along with her hat. She caught her reflection in the mirror and thought how unattractive she looked – tired, with her make-up all worn off and her hair cut into a short bob. She ran her fingers through her honey brown hair, wishing it was still shoulder length and wavy. The army had demanded she put it in a bun, so she'd decided to have it cut short instead. It was easy to look after, but this evening, she would have liked to look more feminine. She wished she could put on some pretty lipstick and perhaps a little perfume.

Taking a deep, steadying breath, she turned to face Harry Kemp.

He wasn't looking at her, however. He was staring about him at the house and frowning deeply.

'Is something the matter, Harry?'

'This house,' he said, waving to encompass the entrance hall's black-and-white art deco floor tiles, the chandeliers overhead and the enormous gilt-framed mirror above the mantelpiece and then, incongruously, the stirrup pump and bucket standing ready to put out a fire. 'I expected a little flat. But this is palatial. Did you really say this is *your* place?'

'Well, it belongs to my family, to my father, of course.'

'Of course,' he said quietly, with a slow smile that was now only slightly bewildered. 'But honestly, George, I don't want to impose on your family.'

'Oh, don't worry, there's no one else here. My parents are down in Cornwall, and they'll be staying there for the duration. My sister's in some little cottage in God knows where. Her husband's in the RAF and she has to keep following him from pillar to post. Come on,' she said, beckoning. 'This house is a bit of a rabbit warren, so we've closed off all the other floors. For one thing, it saved making endless blackout curtains. These days I spend most of my time below stairs, mainly in the kitchen.'

Before worried second thoughts about bringing Harry into the house could take hold, she hurried on with a running commentary. 'There aren't any servants down here now, of course. Our men have all joined up and the women are doing war work, so there's only James. He was our footman, and he couldn't join the military because of his weak chest, so he has a little room at the back of the house and he keeps an eye on the place for us, but most of the time he's being terribly important and busy as an air raid warden.'

As Georgina said this, a menacing drone of aeroplanes sounded overhead. She shot a glance to Harry and found him watching her with obvious concern.

'They take a bit of getting used to,' she said.

He nodded but made no comment, then gave a little shrug and she realised that his concern was for her and not for himself. She found this incredibly comforting.

They reached the kitchen with its long scrubbed table where the servants used to dine. Against one long wall stood a huge dresser crowded with crockery and on the opposite wall, shining rows of copper pots and pans hung above the cooking range.

'This is quite amazing,' Harry said. 'Your father's not a duke, or a lord or something, is he?'

'A baron,' Georgina said lightly. Then quickly, to cover any nervousness, she tried to sound efficient and businesslike. 'Now, if you'd like to come with me and collect a little more coal from the scullery, I'll get the things I need to make our supper.'

Harry smiled again and she wondered if he'd caught the note of pride in her voice and had guessed that cooking was a newly acquired skill for her.

Self-consciously, she added as they reached the scullery, 'I have plenty of eggs.'

'Fresh eggs?'

'Yes. They're from our place in Cornwall. Mummy sent fresh supplies up to London last week, so I have hens' eggs, milk and butter straight from the farm *and* blackberry jam. Proper jam, not the thin miserable stuff the shops sell these days. I'm rather spoiled, actually.'

To her relief, she felt quite comfortable with Harry in the kitchen. As a new wave of German planes thundered overhead, he set to lighting the stove while she broke eggs into a bowl to make an omelette.

'So whereabouts in Australia do you live?' she asked him as she beat the eggs and a little milk with a fork.

'We have a cattle station called Kalkadoon. It's in north Queensland in the outback.'

Georgina liked the sound of a cattle station and she gave a nod of approval. 'I love the countryside. I've always preferred it to the city, although I'm afraid I don't know one end of Australia from the other. I do have an aunt and uncle living in New Guinea, though. They're on the island of New Britain.'

'Well, north Queensland's closer to New Guinea than to Sydney.'

'Is it really?'

Harry was smiling and Georgina found herself smiling back. In fact she wanted to grin she felt so ridiculously happy.

'When the war started, Aunt Cora was very keen for me to go out there to stay with them.' The memory brought another smile. 'It would have been safer, of course, and I was very tempted. Who wouldn't want to escape this horrible war and go to a tropical island instead?'

Harry looked amused. 'Coconuts and palm trees and sunny skies.'

'Exactly. No planes or bombs. It would have been lovely.' As she finished whisking the eggs, she shrugged. 'But I couldn't bring myself to rush off and abandon poor old England.'

Harry nodded at this, then stood with his arms folded across his considerable chest, watching as she set a pan on the stove, poured in the eggs, and tilted the pan until they covered the base.

'You're a dab hand at this,' he said with clear admiration.

To Georgina's dismay she felt her face burn with an obvious blush. 'Omelettes are about the only thing I know. I learned how to make them when I was ten years old. Our gamekeeper's son taught me. We cooked over an open fire using wild birds' eggs.'

'Fair dinkum?'

'Fair –? Uh, excuse me?'

Another grin lit his face. 'Sorry. I just meant that it sounds like a lot of fun.'

'It was.'

She shouldn't have looked at Harry again then. His eyes gleamed not just with interest, but with a deeper appreciation that sent fine tremors running through her. It was only with the greatest difficulty that she concentrated on not spoiling the omelette. Even so, a kind of singing excitement danced under her skin as she reached for a wooden spoon to gently lift and stir the egg mix, before tilting the pan so the uncooked eggs ran underneath.

'I'm afraid I don't have any ham for a filling,' she said. 'There's a little bacon, but it might be best if we save that for breakfast.'

'This will be perfect.'

'It will be even better with a little wine to wash it down.'

And indeed it was. In fact it was ridiculously perfect to sit in the kitchen in Belgravia opposite the handsome Harry Kemp from Australia, sipping one of her father's best Bordeaux clarets and sharing a simple but perfectly golden omelette.

So very different from her life twelve months ago. Again, Georgina's mind flashed back, this time to the Queen Charlotte's Ball, which was supposedly one of the highlights of the season's calendar, when she and the other debutantes, all dressed in the mandatory white gowns, had paraded down the grand staircase and into the ballroom of Grosvenor House to curtsey to a giant cake.

Admittedly, there'd been an enormous amount of money raised for the famous Queen Charlotte's maternity hospital, but the carry-on seemed so bloody ridiculous, even more so now, looking back.

From outside came the sound of gunfire, soft and muffled in the distance.

'Do you want to listen to the news on the wireless?' Georgina asked.

Harry shook his head. 'Not tonight.'

'Good. It's nice to take a break from bad news and not think about the war. Tell me more about your place in the country.'

He gave another of his slow, incredibly charming smiles. 'It's nothing like the English countryside. The outback's very remote and rugged.'

'I like wild places. Is it a big property?'

'It is compared with properties here.' Harry took a sip of wine. 'I guess Kalkadoon might be the size of one of the smaller English counties.'

She laughed, but she was also deeply impressed. She thought briefly of her Aunt Cora and wondered if this exciting, edgy fluttering and happiness was how she had felt on the night she'd met her romantic Lord Teddy.

'Do you have servants?' It was impolite of her to ask Harry this, but she was too curious to hold back, and she wanted him to keep talking. She liked hearing the lazy mix of amusement and confidence in his voice.

'We have stockmen to help with the cattle,' he said. 'And a cook. They're mostly Aborigines —' He stopped and then grimaced, looked almost embarrassed. 'Stockmen, footmen. I guess they're kind of the same – only different.' Picking up his wine glass, he smiled wryly. 'Very, *very* different.'

Georgina found herself leaning forward, elbows on the table. 'What do you love about where you live?'

At this, Harry let out a surprised huff, then frowned as he dropped his gaze to his glass.

'I only ask because I'm genuinely curious,' Georgina added, in case he thought she was simply trying to make conversation.

'And it's a good question. You see, my home is remote and rugged and not the slightest bit pretty like England, but it has its own unusual kind of beauty.' He looked thoughtful for a moment. 'As for choosing things I like, there's waking in the morning to the sound of magpies – ours are a lot more musical than the ones you have here. Or riding my horse at full pelt across plains that stretch all the way to the horizon. Just quietly walking the horse under the melaleuca trees down along the creek bank. There're the smells, too – the eucalyptus smell of the bush, or the smell of the first summer rains hitting the dry dust.'

His mouth tilted in a crooked smile. 'And then there's the sound of kookaburras laughing.'

'Do they really laugh?'

'Yes, they're hilarious.' Now he was flashing her a cheeky grin, and then he let his head drop back and began to make an astonishing *kook-kook-kook* sound. To Georgina's surprise he kept going. '*Kook-ha, kook-ha, ha, ha, ooh, ooh, ooh.*'

The sounds continued, flowing and ridiculous, and utterly contagious. Georgina began to giggle and once she started, Harry made even louder kookaburra sounds. She couldn't stop laughing now. Soon she was doubled over, holding her stomach.

'I believe you,' she gasped, when Harry finally stopped and she caught her breath. But oh, how good it felt. She couldn't remember the last time she'd laughed like that. Surely it was years ago that she'd felt so giddy and untroubled?

'I'd love to hear a kookaburra in the wild.' There was next-to-no chance that she would, of course.

Perhaps the same thought occurred to Harry. He took another sip of wine, then said, 'Enough about me. Tell me how you came to join the army.'

'Well, it certainly wasn't because I wanted to look fetching.' Georgina cast a downwards glance at her uniform. 'Most of my girl-friends joined the navy because of the Wrens' lovely blue uniforms. These ATS ones are so ugly. Shapeless khaki skirt, khaki blouse.'

'Nowhere near ugly,' Harry said softly and the look in his eyes might have melted her on the spot, but there was a sudden *boom-boom* of heavy bombs close by, followed by the *crump-crump* of a building being torn apart, and then the sound of breaking glass and slates falling.

They looked at each other.

'That one sounded a lot closer, didn't it?' Georgina said.

'Perhaps.'

Harry didn't look worried and she felt her fear calmed by the steadiness in his eyes. She poured the rest of the wine into their glasses.

'I joined up because my father and grandfather were both in the army,' she continued more soberly. 'If there'd been a son, he would have been in the army as well, but there's only my sister Alice and I, and Alice was married at the start of the war, so she's been busy with her pilot.' She gave a shrug. 'I knew I didn't want to be a nurse, so I put my hand up for the army.'

Georgina didn't add that when war was declared – even though she'd known she should dread what might come – she'd been secretly hoping for a little excitement and possible adventure. Nor did she mention that her mother had been worried she would fall in love with a lowly sergeant and had urged Georgina's father to pull rank, with the result that George was made a clerk to one of the officers, Captain Ian McNicoll, who'd lost his right arm in the

First World War just as her Uncle Teddy had, and was subsequently posted to a Royal Army Service Corps office in Dulwich.

It had all been quite an eye-opener for Georgina when she first arrived. The scale of the task of transporting, clothing and feeding the British Army had seemed overwhelming. As well as coordinating road and rail transport for troop movements, there were also thousands of tradesmen, carpenters, bakers, mechanics and even foresters employed as part of this effort to support the soldiers.

Thinking about the men at her work, many of whom quite happily entertained women who were not their wives, she said, 'I suppose I should ask if you're married or attached, or anything.' With his looks, Harry was bound to have had opportunities.

He lifted a dark, amused eyebrow before he slowly shook his head. 'No wife, no fiancée or girlfriend. There are certain social limitations to where I live. But I'm sure it must be different for you, a lovely girl living in London.'

'Ah, but I'm choosy.' Georgina willed herself not to look coy because he'd called her *a lovely girl*. 'Besides, there's not a lot of point in getting too caught up with someone at the moment, is there?' she quickly countered. 'Not with the war and everything.'

'I don't suppose so.'

He sounded so calm, so at ease in his skin, she felt foolish for having raised the subject. She needed a quick change of direction. 'Would you like pudding? I could offer you toast and jam, but not much else.'

'I don't want to use up your rations.'

'You won't. I assure you, the supply of fresh produce from Cornwall is steady.'

So they ate two thick slices of bread each, spreading them generously with butter and blackberry jam and washing them down with scalding cups of tea. It was incredibly cosy in the warm kitchen and so easy to be with Harry.

Georgina found herself thinking again about the fuss of last year's season – the drama of choosing the right gowns, of learning how to process through the royal palace and to curtsey before the King and Queen, the pressure to be seen with all the right people, at all the right places, at the most glittering parties. The expense, the glamour, the bright lights, the music and the handsome young men, all looking so dashing in their full evening kit.

So much had changed so quickly. Almost all of the young men she'd danced with last year were in uniform now. Some had been killed already – Freddy Mathews, Charles Hawthorne, Michael St George.

Even for her, there'd been massive changes. Before the war, she'd hardly ever stepped below stairs to this kitchen. And now, this night . . .

Sharing tea and toast with a man from another world, a man who at any moment would be sent to somewhere terrible.

Watching Harry over the rim of her teacup, she tried to imagine where he might be heading. What lay in front of him? What might this war demand of him? She shivered. 'Do you know where you'll be sent next?'

'No idea. We're here to defend England, waiting for orders.'

Outside there was another burst of gunfire, another explosion. A small impatience flashed in Harry's eyes. 'I must admit we're pretty keen to get stuck into Jerry.'

He drank the last of his tea and set the cup down in its saucer. 'Thank you. I can't remember a meal I've enjoyed more.'

Nor could Georgina, but she wasn't quite brave enough to say so. She collected their plates and cups and wine glasses and took them to the sink in the scullery.

'Would you like a hand with the washing up?' Harry asked from the doorway.

'No, thank you.' She raised her voice over the thumps of guns shooting at planes overhead. 'A daily help will pop in for an hour or two tomorrow and she can look after these.' Her heart was beating fast. It was time to discuss their sleeping arrangements, which weren't straightforward now that most of the house was closed up. 'You haven't told me what sights you want to see after you've finished with your business in the morning,' she said, still skirting the awkward topic. 'I – I suppose you'll want to see all the main attractions – the Tower Bridge, Buckingham Palace, Big Ben.'

'That'd be great.' Harry casually leaned a shoulder against the doorjamb. 'I had been hoping to see a painting in the National Gallery, but I heard they've evacuated everything out of there.'

'Yes, I'm afraid all the paintings have been ferreted away for safe keeping.' Curiosity compelled her to ask, 'Which painting did you want to see?'

'Oh, it's just a small thing my father told me about. A watercolour called something like "The Dales at Dawn". Apparently, it was painted by my great-grandfather.'

'Really? He must have been jolly good to have something hung in the National Gallery.'

Harry simply smiled. He was still standing in the doorway to the scullery, virtually blocking her path. Quietly, he said, 'It's occurred to me, George, that you're not the run-of-the-mill upper-class English girl.'

It took a moment for her to catch her breath. 'And I suspect you're not the run-of-the-mill Aussie soldier.'

His light-grey eyes blazed in his brown face and the air between them seemed to crackle with tension. She sensed that Harry wanted to kiss her and she knew, without question, that she wanted him to. But annoyingly, she heard her mother's voice.

You must never let a man kiss you unless you're engaged to marry him.

The effects of this unsolicited advice must have shown in her face, for instead of stepping towards her, as she was sure he would, Harry frowned and moved away, allowing her to pass easily through to the kitchen.

Drenched by maddening disappointment, she wanted to cry. She wished they could go back to the start of their 'run-of-the-mill' conversation. It had been so brimming with flirtatious promise. Why on earth had she given a moment's thought to what her mother might have said aeons ago, before the war arrived to turn everything upside down.

Nothing was the same now. Nothing.

Nothing.

'George?'

Her head snapped up. 'Yes?'

'You look upset. Would you like me to —'

'Yes,' she broke in quickly.

'Excuse me?'

'Yes, I'd like you to kiss me.' Before she completely lost her nerve, she added, with a timorous smile, 'Please.'

A painfully long beat passed before he lifted his hand to touch her cheek. A moth-like touch. 'Hasn't anyone ever told you that it's dangerous to say please?'

'I – I think I'd rather like to live dangerously.'

They stood facing each other in the silent kitchen. The only sound was the ticking of the kitchen clock and then the distant clanging of a bell – an ambulance or a fire engine rushing to yet another scene of devastation.

Then, to Georgina's intense relief, Harry Kemp gathered her in and kissed her.

9

In the little room beside the kitchen, which Mrs Rogers, the house-keeper, had formerly used as an office, a shaded lamp now cast a gentle glow, a small circle of light, over the rumpled bedclothes where they lay.

Weeks ago, Georgina had turned it into her own bedroom, organising for the lamp, along with the double bed, to be brought down from one of the now disused upstairs rooms. She'd also brought pretty frilled cushions and a chintz coverlet to make the serviceable little room more feminine.

Harry turned to her in the soft light. 'Why didn't you tell me?'

'Tell you what? That I was a virgin?'

'Yes.'

'And what would have happened if I'd told you?'

With a gentle hand, he tucked a strand of her hair behind her ear. 'I would have had second thoughts . . . about this.'

'Which is exactly why I didn't say anything. I'm sorry, Harry, but I *wanted* you to make love to me and I'm ever so glad you did.'

She saw the movement of his throat muscles as he swallowed. 'It – it was – wonderful,' she said softly.

He drew her against him and pressed a kiss to her forehead. Happy, Georgina closed her eyes and lay against his warm solid chest, listening to the steady, comforting thud of his heartbeats.

After a bit, she asked, 'Is this your only night in London?'

'I'm afraid so. I have to be back in barracks by tomorrow evening.'

'Then I'm especially glad about this,' she said and then she spoiled the moment by yawning.

'You should go to sleep.'

'I'm not sleepy.'

'Of course you are.'

'Not really.'

'You're exhausted. You fell asleep on the train.'

'Oh yes, that's right. Thank heavens I did, though, or I might not have met you.'

He made a soft sound that might have been a chuckle or a sigh. 'Good night, George.' He pulled the bedcovers back over them, and tucked the sheet high under her chin, then turned out the lamp. The room was now completely dark. Dark and warm and safe with Harry beside her.

'Good night, Harry.'

She settled into her pillows and they lay in silence, their bodies nestled, but of course she couldn't possibly drop straight off to sleep. She had far too much to think about. She wanted to remember every detail of this amazing night. The life-changing moment of meeting Harry on the train. Their cosily intimate supper. Harry's thrilling, beautiful kiss that had ended with them hurrying to this bed.

After the initial, exciting shock of being naked together, she'd been swiftly overwhelmed by the utter magic of Harry's tenderness and passion. She'd had no idea that sex could be like this. He'd made her feel incredibly desirable and cherished.

I've been waiting for him, she thought happily.

But then, not quite so happily, *Trust me to fall for a man who's neither an officer nor British.*

Her mother would have such a fit if she knew.

An Australian!

Georgina could so easily imagine the snobbish, horrified sneer in her mother's voice.

Sadly, it didn't really matter. The unpleasant truth was that after tomorrow, Harry Kemp would be gone to God-knew-where and Georgina was unlikely to ever see him again. She lay awake for ages thinking about that.

They both had a restless night, but their tossing and turning had little to do with the German planes overhead. Georgina wondered if or rather hoped that Harry might take her into his arms again, but he made no further attempt to seduce her. She wondered if her virginity had scared him off.

Eventually she fell asleep, but she woke as usual just as daylight crept greyly around the edges of the blackout curtains. Her first thoughts were about Harry, but when she rolled over, the bed beside her was empty. Then she heard a small clatter in the kitchen and she reached for her dressing-gown, slipped her feet into fluffy slippers and hurried to find him.

His hair was damp and she could see that he'd already washed and shaved, and had dressed in his uniform. He had the stove lit, too, and the kettle was humming, close to boiling.

'Morning, George.' His smile this morning was a shade less confident. Perhaps sadder.

Georgina felt rather sad, too. Last night's romantic tryst should have been nothing more than a simple fling, time-out from the beastliness of the war, but she knew that her heart had become inextricably involved, and when she thought about Harry leaving today, she was engulfed by a wave of awful, gut-wrenching loss.

But she managed to smile as she said, 'Good morning,' and then quickly, as she headed for the scullery, 'I'll get that bacon I mentioned last night. It will go down well with tea and toast.'

They worked quietly together, almost like an old married couple, with Georgina frying the bacon while Harry made the tea and buttered the toast, and in no time they were once again sitting opposite each other.

'I hope you don't mind my eating in my dressing-gown,' she said.

'Of course not. It's your day off. I'd say it's compulsory.'

His gaze warmed her, like sunlight on her skin, and she felt sadder than ever. 'Tell me more about Kalkadoon,' she said, suddenly anxious to know as much about him as she could. 'What does the name mean? It sounds Scottish.'

Harry merely shrugged. 'The outback is about as different from Scotland as you could possibly imagine. My grandfather named the property after the local tribe of Aborigines. They're fearsome warriors, so I suppose that's something they have in common with the Scots.' A gleam of the old amusement shone in his grey eyes. 'So, what's your next question?'

'Am I being too nosy?'

'I don't mind.'

With a piece of bacon poised on her fork, she asked the first question that leaped into her head. 'What do cattle graziers eat for breakfast – when they're not away fighting wars?'

'Steak, of course. Steak and eggs.' Still smiling, Harry narrowed his eyes. 'What about minor baronets and their families? What do they dine on for breakfast?'

'Well, I should think that apart from their farm produce, my parents are on rations now, pretty much like everyone else, but before the war, there would have been bacon and eggs, kidneys, salmon, kedgeree, coffee . . .'

Harry's smile sobered.

'What's the matter? Did I say something wrong?'

'No, 'course not.' But his mouth was firm, his expression serious. There was a perfectly good clock on the kitchen wall, but he slipped back the cuff of his uniform and unsnapped the leather cover on his wristwatch. 'I need to get to that meeting by eight, so I'd better get cracking.'

'It won't take you long on the Underground, but of course, don't let me delay you.'

He drained his teacup then stood. 'I'm not sure how long this will take. Can we meet at midday? I'd like to take you to lunch.'

'That would be lovely. Perhaps we should meet at Piccadilly Circus?'

'Sounds good to me. How will I find you?'

'I'll wear a red carnation in my buttonhole.'

At this Harry grinned a lovely, face-lighting grin, and for Georgina the whole world felt better.

'Actually, I'll be waiting right in the middle of the intersection. There used to be a statue of Eros, but it's been dismantled and covered in sandbags and huge ads for war bonds. You won't miss me there.'

'Right.' He came to her side of the table and leaned down to kiss her cheek. 'I wouldn't want to miss you.'

After he'd left, Georgina vowed to be sensible. She would make the most of this one day and let tomorrow take care of itself. After all, the war left her with little choice.

She took the breakfast dishes through to the scullery and, as the daily help was inclined to gossip, she changed the bed sheets, took them to the laundry and set the washing machine going. Then she had a long bath and washed her hair. Wrapped again in her dressing-gown, she drew back the curtains.

The sky had clouded over but at least it wasn't raining. She looked out at the neighbours' houses, which were all, thankfully, still in one piece, although bearing the effects of war with their sand-bagged doorways and windows crisscrossed with tape to stop glass from flying in a bomb blast.

She paced restlessly while her hair dried. It was still far too early to meet Harry, but she changed into a grey woollen skirt and a deep cherry angora sweater tucked into the skirt's belted waist. She thought about wearing her pearls but opted for a more casual, floaty silver scarf. She carefully put on make-up and sprayed scent on her wrists.

Then, unable to sit still, she decided to leave early and she walked to the corner to catch a bus to Piccadilly Circus. The view from the bus window was grimmer than ever. Office blocks had storey after storey of blown-out windows, shopfronts were boarded-up, a brigade of civilians was sweeping rubble into the gutters with wide, stiff brooms.

St James's church was a dreadful sight with its toppled steeple, the roof burned and collapsed and the lovely stained-glass windows gone, and there was a huge bomb crater on the opposite side of the road.

But Harry was ready and waiting for her – such a lovely surprise. 'I got away a bit early,' he said, 'so I grabbed a carnation.'

What he offered her, however, was not one carnation, but an entire bunch of bright crimson blooms.

His smile was infectious and Georgina was grinning as she buried her nose in the scented bouquet. 'Where on earth did you find these?'

'Covent Garden.'

She knew they must have cost a small fortune. Almost all the flower gardens had been given over to growing vegetables as part of the Dig for Victory campaign.

'Have you any idea what a thrill it is to let famous names like

Covent Garden just trip off my tongue?' Harry said.

'Then we'll have to make it our mission to fit as many of those famous names as we can into one afternoon.'

'But first, I promised you lunch. I've been paid, so I'm flush.'

He took her to the Criterion, which wasn't Georgina's favourite restaurant, but it hardly mattered when she was there with Harry. The place was warm and smelled of good food and the inevitable cigarette smoke and it was filled with men in uniform and elegant women, who may have been the men's wives but probably weren't. And it was suitably impressive with its imposing arches and ornate décor, especially the curved ceiling of glittering golden tiles.

Apart from all the people in uniform, there was no hint of the war, which was perhaps the best thing of all.

'We can't stay here too long if you want to do some sightseeing,' Georgina warned as Harry helped her out of her coat.

'Yes, but we'll still need a drink.'

They were shown to a table. Georgina set her flowers between them and Harry ordered a bottle of champagne, which came with gratifying speed.

'Cheers,' he said as he raised his glass.

'Here's mud in your eye,' Georgina responded, quoting her father's favourite toast.

Harry took a careful, almost cautious sip.

Watching him, Georgina said, 'Don't you like champagne?'

'Must admit, it isn't my usual poison.' He took another sip and grimaced.

Oh dear. 'You really don't like it, do you?'

Harry shrugged and gave a lopsided grin. 'I guess aerated vinegar is an acquired taste.'

'Well, it's very kind of you to buy it for me anyway. Thank you. I happen to love champagne.' To prove it, she took a long, appreciative sip before she set her glass down. 'Have you had a successful morning?'

'All the necessary plans are in place.'

'That's good. And don't worry, I won't pry, Harry. Honestly. I know from my own work that you can't talk about these things.'

'Oh, it's not top secret. Your brass will be jawing about it soon enough. They're going to have a parade with the Australian troops marching across Westminster Bridge. I was just sent up here to do the leg work.'

'When are you marching?'

He named a date about three weeks away.

'So, you'll be coming back to London. That's —' Georgina was about to say wonderful, but hesitated. She had already decided it was completely foolish to think that she and Harry had any kind of future beyond this day. 'That's nice,' she finished lamely.

'It won't be all that nice, trying to round up my mob and get them spit and polished.'

'A little like herding your cattle?'

'More like herding cats.'

Harry's smiling gaze connected with hers and the crowded restaurant faded until nothing mattered but the two of them. And again Georgina could feel that delicious stirring of unbearable excitement. It was like hearing the first familiar bars of a heartbreakingly beautiful piece of music.

'I suppose the parade is a morale-boosting exercise,' she said, trying to ignore the melting sensation Harry's proximity roused. 'To demonstrate the Empire rallying to the aid of the mother country.'

'Actually, that's a bit of a sore point with the Aussies. We don't talk about the Empire these days. It's the Commonwealth now. And to set the record straight, we haven't been rounded up by the King. All the Aussies over here have volunteered.'

'For which we're very grateful.' Georgina raised her glass again and gave a little bow of her head. 'And full of admiration.'

'Well, enough of that.' Harry's tone was dry, his eyes alight. 'Let's check out this menu.'

It all went too quickly of course. The champagne lunch and the hasty tour of London's sights: the promised Buckingham Palace along with Oxford Street, Savile Row, the cathedrals and castles. At some point during the afternoon, they stopped playing it safe and they walked as lovers, with arms linked, or holding hands, or with Harry's arm around Georgina's shoulders.

In the taxi on the way to the Tower of London, Harry stole a long and lovely kiss. On the Tower Bridge, in broad daylight, Georgina stole one back. Such a heady experience, a sense of her feet not touching the ground, of knowing that she was living inside the most delicious, happy dream from which she never wanted to wake.

Too soon the daylight faded and blackout curtains were drawn. A chilling wind swept up the Thames and they hailed a taxi that took them to Waterloo station.

The platform was crowded and it was as if they'd come full circle. Was it really only twenty-four hours ago that they'd met?

Harry's train pulled in and Georgina tried valiantly to smile. The doors opened and passengers clambered out, looking tired and hassled. Her lips were trembling so badly, her smile wouldn't hold.

'I'll ask if I can have time off,' she said. 'So I can come to wave at your parade.'

'It might not be worth the trouble.'

'It doesn't matter. I know you won't be able to talk to me or anything, and you probably won't even see me.' But she would see him, she would watch him marching, looking soldierly and stiff and staring grimly ahead. It would be something.

Harry looked away and swallowed. 'I've got your address, so I'll write to you.'

'That would be lovely.'

People were boarding the train. At any minute the guard's whistle would blow.

'And, of course, I want to thank you.'

'No, don't, Harry.' Hot tears stung her eyes. 'Saying thank you makes it – I don't know – as if I've done you a favour or something, but it wasn't like that, was it?'

His eyes shimmered and she heard the way he drew a quick breath. 'Bloody hell, George.'

'Yes, bloody hell,' she said softly. 'That about sums it up, doesn't it?'

The train's engine gave an impatient wheeze. A man's voice called, 'All aboard!'

Harry cracked a very lopsided grin. 'Maybe you'll come to Australia when this is all over and I can show you around.'

'I might hold you to that.'

They shared tremulous smiles.

'Bye then.'

Just one kiss, short and sweet.

Her throat was painfully tight, but she forced the words out. 'Bye, Harry. Stay safe.'

The guard's whistle blew and she watched through a blur of tears as he jumped on board.

'Excuse me, sir?'

Captain McNicoll looked up from the pile of paperwork on his desk. 'What is it, Lenton?'

'I was hoping to have a little time off next Tuesday morning. I have an appointment.'

Her boss, a blue-eyed, sandy haired Scot with high cheekbones and a long, firm jaw that hinted at Viking heritage, watched her over the rim of his glasses as he waited for her to elaborate.

'It's a meeting with my family's lawyer, sir. My father has asked me to see him.' This wasn't in any way true, and Georgina felt frightfully bad about lying. She hadn't dreamed that she would go to such lengths to see Harry again, and the risk certainly came with a price in the form of her uneasy conscience. She took her job at the RASC very seriously.

Their unit was responsible for getting ambulances and drivers into the field as fast as British industry could deliver and, as well as their usual commitments, they were currently turning out one hundred newly qualified drivers each month. This meant that everyone in the office was busy – the men housed in small temporary offices and cubicles, the women in rows, working as typists and filing clerks, the runners and motorcycle dispatch riders. People were constantly on the phone, constantly coming and going.

It was like working in a busy beehive, a productive beehive with a purpose, thanks to Captain McNicoll, who made sure that his unit understood the importance of their work.

Early in the piece, he'd lined up all forty of the staff and had addressed them, not in his usual quiet tones that came with the remnant lilt of a Highland accent, but with the surprisingly passionate ferocity of a man who'd suffered in the trenches in the last war.

'The boys in the frontline depend on the flow of our supplies. It will be winter soon and I've seen my friends die in their sleep for want of a hot drink or a warm blanket – it's up to us to get these supplies through. We must never take the simple things for granted.'

Georgina's job mostly involved typing memos and orders that would have been difficult and time consuming for Captain McNicoll, a natural right-hander who'd lost his arm in the Great War and was now struggling to use his left hand. She also acted as his driver and stepped in as his scribe at training and admin sessions, a task she'd quietly taken on without any fuss as soon as she'd seen him struggling with the blackboard.

But even though she was conscientious about her work, the Australians' parade, scheduled for the following Tuesday, had become vitally important to her. How could she give up another chance to see Harry? She was planning to follow the marching soldiers till they came to a halt, and if there was the tiniest chance that she could speak to Harry, she would grab it.

'There are no meetings scheduled for next Tuesday morning,' she told Captain McNicoll, although they both knew that an unforeseen emergency could arise at any moment.

To her relief, he nodded. 'Very well. At this point in time, I can't see a problem.'

'Thank you, sir.'

The Fates, however, were not on Georgina's side. There *was* a problem the following Tuesday morning, and it came in the form of a roadblock, which she stumbled into while she was driving her boss back from a meeting at HQ.

An ARP warden with a red face and a walrus moustache informed them that a demolition squad was at work on an unexploded bomb.

'We've cordoned off all the streets in the block surrounding the emergency,' he told them with an air of self-important officiousness. 'And we're clearing the entire area of all residents, pedestrians and traffic.'

Georgina might have been able to turn the car around to take a different route back to their office, but before she could attempt this, they became hemmed in by traffic backing up behind them. It was quite some time before a policeman arrived to redirect the flow, and by then vehicles were banked up for several blocks. It was clear it would be ages before everyone was moving again.

Miserably, she told herself that this was her punishment for telling the captain a lie.

The minutes crawled and they'd made no progress at all by the time the parade was due to begin. She tried not to think too much about it, but it was hard not to imagine the band music and the crowds. And Harry, marching with his fellow Australians. People on footpaths would be waving and cheering. Cheering Harry, while Georgina was stuck in this blasted jam.

She tried to tell herself that it didn't matter. There was no point in getting all worked up about a tiny glimpse of a man marching by. But foolishly, she'd spent every night of the past three weeks imagining this day. She'd been so looking forward to another chance to see him, another slim but tempting possibility to say goodbye – this time with a smile instead of a tear.

'Lenton,' Captain McNicoll said, watching her with concern. 'Don't worry about taking me back to the office. As soon as we get moving again, you should drive directly by your lawyer's rooms. I can wait in the car while you have your meeting with him.'

Georgina's cheeks burned. 'Oh no, sir, I couldn't ask you to do that. It – the appointment's not that important.'

'I'm sure your father wouldn't agree, Lenton. In times of war, it's very important for families to have their legal matters sorted.'

'Yes, sir.' Georgina swallowed guiltily and found herself wondering about her boss's family circumstances. She knew very little about him, just that he was a widower and that he had a son in the navy, a very handsome young man, judging by the photo on the office desk. 'I'll ring Mr Hartley as soon as we get back,' she said. 'I might still be able to see him later today, or perhaps I can reschedule my appointment.'

Captain McNicoll nodded. 'Very well. And you should use my phone. It will be more private.'

Georgina's cheeks burned hotter than ever. 'Thank you, sir.'

It was another hour before they finally got back to Dulwich, an hour during which Georgina thought almost constantly about Harry.

'Sir?' she found herself saying on an impulse, as she pulled into her boss's allotted parking space.

'Yes, Lenton?' Already, his left hand was poised on the door handle.

'I wondered —' Sudden perspiration beaded her upper lip. Her heart fluttered wildly. 'I wondered if you've heard any word about where the Australians might be heading.'

'The Australians?' Captain McNicoll looked almost as surprised as Georgina's mother might have looked under similar circumstances. 'Why do you want to know about the Australians?'

Her hands were white-knuckled on the steering wheel. She couldn't remain calm if she tried. 'It's just —' Her mouth was dry and she had to run her tongue over her parched lips. 'I – I met an Australian chap and I . . .'

She couldn't finish the sentence.

An interminable age seemed to pass before Captain McNicoll said quietly, 'And you're worried sick.'

'Yes, something like that, sir.'

'Well, my dear girl, it will be in the newspapers soon enough. I'm afraid the Australians are going to take on Mussolini. They're heading for North Africa.'

10

As Lucy pulled up outside her grandfather's house, she was rather relieved to see that it still looked the same, from the street, at least. A simple worker's cottage, half hidden by two shiny-leaved New Guinea frangipani, it was built of timber and painted pale blue with white window frames and deep-blue guttering. The roof was silver ripple iron and the front verandah was enclosed by white wooden shutters.

The gate squeaked as Lucy pushed it open and brown frangipani blooms lay wilting on the path among the weeds that sprouted from cracks in the concrete.

The ruby-coloured glass panel in the front door was smeared with dust, the corners filled with fine cobwebs. Clearly there were limits to the assistance Blue Care provided. But that was okay, Lucy decided. She needed a project.

Standing on the front step, though, she had to take a deep breath as memories rushed in, distant memories of days in childhood when she'd trailed after her Harry-pa in his backyard, helping him to stake tomatoes and to pick slugs off his lettuce. She'd also gone down to the mangrove creek at the back of this house and helped Harry to pull up crab pots, and she'd sat on the back steps with him, eating fresh crab sandwiches made with soft, white bread and plenty of salt and pepper. Whenever her mum had gone out on a date, Lucy had slept here to be woken in the morning with a proper grown-up cup of tea and an oatmeal biscuit.

Gripped by nostalgia, she knocked and heard footsteps inside, slow and shuffling. Harry would be making his way down the hallway and, as she waited, the precious memories kept coming, tumbling and rolling – Harry cheering from the sidelines when she scored a goal at soccer, Harry consoling her when she got chicken-pox and missed the finals, Harry smiling with a complicated mix of concern and pride when she told him that she'd enlisted.

Her throat was tight with emotion by the time the door opened and she saw her grandfather's beloved wrinkled face.

'Lucy!' He looked frighteningly frail and stooped, standing there, clutching the doorknob for support. But beneath the shock of white hair, his light-grey eyes were as twinkling as ever. 'Come in, come in.' He stepped back to let her into the house. 'It's so good to see you, my darling girl.'

'It's good to see you too, Harry.' Lucy resisted the urge to give him a bear hug. Instead she hugged him gently, kissed his thin cheek and then blinked madly to clear tears from her eyes.

Up close, she was reassured to see that the verandah looked much the same as ever, with Harry's canvas-lined squatter's chair, a cane occasional table and his tall timber bookcase still filled with old, faded hard-cover copies of the complete Sherlock Holmes and newer, thick paperbacks by his favourite authors – Ian Fleming, Clive Cussler, Alistair MacLean, John le Carré.

They went down the familiar hallway that divided the house down the centre. Opening to the right were the lounge and dining rooms, and to the left, the bedrooms – first Harry's and then the lit-tle spare room where Lucy had so often slept. At the back of the house was the kitchen and even before Lucy reached it, she could see sunlight sparkling on the row of white daisy-glass windows. Off the kitchen were a bathroom and a separate loo and then, two steps down, the laundry.

Such a simple, humble home, but for Lucy a happy haven of love; a secure and cosy nest that had barely changed since she was in nappies. Through all the years of instability in her own family home, Harry had always been here. Steady, reliable and loving. Filling the gap left behind by the father who'd deserted her before she'd learned to crawl.

'Sit down, Harry,' she ordered as they reached the kitchen. 'I'll put the kettle on.'

To her surprise, her grandfather obeyed without question. The short trip to the front door and back had tired him, which was rather unsettling.

'I'm so sorry you've been in hospital.'

'It's damn good to be home. I don't like hospitals. Never have.'

'Are you feeling okay now?' It was a silly question. How could he be okay when he'd been told that his kidneys had packed it in? In six months, a year, he might . . .

'Yes, yes,' Harry said brusquely. 'I'm fine. Truly. I might look shaky on my pins, but I'm still mobile and I don't seem to have lost too many marbles.'

'So you can still argue the toss?'

He laughed. 'Just try me.' His eyes glistened. 'I'm just so pleased you're home, Lucy-girl. Out of that damn war zone.'

She managed a wobbly smile. It was so like Harry to be worrying about her instead of himself. Quickly she turned and reached for the kettle and for the next few moments she kept herself busy by finding mugs, teabags, milk and sugar.

Through the open window came the sweet cloying scent of fallen mangoes lying in varying states of rottenness in the ankle-high grass. She could see the empty chicken coop under the mango tree and the old fibro shed where Harry garaged his car and kept an untidy workbench littered with tools and rusting paint tins. By the fence was the veggie patch where withered tomato vines hung from stakes. Lettuce and parsley had gone to seed. There was plenty of work to be done, reinforcing her decision to make Harry's yard her new project.

Given Sam's bombshell, she needed to keep busy.

The kettle came to the boil and she filled their mugs. 'I brought ginger biscuits,' she said, knowing they were Harry's favourites.

When she joined him at the table, his eyes twinkled again as he raised his mug in a salute. 'It's so good to have you home safely,' he said again. 'Out of harm's way.'

'Yeah.' Lucy wished she felt happier about being home. She was still adjusting to Sam's dummy spit, to her mother's move from Mango Avenue and Harry's failing health.

'So, tell me. How was it over there in Afghanistan?' Harry asked.

'For me?' Lucy pulled a face. She could tell him about the long hours working in logistics, organising the re-supply of fuel by air and road, of getting in enough food for the base, sourcing motor vehicles and their parts. Or the interesting, sometimes dangerous work she had done in the community, meeting with Afghan women as part of a female engagement team.

But Harry rarely spoke about his own war experiences, so she answered cautiously. 'You know the army. Loads and loads of paperwork.'

He sent her a smile of sympathy. 'It's always been like that. Nothing's changed. So you're feeling okay, love?'

'Yes, we had a good debriefing. Five days at Al Minhad in Dubai with teams of psychologists et cetera.'

'That's good to hear.'

'Better than in your day, huh? When you were simply demobbed after five years of fighting.'

'Yep. No victory parade for our lot.'

'By the way,' Lucy said, reaching into the shoulder bag she'd slung over the back of a chair. 'I brought this back for you.' She set his old biscuit tin on the table. 'I'm assuming you didn't want to leave this at Mum's forever.'

Harry looked surprised.

'Mum had it stored in the room where I'm staying.'

'S'pose Ro's too busy to bring it here herself.'

Lucy hurried to defend her mum. 'Well, she knew I was keen to see you.'

He gave a resigned nod. 'Thanks.' Took a noisy sip of his tea.

'I took a quick look at your medals,' Lucy said. 'You have quite a collection.'

This brought a brief grunt.

'You never told me you were a Rat of Tobruk, Harry. I was stoked when I saw your Rat badge. That's really special. And you were at Kokoda, too. That's a *huge* deal.'

Another shrug. 'It was all such a long time ago.'

'But they were both such big battles. So important for Australia. I'm surprised you never talked about them.'

Her grandfather didn't respond to this but simply sat, fingering the edge of the tin with a bony, scarred finger. 'Every battle's important for the poor buggers who have to fight them.'

True, Lucy thought, but she had been reading up on Tobruk and its reputation hadn't been earned lightly. The Aussies had endured 241 days defending Egypt and the Suez Canal against the Italians and Germans who were under Rommel, and they'd done it in the grimmest of conditions.

The desert ground had been so hard and stony they'd only been able to dig shallow trenches, little more than a metre deep in most places, which meant they'd had to crawl everywhere on all fours, the whole time putting up with a daily bombardment from mortar or field guns and snipers. And they'd slept in tiny, two-man dugouts roofed by beams covered in sandbags.

'It must have been terrible out there in the desert,' she said. 'I've been reading about the huge problems with the water being all brackish and salty. I don't know how you drank it.'

At this, Harry cracked a small smile. 'S'pose I'm fortunate my kidneys have lasted this long.'

'I guess,' she said softly. Then, needing to quickly change the subject, 'And what about the thousands of flies, Harry? They must have been unbearable. Flies and maggots during the day and armies of fleas at night.' Not to mention the dysentery and desert ulcers the men had to deal with.

'Yeah, well.' Harry reached for a ginger biscuit. 'It helped to have a sense of humour.' For a moment he sat, the biscuit forgotten, as he stared into the distance, no doubt thinking about the past. Then he chuckled. 'You mentioned all the paperwork. It was even like that in Tobruk. There we were, struggling with Rommel and his Panzers on the frontline and our captain kept getting these bloody forms to fill in.'

Lucy smiled.

'Lucky for us, our captain had a brilliant sense of humour, and in the end he mocked up a form of his own. Made it look official and sent it back to HQ. Called it the Fly Report.' Harry was grinning broadly now. 'He even invented all these categories of flies that had to be filled in. Number of flies killed per unit, method of destruction – whether they were killed by fly swat, spray, sticky paper – type of fly.'

Lucy was laughing. 'Oh, that's priceless. Even the type of fly?'

'Yeah. Small, black fly. Large green. Blue arsed.' Harry chuckled again. '*That* should have been a dead giveaway, but there were some units that actually filled in the report.'

'You're joking.'

'Even had them signed off by the authorising officer.'

'Oh, I love it. That's fabulous.' Across the table they grinned at each other and Lucy was delighted that Harry had finally shared a tiny snippet from his past, even if it was only a funny story. 'No wonder the Rats became famous.'

Harry's smile faded. 'There was no fun like that in New Guinea, especially Kokoda. Don't ask me about that, Lucy.'

He looked haunted suddenly. 'All right, I'll remember not to ask,' she said quickly.

With a shake of his head, he added, 'But I reckon wars are getting harder to fight.'

'Oh, I don't know. You must have —'

He ignored her attempt to interrupt. 'In my day, we had a frontline. We knew where the enemy was and what we were up against. But it's different now. Your enemy manages to infiltrate everywhere, all around you. In the towns, even in the bases. I read the papers. I keep up with the news. You must have never really known where your danger lay. I bet you were always looking over your shoulder.'

'That's true,' she said softly. There'd been several scary incidents when she'd been out in villages with the female engagement team, and a couple of times when the base had been hit by rocket fire.

Her mother and Sam had both acknowledged this danger, but at the same time they'd also resented her presence in a war zone, almost as if she'd gone there deliberately to upset them. It was reassuring to know that Harry understood exactly what she'd been through, and she appreciated that he commented without accusations.

But when she looked at the battered old tin sitting on the table between them, she couldn't help wishing he'd shared more about his own experiences. She wanted to ask him about *all* of his medals, about his life out west on the cattle property, Kalkadoon. Most of all, she wanted to know about the mysterious and beautiful George.

'There's so much I don't know about you,' she said, unable to keep quiet. 'I know practically nothing about your life before you moved here to Townsville.'

Harry quickly dropped his gaze to the tin and frowned. 'I suppose it's a habit I've fallen into. Your mother went through a really rough patch when she was younger, before you were born. That's when I left Kalkadoon and after that, she never liked me talking about the place, or the past.'

Lucy could well believe this. Her mother was even more tight-lipped than Harry about her past, and she'd gone ballistic over that letter.

'I wasn't the father I should have been,' Harry said sadly.

Lucy very much doubted that this was true. Reaching over, she placed her hand on his. 'Well, you've been a bloody fantastic grandfather.'

'Thanks, love.'

They sat for a bit, his hand in hers, savouring their special bond. *Poor Mum*, she thought. *You've missed out on so much*.

Watching her, Harry said, 'You should focus on the future, Lucy, not the past. You should be thinking about that young man of yours.'

That young man of yours.

Sam. Lucy gripped the handle of her mug so tightly it was a wonder it didn't snap. She still hadn't heard from Sam. Sure, she could always try to ring him, but no way was she going to beg and plead.

After all, Sam was the one with the problem. But his silence made everything pretty damn clear and final. Even so, a tiny corner of her stupid heart was still hoping . . .

She couldn't bring herself to explain this to Harry. Not yet. He would only worry. He might even assume she was following in her mother's footsteps – becoming a relationship tragic.

But . . . *Oh God*. By not telling Harry, she was being as secretive about her private life as he was. Uncomfortably aware of the irony, Lucy decided she couldn't press Harry for more personal stories today. There was still time.

Instead, she said, 'First up, I'd like to focus on doing a few odd jobs around here. There's plenty to do in your yard.'

Harry frowned. 'You've got better things to do than worry about my yard.'

Showed how little he knew. Here she was, home on leave, with Christmas coming and weeks of leisurely summertime to fill, and with absolutely no idea what she was going to do with her time. With her life.

Her friends had all scattered, most of them, including Kaz, taking off down south to spend Christmas with family and friends. Her fiancé had dropped her and her mum had moved into a brand new apartment with a nice new man, which meant that hanging around them, Lucy felt a big fat gooseberry.

She sent her grandfather her warmest, most convincing grin. ''Course I want to help you. I'm used to working hard – long hours and no time off. It feels weird to have so much spare time on my hands. Honest, you'd be doing me a favour, so if you've got a pen and paper, we can make a list.'

'Not more paperwork.'

They both laughed. It felt good.

Lucy ran hard along Townsville's Strand, weaving her way around dog-walkers, past joggers with the latest-model fitness trackers strapped to their biceps, and young mothers in gym gear pushing state-of-the-art prams.

The path was set in parkland, rimmed by palm trees and beach and, beyond, the shimmering pale sea lay as flat and still as a swathe of blue silk. On the other side of the park, restaurants and apartment blocks and cafés spilled onto footpaths where cyclists in fluorescent lycra sipped their morning lattes.

So different from the world she had left behind in Uruzgan province, where people still travelled on donkeys and women and girls carried their family's water supply on their heads. By comparison, her hometown was like a futuristic planet.

The sense of dislocation had hit her especially hard this morning. She'd visited Anna Duncan yesterday and had subsequently spent a night battling bad dreams, only to wake and find herself yet again in her mother's pristine white-and-cream apartment.

Her sense of loss had hit harder, too. A quick check of her phone had shown that Sam still hadn't tried to make contact, which meant it was four days now since she'd seen or heard from him.

This stupid silence had gone on long enough. She would have to make contact, bring things to a head. She felt sick at the thought.

Reaching the rockpool at the end of the Strand, she paused briefly to take in the view across to Magnetic Island and to grab a deep swig from her water bottle, then turned and retraced her steps. Running back along the waterfront, she continued on through Anzac Park, veering along the eastern end of Flinders Street past the museum and marine aquarium and over the bridge that spanned Ross Creek.

It was only eight-thirty, but already the tropical sun whacked a sting and she was sleek with sweat.

Not the best condition in which to encounter a familiar figure as she turned the next corner.

Sam.

Lucy almost stumbled. Forgot to breathe.

Sam, in blue jeans and a white T-shirt that showed off his gym-taut body, was obviously waiting. For her.

Her heart leaped, bounding like a hurdler. Her legs were unsteady, her knees threatened to buckle.

With a casual lack of haste, Sam took his hands from his pockets and rested them loosely on his hips. He appraised her without smiling. 'Hey,' he said.

It wasn't a promising start.

'Hi, Sam.' Lucy drew a deep, very necessary breath. At least she wasn't panting. 'I'm guessing that Mum must have told you where to find me.'

He nodded. 'I thought we'd better sort this out.'

This – such an unhelpful word under the circumstances.

Lucy wiped her sweaty hands on the backs of her running shorts. 'Do – do you want to talk here? Go somewhere for coffee?' There were places open on Palmer Street.

Sam's blue eyes were narrowed and shrewd. 'That depends.'

'On?'

'On why I haven't heard from you.'

Lucy gasped. 'Why *you* haven't heard from *me*?' She glared at him. 'I've been waiting to hear from you. You were the one who —'

'You were the one who walked out,' he cut in tightly.

'True, but I walked out to avoid a fight. You know that. You were the one who had the problem.'

'Whatever, Luce.' He gave an irritated shrug and he looked and sounded bored.

Damn him. Lucy's eyes were stinging, but she was too angry to show any hint of her hurt. 'What do you want to hear from me? That I'll resign from the fucking army?'

He didn't answer, simply stood there, his expression wooden.

'Perhaps you need to spit it out, Sam. We're over, aren't we?'

'Is that what you want?'

She gritted her teeth. Not only was Sam playing games, parrying her question with a question of his own, but he hadn't shown the slightest hint that this conversation was in any way upsetting.

Bastard. What the hell had she ever seen in this guy? He might be handsome – *cute* was the word her girlfriends had used – but it was damn annoying that she'd been so smitten, that she'd actually fallen in love. If only she'd realised sooner there was way too much ego to match his pretty face.

'Let me get this straight,' she said, needing to sock it to him fair and square. 'First, you drop a bombshell, claiming you can't marry me because of my job. Not because my work's dangerous and you actually care, but because you think my role in the field has higher status than your desk job. And when I leave to avoid a heated argument on my first night home, you go sulky and silent. Now you're trying to tell me that it's all my fault.'

And he wasn't lifting so much as a finger to try to win her back.

Lucy's fury burned white hot. 'You know what?' she demanded, glaring with a fierceness to match his.

Sam rolled his eyes. 'I'm sure you're going to tell me.'

Yes, she bloody well was. 'You're a prick, Sam Harrison. And there's no question. We are most definitely over. So goodbye and —'

She whipped the tiny diamond from her finger – lucky she was so sweaty it slipped off easily – and thrust it roughly into his hand.

'Good riddance!' she yelled over her shoulder as she jogged away.

11

Lucy didn't look back to check out Sam's reaction. She ran hard, on past her mother's apartment block, turning into a leafy, quiet suburban back street. Here she eventually slowed to a walk, taking deep breaths. Morning sunlight streamed through overhead poinciana trees. She could hear the sounds of children's laughter spilling from a nearby house, saw an elderly woman watering her front garden before the day got too hot. The street was peaceful and ordinary and Lucy was no longer engaged to be married.

Out of nowhere came a miraculous sense of relief.

She could admit it now. Loving Sam had been hard work, much harder than it should have been. If she was honest, she'd never been truly relaxed and certain about him and, amazingly, the prospect of a future without him was like having a fresh breeze blow across her face, a whiff of beckoning freedom.

Rather shocked by such an immediate feeling of reprieve, she looked up through lacy green branches laden with red to the bright, cloudless blue sky and she wondered if this new sense of lightness was how her mum had felt when her relationships had ended. Was this why her mother was able to start again, over and over, each time with fresh hope that with the next new man everything would be rosy?

Shit. She didn't want to be like her mum. She couldn't bear to fall into that kind of pattern.

I'm not.

I'm not like her.

Lucy was sure she didn't share her mother's neediness or lack of confidence. Even as a child, she'd sensed her mother's emotional fragility, but she'd never really understood how this could have happened when her mother had been brought up by Harry. But there'd always been that tension between Harry and her mum, the tension that Lucy had never understood.

She was sure it had something to do with their past. *Perhaps it is connected to that letter Mum screwed up.*

As she turned into another street lined with sprawling timber Queenslanders set back behind clumps of palm trees or bougainvillea, she thought about the turmoil in her mother's face when she'd snatched the Englishwoman's letter out of her hands. The letter writer had begged and cajoled Harry into giving up his daughter, demanding that he send her to England where she'd be so much better off, where she could mix with her 'own kind' and be 'properly' educated.

It was such a snobby thing to say.

Her mum, who obviously knew the woman, had called her a bitch. And Lucy could imagine that was true. A snobby bitch.

Lucy was glad she'd retrieved the woman's letter from the kitchen tidy bin. She'd felt only slightly guilty and she'd soon reconciled her conscience. Surely a letter like that was too significant to throw away?

After all, with Harry never talking about his glamorous George or his part in the war, and with her mum jamming up whenever she asked questions about Kalkadoon Station or her time in England,

Lucy was sick of all the secrets in her family and fed up that they wouldn't tell her anything.

It occurred to her now that Harry's George came from England, as well. One way or another, these family secrets all seemed to be connected in some inescapable way to England.

And by a weird coincidence, if things had turned out differently, Lucy would have been heading off for England right now.

Months ago, before she'd been distracted by Sam's marriage proposal, she and Kaz had planned to spend their Christmas leave by going to London and then hiring a car to see England and Ireland. Despite being smitten with her boyfriend, Kaz had been mightily disappointed when Sam's proposal had prompted Lucy to pull out of the trip.

Remembering this, another sickening thought struck. Sam had only proposed to her after she'd told him about her travel plans.

Realising this now, her anger kicked in again with a vengeance, but she would only make herself sick if she tried to analyse the deeper implications of Sam's timing. She'd wasted enough of her life agonising over that guy.

One thing was coming through very clearly, though. She was pretty damn sure that she knew how she was going to spend the rest of her leave.

Following swiftly on from that thought, Lucy impulsively retrieved her phone from the pocket of her shorts and keyed in Kaz's number.

Her girlfriend answered quickly. 'Hey, Lucy, how are you? How's Sam?'

Lucy winced. 'I'm . . . so-so. That's so-so, as in, not so great, actually. A bit gutted, to be honest.' She swallowed to ease the tension in her throat. 'Sam and I just broke up.'

There was a gratifyingly shocked gasp on the end of the line. 'That's terrible, Luce. I'm so sorry.' A small silence fell, but Kaz clearly couldn't hold back. 'What happened?'

To her annoyance, Lucy struggled to get out the words. 'Basically, Sam wanted me to leave the army.'

'Oh.' A brief pause from Kaz. 'I suppose he's like my Brad. Worried about another deployment and he wants to keep you home safe and sound.'

'Not exactly.' Although that would be a logical explanation, and one Lucy probably could have lived with. 'For Sam it was more of an ego thing.' She could feel the tension tightening her throat and she drew a deliberately calming breath. This was going to sound so damn lame. 'It's pretty crazy, Kaz. He's unhappy because he's stuck in a desk job while I'm on active duty.'

'You're joking.'

'No. Unfortunately, that's the story. If I stay on as a soldier, it will upset the balance in our relationship.'

'What century does that guy think this is? Doesn't he know that sort of thinking went out in the Dark Ages?'

'Well, clearly, he has a very tender ego.'

Kaz made a scoffing sound. After a bit, she asked somewhat awkwardly, 'So was it your idea to call the engagement off?'

Lucy sighed. 'Yeah, I guess. Actually, it was pretty much mutual. A kind of implosion. Everything seemed rosy and then it suddenly turned to shit.' Lucy felt her mouth twist out of shape as she relived the evening in Sam's flat when the truth had hit home.

Now she had to take another steadying breath.

'I'm so sorry, Luce,' Kaz said gently. 'If only I wasn't down here at the Gold Coast, I'd come over. Take you out for a drink or three.'

'I would kill for that drink with you, Kaz.' Lucy indulged in a moment of feeling completely sorry for herself. 'Actually,' she added quickly before she did something stupid like crying. 'I've been thinking about our travel plans. You remember how we were going to do England and Ireland together?'

'Yes.' Kaz sounded cautious.

'I don't suppose you'd still be interested? I know it's last minute, but the flights aren't too expensive. It's low season over there – mid-winter.'

'Oh, Luce, I'm sorry. Brad and I are going to Thailand. We booked two days ago and we're heading off straight after Christmas.'

'Oh, right. That's okay.' Lucy's voice cracked at just the wrong moment, making a mockery of her attempted nonchalance, but she soldiered on. 'That's fine. It'll be – ah – fabulous for you both. You'll have such a fantastic time. That's wonderful. I'm so pleased for you.'

'Brad would never forgive me if I tried to wriggle out of it now.'

'Of course. Don't even think about it. God no, Kaz. It was just a crazy suggestion off the top of my head. Spur of the moment.'

'But you should go to England, Lucy.'

'Yeah, I'm thinking I might.' Had she really said that?

'Don't think twice, just do it.' Kaz sounded genuinely enthusiastic now. 'It would be magic to see England in winter. The total opposite of Townsville and, under the circumstances, I reckon that's exactly what you need.'

'Yeah.' The idea of a solo adventure was taking root, making more sense by the second. The only stumbling block would be her mum, who had major hang ups about England and would probably put up a fight just like she had when Lucy had told her about her original travel plans. But there was no point in postponing it. She would head straight back to the apartment, have a shower and then start investigating bookings. When everything was settled she'd confront her mum.

Right on cue, Ro had the predicted meltdown when she heard Lucy's change of plans.

'Not England again. I can't believe you'd want to go there

in winter. Honestly, it's just like when you joined the army,' she wailed. 'You raced off then and did your own thing. You wouldn't listen to me. You never do, Lucy. I couldn't even guide you or influence you when you were little – not about anything – hair, clothes, your friends.'

Lucy garnered as much patience as she could muster. 'I think you're overreacting, Mum.'

'Overreacting?' Tears filled her mother's eyes. 'How can you say that, girl? You know you rushed headlong into the army. I could have helped you to find a much more suitable career.'

Lucy resisted the temptation to point out the flaws in her mum's own career path. 'The army's been great for me,' she said.

This was met by a stubborn shake of auburn curls. 'Great for you, maybe, but what about me? You did everything you could to get into a war zone.'

'It's not as if I was fighting in the frontline.'

'You didn't have to be. You were still in danger. There were people killed on the base, as you very well know. You visited that poor soldier's widow yesterday, and took presents to his fatherless kids.'

'Yes, but —'

Dramatically, her mother flung her arms wide. 'How do you think I felt, worrying every day, listening to the news and reading the papers, waiting for the knock on the door?'

This set Lucy back. 'You never said a thing.'

'There wasn't any point, was there? You wouldn't have listened.' Now her mother pouted. 'Daughters are supposed to listen to their mothers. I never had a mother to give me advice, but I bloody well would have listened if I'd had half a chance.'

'You reckon?' Lucy wasn't prepared to take this lying down. 'You had a father, Mum. Harry was a wonderful father and you've practically ignored him.'

This time, her mum opened her mouth to protest, then seemed

to change her mind and shut it again.

Lucy seized the chance to push her point home. 'And if we're going to have this argument, what about the fact that I never knew my father and I've often wished I did? You wasted a fantastic opportunity with Harry.'

The triumph of firing this missile was momentary. When her mother's face crumpled, Lucy immediately felt guilty. Given the two-way tensions between them, she knew there was an element of hypocrisy in her own accusations. Just the same, she wasn't going to be manipulated by her mother's emotions. It had happened too many times in the past.

Besides, she wasn't going to England simply to escape. She was hoping to find out more about George – Georgina. She had a right to know about her own grandmother, surely? She had a sense that she might understand her *self* better if she knew more about her family's past.

'Could you try to look at this from my point of view?' She was trying her hardest to sound calm and reasonable. 'I've taken a big hit from this breakup with Sam and I need to get away for a bit, to be somewhere completely different.'

'But you've just come back from somewhere completely different.'

Lucy sighed. Clearly this was going to take a while.

Harry's yard was looking pretty good now. Lucy had cleared the straggling veggie patch and weeded the other gardens. She'd gathered up the fallen mangoes and mowed, whipper-snippered and raked the grass. They were sitting under the mango tree, enjoying a cool drink while the sprinkler hissed softly in the background, when she told him about her travel plans.

She had already told Harry about Sam and once he'd realised she wasn't too devastated, he'd reacted with surprising equanimity.

Eventually, she'd felt compelled to ask. 'Did you like Sam, Harry?'

He'd taken his time to answer, before he'd eventually said, 'Well, you know, he struck me as a young man who believed his own PR.'

Lucy suspected that this rather damning description of her former boyfriend should have upset her, but it hadn't.

Now, having told Harry about going to England, she said, as casually as she could, 'I was wondering if there's anyone you'd like me to look up while I'm over there – like my grandmother's family in Cornwall.'

If Harry was surprised, he didn't show it, but he took a while to answer. 'It's a long time since I've heard from any of them.'

'I'm just curious, you know. About my ancestors and everything.'

'I guess it's up to you, Lucy. Just don't expect too much.'

'Well, no, I won't. I know Mum had a tough time over there.'

His eyes narrowed. 'Has she told you about it?'

'No. She just gets angry if the subject comes up.'

'Yes, that would be right.' Harry sighed.

Lucy's head was swarming with questions she longed to ask, but she'd decided to take her cues from her grandfather. If there were things he wanted to tell her he would. If not, she at least knew that she had a branch of the family – descendants of the dreaded letter writer – still living over there. And she had their address.

———

Boxing Day found Ro at the airport, the last place she wanted to be, but as had happened so many times in the past, she'd lost another battle with her daughter.

Now, Lucy was on her way. Already, the plane was a small dot in the sky above Palm Island, heading north to Cairns, and from there Lucy would take a flight on to London via Hong Kong.

It was all so very disappointing. Her daughter had been home for such a short time and Ro had nursed such high hopes. Almost nothing had worked out the way she'd imagined. There would be no wedding plans. No pleasant mother-and-daughter mornings in bridal shops. No handsome son-in-law. No chance of a sweet little grandchild . . .

So extremely upsetting.

Ro had been desperately hoping that everything would be perfect this time, in the lovely new apartment with her lovely new man. She had dared to let her imagination get carried away, picturing an engagement celebration with champagne on the apartment's balcony – and then all the happy plans that would follow.

Instead of shopping for her mother-of-the-bride ensemble, she was clutching a bunch of mascara-streaked tissues and making her teary way to the airport restrooms where she needed to wash her face. She couldn't possibly go home to Keith looking such a mess. She certainly didn't want him to know how upset she was.

She just needed a moment, a little personal space to feel sorry for herself. And yes, to acknowledge that she was angry with her daughter. Not just angry with Lucy for calling off the wedding, or for racing off to England, but also for stirring up the problems from the past that Ro had been trying, desperately, to put behind her.

Ro had tried to argue her case, but she hadn't liked to fight too hard when she knew that her daughter was hurting about Sam. After all, she'd been rejected enough to understand the pain. She just wished Lucy had chosen anywhere to run to but England.

England!

Ro cringed as she remembered Lucy's questions.

'What happened in England? Why is it such a big dark secret?'

'I blotted my copybook. Okay? Can we leave it at that?' But any kind of admission to Lucy was a mistake.

'Blotted your copybook leaves a lot to the imagination, Mum. Are we talking about major blottage?'

Ro hadn't replied. Not only did she hate to admit to the mistakes she'd made, but she also couldn't bear the emotions that accompanied her memories of those years she'd spent in England against her will – *the secret years*, Lucy had called them. She simply wasn't prepared to revisit that time, to dredge up the intense anger and betrayal she'd felt at being sent away from Kalkadoon to live among snobby, aloof strangers.

Was it any wonder she'd dug in her heels, refusing to be called Rose and behaving atrociously? Getting herself into trouble of the worst kind?

There was little to be gained by confessing to her daughter. The past was dead and buried. It had to be. Ro was moving on.

With Keith.

Unfortunately, though, Ro knew exactly where Lucy was heading. And why. She was well aware that the crumpled letter had disappeared from the kitchen tidy bin, complete with the address in Cornwall.

When it had come to challenging Lucy about it, however, she'd backed down. It would have brought on another barrage of those difficult, searching questions from her daughter and she'd already been through the third degree.

Now, as she stared at her pink-eyed, blotchy reflection in the restroom mirror, fresh tears welled, but before they could take hold, she splashed her face with cold water, which was fortunate timing, as a trio of giggling teenagers suddenly burst into the Ladies'.

Lord, she had to get a grip.

She patted at her face with a paper towel, reached into her handbag to feel for her lipstick and powder, and vowed to stop this self-pitying.

After all, there was plenty to be thankful for. Christmas Day had been lovely, the Christmas of her dreams. She'd decorated the apartment tastefully with brand new ornaments, and set the table elegantly with white and silver. The seafood and champagne had been of the very best quality, and Lucy had got on beautifully with Keith and his daughters.

It was time to be grateful for what she had. Time to let go of the past once and for all, or at least until her daughter came home and stirred things up again. With any luck, Lucy would be surrounded by exciting new sights and people in London and she would forget all about digging up trouble in Cornwall.

Fixing her smile firmly in place, Ro reminded herself of the good news from the astrologer she'd visited a few weeks back. Her life was on an upward trajectory.

At last.

12

Cornwall in January was all blustery winds, dark sheeting rain and even darker seas. Lucy, watching the huge waves explode onto rocky sea cliffs, was reminded of the books she'd read back in her school days about pirates and shipwrecks and smugglers flashing lanterns to send messages through the storm-lashed night.

It was a damn exciting destination, she decided, although she could imagine that her mum, arriving as a child and alone among strangers, might have found the place rather grim and forbidding.

Lucy, on the other hand, was rather enjoying her independence as a solo traveller. She'd caught a train from London to Penzance, and had loved every moment of the journey past pretty English villages, and fields bordered by hedgerows, and the astonishing, gobsmacking green of the hills dotted with black-and-white cattle, the forests of leafless trees. Then she'd picked up a hire car and had driven on, across more picture-perfect countryside with quaint, thatched farmhouses and little villages that seemed to cling to the cliff tops like barnacles.

Night fell early though – about mid-afternoon – and of course it was raining, so Lucy's journey had been a little scary at times. She made her way slowly, windscreen-wipers thrashing madly, down narrow, winding country lanes, which on occasions were bordered on both sides by alarmingly tall hedges.

With next-to-no visibility, it was particularly scary when a tractor appeared out of nowhere, completely blocking her way. But *phew*. She'd finally made it. Or at least, she'd made it to the seaside town of Portreath, which, according to the map, was very close to Penwall Hall, the address on the letter.

Relieved to have arrived, she pulled into the very last spot in the tiny, crowded car park next to a white-walled pub called The Seaspray Arms.

With the wind whipping at her heels, she snapped the central locking and dashed through the icy rain and into the welcome warmth of the pub to find a low-ceilinged room with dark beams, a flagstone floor and, best of all, a blazing log fire.

Locals in thick sweaters or tweed jackets were gathered in happy groups, and there was music playing – something low but jaunty – in the background. It could have been the setting for an episode of *Doc Martin*.

Eyes turned her way as she unwound her scarf and hung it with her new designer trench coat on a rack near the door. She didn't mind the none-too-subtle stares as she ran her fingers through her damp hair. She was feeling pretty good about her appearance tonight.

She'd bought a fab, morale-boosting wardrobe of new winter gear in London and tonight she was wearing Le Skinny charcoal jeans and ankle boots, and a fine wool, cherry-coloured sweater with a polo neck. After growing up in tropical Townsville, where the winters had never really been cold enough to bother with more than the occasional cardigan, it was a novelty to dress stylishly for the cold.

Now, walking up to the bar, Lucy felt a new confidence. It was surprisingly liberating to be so far from home and from everyone she knew. Away from Sam. Returning to singledom was not such a bad thing after all.

'So, what can I get you, love?' The barman was a cheerful chap, middle aged, with a round, ruddy face and a fringe of hair circling his bald patch that made Lucy think of Friar Tuck.

'I'll have a whisky, please.' It was too cold for beer. 'And a packet of crisps.' Already she'd learned not to call them chips.

'Would you like water with your whisky?'

'No, neat's fine.'

'You're an Aussie.'

Lucy grinned. 'I am indeed, mate.' As she drew up a barstool and he set the drink in front of her, she wondered if Australian girls had a reputation for drinking their whisky neat.

'On holiday?' the barman queried politely.

'Yes.'

He looked apologetic. 'It's not the best weather for it.'

'Maybe, but I don't really mind.' Then she felt compelled to justify her vacation choice. 'I'm looking into my family history while I'm here.'

Now he nodded sagely. 'Genealogy.'

'Well, sort of,' she mumbled, before taking a sip of her drink.

He left her then to attend to other customers. Lucy took another sip of the whisky and felt it warming her insides all the way down. She opened the packet of chips and looked around her. It was all so very different from her favourite pub in Townsville, which was open and airy and had views of the river and the tropical beer garden at the back.

This place was snug and colourful, with overhead lights reflected in the rows of hanging glasses, so that they shone like chandeliers. Rows of colourful liqueur bottles added to the ambience, as well as decorative old brass ships' fittings and framed prints of marine charts and of sailing ships in the harbour. Someone had written a sign on a blackboard in curvy script: *Life isn't about waiting for the storm to pass, it's about learning to dance in the rain.*

Lucy smiled. In Townsville, the sign would be more likely to say: *No shirt, no beer.*

The locals, after their initial quick inspection, were no longer taking any notice of her, so she was free to observe them. Quite a mix, really – elderly couples, men she guessed were farmers or fishermen, groups of laughing young people. There were none of the suits and ties she'd seen so much of in London.

Everyone seemed to know each other and they were all now back in conversation, probably discussing small details of their lives, the state of the world, sharing jokes, by the looks of things. She felt quite comfortable about sitting alone, however, and was enjoying herself – trying to imagine living here for a few months, making friends, fitting in. She wondered why her mum seemed to have such bad memories of the place.

She was still looking around and reaching for another chip, when one particular, very masculine figure caught her eye.

Dressed in jeans with a V-necked, black knitted sweater over a white shirt, he was leaning a massive shoulder against the post at the end of the bar while he chatted with a group of farmer-ish types. Lucy decided that he must have been partly obscured before, because he was incredibly eye-catching, with a lot of thick, rather messy black hair and high cheekbones and strong – well, strong everything, really – brow, nose, jaw.

Lucy hadn't meant to stare, but she couldn't really help herself. He was so very watch-able.

Just her luck, he turned while she was still checking him out. He looked directly at her.

Gulp.

Her reaction was disconcerting. She had never, until that

moment, experienced an across-a-crowded-room lightning flash, but catching the eye of this man was like being zapped by an unseen laser. The merest connection of his dark-eyed glance, and proverbial sparks scorched all the way through her.

It wasn't supposed to happen to a young woman who was nursing a broken heart.

To make matters worse, Lucy had been in the process of swallowing a chip, but now a sharp corner stuck in her throat, and she spluttered, desperately in need of a drink to wash it down. Sadly, the only drink to hand was her whisky, which made her breath catch and resulted in a coughing fit.

Talk about embarrassing.

As she wheezed and went red in the face, she was aware that the source of her dilemma had not once shifted his cool, appraising gaze from her. And her friendly barman had deserted her, so there was no chance of changing her mind about the offer of water.

Dismayed, she turned her back on the unsettling attention.

Classy effort, Luce. You catch sight of a hot Englishman and then react with all the finesse of a thirteen-year-old.

She tried to shrug this gaffe off as she downed the last of her whisky, but the aftershocks of locking gazes with Black Sweater stayed with her. She was relieved when the barman came back and she could turn her attention to practical matters, like asking him for directions.

'I believe Penwall Hall is near here?' she said.

The barman nodded. 'About a mile up the road on the way to Camborne. I'm not sure the Hall's open just now, though.'

'Oh, it is. I've already booked a room there.' She'd had a stroke of luck when she'd Googled the address, discovering that Penwall Hall included a B&B.

Lucy was hoping to meet her great-aunt's descendants, although she was a bit vague about what might happen after that. She knew she couldn't expect too much from a brief meeting with very distant relatives. But even if there was only a slim chance that she could shed any light on the mysteries in her family's past – especially George's – she felt it would be worth it.

The barman was looking surprised. 'Are you sure you want to stay out there? There won't be many young people, and they have nice rooms here at the pub, you know.'

'Thanks. I'm sure the rooms here are lovely, but I'll give the B&B a try. I've already made the booking.'

'Oh, aye.' He shrugged. 'The grandson from Penwall Hall is here tonight.' He gave a nod towards the far end of the bar. 'The tall fellow in the black sweater. Young Mr Myatt.'

Lucy swallowed a groan. He *had* to be joking. She knew there was only one tall fellow in a black sweater at the end of the bar, and now, as she took a surreptitious peek, her fears were confirmed.

Yep. She'd just coughed and spluttered and blushed in response to a glance from the grandson of Penwall bloody Hall. Which also meant she'd just wasted all that schoolgirl blushing on a guy she was probably related to, albeit distantly.

At least he was no longer looking her way so she stole another sneaky glance, and yes, he was still very hot-looking. Lucy supposed some people might say that he looked *distinguished*, but now that she knew he was a descendant of the snobby woman who had caused her mum so much grief, she wasn't inclined to be generous.

'Did you say his name was Myatt?' she asked the barman.

'That's right. Nicholas Myatt.' The chatty barman leaned closer, lowering his voice, like a conspirator. 'The family were about to sell Penwall Hall. Same old story, couldn't afford the upkeep in this modern day and age, but then young Nick stepped in and turned the place around. You know, like on the TV show, *Country House Rescue*. Opened it up for weddings and tour groups and turned the wing where you'll be staying into a B&B.'

Lucy didn't glance at 'young' Nick Myatt again. She'd seen enough to know that he was probably in his mid-thirties, which *did* seem a bit young to have achieved so much. She'd had little to do with high achievers and it was hard to believe he was actually related to her, as a second cousin or whatever. The name Myatt didn't ring any bells either, but then, she knew next to nothing about her family's Cornish connections.

But damn, just her luck, the man who'd so closely observed her humiliating splutter was a member of the one family in all of England that she had actually needed to meet and impress. She wished she could shrug it off, as she normally would, but there was something about this guy that rattled her.

One thing was certain: if she wanted to tackle him about her family history it would be best to start afresh, so the smart thing would be to make a quick getaway now. This decided, Lucy thanked the barman and said goodnight, then, on the off-chance that Nick Myatt might glance her way again, she slid from the barstool with as much dignity as she could muster and kept her head high as she crossed the room to the coat rack.

Of course, she gave an ever-so-subtle sway of her hips as she walked and, of course, she resisted the temptation to look back.

Outside, Cornwall was colder and wilder than ever. Lucy's cheeks stung and the ends of her scarf flapped madly as she hurried to the car. As she started up the motor, she consoled herself with the realisation that Nick Myatt was too young to know anything about her mother or her grandmother, so she didn't really need to speak to *him*. To get any sort of useful information, she needed to meet someone from his parents' generation.

The road left the village behind quite quickly, climbing upwards to sweeping moorland. Lucy had her headlights on high beam and as she peered between swipes of the windscreen-wiper blades, she caught glimpses of drystone walls and leafless trees bending low in the wind. A white-tailed rabbit scampered across the road.

She wondered if the Myatt's family home would be like Wuthering Heights, all Gothic and ghostly and lonely, but before her imagination could get carried away she reached an impressive set of iron gates set in a high stone wall and a sign that showed she'd arrived at her destination.

Nerves kicked in when she slowed the little hire car and turned through the gates. Her chest tightened as she thought of her mum, arriving here, a lonely ten-year-old surrounded by snooty strangers.

Driving sedately now, Lucy headed along a drive lined with huge ancient trees, bare of all leaves. Parkland stretched beyond the trees and every so often her headlights caught a fence line, a winter-bare orchard, a tall barn-like building covered by the twisted ropey stems of a leafless creeper. She sensed that the grounds were extensive, but even so, she hadn't expected anything quite so grand as the building that greeted her when she rounded the next corner.

She wished it was daylight and not raining so she could see the place properly. But there was enough light from the lamps in the courtyard and the double row of tall, multi-paned windows to show her that the house Nick Myatt had rescued for his family was not only impressively large, but also very beautiful. With grand proportions and elegant columns guarding the front entrance, Penwall Hall was a stately English home in the best aristocratic tradition; built in stone that had stood the test of centuries.

Lucy smiled, thinking of her childhood home, a rather ramshackle box on stilts, and of her grandfather's humble worker's cottage. This was so far out of their league that it was hard to believe there was a family connection.

A light shone over a door at one end of the house. The door was set in a kind of rounded turret, and above it there was a sign announcing the reception. Somewhat overawed, Lucy pulled up, climbed out of the car and soon found herself inside a very pleasant, cosily warm room, complete with chintz-covered armchairs, Tiffany lamps and cut-glass bowls filled with roses.

The plump woman behind the counter had salt-and-pepper hair and was probably around fifty. Putting aside the romance novel she'd been reading, she welcomed Lucy with a bright smile.

'So, you must be Lucy Hunter?'

'That's right.' Clearly there weren't many guests expected this evening.

'Wonderful. I'm Jane Nancarrow.'

'Lovely to meet you, Jane.'

'I'm so glad you've made it here safely. It's such a terrible night to be out on the roads.'

Lucy was relieved by the warmth of Jane Nancarrow's welcome. She had, rather rashly, made a booking for seven nights and now, despite the shaky start at the pub, she knew she would be able to relax here, and to once again feel optimistic.

'So here's the key to your room,' she was told as she finished filling in the form with her details. 'You have a view all the way to the sea.' Jane smiled. 'Well, you *will* have a nice view if it ever stops raining.'

Lucy smiled back at her. 'I don't really mind about the weather.'

'You've come from overseas,' Jane said, reading the Townsville address on the form.

'Yes, from Australia.'

'Oh dear. You'll be used to all that sunshine.' She gave a smiling shrug. 'Well, at least in January, you won't be jostling elbow to elbow with tourists. In fact, you'll have Cornwall almost to yourself. And because it's so quiet, we've upgraded your room.'

'Goodness. Must be my lucky night. Thank you.'

'But I'm afraid the main Hall isn't open for tours in winter,' Jane said next.

This was a disappointing blow that Lucy hadn't foreseen, but she didn't want to dwell on it now. Perhaps she would pluck up the courage to announce her connections. Somehow or another, she would find a way to tour the Hall and meet its residents. She had plenty of time to sort something out.

'There are all kinds of wonderful walks over the moors and along the seafront, though.' Jane pointed to a pile of coloured brochures and maps. 'Take some of these to browse through. There are fine art galleries in the area, too, if you like that sort of thing.' Her dark eyes twinkled. 'And you'll always find hot chocolate and a blazing fire here when you get back.'

'What more could I want?' Lucy rewarded her with another broad smile.

'Now, have you eaten?' Jane asked next. 'I'm afraid we don't have a restaurant, but there's quite a good pub just down the road. The Seaspray Arms in Portreath.'

'Oh —' Lucy had no plans to return to The Seaspray Arms this evening and she wondered if half a packet of crisps could sustain her till morning.

'Or we can do a nice homemade supper on a tray,' added Jane. 'Toast and scones and hot tea? Perhaps a little pâté and a pot of jam?'

Lucy almost hugged her. 'Jane, that would be perfect.'

Her room, she soon discovered when she went up the two flights of thickly carpeted stairs, was also perfect. Despite being generously proportioned with high ceilings, it wasn't intimidating or too dauntingly old-fashioned. It was all very tasteful, with pink floral curtains and a framed mirror, a vase of tiny cream roses on the chest of drawers, pretty lamps by the bed, an antique writing desk and chair, as well as an armchair upholstered in rose brocade. It wasn't the sort of room Lucy had ever really yearned for, but here in this house, it felt just right.

After a hot shower and Jane's tasty supper, delivered, as promised, on a tray, she went to bed early and slept soundly.

Miraculously, the rain stopped during the night. Lucy had forgotten to draw the curtains and she was woken by pallid grey dawn light streaming through two tall windows. She slipped out of bed to get a better view and her breath caught. Jane was right. She had a wonderful view over the garden terraces and flights of stone steps to the sloping, winter-pale fields that ran all the way down to the sea.

As she watched, she saw a small boat plough valiantly out through the choppy waves. Then a bird, a proper English robin redbreast, flew onto her windowsill, and it looked so alert and bright and alive, she felt a sudden impulse to dress and hurry outside.

There was time for a little exploration – fortunately, breakfast ran quite late in winter – so she rugged up against the biting cold, and went downstairs and out through the vacant reception area.

Outside, her running shoes crunched on the frosty gravel drive as she crossed to a small, green door in a stone wall. It opened easily and she followed a path to the back of the house where she found a terrace edged by a low wall and huge urns that no doubt spilled over with colourful flowers in the summertime. A broad sweep of stone steps took her down to another terrace with potted shrubs and trees and elegant garden furniture.

After yet another short flight of steps, Lucy reached a long grassy field covered in a heavy dew that sparkled like diamonds in the morning sunlight. The air had a bracing, good-to-be-alive crispness and, in the distance, she could see the choppy sea already changing from grey to a smoky blue. After the stormy night, the morning was so clear and beautiful, she felt compelled to run across the fields and all the way to the dazzling, dancing bay.

She was enjoying every step of her run until she rounded a rocky headland and came face-to-face with a galloping horse.

Of course she shrieked. She couldn't help it. And the horse shrieked, too. Or at least, it let out an ear-splitting whinny as it reared up, with its black hooves striking at the air.

Horrified, Lucy shrank back against the rock, throwing a hand up to protect herself and instinctively shutting her eyes.

When the whinnying stopped, she was miserably aware that her army training had been completely useless in this sudden emergency. She forced her eyes open.

The horse was no longer prancing and rearing, but standing quite sedately, constrained by its grim-faced rider's tight grip on the reins.

Lucy took a second look at the rider. From her cowering position she had to look up. Up past the magnificent, shiny black stallion, and up –

Oh, for crying out loud. No, it couldn't be.

But it was.

Still with that shock of black hair, made even wilder by the wind, Nick Myatt looked more impressive than ever in a rusty brown riding jacket, thigh-hugging jeans faded to a soft blue and a tattered tartan scarf knotted at his throat.

Lucy was grateful to remember the useful cliché about good looks being skin deep. It was a lesson she'd learned from Sam and it had well and truly sunk in.

Not that it mattered in this instance, as Nick Myatt was no more pleased to see her than she was to see him. A dark scowl marred his fine looks as he dismounted.

It was so Jane-Eyre-meets-Mr-Rochester that Lucy might have laughed if she wasn't so nervous.

'Are you all right?' he asked gruffly.

At least he had the grace to appear concerned.

Lucy nodded, and then, because she was determined to improve on last night's flustered spluttering, she lifted her chin. 'I'm sorry I startled your horse. I didn't see you coming until it was too late.'

'Well, you don't seem to have done him any harm.' He ran an expert eye over his mount and gave its mane a soothing pat, but when he turned back to Lucy, his dark brown eyes narrowed again.

She was pretty sure that he recognised her as the silly, red-faced girl in the bar. Instinctively, she squared her shoulders.

'You're the new house guest from Australia.'

'How did you know?'

He smiled – and wow! What a difference a smile could make. 'Word spreads fast around here, and your accent's not easy to miss.'

'So, that's me sorted.'

'Not quite sorted,' Nick Myatt replied. 'I don't know your name.'

Now that he'd stopped scowling, she could almost enjoy this exchange and she could feel her old mojo returning.

'The name's Lucy,' she said, holding out her hand. 'Lucy Hunter.'

'How-do-you-do, Lucy. I'm Nick Myatt.' His handclasp was strong, but at least it wasn't bone-crushing, and his English accent was truly beautiful – cultured, but not too toff. 'I live at the Hall.'

'Nice to meet you, Nick.' Resisting the cheeky impulse to drop a quick curtsey, Lucy gave a polite nod, which he returned.

'I hope you enjoy your stay here.'

'I'm sure I will. Jane Nancarrow's given me plenty of sightseeing brochures.'

'Jane's a good stick.'

It was all so jolly polite now, but as far as Lucy was concerned, inadequate. She had far too many questions to ask and, with the Hall closed for winter, she knew she shouldn't waste this chance to open doors.

Already, Nick Myatt had his foot in the stirrup, preparing to mount his horse.

Grasping at straws, Lucy nodded towards Penwall Hall with its long double rows of deep windows glittering in the morning sun. 'You don't live *alone* up there, do you?'

Wariness crept into Nick's eyes. 'Not normally, no.'

'It's just – it's just that it's so huge. I can't imagine what it must be like.'

He withdrew the foot from the stirrup and assumed an expression of cautious mistrust. 'I'm afraid the Hall's closed to visitors during the winter.'

'Yes, so I was told.' It was hard to not be intimidated by the suspicion in those smouldering dark eyes. Lucy dropped her gaze and felt so stupidly nervous again, she almost chewed a fingernail. 'The thing is,' she said quickly before she lost her nerve, 'I'm not exactly your everyday average visitor.'

After a beat, he said quietly, 'And why is that?'

Lucy swallowed. 'I believe we're related.'

A flicker of shock flared, but Nick recovered in a heartbeat. 'You do?' he asked coolly.

'*Distantly* related,' Lucy amended.

He didn't reply to this and his face was now as stony as the walls that lined his fields.

To Lucy's annoyance, she began to feel as flustered as she had last night. It was so galling. She was used to holding her own with intimidating army officers. A snooty English gentleman should be a breeze. 'Look, I'm not here to steal the family silver, Nick. I won't be putting in a claim for the place or demanding a key to the castle.'

This brought a very slight lessening of the suspicious glint in his eyes.

Taking advantage of this brief reprieve, Lucy added, 'I believe my grandmother used to live here.'

He was clearly so surprised he forgot to frown. 'What was her name?'

Lucy's confidence faltered as she came face to face with the yawning gaps in her knowledge of her family. Before she'd left Australia, the atmosphere at home had been so fractious, she hadn't liked to pester her mother with too many questions.

'I'm afraid this is going to sound really dodgy,' she admitted. 'But I only know her married name. It was Georgina Kemp. She was my mother's mother, and I believe my grandfather used to call her George.'

13

Harry's letter from Tobruk arrived on a Friday evening, at the end of a long and difficult week.

Georgina and her two closest friends from the RASC were too weary to go out on the town, but after the huge push to get provisions to British troops in Egypt, which had involved working long hours with inevitable frayed tempers, the girls felt a need to let their hair down.

When Georgina suggested going back to her house for a light supper and a drink, her friends had accepted with flattering enthusiasm.

Dodie and Enid had been to the house in Belgravia a couple of times now, so they no longer oohed and ahhed at the size of the place, or begged for peeks at the upstairs bedrooms.

They were more than happy to gather in the warm kitchen downstairs. In fact, they even declared it was their turn to cook the supper.

Already this evening, on the tube ride home, they'd sorted out recipes and ingredients and had made their plans. Dodie's responsibility would be Potato Jane, a recipe from a Ministry of Food leaflet involving potatoes and carrots baked with layers of bread-crumbs and grated cheese, while Enid planned to make a marmalade pudding. Georgina's contribution would be the venue and a nice bottle or two from her father's cellar.

With the night in hand, their spirits were riding high by the time they reached Victoria station and they were laughing at one of Dodie's terrible jokes as they turned the corner to Wilton Street. It was a clear moonlit night, but there hadn't been any bombing raids in the past few weeks and Londoners were almost daring to believe that they'd seen the end of the Blitz.

As Georgina pushed the front door open, she saw the letter on the hall table almost immediately. She supposed James must have left it there for her and she was only mildly curious. The envelope was very thin and grey and a bit creased and dirty and, although it was addressed to her and not her father, she didn't recognise the spiky handwriting.

Picking it up, she saw that the postmark was faded and foreign and hard to read. She wondered if it had come from her Aunt Cora in New Guinea, but when she turned the envelope over, she saw the sender's name.

Lt H J Kemp.

Her heart took a frantic leap. And then the envelope fluttered in her shaking hands as she stood, staring at it.

Harry.

After months of wondering and waiting and worrying, of losing sleep, of never daring to hope . . .

'Are you all right, George?'

'Oh dear, you've gone all pale.'

'No, I'm fine.' Georgina forced a shaky smile as she slipped the envelope into her skirt pocket.

Enid, a pretty, fragile blonde, was watching her closely. 'Why don't Dodie and I leave you to read your letter in peace? Go on, don't mind us.' Her finely arched eyebrows lifted as she sent a significant glance to Dodie. 'We can get started on the supper. Can't we, Dodes?'

Georgina shook her head. 'It's all right, I can read this later.'

Harry's letter was too important for a quick, furtive skim. She wanted to savour it in complete privacy, to be able to linger over it for as long as she liked. Besides, no one in the RASC office knew about Harry, apart from Captain McNicoll, and she wanted to keep it that way. She couldn't bear to be the focus of gossip, and a romance with an Australian would most definitely set tongues wagging. As it was, there'd been enough whispering about her father and his title and the fact that she didn't go out much. The general assumption was that she had a serious boyfriend, almost certainly titled, who was away fighting.

Georgina was happy to leave it at that. There was always a danger that gossip about Harry could filter through the army loops until it reached her parents, and the last thing she needed was her mother on her doorstep demanding an explanation. But this evening, as she went down to the kitchen, she could feel Harry's letter burning a hole in her pocket.

'Smashing night, George.'

'Yes, smashing.' Dodie giggled. 'Does us good to have a quiet night in now and again.'

It was late when the girls finally left, and they were both a little tipsy as they headed off for the tube station, arm in arm, singing, 'Wish me luck as you wave me goodbye', slightly off-key.

Watching from her front doorway, by the light of an almost full moon that sailed blithely above the rooftops, Georgina waited until they turned the corner. The street was empty and, as ever, all the lights were out. A chill wind whisked out of nowhere, gathering fallen leaves into a spinning dance. With a shiver, Georgina tugged her cardigan tighter over her chest and closed the door, then she went back down to the kitchen where a half-full ashtray, empty glasses and a wine bottle still littered the table.

After supper, Dodie and Enid had lingered and, with the lights low and the wireless playing Glenn Miller softly in the background, they'd been content to regale her with hilarious stories of their many and varied romantic adventures. And they had done this without pressing her to share similarly intimate details of her private life, for which she was deeply grateful.

But now . . .

At last. Georgina turned on a lamp by the ancient brown leather armchair in the corner, where their cook had been in the habit of resting her bunions at the end of a long day. She took out Harry's letter and made herself comfortable with her stockinged feet tucked beneath her while she read.

Tobruk
10 September 1941

> *Dear George,*
>
> *Here's hoping this letter reaches you and finds you safe and well. I wanted to let you know that I'm still in one piece here in the desert. The conditions are pretty tough, but that's what you get in a war, isn't it? No one's having it easy.*
>
> *At least we've had news that the bombing raids on London have been easing off, so that's a big relief, I can tell you.*
>
> *There are a lot of other things I'd like to tell you, my dearest George, like the way I lie awake at night remembering every sweet detail of our twenty-four hours together, and how I think about you all the time. But I know I mustn't pile it on too thick. It would be presuming too much after such a brief time together. Although I do need to tell you that our night*

meant a great deal to me, George, perhaps more than you can possibly imagine.

This letter is mainly to let you know I'm alive and kicking and we've given old Rommel a bloody nose. Also, I could be moving on to a new role soon. Can't say too much about it, but I'll try to keep you posted.

Your mob, the RASC, are here delivering fuel and supplies and I cornered one of the young officers and made him promise to get this letter to you. It will still have to go past the unit censor, of course.

In the meantime, stay safe.

I smile whenever I think of you, and I would love to hear from you.

Harry

By the time Georgina went to bed, having first cleared away the glasses and ashtray, she'd read Harry's precious letter so many times she almost knew it by heart.

I lie awake at night remembering every sweet detail of our twenty-four hours together . . . I think about you all the time . . .

In the little bedroom where they'd spent that one precious night, she turned out the light and opened the curtains so she could look up at the small corner of sky that wasn't blocked by their neighbours' roofs. A cluster of shiny stars hung in the black sky, and she thought how distant and pure they looked – so innocent and removed from this terrible war.

She wondered if Harry was lying in some ghastly desert trench, or if he'd already moved on to his new posting. She wondered what stars he could see.

'I think about you, too,' she whispered. 'All the time. Stay safe, Harry. Please, stay safe.'

It took several attempts the following morning before she was satisfied with her answering letter to Harry. It was so hard to hold back from telling him everything that lay in her heart, but she took his lead and stopped short of revealing the true depth of her emotions. After all, he was in the thick of an exhausting and gruelling battle, and telling him how much she worried about him and longed to see him couldn't possibly be helpful. He had more than enough to deal with.

In the end she kept it as short and to the point as he had.

3 Wilton St.
Belgravia
London, England
5 October 1941

>Dear Harry,
>
>Thank you very much for your letter. You have no idea how pleased I was to hear from you. I've been following the news of the war in North Africa very closely and I know you Aussies have done a magnificent job in defending Tobruk.
>
>Ever since you left here, whenever I've felt inclined to be sorry for myself about the Blitz, or to complain about how little we can buy here in London with our ration cards, I've thought of you with tins of bully beef in those hot desert trenches and I've given myself a mental slap.
>
>If you've been moved to a new posting by now, I hope it isn't too grim, and I hope this letter finds you. You'll send me another letter with an address, won't you?
>
>Thank you for telling me that you smile when you think of me. If I thought it would make you smile I'd tap dance or sing a song, even cook another omelette. But as I can't

> *do any of these things, I'm enclosing a photograph. A small memento. I hope you like it, Harry. It was taken just before the war, before I had my hair cut short and when I was still looking rather glamorous.*
>
> *I hope that it might make you smile.*
>
> *Oh, and I nearly forgot to congratulate you on being promoted to lieutenant. Well done, but stay safe, Harry.*
>
> *Love,*
>
> *George*

She dithered for ages before she finally added:

> *PS I sleep with your letter under my pillow.*

Captain McNicoll didn't look up from the pile of paperwork on his desk as he beckoned Georgina into his office.

'Excuse me, sir, there are two rather urgent letters here for you to sign.'

She set them with their carbon copies in front of him and, with only the briefest survey of the contents, he scrawled his signature – a simple task for most, but one that was still difficult for him and involved a grim downward curve of his mouth as he curled his left hand awkwardly over the pen.

'Thank you, Lenton.' He gave a brief nod when he was done, and Georgina was about to retrieve the letters and leave when he looked up. His normally mild blue eyes narrowed and seemed to pierce her. 'Tell me, are you still in touch with your Australian chap?'

The question was so unexpected, Georgina felt her face burst into flames. 'I – we – we've exchanged letters, sir.'

Apparently satisfied, Captain McNicoll nodded. 'I suppose you've heard that the Australian Prime Minister has withdrawn his troops from the Middle East.'

'Yes, sir.' The Australian withdrawal had been ordered as a result of the increasing threat from the Japanese. Georgina had been following the news reports closely, but so far she'd heard nothing from Harry and she had no idea where he'd been sent. And now the Japanese had bombed Pearl Harbor and had invaded Malaya.

But none of this involved their RASC office directly. She wondered why her boss had chosen this moment to talk about it.

He dropped his frowning gaze to his desk and appeared to be deep in contemplation.

Confused, Georgina picked up the signed letters and began to back out of the office. 'I'll get these into the post straight away, sir.'

'Before you go,' he said, still frowning. 'I had a drink with Gerald Duffy last night – he's a major with Army Intelligence.'

'Should I know him, sir?'

'Not necessarily. The thing is, he told me that he's being posted to Australia. He'll be attached to the British Embassy in Canberra and answerable to the British military attaché, Colonel Pinter. Pinter reports, via the embassy, directly to the War Office here in London.'

Georgina swallowed. Her boss had never been one for idle chatter and she had no idea why he was telling her this.

'Major Duffy's new role in Australia will include making an independent assessment of the situation in the south-west Pacific,' Captain McNicoll said next. 'As you know, the Japanese have been moving at a cracking pace ever since Pearl Harbor and it's not in Britain's interests to rely exclusively on Australian or American reports.'

'I – I see,' Georgina said, although she felt more puzzled than ever.

'The situation's tricky,' her boss went on. 'You might not have heard about the friction over Churchill's "Beat Hitler First" doctrine, but the Australian Prime Minister, John Curtin, is very concerned about the growing threat to his own region.'

'Yes, sir.' She had no idea what else to say. She was quite sure that her boss wasn't asking for her opinion, although, if she had been asked, she found it perfectly reasonable that Australia's focus should not remain in Europe, but rather on what Churchill regarded as the 'lesser war' in Asia and the Pacific.

'Duffy will be taking a subaltern with him,' Captain McNicoll continued. 'And he was asking me if I knew of any good secretaries who might be prepared to go to Australia.'

'Oh.' Now the penny dropped and Georgina's heart took off like a runaway horse. 'Were – were you thinking of me, sir?'

'Well.' Her boss's smile was complicated, a mix of regret and sincerity. 'I certainly wouldn't be happy to lose you, Lenton, quite the opposite in fact, but your name did spring to mind. You're very competent and have the confidence that this particular job requires. Of course, I wouldn't say anything to Duffy without speaking to you first.'

He opened a drawer in his desk and pulled out a small folder. 'I've investigated the details of the position, though, in case you are interested. But I'm afraid you'd need to make a quick decision. Time is of the essence.'

There was another letter waiting on the hall table when Georgina arrived home, her mind still whirling with all the questions and possibilities raised by Captain McNicoll's surprising suggestion. She pounced on the envelope as soon as she saw it, but this letter had not come from Harry.

Kokopo Ridge Road,
New Britain
22 December 1941

Dearest Georgina,
    I've already written to your parents but I know you're

living in London these days, so I wanted to write to you as well. By now you've probably heard about the rapid advances the Japanese are making through Malaya and the Dutch East Indies, which sets us here in New Guinea rather squarely in their path.

My dear, to think I tried to persuade you to join us down here! In my naivety, I thought you'd be safe. Who could have imagined that this dreadful war would spread all the way to our little island paradise?

As I write this, the women and children are being evacuated from New Britain – the European women and children, that is – but I've chosen to stay here with Teddy. Darling, please don't worry. I know I've made the right decision. If I had children to consider, it might have been a different matter but, as you know, our Gus is busy flying over Europe with the RAF, so it's just Teddy and I and our dear Tolai people who work for us on our plantation. They are almost like family to us now, after all this time, and I would feel terrible about deserting them.

As you know, poor Teddy was badly shaken by the last war, which is why we came down here on our honeymoon, seeking refuge and peace. In Darwin we joined a Burns Philp cruise to the islands that brought us to New Britain and, after one night in beautiful Rabaul, we fell in love with the place. I'm so sorry that you have never been able to visit us here. I know that you, of all the family, would have understood why we love our island home on the edge of the Coral Sea.

Forgive me for rambling, Georgina, but I am feeling very nostalgic about New Britain right now and it seems important to tell you about it. Despite the volcanoes that ring Rabaul – which is why we chose to live a little distance away at Kokopo – it has always been such a pretty town, with streets lined with mango trees and frangipani, a bustling waterfront, and dark, rugged mountains as a backdrop.

There's the beautiful harbour with wharves and copra sheds and, out on the water, all manner of merchant vessels and sailing skiffs. So many adventurers wander in here and there are outrigger canoes, paddled by natives, loaded with fruit for sale.

If you were to saunter down Rabaul's streets you would see quite a cosmopolitan mix of people, with the local Tolai natives mingling with Chinese and Malay, as well as suntanned businessmen, mostly but not exclusively from Australia, dressed in white cotton, tropical suits, and women, almost always wearing bright floral cotton frocks, which seem so right in this setting.

There's a Chinatown with exotic shops and the Chin Hing Hotel on Yara Avenue. And of course I would take you to The Bung, a colourful market with rows of stalls piled high with pineapples, coconuts, pawpaws and shellfish, not to mention the chance to see cheerfully bare-chested local men in their colourful sarongs.

I know none of this sounds exciting compared with London and Buckingham Palace and debutante balls at the Savoy, but Teddy and I have a comfortable home, a good network of friends and, until now, a wonderfully peaceful lifestyle.

For all these reasons and so many more, Teddy refuses to leave our plantation. He believes the enemy will be stopped and I'm sure you'll understand that I couldn't possibly abandon him. Don't worry about us. We'll have each other, my dear, so we'll be fine. We'll see this through, inspired by the way you in London have so bravely endured the Blitz.

Sending much love to you always and forever,
Aunt Cora

After Georgina had closed the letter and tucked it back into its envelope, she went to the drawing room, which was normally closed up, and began to anxiously pace behind the drawn curtains. Wending her way between pieces of furniture covered in dust sheets, she sank deep into thought.

Ever since the afternoon's conversation with her boss, she'd had so very much to think about. Right now, she felt overwhelmed by the disturbing undertone of heartbreak in her aunt's letter, by the uncharacteristic, almost nervous detail, and the very real peril that her aunt and uncle faced. In many ways, this worry was even more overpowering than her longing to see Harry again.

The timing of the letter's arrival was uncanny. Coming so soon after her boss's news, it almost felt as if fate or the hand of God had intervened. Georgina had the strangest presentiment that she'd been sent a message – and one that was almost impossible to ignore.

Should I go to Australia? Am I meant to?

There were good reasons to go. Her desire to see Harry again, even if the possibility was slim, combined with worry about her aunt and uncle, was strong, frighteningly so. Added to that, she'd always been the adventurous one in her family and here was a chance to visit an exotic location instead of remaining stuck in the office in Dulwich for the rest of the war. She'd heard her Aunt Cora speak glowingly of Sydney with its beautiful beaches, blue ocean and sunshine, and apparently, the social life was quite sophisticated as well. If she went there she should probably pack an evening dress.

But, of course, this decision was far too important to jump into rashly. She had to think it through carefully, had to ask herself why seeing Harry was *so* important.

Georgina was worldly enough to know that a girl shouldn't be hung up on her very first lover and yet, deep down, she was certain that her feelings for Harry were profound and powerful – an emotional connection that couldn't be explained logically.

Of course, she didn't really expect that a job in Australia with Major Duffy would result in her being able to see Harry. He could be anywhere in the South Pacific. And she probably couldn't assist Cora and Teddy in any practical way, but her chances of doing either of these things had to be greater than if she stayed in London.

Pausing to look about her, she found herself remembering the drawing room without the dust covers. Here in this very room, at the height of the season in 1939, she'd thrown a party, and the drawing room had looked so fresh and summery with upholstered sofas and armchairs of cream and gold brocade, set against the pale green carpet.

She and her mother had arranged flowers in enormous vases and the room had been filled with the scent of lilies and with the laughter of young people who were enjoying smoked salmon sandwiches and champagne. Lights from the chandeliers had reflected in mirrors and on the sparkling glasses.

What a success that night had been!

Georgina could remember Bunny Featherstone, so sophisticated in an almost sheer black evening dress, perched on the arm of the sofa near the piano, with at least three smitten young swains practically kneeling at her feet. And over there, by the window, Primrose Cavendish had fallen in love with Stephen Wade.

Georgina's dress that night had been divine, a Parisian halterneck, made of a gorgeous silvery-green lamé with a net skirt covered in four-leaf clovers.

'Just breathtaking!' Michael St George had told her.

Sadly, Michael and Stephen had both been killed in France six months later. And now, Bunny had joined the Women's Royal Naval Service and was based in Portsmouth and Primrose was practically running her family's farm in Cornwall single-handedly. The whole world had been consumed by this dreadful, devastating war, which now covered both hemispheres of the globe.

Georgina thought again about Cora and Teddy and shivered. She remembered what Harry had said in his letter.

But that's what you get in a war, isn't it? No one's having it easy.

With a sigh that could have been caused by either anger or despair, she began to pace again, but she had only taken a few steps when any lurking doubts were overtaken by the growing weight of her new certainty.

Abruptly, she stopped, turned, and went straight to the telephone in the hallway, where she asked to be put through to Captain McNicoll's home number.

'Ah, Lenton, so you've made up your mind?'

'Yes, sir. I'd like to apply for that position.'

14

Colonel Ralph Pinter, the British military attaché in Canberra, had a bright shock of ginger hair and a surprisingly ruddy face, which sat at odds with the gravity of his expression as Georgina and her new boss, Major Gerald Duffy, were ushered into a small, mustard-walled meeting room for a special briefing.

Unfortunately, they were not shown to a seat near a window and Georgina couldn't see a fan in the room, so she prepared to suffer. January in Australia was blisteringly hot.

It was hard to believe she was actually here. Everything had happened so quickly after her successful interview with the major. Her first ordeal had been giving the news to her parents and then handling their reactions, which amounted to quiet concern overlaid by a hint of pride from her father, and near hysteria from her mother. Then had followed the whirlwind of finishing up in the office in Dulwich and farewelling her friends. Dodie and Enid, in particular, had wept buckets.

'We'll never see you again,' Dodie had cried, only to receive a sharp dig in the ribs from Enid.

'Don't tell her that,' Enid had admonished and she'd pressed a rather flea-bitten rabbit's foot into Georgina's hand. 'Here,' she said. 'I got it from a stall in Covent Garden. My Dad had one just like it. It was his lucky charm in the last war and he came through it safe as houses. Carry it for good luck.'

Then there had been the packing, and the rather terrifying ordeal of the long flight to Australia via Singapore.

And now here she was, a mere week later, still quite exhausted, in a roomful of military and political officers in Canberra, and in a uniform totally unsuited to the Australian heat.

'Gentlemen,' Colonel Pinter began rather pompously. 'For the benefit of the new staff,' – he nodded to Major Duffy and Georgina, who had earlier been introduced – 'I'll start by recapping the current situation in this region.' He paused and eyed his audience grimly. 'To put it bluntly, the Australians, the Americans and we British, including, or should I say *especially*, our own Prime Minster, have all underestimated the capacity of the Japanese Imperial Forces.'

There was a significant pause before he went on. 'Churchill was shocked when the *Prince of Wales* and the *Repulse* were sunk last month off Malaya. The Japanese were well equipped, using both land-based bombers and torpedo bombers, and now, as the rest of you here already know, there is a growing fear that Singapore will fall.'

Georgina had been sitting with her pen poised to take notes, but now she looked up in shock. Surely this was impossible? Everyone – the British Prime Minister, the journalists, the military spokes-men – absolutely *everyone* had stated with complete certainty that Singapore could never be captured.

Now the colonel pointed to a large wall map of Australia and South East Asia. Until this moment, she'd never really noticed how close to the north of Australia those Asian countries and islands were. Not as close as Europe was to Britain, but still . . .

The colonel turned back to his captive audience. 'This infor-mation remains strictly within these walls, of course. Publicly, the war office is still expressing every confidence in Fortress Singapore, but I'm afraid the Japanese air superiority is obvious. Their shipping and logistics are almost impossible to stop and they have a very strong and mobile force on the ground pushing our units back down the Malay Peninsula.'

Georgina's pen was flying across her notebook when Colonel Pinter made a rather noisy and deliberate throat-clearing sound, and Major Duffy nudged her with his elbow.

Looking up, she found the colonel watching her coldly. 'No note-taking during this conference, thank you, Lenton.'

'Yes, sir.' Her cheeks felt a bit pink as she closed her notebook and she was aware that every single man in the room, except her boss, was frowning at her. But she refused to be intimidated and instead of looking apologetic, she remained at her most dignified.

Her mother would have been proud of her, she thought, swallowing an urge to smile, and she kept her hands folded demurely in her lap as Colonel Pinter went on with his briefing, informing them that Australia's military capabilities were totally inadequate. Until now, Australia's focus had been on the defence of Britain with the result that they'd given insufficient strategic thought to the defence of their homeland.

As it stood, Australia's only forward lines of defence were in various strategic islands to the north and west.

'But these defences are nowhere near adequate,' the colonel said dourly. 'And last month Prime Minister Curtin appealed to Roosevelt to come to Australia's aid in the Pacific Islands without success.'

'What about Rabaul and New Guinea?' Major Duffy asked. 'What's the situation there? As far as I can see, they're vital. Their capture would give the Japanese a tactical stranglehold on South East Asia.'

An icy shiver ran down Georgina's spine. Cora and Teddy practically lived on Rabaul's doorstep.

'The island of New Britain is crucial,' agreed the colonel. 'Rabaul has a big, deep, natural harbour. In fact, we believe the Japanese plan to turn it into one of their greatest air and sea bases in the South Seas.'

As he said this, the colonel turned back to the map, his expression doleful. 'Unfortunately, we also understand that Rabaul is poorly protected. From the intelligence we've received, there's a small unit called Lark Force, with about twelve hundred men, a local expat unit of New Guinea Volunteer Rifles, a small anti-aircraft battery and a few coast watchers.'

'But that's ridiculous,' Major Duffy spluttered. 'It's untenable.'

'It is indeed,' the colonel agreed. 'Especially as the Japanese already have a huge force on Truk, only two hundred miles away.'

'Surely more forces will be sent?'

'Word is that Curtin doesn't have the intention or the capacity to send extra troops.'

Georgina's heart began to thump madly. Her aunt had written so calmly, claiming that she and Teddy would be fine, but clearly they were in very grave danger indeed.

Major Duffy was staring at the map, his forehead creased by a worried frown. 'New Britain is a simple stepping stone to Australia.'

'Exactly. We suspect the Australian government is either downplaying the risk, or simply underestimating it.' Colonel Pinter squared his shoulders as if to impress on them what he had to say next. 'Either way, we in the British Army need better intelligence about this situation.'

It was an hour or two later before Georgina discovered exactly how this 'better intelligence' was to be acquired. She was trying to set up some kind of filing system in the shoebox-sized office she'd been allocated, when Major Duffy came back from a private meeting with Colonel Pinter.

'I'm off to Rabaul in the morning,' he told her.

'You, sir?' She knew it was insubordinate of her to question her boss, but she was so surprised it had jumped out. Fortunately, the major didn't seem to mind.

'Just a quick flight up and back. I'll be travelling via Townsville and a flying boat from Port Moresby and I'm to liaise with Colonel Scanlan of the Lark Force. I want to evaluate the true situation in New Britain.'

'I see, sir.'

'As you must have gathered this morning, we're not entirely happy with the way the Australian government is handling the Rabaul situation. They want to make a stand, but to us it looks rather hopeless. Unless they have something up their sleeves.'

'Yes.' Grabbing a quick breath, Georgina said, 'May I come too, sir?'

A shocked, scoffing sound broke from her boss. 'Certainly not. Great Scot, Lenton.'

'But, sir, it's my job, isn't it? If I were a man, you'd be taking me.'

'But you're not a man and we've had reports that Japanese Zeroes have already started bombing New Britain's two airports.'

'Then it's even more important that I go.'

'Don't talk nonsense.' Major Duffy frowned at her. 'You're not making sense.'

'Sir, I have an aunt and uncle living on New Britain. Last time my aunt wrote, they had no plans to leave. I don't think they realise how vulnerable they are.'

'Well, I'm sorry to hear that, but I can't wait while you try to find out where they are now.'

'I know exactly where they are,' Georgina said bravely. 'So, let me come with you.' The last thing Georgina wanted was to get on another aeroplane, but what choice did she have? She couldn't bear to think of her beautiful Aunt Cora and gentle-natured Teddy falling into the hands of the Japanese. After she'd come all the way from England, she had to grab this chance. 'I'm sure if I were able to speak to them, they'd listen.'

Major Duffy gave an annoyed shake of his head and was in the process of turning away when he stopped and his eyes narrowed, as if he were remembering something. 'What are your aunt and uncle's names?'

'Lord and Lady Harlow.'

Now he stared at Georgina, his eyes blazing with disbelief. A muscle flexed in his jaw and she could see the fact that her family was titled was making an impact. It was some time before he spoke. 'The plantation owners have all been evacuated.'

'I don't think so, sir. The letter from my aunt only came a few days before we left England and she said that she and Uncle Teddy planned to stay on New Britain. They've lived on the island for so long, you see, and they love the place and they feel loyal to the locals who work for them. Aunt Cora sounded quite determined.'

'Good God.'

The poor man looked both disturbed and shaken; Georgina could see that he believed her.

'Please let me go with you, sir. I know they'll get a terrible shock to see me, but I think I could use that to my advantage.' Crossing her fingers behind her back, she said, 'I'm confident I could persuade them to leave. Although, of course, that would be secondary to any other duties I might have to support your inquiry.'

Major Duffy let out a heavy sigh.

But at least he didn't say no.

Georgina had no idea what to expect when she reached Rabaul. Despite her aunt's eloquent descriptions, she hadn't really been prepared for the stunning natural beauty of New Guinea. Seen from the air, the colours of the rugged, dark emerald mountains and the glowing peacock-blue seas were more intense than she could have dreamed, so different from the muted, misty tones of the English countryside.

But as the Catalina seaplane made its low swooping descent over the crescent-shaped island of New Britain, chilling signs of destruction became apparent, marring the pristine beauty.

Smoke was rising, not only from the volcanoes that ringed Rabaul, but from blackened buildings along the waterfront and a large ship moored at the wharf. There was no sign of the outriggers laden with fruit coming to greet them on the water. And on land, instead of the colourful market stalls that her aunt had described in her letter, Georgina saw soldiers in trucks, or stripped to the waist and digging trenches, while anxious-faced citizens rushed about, carrying boxes and cartons of food like frenzied ants.

She could almost smell their urgency and fear. Word was out, she and the major were told by the Australian sergeant who greeted them at their moorings. Coast watchers had sent the latest warnings. A large Japanese invasion fleet was looming closer by the hour.

All the military trucks were in use, so the sergeant drove them to the army HQ in a commandeered civilian car. Looking about her at the buzz of frantic activity, Georgina was hit by chilling reality. This was it. She was on the ground in a foreign war zone, no longer just hearing about it in a meeting room or reading about it in the newspapers.

Now, for the first time, panic gripped her, bringing a flood of doubts. Had she been mad to come here? Was she risking her life foolishly? Was there even time to find her aunt and uncle? There might barely be time for Major Duffy to make his necessary reconnaissance with the Lark Force commander and get clear away again before the Japanese arrived.

Unfortunately, she had to be patient while the major went into the large wooden hall that served as headquarters to organise an audience with Colonel Scanlan. Her need for a vehicle and a driver to take her to Kokopo was not their top priority.

Meanwhile, the heat in New Britain was stifling – not the dry, burning heat of Canberra but humid and sweltering, the air thick and damp, making it hard to breathe. Sweat ran in rivulets down her back and between her breasts.

She found a seat out of the blazing sun, in the shade of a large spreading tree, a tree heavy with fruit that might have been mangoes, she wasn't sure. The faintest breeze blew up from the harbour and she undid the top button of her shirt and the buttons on the cuffs of her sleeves and rolled the sleeves back. At least no one here would reprimand her for not being properly in uniform.

From her post, she looked down to the deserted, smoking wharves, and across to a distant hill where timber houses with deep verandahs climbed the gentle slopes. One or two of the houses looked damaged and at the very top of the hill, anti-aircraft guns were positioned, partly camouflaged by rocks and sandbags.

She wondered if she was going to die here on an alien island in the South Seas. *Like Robert Louis Stevenson*, she thought, although she didn't find the thought comforting. Strangely, she felt more frightened now than she had in London during the Blitz. Of course, it had helped to be living in a large solid house with a basement and to be surrounded by familiar things. Now, if Japanese Zeroes suddenly appeared out of that bright blue sky, a mango tree wouldn't be much protection.

The major reappeared on the verandah and Georgina could tell at first glance that he wasn't happy.

'No need to hang about out there in the heat, Lenton. You may as well come inside.'

'Have you spoken to Colonel Scanlan?'

'No.' He gave a shake of his head for emphasis. 'It doesn't look like I'll get anywhere near him.' An irritated sigh escaped him. 'I knew they weren't going to roll out the red carpet for us, but —'

He hesitated, and seemed to change his mind about finishing the sentence. 'Anyway, there's a group of young mid-rank officers in here, and they seem pretty professional. Come with me. We're going to have to intrude and demand a few answers. Get the job done, one way or another.'

Georgina almost smiled at his stiff-upper-lipped British bravado as she followed him into the hall where soldiers were busily transporting boxes through a side door to a waiting truck. Three or four officers were grouped at a table, absorbed in a low-voiced, tense conversation as they sorted through documents.

The major promptly marched to these officers and introduced himself. 'Hello there. I'm Major Duffy of the British Army. You should have received a signal that I was coming.'

Georgina remained at a discreet distance, looking around her at the hall, which was no more than a large room with a stage at one end, as if it had once been used as a theatre. Maps had been hung on the walls, but there was also a photo of King George VI, looking somewhat incongruous in this antipodean setting. A field telephone sat on a separate desk next to the officers, its cable lines running outside through an open window.

At another table in the corner, a lone officer was leaning over a map spread on the table. He was tall and wore a khaki beret at a rakish angle. His hair was dark and he looked so much like Harry that her heart did a somersault.

Oh my gosh.

It *was* Harry. Thinner than before and more suntanned than ever, but every bit as handsome.

In shock, Georgina could only stand there, staring, while her knees threatened to give way. She glanced again at the major. He had interrupted the Australian officers in the midst of their heated discussion and he didn't seem pleased by their polite but rather curt responses.

With a frustrated harrumph, the impatient major turned back to frown at her, then concern spread across his reddened face. 'My God, Lenton, what's the matter? You're as pale as a ghost.'

'I think I've seen someone. Someone I know.'

'Who?' Major Duffy looked understandably puzzled.

'Harry. Harry Kemp.'

The major's eyes widened and he scanned the hall. 'You know one of these men?'

'Yes, sir.' Georgina's voice was trembling with shock. With fear. With joy. 'The tall fellow in the corner with the beret. I – I met him in London, before he was sent to Tobruk.'

'And now the poor sod's here,' the major muttered, almost beneath his breath. Then, 'You said his name's Kemp?'

'Yes, sir.'

'Right, that's handy. These other fellows are busy, so he's our man.'

With that, the major zeroed in on Harry.

'Excuse me,' he said. 'Lieutenant Kemp?'

Harry's head jerked up. He looked first at the major and then at Georgina. Shock flared in his grey eyes. His mouth opened but he was clearly lost for words. He swallowed. Blinked. Looked around him, as if somehow this would provide an explanation. When he looked at Georgina again, his gaze seemed to burn her.

Major Duffy intervened. 'I believe you know my subaltern, Lenton.'

Harry stood stiffly, his eyes now drinking Georgina in and she longed to launch herself into his arms, to press her face to his chest, to cling to him. Claim him.

Somehow she managed to restrain the inappropriate impulse. She held out her hand. 'How are you, Harry?'

'George.' He sounded as shaken as he looked and his hand

gripped hers tightly. 'What in God's name are you doing here?'

'I can explain,' Major Duffy said, smoothly overriding the tense undercurrents. 'Is there somewhere private we can talk?'

Harry nodded towards the door. 'The verandah's as good a place as any.'

Abruptly he excused himself from the group of men at the next table, who were so intent on their discussion, they scarcely paid any attention to the interruption, and Georgina and the major followed him outside.

There was no time for small talk.

'I'll come straight to the point,' the major said quickly. 'I represent the British forces out of Canberra and I'm trying to assess the situation here.'

'I'm on a similar mission,' said Harry. 'With the 1st Independent Company, based on New Ireland.'

'You're a commando?' Major Duffy was clearly impressed.

Harry acknowledged this with a curt nod. 'Selected for commando training after we left Tobruk. Came over here this morning by boat for a quick reconnaissance.' He spoke civilly enough, but his gaze kept flicking to Georgina and he looked angry.

'I regret that Lenton's involved,' Major Duffy said, clearly sensing the immediate source of Harry's disquiet. 'We hadn't realised the situation was so desperate.'

'Desperate is the word all right.'

'Does this mean the defences here are as bad as they appear? From what I can see, there aren't enough heavy weapons and artillery to stop an invasion.'

Harry scowled at the blazing tropical sunlight and at the guns in place on the distant promontory. 'It's a mess,' he said with quiet resignation. 'Every bit as bad as it looks. The artillery is antique. Lark Force has a few mortars and machine guns. That's it. Basically, they only have small arms.'

'I see.'

The men eyed each other solemnly and Georgina could easily guess what they were not saying. Rabaul would fall and Lark Force would be annihilated.

Despite the heat, she felt cold. Cold with dread, with fear for the men, for herself, for her aunt and uncle.

'You should both leave here now,' Harry said next, his eyes flashing to Georgina as he rasped the words between gritted teeth.

'Yes,' replied the major. 'I've got to report back. I can't afford to be caught. We'll get straight out on the next Catalina. I'll organise our departure immediately.'

Panic surged through Georgina. Surely she couldn't be turned away without even trying to make contact with her aunt and uncle? 'But I've got to get to Kokopo.'

Harry's gaze was as fierce as it was horrified. 'Jesus Christ, George. Why?'

She explained as quickly as she could about Cora and Teddy. 'That's why I've come here. I can't leave without trying to see them.'

A muscle jerked in his jaw. 'I'm sorry. It's too late. They should have evacuated by now.'

'I'm sure they're still here. They're stubborn, Harry.'

He seemed to grind his teeth as if he was biting off an expletive. After scowling into the distance for several long, nerve-racking seconds, his gaze finally softened, but his throat worked as if he was dealing with a difficult emotion.

'You'll have to go with Corporal Palmer,' he said finally, nodding to the vehicle that had brought them from the harbour. 'I presume you've sanctioned this, sir?' he added, addressing Major Duffy.

'Yes, yes, as long as it's quick.'

Harry nodded grimly. 'Palmer's taking a delivery to the Three Ways and Kokopo's not much further. He can drop you off. But you'll have to do some very fast talking with these relatives of yours.'

'I will,' Georgina assured him.

'And one other thing.' Harry spoke more gently now and his grey eyes shone extra brightly in his suntanned face.

'Yes?' Georgina almost took a step closer. She longed for him to touch her. Just a brush of his hand, a tiny kiss on the cheek.

'Make bloody sure you're back quickly and on that Catalina,' was all he said.

15

'So you need to get to the Harlow's plantation.' Corporal Palmer was now wearing a helmet as Georgina climbed into the car beside him.

'Yes, please. Do you know it?'

He gave a curt, tight-lipped nod but then he frowned and, for a moment, he looked as if he was going to say something else. By the curl of his lip, Georgina suspected that he wanted to comment on the stupidity of her mission, but he must have thought better of it, for he suddenly took off, roaring along the road out of town.

In no time they were heading through thick jungle where the air smelled dank and the tree branches, roped with dangling vines, met overhead. The road climbed through this tunnel of greenery until the forest eventually broke away and they were in open country. Here the road hugged the ridge and below she could catch views of the jewel-bright sea, looking deceptively serene and harmless.

They passed a cluster of little thatched bamboo huts that must have belonged to natives. A similarly structured but larger building with a cross was clearly a church. Georgina saw a group of women in grass skirts with babies on their hips. Nut-brown children, naked and laughing, chased each other. Georgina had only just taken these sights in when the corporal took a sharp turn down a narrow track between lines of forest fringed by rows of coconut palms. Finally, the track opened out onto a plateau lush with spreading green lawns and gardens.

In the middle of the gardens sat a low, sprawling bungalow, pristine white against the bright green of the vegetation. Beyond the house, natives were digging deep holes that Georgina decided must be trenches.

'I'll be back in twenty minutes to collect you,' her stern young driver warned. 'You'll have to leave then, no matter what.'

'Yes,' Georgina told him. 'I understand. Thank you.'

So.

Here she was – standing on the damp lawn outside a house that was different from any she'd ever seen. It appeared to be completely open, with floor-to-ceiling shutters that folded back, and the house flowed all the way into a garden filled with glossy-leaved shrubs and bright exotic flowers – bougainvillea and frangipani.

It was appalling to think that war might destroy such a peaceful scene of natural beauty. Somehow it seemed even worse than the Nazis' bombing of London.

As Georgina made her way along a path made of crushed shells and pebbles, she could see the smooth-tiled floors of the house's interior. There was an elegant cane dining table and chairs, upholstered cane lounges, huge pink pots filled with ferns and palms.

'Hello?' she called uncertainly when she reached a doorway and, just like that, a woman appeared.

Aunt Cora. Her dark hair streaked with white, but looking as elegant as ever in an aquamarine silk blouse and slim white trousers, her feet encased in beautifully embroidered gold cloth slippers.

Oh, God love you, Georgina thought with a fierce rush of affection. Here was her aunt, about to be invaded by a fearsome enemy, and she looked almost as glamorous as she had in her tiara and diamonds at Buckingham Palace.

But although her aunt was keeping up appearances, she didn't look calm. There was high colour in her cheeks and her eyes were extra bright and, when she saw her visitor, she stopped abruptly, pressing a shaking hand to her throat.

'Georgina?'

'Hello, Aunt Cora.'

'Good heavens.' Cora's mouth trembled, as if she was on the verge of breaking down. 'What on earth are you doing here?'

'I've come to tell you that you have to leave. There's room on a seaplane. You can go to Australia, but you have to get out now.'

'You haven't come all the way from England?'

'I was posted to Canberra and I've come here to New Britain with Major Gerald Duffy.'

'Good heavens.'

Now her aunt seemed to recover from her shock and she was suddenly her old self, smiling warmly, holding her arms out in greeting. 'Darling,' she said, pressing kisses to Georgina's cheeks and hugging her. 'How wonderful to see you.' As if Georgina had arrived as a long-awaited house guest. 'Would you like some tea? Come and sit down. I'll get Flo to make us a fresh pot.'

Cora gestured for Georgina to sit in one of the deeply cushioned cane armchairs.

'Aunt Cora, we don't have time for tea. The Japanese fleet is almost here. You do understand how urgent this is, don't you?'

Her aunt's smile was somewhat bewildered.

'The Japanese are going to —' Georgina broke off in mid sentence as the *boom-boom* of an explosion sounded in the distance. 'See!' she cried, panic flaring in her chest.

'They've been doing that for weeks now.' But her aunt looked worried, even as she dismissed the explosion with a wave of her hand. 'You've been through the Blitz. You know what it's like.'

'This is different, Aunt Cora. I have it on good authority. The Japanese mean to take Rabaul. It will become an important base for them. And there aren't nearly enough Australian forces here to defend the island. I only have twenty minutes to get you out of here.'

As Georgina said this, there was another explosion and, after it, the menacing drone of planes and the snapping of gunfire.

Her uncle appeared from one of the house's inner rooms. Looking very suntanned and thin, he was dressed all in white, with the loose sleeve of his open-necked cotton shirt casually knotted below the stump of his missing arm.

'I heard gunfire in the distance. Sounds like things are hotting up again,' he said, and then he stopped and stared at Georgina. 'Good God.'

'It's all right, Teddy,' said Cora. 'You're not hallucinating. Georgina's come to help us.'

'Good God.' It seemed to be all her uncle could manage.

'Hello, Uncle Teddy.' Georgina crossed the room and gave him a kiss, which he returned almost absent-mindedly.

'There's a car coming back soon,' she told him. 'And you have to leave, Uncle. There's a huge invasion fleet on its way.'

With a worried frown, Teddy walked to the edge of the open verandah where he stood, his one hand sunk in the pocket of his white trousers, and looked out to the edge of the lawn where the natives were busily digging the trenches and lining them with sand-bags. Beyond this, there was a gap in the trees that offered a view of the distant harbour. As he stood watching, a dark wave of planes appeared, like an enormous flock of menacing birds. Then there were streaks in the sky as bombs began to fall, followed by explo-sions and thick clouds of black smoke.

Teddy turned back to them. 'We were going to leave last week,' he said, directing his words to Georgina. 'There was a Burns Philp freighter, the *Herstein*, willing to take evacuees, but then the Australian government in its wisdom insisted they take a full load of copra. No person was to take the place of copra.'

Georgina was so appalled she couldn't think of anything to say.

Tears glittered in her aunt's eyes.

Teddy's face twisted in an attempt to smile at her. 'My dear, the time has come. Georgina has brought us another chance.'

'Are you sure?' Cora asked him softly.

He looked again to the natives digging the trenches and lugging sandbags, and his throat worked. A tremor seemed to run through him.

Another wave of planes arrived, zooming out of the blue, arrowing straight for Rabaul.

With a shaky smile for Georgina, Teddy said, 'How could I not be sure when our dear little goddaughter has come all this way from England to save us?' He gave Georgina a faint nod. 'We're ready. We do have a small emergency bag packed, you know.'

'Oh, thank goodness.' Awash with relief, Georgina rushed to hug him.

Teddy accepted her hug, but quickly broke away. 'I have to tell my workers to flee. They should head for the bush.' With that, he hurried out of the house and across the lawn to the natives working on the trenches.

Watching, Georgina saw him speak to them, saw him patting their backs, shaking one man's hand and then another. Her throat ached on a painful knot of emotion as one of the men hugged her uncle and wept on his shoulder.

'Oh, dear Lord,' her aunt said softly from behind her. And then, 'I'd better get changed into something more suitable for travelling.'

The bombing over Rabaul grew louder and the pall of black smoke plumed thickly. From time to time, there were ghastly explosions in the sky as planes were hit. The terrible thump and crump of bombing grew closer.

'They're probably attacking the airfield at Vunakanau,' said Teddy.

Georgina was afraid it was already too late to try to fly off the island, but she didn't give voice to these thoughts as she sat with her aunt and uncle, drinking tea and eating Flo's coconut biscuits, while they waited for the return of Corporal Palmer's vehicle.

'When did you say the soldier would come back?' her aunt asked.

Georgina looked again at her watch, dismayed to see that almost three-quarters of an hour had passed. 'He should be here any minute.' She tried not to sound as anxious as she felt.

She was terribly worried, though. For all she knew, Corporal Palmer's car had been bombed, or he might have been given orders that overrode his earlier instructions to collect her.

In tune with her lowering mood, the blue sky had become overcast with thick, heavy clouds that pressed close. It wasn't only the Japanese who approached. A storm was rolling in from the sea.

'I've been hearing a lot of trucks on the road,' her uncle said. 'Sounds to me like the army's on the move.'

'Perhaps we shouldn't wait then. We should take one of our own vehicles,' said Cora.

Her husband frowned at her. 'Where would we drive to? I don't really fancy our chances of leaving Rabaul now.'

'Perhaps we could go up to the mission. Safety in numbers.'

'Or perhaps we should wait just a little longer for Corporal Palmer?' Georgina suggested carefully.

'Yes, of course,' agreed her uncle.

Five minutes later it began to rain, falling first in fat heavy drops and then gathering force until it became a thick curtain that completely obscured their view.

The housemaid, Flo, had already left under Teddy's orders, so Georgina helped her aunt to clear away their teacups and saucers. Cora closed some of the shutters and lit several pretty lamps. The house was still surprisingly warm and cosy, despite sections of the wall left open to the rain, and if Georgina hadn't been so worried, she might have enjoyed sitting there, warm and dry in the beautiful lamp-lit house, while a tropical storm thundered above and around them.

As it grew darker, the air raid died down, but conversation became strained and they sat, ears alert, hoping to catch the sound of an approaching vehicle. Hating the tension, Georgina told her aunt and uncle every shred of news from home that she could think of – about her work in London and about her parents coping rather badly without servants and how Primrose Cavendish was running her parents' farm.

'She's so incredibly busy, with all her brothers away fighting and her father unfit after being gassed in the last war. She only has a girl from the Land Army to help. Between them they do all the milking, and mucking out the stables, caring for the chickens, picking the fruit, making jam. But Primrose looks wonderfully fit and well. I think she's loving the war, to be honest!'

She told them that her sister Alice was hoping for a baby, but so far had been unlucky with getting pregnant.

'That's not such a bad thing. This is a terrible time to bring a baby into the world,' Aunt Cora said rather tightly.

Georgina felt obliged to defend her sister. 'But poor Alice would adore a baby and she's lonely. James is with the RAF and he gets such sporadic leave.'

'She could always follow your example and get a job.'

Not Alice, Georgina thought to herself. Her sister was like her mother. Alice had been horrified when Georgina joined the ATS. 'They'll have you driving ambulances and changing truck tyres,' she'd said with a look of disdain, as if this was completely beneath her.

But now, as the sound of planes and gunfire renewed, was no time for disloyal thoughts about family, and Georgina had run out of news. Even so, she didn't like to ask Cora and Teddy about their life here on the plantation when they were about to leave it and had no idea when they might be able to return.

Restless, she rose from her chair and went to the open doorway to look out. It was almost dark now and the rain had eased, although water continued to drip from the trees, and the dusk was filled with the scents of damp earth and decomposing vegetation and the sounds of noisy insects and frogs. Georgina had never heard so many frogs.

She was about to agree with Teddy that they should make their own plans without waiting any longer, when she heard something else – the sound of a motor quite close. Not the full-bodied roar of a truck or car, but more of a purr.

'I think someone's coming,' she said. 'Can you hear that engine?'

Teddy, joining her at the doorway, listened and frowned. 'Sounds like a motorbike.'

And sure enough, as they peered into the gathering gloom, they saw a single light bobbing and weaving down the track. Moments later, a motorbike roared onto the lawn. Its rider was in khaki and he had a backpack and a rifle slung over one shoulder.

He killed the bike's motor and dismounted. He wore a commando's beret.

Harry.

She thought for a moment that her heart had stopped beating. 'What are you doing here?' she called. 'What happened to Corporal Palmer?'

'Don't know,' Harry said grimly. 'We haven't heard from him.' His deadly serious gaze quickly took in her aunt and uncle. 'Here's the situation,' he said without waiting for introductions. 'Three

Wirraways have been shot down and two others have crash landed. A massive Japanese fleet is just offshore and Rabaul's been evacuated. The men in Lark Force have been told to hold Kokopo Ridge Road open for as long as possible, but after that, they have to fend for themselves. Civilians have stockpiled food and if they're young and fit enough they're heading for the bush and the mountains. Otherwise they're taking refuge in the missions.'

Teddy and Cora looked at each other, their gaze troubled, yet somehow resigned.

'We wouldn't last long in the jungle,' Teddy said. 'We're not as fit as we used to be, and I'd only be a hindrance with one arm.'

'And I'd much prefer to go to the mission.' Cora even managed a small smile. 'At least they have beds.'

'Do you have transport?' Harry asked them.

'Yes,' said Uncle Teddy. 'We have a car.'

'Then I suggest you drive to the mission at Talligap.'

Teddy nodded. 'We can do that. So there's absolutely no hope of getting out via Rabaul?'

'None at all, I'm afraid.' Harry turned to Georgina. 'Your major had to leave. He didn't want to go without you, but he had to get back to Australia safely and the Catalina couldn't wait.'

Georgina was now almost too terrified to think straight, although one part of her frantic brain registered that Major Duffy had a duty to get back to the embassy and deliver his report. If he'd come searching for her and risked being captured, he could have faced a court martial.

Harry's mouth tightened. 'I assured the major I'd get you out.'

'But you shouldn't have to worry about me.'

He didn't reply, although she fancied she saw the merest flicker of a softer emotion, but it was gone too quickly to be sure.

'We're packed and ready,' said Cora. 'And we could take Georgina with us.'

Harry turned to George. 'Under the circumstances, your best bet is to come with me,' he said. 'It'll be damned uncomfortable and dangerous, but I promised Duffy I'd get you out. At least I've had jungle training. My role here is to help retreating infantry men.' His bright glance rested on her. 'Or women.' He dragged a deep breath. 'With luck, we'll get across country to one of the bays and then a boat off the island.'

'But I'll slow you down, Harry. You have a duty to your men.'

'Georgina,' said her uncle. 'Don't argue. You're young and fit. Go with this man. If you go to the mission, you'll probably have to surrender and be taken prisoner.'

She stared at Cora and Teddy in dismay. 'Is that what you think will happen to you?'

Her uncle shrugged, then nodded.

Oh, dear Lord.

The tropical night closed in and Georgina's tension skyrocketed. In truth, the thought of fleeing through a jungle terrified her and she much preferred the sound of the mission, even if it meant being taken prisoner, but Harry was the expert. She had no choice but to trust him.

So.

One last, too quick, too desperate hug of Cora, and then her aunt and uncle hurried off, while Georgina climbed onto the back of the motorbike. Harry kick-started the motor and the bike took off with a snarling leap while she wrapped her arms around his waist and hung on for dear life, grateful for his reassuring strength.

As they reached the main road, a truck hurtled past with soldiers on the running board, while others clung to the canvas on top. After several winding corners, they were in open country again, passing through the Three Ways and bumping along a rough track heading inland. And it was there that Georgina saw, in the brief flash of the bike's headlights, a shiny black vehicle upended in a ditch by the side of the road.

'Harry!' she shouted, pointing as she recognised the car.

He slowed to a juddering halt.

'I think that's Corporal Palmer's car,' she yelled.

Harry nodded.

'Should we check to —'

Harry had already cut the motor. 'Stay with the bike,' he ordered gruffly before he hurried to the ditch and made his way, slithering on his behind, to the vehicle.

It was too dark for Georgina to see him clearly and she schooled herself to remain calm as she waited. The warm night pressed around her and she tried not to think about what perils lay ahead of them in the jungle, tried to forget the comforts she'd left behind in the house in Belgravia.

She imagined Cora and Teddy arriving at the mission, being greeted with kindness and given a hot meal.

Harry was back. 'Zeroes shot him up,' he said as he climbed back onto the bike. 'I'm afraid there's nothing we can do here. We have to get cracking. Hang on tight.'

16

'Hey there, how's my girl?' Keith's cheery greeting was followed by the sound of the front door closing and his footsteps coming down the hallway. The footsteps stopped abruptly as he reached the living room. 'Ro, what's the matter?'

Ro was stretched on the sofa, clutching a cushion to her chest. She sighed. 'Nothing. I'm fine. Just a bit tired.'

'Are you sure that's all?' Keith came closer, his kind face creased with concern.

'I'm missing Lucy,' she said, offering the first explanation that sprang to mind. She didn't want Keith to worry, as he was inclined to, after nursing his wife, Deirdre, through a long and harrowing illness.

Unfortunately, her explanation didn't seem to satisfy him.

'But Lucy's only been gone ten days. She was away for months when she was in Afghanistan and you weren't like this.' His frown deepened. 'You've been different ever since she left for England.'

Ro sighed, wishing she'd thought this through before she grabbed Lucy as her excuse.

The sorry truth was she'd spent a lovely afternoon wallowing in self-indulgent misery, a luxury she hadn't allowed herself in ages, not since she'd moved into this apartment with Keith.

It had seemed necessary after six weeks of trying so damn hard to be perfect. She had given up smoking – for good this time – and she'd stuck to drinking no more than two glasses of wine in the evenings. She'd kept the apartment spotless and she'd even hosted a successful dinner party for Keith's best friends. That event had been pretty scary, given that his friends were two super respectable and very nice couples who'd been married for decades and had known Keith and Deirdre since their children's playgroup days.

Ro had also bent over backwards to be the best possible stepmother for Ashley and Morgan, Keith's two grown-up daughters. She'd lavished the girls with compliments and had never once criticised them or offered a contrary opinion, even though they had implied, ever so subtly, that Ro would benefit from shedding a few kilos and joining a granny gym.

With commendable self-control, Ro had refrained from telling the girls that their father seemed to enjoy her curves. Instead she'd simply smiled serenely and bought them little gifts. Nothing too over the top – a handmade soap, or a glass bead bracelet from the Sunday markets in the Mall. And whenever the girls dropped in to visit their father, Ro had cooked them the nerdy, health-conscious tofu stir-fries or couscous salads that they adored. *And* she'd made sure that their father's shirts weren't in a tangle on the laundry floor, but washed and ironed and hanging in his wardrobe.

As for Christmas! She'd been a gold-plated domestic goddess.

Sustained self-discipline, however, was exhausting. And today Ro had allowed herself to hang up her halo and take an afternoon off, to indulge in a few hours of reversion to the old, up-and-down, less-than-perfect Ro Hunter.

It was Friday, after all, and with the help of a chilled sauvignon blanc, she'd recollected, as she had done so many times in the past, all the justifiable reasons she had to feel sorry for herself. The memories were a record of her messed-up life, starting way back when she was a child and progressing through her disastrous teenage years in England and her succession of equally disastrous adult relationships back in Australia, including her ongoing rocky relationship with her daughter.

She'd made herself thoroughly miserable, but so what? It was impossible to be an upbeat Pollyanna all the time, and she decided this was a necessary lapse.

Now, however, Keith's frown deepened as he picked up the empty wine bottle from the coffee table beside Ro, then dropped a glance to the almost empty glass, set handily within her reach on the floor.

'Have you drunk all of this on your own?'

Ro pouted. 'What if I have?'

He was looking so concerned and surprised, she decided not to tell him that she'd also downed the half bottle they'd left in the fridge.

'Can I get you a glass of water, Ro?'

'No, thanks,' she said tartly.

With a shrug, he went to the kitchen and hung his car keys on the convenient row of hooks he'd screwed to the wall. Then he carefully removed his wallet from his pocket and set it on the kitchen counter in the same spot he'd chosen when they first moved in. A man of tidy habits, her Keith.

In front of the fridge, he hesitated. 'Did you have anything in particular planned for dinner?'

Ro sighed again, more loudly this time. Today was the first day since she'd moved into the apartment that she hadn't been interested in planning dinner. This evening she felt awash with the Friday-night-let's-dial-a-pizza weariness that she'd so often succumbed to before she met Keith. 'I thought we could wander down Palmer

Street and have something simple. Maybe a fresh salad.'

'Okay,' Keith said. 'But you'd probably be better with something more filling.'

Annoyed, Ro sat up, placed the cushion precisely in the corner of the sofa and straightened her skirt. 'I'm not pissed, Keith. I don't need something to soak up the grog.'

'But you do look tired,' he said carefully. 'I'll go down the street and get takeaway fish and chips and we can —'

'I'd rather have grilled fish and salad.' Secretly, Ro rather liked the sound of fish and chips, but she was in an annoyingly obstinate mood. 'I'm on a diet, remember?'

His light-green eyes widened and Ro half-expected him to point out the number of liquid calories she'd already consumed. Instead, he said in placating tones, 'All right, that's fine. Grilled fish it is.'

'And you don't have to go on your own,' Ro added. 'If you wait five minutes, I can change. I could even have a quick shower while you're relaxing with a beer.'

Keith always had a beer or two on Fridays.

But now he was frowning again. 'Are you sure you want to bother with going out?'

The extra careful way he asked this added to Ro's annoyance.

'What's that supposed to mean? Don't you want me to come with you?'

'I just thought —'

'You think I'm going to stumble down the footpath? Throw up in the gutter?'

Keith's face twisted into a grimace of dark vexation, an expression she'd never seen on him before. 'No, Ro,' he said now, with the exaggerated patience of a parent dealing with a teenager on the edge. 'I just thought you might like to eat *in* tonight. An easy dinner on the balcony.'

She knew this was reasonable. She'd told Keith often enough

that their balcony was her favourite place in the whole world. And actually, she *was* starting to feel rather tired. She shrugged. 'All right, whatever.'

When she got to her feet, she was – *oops* – a little unsteady. She hoped Keith didn't notice. 'Maybe I'll have that shower anyway,' she said, hoping the steady stream of warm water would revive her.

In the bathroom, Ro vowed this would be her one and only fall from grace. She actually liked herself much better when she was being 'good' and it hadn't been all that hard to be the kind of woman Keith expected and deserved. Not really. She was already regretting her impulse to indulge.

Now, as warm water and the scent of lavender and patchouli soap helped to soothe her, she promised herself this would not happen again. She shampooed her hair for good measure.

She only felt a little woozy when she stepped out of the shower and reached for a towel, and she was wrapping it around her when Keith put his head around the doorway. She thought he might have come in. She would have liked him to take her, naked and willing, into his arms.

He said, 'I'll pop down and get that fish.'

'All right.' Disappointed, Ro felt a small cloud of inexplicable sadness settle over her as she began to towel herself dry. Her bathrobe was hanging on a hook behind the door and she pulled it on, yawning as she tied the waist. With a towel wrapped around her damp head, she went through to the bedroom.

Keith would be away for at least twenty minutes, so there was time for a lie down. A short refreshing nap was all she needed.

The mattress was a pillow top, such a wonderful invention, and it seemed to welcome Ro as she settled into its cloud-like softness. With her eyes closed, she relaxed and, almost immediately, the same memories that she'd wallowed in all afternoon came streaming back. Happy memories at first, of her childhood at Kalkadoon. The bright flashing smile of her best friend Dougie. Swimming and fishing in the creek with Dougie and his cousins and then eating the fish they baked in the coals of a camp fire. The sound of his uncles' clap sticks and their voices singing in language down on the creek bank.

She remembered riding out over the paddocks with her father. When she was little, her father had set her on the saddle in front of him with his strong arm holding her safe, and then when she was older, she'd had her own pony that she'd called Prince Charles.

Abruptly, with chilling sharpness, Ro remembered the English aunt who'd come to Kalkadoon for a second time when she was ten. Remembered the earth-shattering discovery that her father had gone back on his word. Broken his promise.

This time he had let her go . . .

A groan broke from Ro now and she curled into a clenched ball as she blanked out the most painful memories of all – leaving Kalkadoon and travelling with the strict English nanny on the long plane journey to England. But despite her best efforts, her relentless mind still threw up images of Cornwall, forcing her to once again relive the heartbreak and homesickness.

She'd left her beloved Kalkadoon, the simple timber homestead surrounded by open verandahs and sunny plains, to live in a great rattling cold stone house called Penwall Hall, with stone stairs on the inside that led up to rows of bedrooms, most of them also cold and strangely empty.

In Cornwall, instead of a sleepy slow outback river dappled by overhanging paperbarks, there'd been a wild, angry sea, a sea that constantly battered the cliffs as if it was trying to destroy them. And there'd been an earnest, straight-laced family. An aunt and uncle and two cousins, a boy and a girl, who could never, in a million years, have replaced her father and Shirleen and Dougie. But that was what the Cornish family had expected.

As for boarding school, from the start Ro had never fitted in. She didn't try very hard, of course, and the other girls hadn't made it easy. They were all so chummy and they played team games like cricket and hockey, which Ro had never played. Bottom line, they'd been very *English*.

And she'd felt so dumb. In the classroom she was way behind the girls of her age. Clearly the governess she'd had at Kalkadoon hadn't been up to scratch. Embarrassed, lonely and homesick, Ro would have tried to run away if she'd known where to run to, but her home was twelve thousand miles away. She had nowhere to go, which had made it so much worse.

The injustice and the sheer futility of being sent there had always angered her. Surely, her father must have known that she would hate it? And yet, despite the earlier promise he'd made when she was six, he'd sent her away as if he didn't really care, as if the love he'd always shown her was only a pretence.

Of course, he'd tried to explain his motives later. He'd only done what he thought was best for her, yadda yadda yadda. But Ro had never been convinced and all these years later, the hurt was still there, lying deep within her, along with the guilt she'd felt for the way she'd behaved. Inescapable wounds.

She knew she shouldn't be crying again now, knew all too well that tears only helped momentarily, and that the pain always came back. She had decided long ago that the only sensible way to deal with this business was to forget, to simply carry on as if it had never happened.

Of course, she'd never really felt close to her father again, and he'd known that. When Lucy was born, he'd switched his allegiance to the baby.

Actually, Ro was proud of the way she'd stepped back, allowing Harry and Lucy to form a close bond. The decision had been instinctive, or perhaps it was a form of self-preservation. She'd stuffed up so many things in her life, but the bond between her father and her daughter had become sacrosanct. Looking back, she believed this was possibly her greatest achievement.

But enough with the bloody navel-gazing.

It was time to stop thinking about all that. She'd schooled herself to compartmentalise her life, to keep the really painful stuff locked away. Buried. And her plan had been working pretty damn well until Lucy chose to go over to England, wanting to ferret up the past and to ask all kinds of pesky questions.

With another groan of impatience, Ro rolled onto her side. *Oh no, not a good idea.* Her stomach rebelled. Maybe she was more pissed than she'd realised.

She lay very still now, willing her stomach to settle. She didn't want to be sick. *God no, please, no.* She couldn't bear to have Keith come home to find her hunched over the toilet. She tried to relax, to let the boozy weariness wash over her.

That was better. Enough with the memories. All she really needed was sleep.

The apartment was in darkness when she woke and it took a good few moments to remember why she was lying on top of the bedspread in her bathrobe.

Shit. Keith had gone to get the fish for their dinner.

Where was he now?

She sat up quickly and winced as her head threatened to split open. *Bloody hell.* She needed aspirin and water. Gallons of water. Damn it, why hadn't she remembered to drink water? For that matter, why hadn't she remembered that drinking a bucket of wine on an empty stomach made a person feel like dying?

Gingerly, she edged off the bed, wondering if Keith was in the living room watching the cricket with the lights out and the sound turned down. Her hip bumped into the doorway as she left the dark bedroom. She'd forgotten to turn a lamp on and there was no light coming from the television screen. No sign of Keith.

For a moment she panicked, worrying that something terrible had happened while Keith was out and he hadn't made it home. But then she told herself that someone would have phoned.

Oh God, she felt sick.

Feeling her way to the kitchen, she found a light switch and turned it on, flinched at the brightness and quickly flicked it off again. The automatic light in the pantry was a kinder option so she opened the pantry door and was relieved to find a box of aspirin with two tablets left.

With these downed and two glasses of water consumed, she waited till her stomach settled, then felt her way, guided by the soft shaft of light from the living room windows, across the kitchen and down the hallway to the second bedroom. Even before she reached it she could hear Keith's gentle snores, which meant he must have brought their dinner home and found her passed out.

Ro pictured him standing at their bedroom door, wondering whether he should wake her, then deciding not to and eating his meal alone.

Now, he was sleeping in the guest bedroom. Alone.

She felt terrible. Such a failure. She hadn't lasted six weeks with Keith before her cracks showed, and soon he would leave her just as all her other boyfriends had. Except this time there would be one major difference. In the past Ro had been the one who'd kicked her useless no-hoper boyfriends out.

This time, the man in question was faultless. True Blue. Salt of the fricking earth. The kind of partner she had never dared to hope for, the style of man she'd never believed she deserved.

And damn it, tonight she'd just proved herself bloody right.

17

Nicholas Myatt, once again looking far too attractive in his black sweater over a crisp white shirt, was the perfect host when he escorted Lucy around Penwall Hall on her third day in Cornwall. He'd been busy with business the previous two days, which she'd found a bit disappointing, but he was now available and, for once, the sun was out as he greeted Lucy at the grand front entrance to the Hall.

'I hope you've been managing to enjoy yourself here, despite the filthy weather.'

'I've had a great time,' she assured him. 'I've discovered I'm quite partial to standing on the top of sea cliffs and almost being blown off my feet.'

The sudden flash of concern in Nick's dark eyes seemed out of character. Until now he'd come across as confident and commanding. 'I hope you didn't go too close to the edge.'

'No, I saw the warning signs to keep away.' Quickly, because he was still frowning like an over-fussy parent, Lucy added, 'And I've had a fab time exploring the quaint towns. I just love all those steep, crooked little streets.'

At this, Nick seemed to relax and he stepped back, giving the merest hint of a bow as he gestured for her to come inside.

'My parents are still away in London,' he said. 'They should be back on Thursday.'

Lucy had been disappointed to learn from Jane Nancarrow that Nick's grandmother had died a few years earlier.

Nevertheless, the absence of the older generation could prove to be a bonus, if it meant she could relax without worrying about too many airs and graces. That said, she was relieved that Nick's parents were returning before she was due to leave. She was sure they'd be able to tell her much more about George, Harry or Ro than Nick could.

It was a weird situation though. Thanks to her family and their bloody secrets, she found herself relying on a couple of strangers to fill in the gaps in her knowledge about her own mother.

The Hall was grander and more luxurious than anything Lucy had ever been in before, and as Nick escorted her from room to room, she did feel slightly overawed by the sheer scale of everything. There were so many beautiful and amazing details – a music room with an ornate soaring ceiling, a huge library, lined wall-to-wall with old books, classical statues in the great hall, and a precious Qing dynasty porcelain bowl taking pride of place at the foot of the grand staircase.

Any hint of austereness was countered with colourful rugs, and paintings in huge gold frames as well as enormous vases filled with greenery and berries. In spring and summer there would, no doubt, be flower arrangements. It was immediately clear to Lucy that the inside of Penwall Hall was even more appealing than the outside had suggested.

Nick explained a little about the history, and managed to do so without sounding like a tour guide. The house had been built by a baronet called Sir Oswald Lenton back in the early eighteenth century. He'd been an eccentric, given to inventions, but he had also been involved in shipping and had built up quite a fortune. Following him, there had been a straight succession of baronets until just after the Second World War.

'When our great-grandfather died,' Nick told her, 'there were no sons, only two daughters – my grandmother, Alice, who was the elder daughter, and your grandmother, Georgina.'

Lucy liked the way he included her branch of the family, but it was all so new to her that she felt a bit of a fraud. An impostor. Briefly, she wondered if any portion of the family's inheritance had filtered through to Georgina, but she had no idea how these things worked and the question seemed impertinent. Besides, when it came to info-gathering, money and possessions weren't high on her need-to-know list. Right now, finding a connection with the people in her family was what counted most.

It was in the beautiful long dining room that she discovered the collection of family portraits, including a lovely informal portrait of Georgina, which had been painted when George – Lucy liked to think of her as George – had been about eighteen.

Wearing a simple, summery, blue dress, George was sitting beside her sister Alice on a lawn, with two sprawling Golden Labradors as their companions, and a beautiful flowering rhododendron as their backdrop.

Lucy stood transfixed, staring at her grandmother, drinking in the details. George's elegantly waved hair glowed a rich golden honey in the sunlight, and her slim white hand rested companionably on the back of one of the dogs, as if she was in the middle of giving it a scratch.

It was so amazing to think that this woman had fallen in love with Harry and then left this life of luxury and privilege in England to come to live with him in a remote corner of the Australian outback. And she'd borne him a child: Rose, her mother.

Lucy could almost see a likeness, if she searched very hard. Her mum's hair was darker and curlier and she was quite a bit chubbier, but there was something about the eyes and the shape of her face, the set of her mouth.

'I wonder how she met Harry, my grandfather,' she said. 'It must have been during the war.'

'I think I was told that Georgina joined the army and was posted to Australia, but somehow she ended up in the thick of things in New Guinea.'

'Really? How amazing.' Lucy stared at George a little longer, wishing she could have known her. Surely it was wrong to know so little about your own grandmother? 'My grandfather, Harry, doesn't like to talk about the war.'

'That's understandable.'

'Is it? I wish he would. I'd love to know more about how he met George.'

Lucy also wished that George was smiling in this portrait. Her eyes were fixed on some place in the distance, so that even in this simple garden setting, she carried a sense of mystery and even a hint of sadness.

'I wish she looked happier,' she couldn't help commenting.

'She doesn't look *un*happy.'

'No, but it's hard to judge her mood.'

Nick gave a slight shrug. 'My grandmother's not smiling either.'

Lucy turned her attention to Alice, who had written 'the letter'. She had a serious, earnest face that stopped her from being as pretty as Georgina.

'Perhaps smiling for portraits wasn't fashionable in the thirties,' Nick said. 'They might have been trying to look sophisticated.'

Then he sent Lucy a smile of his own. Which caused her all kinds of problems.

Unfortunately, nothing had really changed since she'd first seen him in the pub. He was still disturbingly attractive with all that thick, lustrous, dark hair and those strong cheekbones and intelligent dark-coffee eyes. There was a magnetic quality about him that she found desperately difficult to ignore, especially when he was smiling at her, as he was now.

Her reaction didn't really make sense. Nick was her second cousin, after all, and she hadn't thought it was possible to become attracted to another man so soon after breaking up with Sam. Surely loyalty to Sam demanded a longer mourning period?

But the sorry truth was hard to avoid – getting over Sam had been ridiculously easy and it was pretty clear now that he'd never been The One.

Disconcerted, Lucy switched her gaze to a collection of more modern photographs, displayed in silver frames on an elegant, highly polished side table, and almost immediately, she noticed a photo of Nick.

Noticeably younger, but still tall and broad-shouldered, he was standing with another strapping young fellow, who looked like him, although his hair was lighter and his build a little stockier.

A brother? Lucy wondered. The two young men were outside a church and were dressed alike in dark-grey suits with pink button-holes, pale vests and ruby-coloured silk ties.

'Was this taken at a wedding?' she asked.

Nick frowned at the photo and his jaw tightened. 'Yes. I was an usher for my cousin Harriet's wedding.'

'This fellow looks a lot like you. Is he a cousin? A brother? I never asked about the rest of your family.' Lucy leaned closer to study the likeness.

After a beat, Nick said, 'Yes, that's my brother, Simon.'

'Does he live here, too?'

When Nick didn't answer this, she turned to find him frowning even more deeply. A muscle jerked in his throat as he swallowed, as if the subject was difficult. 'Simon's dead.'

'Oh God, I'm so sorry.' The sudden anguish in Nick's eyes was heart wrenching. Lucy wished she hadn't asked.

'Simon was a doctor – a medical officer in the army,' Nick added tightly. 'He served in Afghanistan.'

A small gasp broke from her, but before she could say anything, Nick hurried on, as if now that the subject had been broached, he wanted to finish his story and be done with it. 'You might as well hear it from me. Simon survived the war. Survived it, physically, at least, but he still came home in a mess.'

'PTSD?' she asked, unhappily guessing how this sad story might have ended.

Nick's gaze flicked to her briefly as he nodded, and in that one glance she saw the painful truth. It was there in the torment in his eyes, in his fists clenched tightly against his thighs.

'I overreacted when you joked about being blown off the cliff. But that's how we lost Simon.' His throat worked as he swallowed again. 'It was officially an accident and he left no note, but I believe my brother took his own life.'

'Nick, I'm so sorry.'

Lucy couldn't think of anything more to say. Suicide was devastating, so very difficult for a family to come to terms with, and so much more complicated than a combat soldier's death in battle. On top of Nick's grief, he would almost certainly be battling a sense of abandonment and rejection, possibly even anger.

Right now, he was standing stiffly with his hands still clenched in fists by his sides. 'The army has a lot to answer for.'

Lucy acknowledged this with a brief nod. There was no point in trying to defend the army. Nick needed to lay blame somewhere and the criticism was fair enough. With PTSD now commonly acknowledged, armies everywhere were working hard to set up effective screening and timely diagnoses. But the unfortunate truth was that veterans suffering PTSD were less likely to seek help than civilians were, and yet they were also more likely to act successfully on suicidal thoughts. Tragic deaths like Simon's were still too frequent.

She almost said something along these lines, but she doubted it would help Nick now. It would be like closing the stable door after the horse had bolted.

One thing was certain. This wasn't the appropriate time to mention her own connections with the army. Nick might very well send her packing.

'Anyway,' he went on, as if he was anxious to change the subject. 'There are only bedrooms and bathrooms upstairs and you've probably seen enough of the inside of the house. Let's go outside while the sun's still shining.' He flashed her another quick, searching smile that didn't quite show in his eyes.

'Great idea,' Lucy said, hoping she didn't sound too enthusiastic. She'd already explored a fair sweep of the grounds, but she was keen to do so again with Nick, second cousin or not.

They left the house by a side door and, from the step, Nick whistled and a dog came bounding from around a corner, a beautiful black-and-white border collie with bright blue eyes and a tail like a plume.

'Come on, Shep,' he said, rubbing the dog between his ears. 'Time for a walk.'

And it was more than pleasant to walk around Penwall Hall's grounds in the weak winter sunshine. The place was quite amazing and gorgeous with fifty acres of parkland, woods, and formal gardens, including all kinds of cleverly designed walks on a network of footpaths. Lucy recognised very few of the trees or shrubs, so Nick pointed out that the clipped hedges around the fountain were box and the high hedges protecting the large orchard were yew. Apparently the orchard was filled with daffodils in the springtime.

It was so, *so* different from north Queensland, she thought, again wondering how George had adapted to her life at the bottom of the world.

Despite being quiet and wintry just now in January, the leafless trees had a special kind of grandeur with their lacy bare branches lifted to the pale sky. Dotted here and there, clumps of yellow gorse flowers added a splash of bright colour to the scene.

Lucy could easily believe that tourists swarmed here in the warmer months to enjoy picnics in the parklands or to explore the bluebell woods. 'Bluebells always sound so romantic,' she said.

Nick laughed. 'They don't last long.'

'Neither do a lot of romances,' Lucy responded, almost under her breath.

This earned her a shrewd narrow-eyed glance, and then he said, 'Speaking of romance, take a look at this.'

They had rounded a corner and now, below them, lay the beautiful lake and, out on a finger of land, stood a delightful, gabled cottage of weathered grey stone. 'It's gorgeous, isn't it?' Lucy had discovered this cottage on one of her earlier rambles and had fallen in love.

The cottage and the lake were stunning against the backdrop of low grassy hills and, further on, the grey-blue sea, which rolled and crashed against the shore.

'It's the old boathouse,' Nick said.

'So that's why it has its own landing.' With her arms folded over her chest, Lucy said stoutly, 'If this was mine, I wouldn't want to share it with the public.'

'That's how my parents always felt.'

'But I suppose someone had to be practical.' She was remembering how the barman at The Seaspray Arms had sung Nick's praises, claiming that he'd single-handedly rescued the family's estate. 'I imagine the boathouse and the lake are popular with your visitors.'

'Yes, we've had a couple of fashion shoots down here and it's been used quite a bit for smaller, more intimate weddings.' Nick grinned. 'Or the odd drunken party.'

Perhaps it was wrong to suddenly think of her mother, but Ro *had* claimed to have behaved pretty badly while she was in England. 'My mother said she didn't like it here,' she found herself confiding. 'But I can't imagine why. Have you heard much about her?'

'Not really,' he said carefully.

'Nothing?'

'Well . . . I don't think she made a fantastic impression.'

'Why do I have the feeling you're being polite?'

'You are persistent, aren't you?' Nick narrowed his eyes at her again, but there was still a hint of a smile. 'Honestly, I've heard very little, and only from my grandmother. And she could be a crusty old thing. Very hard to please. I'm afraid she had quite a talent for snobbishness.'

Lucy thought again about the photograph of Nick's grandmother that she'd just seen, and the letter that she'd found in Harry's biscuit tin. She remembered the singed corners, as if Harry had tried to burn it. Then her mother's reaction – screwing the paper into a ball and throwing it into the rubbish bin.

Bitch.

Watching Shep down at the lake's edge, sniffing in a patch of reeds, Lucy said, 'I don't suppose your parents will welcome me with open arms when they get back from London.'

Nick gave another shrug. 'Oh, you never know. Water under the bridge.' But he didn't sound as convincing as she would have liked.

The sunny day and the setting were too lovely to dwell on negative thoughts, however, and as they walked on Lucy encouraged Nick to tell her about how he'd so miraculously saved this place. He made it sound easy as he ran through the extra money-earning activities that he'd set up – afternoon teas on the terrace, pop-up restaurants in the dining room, outdoor theatres, even shooting parties.

He downplayed his part in the estate's revitalisation, but with a few probing questions Lucy could tell he was intimate with every aspect of running Penwall Hall. From her own job in logistics, she knew this meant he was a very good administrator. Another point to add to her growing list of reasons to admire him.

Not that she was counting.

Or was she?

Actually, if she was honest, her unhelpful reaction to the man was turning into a bit of a problem. Of course, she'd made sure that her conduct was as proper and appropriate as Nick's, and they'd both been super polite and friendly, just the way second cousins were supposed to behave towards each other.

The fly in the ointment was her body's response. Nick's smiles lit spot fires wherever they touched. Not that he was flirting exactly – well, he wouldn't, would he? She was nothing more than a poor Aussie relation. It was out of the question.

Actually, she supposed she might have found Nick less attractive if he *had* flirted. Sam had flirted from the moment he'd clapped eyes on her, and while that had been flattering at the time, looking back, Lucy could see how shallow his behaviour had been. She wondered how she'd ever fallen for it.

Now, she told herself she was glad and genuinely relieved that Nick was most definitely a no-go zone. Even if they hadn't been family, the last thing she wanted or needed was another romance. She was trying to sort out her life, not complicate it.

Until this point, she'd felt as if she didn't have any clear aim. Even when she'd joined the army, she'd never felt a really true calling. But ever since she'd found the letters and photos in Harry's tin, she'd had this crazy sense that if she could understand more about the past, about her mum and Harry and George, she might get a handle on her own life, on who she was, or who she was supposed to be and what she really wanted for the future. She had important decisions to make about her career and she wanted to feel confident that she wasn't just drifting with the tide, but making good choices for all the right reasons.

She just wished she could turn off this attraction vibe.

It wasn't supposed to happen.

She was still wrestling with these annoying internal arguments when she and Nick arrived back on the top terrace and it was time to go their separate ways.

'Thanks for giving up an entire afternoon,' she told him politely. 'I really appreciate it.'

'My pleasure.' He looked slightly amused when she formally offered her hand, which he shook with a predictably firm grasp.

'You have a beautiful home,' Lucy said. 'I can't help wondering why my grandmother ever left all this.'

'I assume she fell in love.'

As Nick said this, his gaze connected with Lucy's. For a beat they were both smiling and then the amusement in his eyes gave way to something deeper. Heat bloomed in her cheeks.

Dismayed, she looked away quickly. 'But Georgina moved from all this to the outback and it's so – so lonely and the life's so rough.'

'Don't you like your outback?' Nick sounded surprised.

'Well, yes, of course.' Although if she was honest she'd spent very little time there, but she had to admit she understood the appeal of an outdoors lifestyle and its inherent sense of adventure. Perhaps her grandmother had been adventurous?

It was an intriguing thought.

'Have you made plans for tomorrow?' Nick asked suddenly.

Caught out, Lucy opened her mouth and then shut it. Any sensible holidaymaker would have made plans. 'Not definite plans,' she hedged. 'I thought I might explore more of the coastline. I'd like to get down to Land's End.'

He nodded. 'And if you're at a *loose* end – sorry, poor joke – you could always come riding in the morning.'

Lucy gulped. 'Riding? On a horse?'

Nick smiled crookedly. 'Unless you prefer broomsticks.'

Her laugh sounded a little nervous. 'I'm afraid I've never ridden either – broomstick or horse.'

There was no mistaking his shock. 'Sorry, I assumed . . . I thought your family owned a cattle property. And – and you look so fit.'

Just in time Lucy stopped herself from explaining that her fitness had arrived courtesy of her army training. She wouldn't mention it now. Her memories of Nick's distress about his brother were still too raw. 'My grandfather did run a cattle station,' she said. 'But he moved into Townsville before I was born and left a manager in charge. I've never been out there.'

It hurt to admit this, to remember that Harry, whom she loved so dearly, had kept a big part of his life hidden. 'Mind you,' she added, quickly shoving the hurt aside. 'There was a time in my pre-teens when I drove my mum mad, begging for a horse.'

'Well, the offer's there, if you'd like to try.'

'Wow.' Surely this was a turnaround too good to ignore? She remembered seeing Nick astride his dashing dark stallion. Remembered her terror of those striking hooves. But it would be different if she was up in the saddle, and it wasn't as if she hadn't had her share of dangerous adventures – fast-roping and parachuting out of planes. How much fun it could be, on horseback, cantering over these long sloping fields all the way to the sea. 'You'd have to show me how.'

His dark eyes were sparkling. 'I don't imagine that will be a chore.'

Now her skin tingled alarmingly and she tried to ignore it. 'I might be too old to learn.'

'Never.' Once again his expression betrayed open amusement. 'How old are you?'

'Twenty-seven.'

'Perfect.'

And damn it, he was smiling again. He was standing there, all tall and dark and stunning, and smiling as his gaze connected with hers, letting his lovely smile reach deep inside her, stirring sparks. And longing. *Forbidden* longing.

He said, 'You'll find it a breeze, I'm sure.'

'Well, I'd love to come riding then.' And she mentally stuck her fingers in her ears, as her better judgement clamoured a warning.

18

Lucy was up early next morning and waiting, somewhat nervously, on the terrace. She hadn't asked Nick about the correct riding gear but she assumed her leather jacket, jeans and RM boots would be suitable. The weather wasn't promising. It had rained again during the night, leaving puddles on the path and, although it wasn't raining now, banks of grey clouds loomed on the horizon and a cold wind blew in from the sea.

She'd pulled her hair into a practical, army-style knot, but, even so, wisps had pried themselves free and already they were blowing annoyingly in her face.

Nick came striding around the corner, all long legs in jeans, and wearing a rusty corduroy coat over a navy sweater. 'We're in luck,' he called. 'It's not raining.' He glanced to the horizon and gave a shrugging smile. 'Not yet, at any rate.'

They dodged puddles as they went to the stables, which were built of weather-stained, mossy grey stone that no doubt had been standing there for centuries. Inside, the place smelled predictably of horses and straw, but Lucy found the aroma rather pleasant. Stooping, Nick sorted through a wooden box on the floor and selected a brush, which he gave to her. 'Hang on to that for a moment.'

Then she followed him down a cobbled passage.

'This is Fenella,' he announced as he stopped at a stall and rested his hand companionably on the neck of a chestnut horse with a pretty white blaze on her forehead.

'Hello, Fenella.' Lucy's nervousness returned. Fenella was very tall and her ears were pricked, her nostrils flared and quivering.

'I'll fit her with a head-collar and bridle,' Nick said. 'That'll make her secure.' The gear was hanging on a nearby post and as he slipped the leather straps over Fenella's head, Lucy found herself distracted by his hands, which were wonderfully large and masculine, with long, strong fingers that looked surprisingly gentle and deft. As he worked he talked quietly to Fenella, calling her a 'dear old girl' and 'a good sort'.

He secured Fenella with a rope to a corner post. 'Now you can have a go at grooming her,' he said. 'You can use that brush.'

Lucy hadn't expected this. She looked down at the brush in her hand and felt a bit self-conscious. 'Is there a right or wrong way to do it?'

'Not really. Just go with the flow. Normally, you'd use a currycomb first, to loosen up any dirt or stray hairs, but she's actually pretty clean, so this is mainly about giving you a chance to get to know her. It's a good idea to become acquainted while she's still in the stall.'

'I see.' It made sense, Lucy supposed, and as she tentatively touched the comb to Fenella's coat the horse appeared to relax, which was reassuring. She pressed a little harder, sweeping the comb in downward motions over Fenella's flank. 'She seems to like it.'

'Oh yes. She'd let you do that all day.'

'Maybe it's a bit like going to the hairdresser's.'

Nick laughed at this and it occurred to Lucy that he understood what it was like for a novice. Admiring a horse's glowing coat and rippling muscles from a safe distance was a very different matter to getting up close and personal.

'She has nice eyes.' Already she was starting to feel more relaxed.

'Yes, she's a calm old girl. You'll be fine.'

And to her relief she was fine when, shortly afterwards, Nick got her to take the rope and lead the horse outside.

'It's important for her to know that you're in charge,' he said. 'Just pull gently and firmly and tell her to *come on*.'

Lucy supposed she shouldn't have been surprised that Nick was a very good riding instructor. He had the same handy combination of inner confidence and outer competence that she'd come to admire in some of the best soldiers, and he was also unexpectedly patient and sensitive.

By the time he'd shown her how to mount Fenella and to sit in the saddle with her butt pressed deep and with the correct alignment of her shoulders, hips and heels, her tension had almost completely evaporated and she was really beginning to enjoy herself.

Annoyingly, she found herself thinking that a man who was both patient and intuitive would also be a wonderful lover.

Bloody hell. She was pathetic.

Hopeless.

The rain held off while Nick collected his horse, the same great stallion he'd ridden on the first morning.

'We won't go too far today,' he said as they steered their mounts out through a gateway and into a long open field. 'Already, you'll be using muscles you don't even know you have, and if you stay out for too long, you'll end up so stiff and sore you won't be able to walk.'

'Well, I feel fine just now. But I'll take your word for it.'

The big surprise was the thrill of the simple things. The feel of the smooth, worn leather saddle and the swaying rhythm of the horse beneath her. It was wonderfully exciting and not at all scary. And when they reached the middle of the open field and Fenella, following Nick's lead, broke out into a canter, the sheer joy of being astride a strong and fluid, sure-footed animal filled Lucy with a cork-from-champagne rush of happiness.

Nick was grinning as he watched her. 'I'd say you're a natural.'

'Really?'

How cool.

It was like discovering something important that had been missing from her life. Her mum had loved to reminisce about riding her horse out at Kalkadoon, and now Lucy regretted not paying more attention.

As she and Nick cantered back and forth along the sloping fields that ran beside the thrashing sea, there was an exciting wildness in the air. Lucy could smell it, feel it, taste it. She wanted to ride all day. She would worry about the aching muscles later.

The rain arrived, however. Just as they turned their horses for the beach, it came in a thick grey, slanting wall, rushing across the surface of the water, thundering over the sand and then drenching them in seconds.

Nick came to a halt and, through the sheeting rain, turned to watch Lucy while she tried to remember everything he'd told her about stopping the horse. *Sit deep in the saddle with your weight back*. She did this and called, 'Whoa.' And, because she couldn't be sure if Fenella got the message, she also pulled on the rein.

Fenella stopped abruptly, and Lucy almost flew over her head.

'Sorry, old girl.' She stroked the damp rough mane as Nick steered his mount closer.

'Better call it a day. We can't send you back to Australia with pneumonia.'

The rain *was* cold and despite her leather jacket, she was already shivering. 'I was beginning to really enjoy myself.'

He grinned. 'I noticed.'

There were towels in the stables and they dried off their clothes as best they could. Lucy was busily rubbing Fenella down when Nick appeared at the edge of her stall and somehow, with his damp, towel-dried hair, he looked more attractive than ever, which surely had to be illegal.

'It's just occurred to me that you've probably missed breakfast.'

'I'll be okay.' Although at the mention of food, Lucy realised she was starving. 'I'm sure Jane will be able to rustle up something.'

'Let's not bother her. What say we go out for a hefty morning tea, or an early lunch? We could go down to St Ives.'

Lucy almost said something foolish like, *You don't have to. I know you're busy.* But how crazy would that be? She could think of nothing she would like more than to dine with Nick in a quaint Cornish restaurant overlooking the sea. She smiled at him over Fenella's broad brown back. 'I'd love to.'

So it was back to the B&B for a hot shower and a change into dry clothes, a hasty blow with the hair dryer, a little lip gloss and mascara, a dab of scent to the wrists and Lucy was ready inside half an hour.

Nick stood for a moment in silence, letting his dark gaze travel over her. His mouth tilted in a slow smile. 'That was a quick and impressive transformation. Most girls I know would have taken twice as long.'

Lucy allowed herself a moment to bask in the heady warmth of Nick's approval, and she chose not to dwell on all the other girls he knew. There was bound to be a host of them, a long line stretching from Penzance to London. 'I was hungry,' she said a little too defensively.

'Right, then let's waste no time in getting you fed.'

It was still raining, but Nick's Range Rover was parked on the driveway and he had a large, black English brolly, which he gallantly held over Lucy as they made a dash for the car. As they were driving out of the estate, however, the experience felt suddenly surreal. Her focus had shifted so completely in such a short space of time. For the past few years, her world had comprised the army and home. Afghanistan and Townsville. Her fellow soldiers, her mum, Harry and Sam.

Now, Sam and Afghanistan were out of the picture. Her mum was furiously trying to reinvent herself with a new man in a new apartment. And Lucy had ended up here in a stately home in Cornwall that was practically a castle. She was whizzing off in a Range Rover with a man who was as close to Prince Charming as she was ever likely to meet, leaving aside the fact that he was her cousin. She almost felt as if she'd fallen down a rabbit hole like Alice in Wonderland. Except there was no Red Queen screaming, 'Off with her head!'

Not yet, at least.

There was nothing fairytale about the weather though. It was still bleak and windy and wet. In St Ives the streets were mostly empty, the gutters running with water. But of course it was very pleasant and cosy inside the little restaurant that Nick chose. After they shed their damp coats, they were shown to a nook in a bay window where the table was set with a crisp white cloth and a brown jug filled with early daffodils.

Better still, the rain had eased enough to give them a view over the crooked rooftops to breakers frothing against the cliffs in the bay.

'Have you tried a Cornish pasty since you've been here?' Nick asked as Lucy opened her menu.

'No. Should I have?'

He reared back in mock horror. 'A hot pasty is Cornwall's

national dish. Part of our county's culinary heritage. You'll have to try one. Actually, a pasty is the perfect meal on a cold and dreary day like this.'

Lucy wasn't finding the day dreary at all, but she was quite happy to order a pasty with her coffee. When Cornwall's famous national dish arrived, she thought it wasn't all that different from an Aussie meat pie. She said as much, but Nick quickly assured her that this was no ordinary pie. The Cornish took their pasties very seriously.

'You can tell these are traditional Cornish pasties because they're D shaped, and crimped along the curved side,' he said. 'They originated among the miners – they made a good nourishing lunch and were easy to hold in one hand.'

'I suppose I'd better use a knife and fork today,' Lucy said with a laugh as she cut into the plump, enticing crescent of golden-crisp pastry. 'Mmm, it smells wonderful.'

After a bite, she released another 'Mmm,' and sent Nick a warm smile and a thumbs up. The steak was so tender and rich and the vegetables were fab, too.

'Potatoes and swede,' Nick informed her.

'Perfect.' Overcome by hunger, she had to tuck in.

They had finished eating and were lingering over a second cup of coffee when Nick asked his awkward question.

'I feel as if I know so little about you or your family. What sort of work do you do?'

Lucy had to think fast to balance the pros and cons of telling him the truth. Given Nick's feelings about the army, any mention of her job could very well spoil their lovely morning. She wished she knew if Simon Myatt had died recently, or some time back. But perhaps it made no difference. Admitting that she was a soldier would almost certainly bring that awful torment back into Nick's eyes.

It was a no-brainer really.

The cons won.

'I'm in logistics,' she said. 'With a government agency.'

Nick nodded politely, but Lucy could see that he was puzzled.

'An agency? Like foreign aid?'

'Well, yes, sort of.' She hoped she didn't look as nervous as she felt. She was uncomfortable about fudging the truth, but she would look a bit silly if she changed her story in midstream.

'We get supplies into where they're needed,' she said, knowing this must sound ridiculously vague.

Nick frowned. 'I thought that sort of work was mostly covered by non-government bodies.'

Lucy lifted her shoulders in a shrug. 'Not always.'

Luckily, Nick was too polite to probe deeper and he dropped the subject, but Lucy felt as if she'd disappointed him. After all, he'd told her quite a lot about the work he'd done at Penwall Hall.

Truth was, her claim to work in a government agency was a response that she and her fellow soldiers often gave when they were out socially in civilian dress. It wasn't that she was ashamed of being a soldier. Far from it. The army had been good to her and she'd worn her first stripes and later her officer's pips with pride.

But like most of her comrades, she felt uncomfortable answering questions about active service, particularly questions about Afghanistan. To answer in brief terms could sound dismissive, and to try to do justice to the memory of her experience there and, more importantly, to those who died there could be too confronting.

Nick had lost a brother in Afghanistan and she didn't want to risk giving him answers that he might not want to hear.

Besides, government logistics wasn't too far from the truth – and she was only going to be in Cornwall for a week.

As Nick paid the bill and they headed outside, however, he said, 'The weather's clearing. Would you like to drive to the Lizard Peninsula? I think it's actually more spectacular than Land's End.'

'Isn't that miles away?'

'Nowhere's very far away down here.'

That was true.

'And you can't leave Cornwall without seeing Kynance Cove.'

'But —'

'It's okay, Lucy. I'm free today.'

She was flattered and secretly thrilled that he was prepared to give up an entire day to be with her. There was only one problem – her original problem with this man – and now she was sinking deeper under his spell.

It wasn't just about Nick's looks any more. He was great company, too. Interesting and attentive. Considerate and fun.

If Lucy was honest, she liked every single thing about the guy.

But being with Nick kept her in a constant state of jangling, bone-deep tension – lusty tension, let's face it – and she didn't know how to turn it off. Her reaction was purely instinctive, defying logic and commonsense.

She only hoped she would survive the next few days without doing or saying anything foolish.

19

Touring the Lizard Peninsula with Nick was both delightful and dangerous for Lucy.

On the one hand, she was able to see the Cornish coast at its most dramatic and beautiful, and to visit famous place names like Helston and Mullion Cove, where Nick entertained her with stories of smugglers and shipwrecks.

Even the weather smiled on them. With immaculate timing, the sun broke through the clouds just as they chose to walk out on the headland at Kynance Cove. The stunning beauty of the churning sea, the jagged, remarkable cliffs and the thatched-roofed, white-washed houses were bathed in gorgeous bright sunshine.

Nick explained that the rocks here were serpentine or soap-stone, famously suitable for carving, and he promptly bought Lucy a lovely souvenir, a polished stone candle holder from a gift shop.

But along with the fun, there was danger, too, and for Lucy the peril came not from the wind and the rain that sent them scurry-ing back to the warmth of Nick's Range Rover, but from the many happy smiles and sizzling glances that passed all too frequently between them.

She knew it was dangerous to enjoy Nick Myatt's company so enthusiastically, to spend the whole day feeling so exquisitely happy and floating. And wanting. There were solid, commonsense reasons why she shouldn't give in to such weakness. Even if Nick hadn't been a blood relation, there was still the small matter of geography and the fact that she would soon be leaving for the other side of the globe. And finally, crucially, there was Nick's justifiable aversion to the army.

Sadly for Lucy, these logical arguments were poor defence against his charms. Each minute she spent in his company, she found him more and more appealing, and it didn't help that he sent out plenty of signals that he found her company as agreeable as she found his.

Eventually, the cloud-shrouded afternoon had sunk into twilight and they drove home over moors covered with thick heather and past winter-bare fields dotted with stark stone farmhouses. By the time they reached Portreath, it was quite dark and Nick turned into the car park of The Seaspray Arms.

He sent Lucy a quick grin. 'We might as well grab a bite of supper.'

She tried not to sound too pleased. 'Might as well.'

As had happened on her first night here, heads turned as they entered the bar, but this time it was Nick who was the centre of attention. He didn't seem bothered though. He simply exchanged friendly greetings or nods with locals as he guided Lucy through the crowded bar to the snug dining area on the far side.

A pretty girl with a perfect peaches-and-cream complexion couldn't quite hide her surprise as Nick asked to be shown to a corner table. Lucy supposed he wasn't in the habit of bringing his girlfriends here. He would probably take them to much fancier restaurants in St Ives or Penzance, or even further afield, perhaps, to London, Paris . . .

They were deep in conversation over a delicious roasted parsnip soup, and Nick was plumbing the depths of Lucy's limited knowledge of the Australian outback, when a woman's voice practically shrieked his name.

Lucy turned to see a group of four – two men and two women – grinning broadly at them and waving excitedly.

'Ah,' said Nick softly, so that only Lucy heard. 'I should have warned you.'

One of the women rushed up to them. She was rather glamorous in a carefully casual way, with stylish fair hair and neat pearl earrings, a grey fur coat, tight designer jeans and knee-high, slim grey boots.

'Darling, Nick,' she cried, flinging her arms around him and kissing him European style on both cheeks. 'How absolutely marvellous to run into you like this, especially with such a lovely companion.'

She beamed at Lucy and waited rather obviously for an introduction.

'This is Lucy Hunter from Australia,' Nick said, touching a hand to Lucy's shoulder.

'Australia? How wonderful.'

'Lucy, Amelia. Amelia Hartford.'

'I'm one of Nick's oldest friends,' Amelia added as she held out her hand to shake Lucy's. 'I don't dare tell you how many years we've known each other. So lovely to meet you, Lucy.'

'Thanks. Pleased to meet you.'

'And here's the rest of our motley crew,' Amelia added as she beckoned to the others, who quickly gathered around her.

A solid, balding man called Guy proved to be Amelia's husband, and with him was a sandy-haired couple, Emma and Michael Jacques. They were all similarly well-dressed in casually tailored clothes that might have come straight from a fashion magazine, and they spoke with plummy accents, but Lucy thought they seemed very warm and genuine. As they introduced themselves, though, they appeared particularly pleased with her – almost as if she was some kind of rare exhibit – which she found rather puzzling and just a little disconcerting. She could only assume that Nick was normally more private than she'd imagined.

'Darlings, we'll leave you to finish your meal in peace,' Amelia said, as she gave Nick an almost motherly pat on the arm. 'But you will come and join us in the bar for a drink before you leave, won't you?'

'Of course,' Nick assured her, but he offered Lucy an apologetic smile as they resumed their meal. 'It's hard to hide in a place like this.'

She couldn't tell if he really minded. 'Do you want to hide?'

His gaze met hers and lingered. 'Sometimes the idea is very appealing.'

Warmth swept through her and she hoped she wasn't blushing. 'I thought they seemed nice.' Trying for a posh English accent, she added, 'Jolly decent chaps.'

Nick smiled. 'Oh, they are. Frightfully decent. And – and they mean well.'

'In what way?'

'They fuss,' he clarified rather uncomfortably. 'At least they have ever since – since Simon, my brother, died.'

Lucy felt an urge to reach out, to give Nick's broad hand a sympathetic squeeze. Perhaps she would have done this if their venue hadn't been so public.

Then again, it was time to be careful. She felt as if she was walking a very fine line between being a sympathetic cousin and a girl on a date. To remind herself of this, she said, bluntly, 'I'm surprised you didn't introduce me as your cousin.'

Nick frowned. 'Why would I do that?'

'Why?' Was he really deliberately thickheaded? 'Because your grandmother and mine were sisters. That's why I'm here. Because we're related by blood.'

'But my father was adopted,' Nick said quietly. 'I thought you must have known that. My grandmother couldn't have children, and my father and his sister were both adopted.'

Adopted!

Lucy felt as if she'd run face first into an invisible glass wall. Perhaps she might have known this fact if her family was normal and actually spoke to each other about such things.

'I believe that's why Granny took such a keen interest in your mother,' Nick went on. 'When Georgina died, Granny wanted to bring her niece, Rose, back to England, to raise her as her own.'

Stunned, Lucy stared down at her now empty soup plate.

Georgina's sister Alice hadn't been able to have children. No wonder her letter had sounded so desperate. But Ro had called her a bitch. Lucy couldn't help wondering what on earth had gone wrong.

But more significant now was the fact that she and Nick were *not* related by blood.

Not kissing cousins . . .

She felt as if this changed everything. Perhaps she really could be just a girl on a date, a ridiculously happy girl. Then again, perhaps it changed nothing. There were still a couple of very convincing reasons to resist Nick's charms.

The waitress materialised to clear their soup plates and, after she'd left, Nick said, 'I know it's a bit forward of me to comment, but I'm surprised you don't have a travelling companion.'

'I came here on the spur of the moment. I tried to persuade my best friend to join me, but her hot new boyfriend made a better offer and she couldn't bear to leave.'

'Fair enough.' Nick's dark eyes shimmered as he held her gaze. 'And what about you?' He spoke super casually. 'Is there a boyfriend? Perhaps several boyfriends?'

'Not currently . . . No.' Lucy felt more flustered than she would have liked, so perhaps it was fortunate that their mains arrived then. As she squeezed lemon over her fish she began to feel calmer, and she realised that she should tell Nick about Sam. Clear the air. Cards on the table.

'Actually, I've just broken up with a guy.' She managed a small smile and then dropped her gaze quickly to her meal. 'We were on the brink of getting married, or at least setting a date, but then we – we realised it wasn't going to work.'

She paid attention to her meal, carefully scooping a piece of succulent white fish onto her fork, and managed to avoid seeing Nick's reaction.

After a bit, he said, 'I'm sorry. That must have been hard.'

'It wasn't fun.' Picking up her wine glass, she took a fortifying sip. Set it down. 'So I guess while we're on this topic, I might as well ask about you.'

'About my girlfriends?' Mild amusement glimmered. 'I'm fancy-free.'

'Really?' She couldn't keep the surprise from her voice.

Nick shrugged. 'Like you, I had a close brush with the altar but I escaped.'

'Gosh. Both of us?'

Lucy drew a deep breath. She knew there must be more to Nick's story, but he was probably as unwilling as she was to supply the gory details. She certainly wasn't prepared to tell him that she and Sam broke up over her job in the army. No point in raising a topic that would completely spoil their evening.

'I'm really enjoying this meal,' she said, clumsily changing the subject. 'I thought Queensland's reef fish were hard to beat, but this is sensational. What's it called again?'

'Turbot. It's very good eating.'

'Mmm. Divine.'

They both opted out of dessert, and went into the bar where Amelia's gang, happily ensconced on sofas near the fire, greeted them with enthusiasm.

It was all rather pleasant. Lucy was subjected to a battery of questions about Australia and how long she planned to stay in England. There was some talk among the men about a shooting weekend. Apparently pheasant shooting was one of the winter activities offered at Penwall Hall. Amelia mentioned it was about time she threw another party.

'Wouldn't it be wonderful if we could fit it in while you're still here, Lucy?'

It was while Nick was at the bar collecting a round of drinks that Amelia leaned closer to Lucy and spoke in a conspiratorial undertone. 'It's just wonderful to see Nick so relaxed and enjoying himself,' she said.

Lucy hoped she didn't look too surprised. Despite Nick's claim to be fancy-free, she was still quite sure he must have any number of pretty girls desperately interested in him.

'I know I'm being forward,' Amelia went on. 'But Nick's a very old and very dear friend, you see, and we've all been rather worried about him. The truth is, he hasn't been out with a girl for ages.'

Lucy knew she was expected to comment, but she couldn't find an intelligent response to this.

Amelia leaned even closer and spoke out of the corner of her mouth. 'At the risk of sounding like the village gossip, you know Nick's brother died last April?'

'Well, yes. I didn't know when, exactly.'

'Before that, Nick was going out quite seriously with a girl called Eleanor, she's from Truro. We all expected an engagement announcement, but they broke up within a few weeks of Simon's death. I don't know what happened exactly. Nick wouldn't talk about it, but he's more or less lived like a Trappist monk ever since.'

Lucy watched Nick now at the bar, laughing at something the barman said. Eleanor from Truro must have been his brush with the altar. And, given the timing of the breakup, it had to be connected to his brother's death. Perhaps Nick had been too grief-stricken to contemplate romance?

'He certainly looks very relaxed and happy this evening,' Amelia said next.

As they watched, Nick was grinning and waving to someone at the other end of the bar and he was still smiling as he picked up the tray with their drinks and made his way back to them.

'Let's hope he's over the worst of it then,' Lucy said.

It had been a long day, starting with the early morning horse ride and ending with Nick's surprising revelations about their family. Lucy was pleasantly tired when she and Nick climbed back into the Range Rover and headed for the Hall.

She almost closed her eyes and sank back against the headrest, but she didn't want to nod off. She wanted to enjoy every last minute of this lovely evening, the perfect conclusion to a perfect day. The rain hadn't returned and as the car climbed away from the coast, she could see a slender new moon sailing delicately between wisps of cloud. If she turned her head, she could see Nick's delicious profile, his lovely strong hands on the steering wheel.

Silly of her, though, to pay so much attention. Despite the wonderful day and the exciting vibes, and despite the not-so-subtle hints Amelia had dropped, there was little point in sitting here eyeing Nick off, even though she could now scratch their blood relationship from her list.

If Amelia was correct and Nick really had been reclusive and grieving for months, the very last thing he needed was some lust-addled Aussie chick complicating his life.

With that settled, she felt commendably composed as Nick

steered the Range Rover down the drive and brought it to a halt in front of the Hall.

He freed the keys from the ignition and then turned to her. 'Would you like to come in for a night cap?'

Lucy was grateful for the darkness that hid her wistful face. 'That's not a good idea, surely?'

'Isn't it?' After a beat, Nick said politely, 'Perhaps you've already had enough to drink for one evening?'

This was probably true, although it wasn't what worried Lucy. She swallowed. 'It's just that having a night cap seems a bit – well, rather like a date.'

Another small silence. 'Is that a problem?'

Lucy couldn't see Nick's face, but she could hear the smile in his voice. Was he playing with her? 'Look, I've had a fabulous day, Nick, and I'm really grateful. I owe you a very big vote of thanks. But you have to admit . . .'

She faltered.

'What do I have to admit?'

In the moonlit dark, Nick's voice sounded deeper and more beautiful than ever. And yes, seductive. Lucy could feel it winding through her, making her wish they could . . .

Stop it.

She looked away through the passenger's side window to the view of the gardens, filled with the silhouettes of trees and the long curving line of a hedge.

When she turned back, she saw Nick's face etched by moonlight. 'I suspect you knew I was clueless about your father being adopted.' When he didn't respond she quickly added, 'Why didn't you say something earlier?'

'I was waiting for the right moment.'

A pulse in her throat leaped into action. Somewhere outside an owl hooted. 'And why was tonight the right moment?'

Now, Nick reached out and rested his hand on the back of her seat. She thought he was going to touch her, and her blood rushed under her skin. Her imagination went wild, anticipating the brush of his fingers against her neck, touching her cheek, her lips . . .

But his hand remained excruciating inches from her shoulder.

'I guess I didn't want to risk scaring you off,' he said. 'Because I've wanted you from the moment I first saw you, Lucy. And I feel as if I've been waiting forever.'

This silenced her. Several ice ages passed before she managed to speak. 'Since that first night in the pub?'

'Yes. I never believed in that "across a crowded room" business until you walked into The Seaspray Arms.'

'But the next morning – you looked so pissed off, when I ran into you with your horse.'

'Sorry. That's because I'd resolved to avoid you. I suppose I was in denial about the way I felt. But now . . .'

He touched her then, just the slightest pressure of his fingers on her shoulder and, despite the layers of winter clothing, her skin burned where he touched.

She yearned to give in, to melt closer to him, to be finally in his arms. She forced herself to sit still, to be sensible, to remember all the other valid reasons why this was wrong.

They were moving too fast. She was going home soon. This could only be a holiday fling. And then what?

But Nick was touching her hair now, lifting a curling tress. 'I've tried to resist you, Lucy.'

A crazy intoxication zinged through her veins. Now she could think of nothing but Nick's fingers in her hair. Of his hands on her skin. And all her logical reasons for keeping her distance were floating away. Zooming out of reach.

'My problem is,' Nick said next, his voice deeper and more sonorous than ever, 'I seem to have reached the limits of my resistance.'

Moonlight was streaming through the windscreen, showing her the lustre of his eyes, the hint of shadow on his jaw, the tempting sexiness of his mouth.

And the longing that had been building in her for days spilled. She needed Nick to kiss her.

'Come here,' he murmured.

And she was already there, tumbling into his embrace. His arms were around her and she could feel the strength of him through the thick wool of his sweater.

Closing her eyes, she lifted her face. His mouth touched her lips once in a soft caress that sent flames flashing deep, and then he kissed her again. Slowly. Confidently. Thoroughly.

Oh my.

Lucy hadn't expected to find herself sinking so quickly. This was seduction at its sweetest, at its most compelling.

When a sudden burst of rain sounded overhead, drumming on the roof of the car, she ignored it. It would be too unfair if the most amazing kiss since the dawn of time had to finish before it had fairly started.

Nick, however, was practical. 'We'll have to get out of here,' he murmured, breaking off the kiss. Already he was turning away from her, reaching over to the back seat for the umbrella.

The driver's door opened and she felt a wash of cool, rain-drenched air. Then his door slammed and a moment later he was helping her out of the car, slipping an arm around her shoulders and they were running together across the driveway, huddled beneath the umbrella, dodging puddles.

Instead of heading for the main front door, he took her to a smaller door at the opposite end of the house from the B&B.

'Where's this?' she asked as he dealt with the lock.

'My flat.'

Of course. It made sense that he would have his own flat. A man of his age couldn't happily live with his parents.

She found herself in a black-and-white tiled front hall.

Nick deposited the umbrella in a stand by the door and then he reached for her. 'Bloody weather.' He took her hand. 'Where were we?'

It was then Lucy realised how truly susceptible she was. Just one playful question from Nick, one touch and she was lost again. Melting, as he took her by the shoulders, as he leaned in to kiss her.

There was no possibility of resistance. She was far too eager to return his warm, teasing, unhurried kiss with one of her own.

'Lucy,' he whispered, making her name sound beautiful and special.

'I'm here,' she replied against his lips. 'Right here.'

He took her down a hallway and pushed open tall, white double doors.

His flat was gorgeous, very modern, with a lot of black and cinnamon and silver. Near the entry there were sofas, a coffee table and a mantelpiece and down the other end a kitchen – sleek glass and stainless steel – with a dining area attached. The lighting was suitably dimmed.

But before Lucy could take in many details, or begin to feel nervous, Nick steered her towards another doorway and gathered her close. 'You've no idea how many times I've thought about this.'

'Ditto,' she whispered back.

His dark eyes shimmered with an eloquent message that made her breath catch. She knew a brief moment of panic as her pesky questions flooded back. What was she doing here? She'd come to find out about her family, not to seduce the son and heir.

But the son and heir had lifted her hand and was kissing the inside of her wrist. When he kissed her mouth again, it was rather too late for quibbles or coyness. Not that she wanted to quibble. Not when his kiss cast such a delicious spell.

Nick shrugged off his jacket and helped her out of her coat and he tossed them both in the direction of a corner chair, before he kissed her again.

'You're trembling,' he said. 'Are you cold?'

'No.' The central heating was doing its job perfectly. She risked a smile. 'But I've never done this in a castle.'

'Not a castle,' he murmured as he slowly slipped his hands beneath her sweater and edged it upwards.

'Next best thing.'

Her sweater went the way of the coat and he traced the curve of her neck, then glided his hand over her shoulder. '*You're* the next best thing.'

He knew exactly the right things to say, and yet somehow he gave the words weight and sincerity. Confident now, Lucy began to unbutton his shirt, and Nick watched her, his eyes smouldering as he watched her hands, watched her face.

No doubt he saw her eagerness, heard the catch in her breath as she peeled the fabric away.

'Wow,' she whispered, letting her hands glide over his chest.

As she let her hands skim lower, she heard him suck in his breath. A beat later, she found herself scooped high in his arms. A heady swoop, and then she was tumbling, landing in a happy heap beside him on the luxurious, big black bed.

20

On Georgina's first night in New Britain, she and Harry slept under an enormous tree at the side of a jungle track with a thin groundsheet as their only protection from the hard, damp and smelly ground.

They'd gone as far as they could on the motorbike, bouncing along rough dirt roads until the track became too rugged and crevassed for even the bike to manoeuvre. It was only then, having abandoned the motorbike, that they'd reached the relative safety and privacy of the jungle, and Harry had finally taken her in his arms and kissed her.

And oh, what a kiss . . . the tough soldier suddenly gentle as he kissed her brow, her cheek, her chin, her mouth.

'George.' Her name was a whisper against her lips, a sigh, a prayer. It was impossible to still feel terrified as he wrapped his arms around her, holding her close. 'I don't know whether it's fate or God that's done this, but if I could, I'd hold you forever and never let you go.'

His words made her cry and she pressed her face into his shirt to blot her tears. 'I'm not crying because I'm scared,' she told him. 'Not any more. I think I'm just . . . overwhelmed.'

''Course you are.' Gently, Harry tucked a strand of her hair behind her ear. 'It's all right to be scared. Being scared will keep you alive.'

She answered with a tiny nod, and Harry leaned back a little, searching her face. Only the faintest moonlight gleamed through the thick tree canopy, but there was enough light to show the deep emotion shining in his eyes. 'Stick with me and you'll be okay.'

'Yes.'

But now the guilt she'd been battling for hours resurfaced. 'I'm worried about being a burden. The last thing you need is a woman slowing you down.'

'Scrap that thought right now. No more talk of burdens.' He dropped another warm kiss on the tip of her nose. 'Besides, worrying won't help.'

Her nanny had told her this so many times when she was a child that now she managed a small smile.

But she did feel bad that she'd landed herself in this mess. With the benefit of hindsight, she had to wonder why she'd been so jolly determined to rush to Rabaul to warn Cora and Teddy. She knew she'd been reckless, but perhaps she would have felt a thousand times worse if she'd stayed in Canberra and done nothing, only to later hear about Rabaul's terrible fate.

At least she'd seen Cora and Teddy's lovely home and she understood how much it meant to them. And they'd been so brave. So British.

Now it's my turn. I have to follow their example.

With gentle fingers under her chin, Harry tilted her face so he could look straight into her eyes. 'You're a brave girl, George Lenton. I saw how brave you were in London. You'll get through this.' It was as if Harry had read her mind.

'Yes, I will.' It was a promise. A promise to Harry. To herself.

'Just remember I love you. Right?'

That first night they ate a tin of bully beef, an item Georgina had found pretty ghastly in London, but this time she was so hungry the taste hardly mattered. It was followed by the luxury of a dessert. They shared a mango, which Harry peeled and sliced with a wicked-looking knife that he wore strapped to his leg. Then they drank a little of his precious water and tried to settle for the night.

'Roll your sleeves down,' Harry told her as he spread out the groundsheet. 'The mozzies here are ferocious and you want to keep as much skin covered as possible. It's lucky you're wearing stockings.'

Georgina did as she was told, but even though they nestled close and she could hear the reassuring steady thud of Harry's heartbeats, she slept badly and woke often. The mosquitoes buzzed and bit at her hands and face and even managed to bite through her stockings, and the rattle and drone of distant machine guns and planes never really stopped.

Added to these discomforts, she kept reliving the dreadful scenes she'd witnessed earlier that evening when she and Harry had fled inland along Bamboo Road. She'd seen the bodies of dozens of young Australian soldiers strewn along the grassy verges like discarded puppets.

It had been unnerving, too, to see Harry, who already carried a pistol in a webbing holster on his hip, calmly salvage a rifle from one of the roadside victims.

He'd looked so different, so cool and calculated as he'd worked the bolt and checked the magazine, and yet she knew he was only doing his job, a job he was clearly very good at. This was war, after all. War on the frontline.

Georgina knew this and yet she still found it hard to believe that instead of working in her nice safe office in Dulwich, she was in a menacing jungle with a fearsome enemy on her tail.

The night wore on and the thick darkness was filled with noises – the screech of flying foxes, the thud of falling mangoes, the whine of mosquitoes, and every so often, the throb and rattle of distant gunfire. Worse were the sounds Georgina couldn't hear but imagined, especially the soft, silent footfall of Japanese soldiers stalking towards them through the black jungle. She was so grateful that Harry was always there, holding her. She suspected that he didn't sleep at all.

When a fresh blast of fury from planes overhead woke her just before dawn, Harry was already up, crouching a few feet away, peering through a patch of scrub.

She sat up. 'Harry,' she called softly, and he whirled around, pistol drawn, frowning. His eyes shot a fierce message as he held a finger to his lips.

Georgina froze, her heart pounding. Surely the Japanese weren't already close enough to hear them? Terrified, she sat very still, watching and listening. The Zeroes were gone now and the morning was silent, apart from the buzzing of insects. And then she heard the chilling sound of a match being struck. Followed by laughter. And then voices . . . Male voices speaking in what could only be Japanese.

Terror strafed down her spine. Next, her heart pounded so loudly she couldn't hear the men any more, could only crouch in the grass, frozen with fear.

It felt like an age before Harry came back to her. 'Japs out there in the bush,' he said. 'I couldn't get a good look at them. But they've moved on now.'

'Are you sure?' she asked fearfully.

He nodded and smiled to reassure her, but she wondered if he did this to stop her from worrying.

'How are you feeling?' he asked next.

'Itchy.' Unable to help herself, Georgina scratched through her sleeve at her armpit.

'Itchy armpits and groin?'

She blushed. 'Yes.'

'It's jungle itch, I'm afraid. Bloody little mites you can't even see.'

'Are you itchy, too?'

'Yeah. No choice but to try to ignore it, George. If you scratch the bites, they'll end up infected.'

Breakfast was a quickly eaten mango, but even before Harry and Georgina set off, it began to rain. Fortunately, Harry had rain capes in his commando pack, along with sulphur patches, bandages, quinine, a billy and tins of waxed matches.

At the first big clump of bamboo he stopped and cut long pieces, about head high.

'They make good walking sticks,' he said, handing Georgina a solid length. 'Use it like a staff to steady yourself on the steep sections. Save your energy.'

'All right. Thanks.'

'Every time you slip or fall it will be harder to get back on your feet. We're in this for the long haul. Right?'

'Right.'

After an hour or two, she felt she had the hang of using the yellow and green bamboo staff to support herself, easing her way along the rougher sections. But although the sticks and rain capes came in handy, the steep ground became slick beneath their feet and Georgina's ATS-issue shoes were soon next to useless.

It was very hard going and if she hadn't already vowed to be brave and to survive this, she might have given up several times on that very first day.

It was the middle of the afternoon when they reached a mission station set in a cleared coconut grove on a high, remote plateau.

A group of very worried missionaries, neatly attired in white, greeted them. 'We're waiting for the Japanese,' they said after the briefest introductions were made. 'But please, come inside and have a cup of tea.'

A cup of tea sounded like the most wonderful luxury in the world to Georgina. She could have kissed them.

Inside the wooden mission hut, they found three Australian soldiers already drinking tea and eating biscuits. Their eyes boggled when they saw Georgina.

'What's a sheila doing here?' a skinny red-headed fellow with astonishingly bright blue eyes asked.

'This is Subaltern Lenton of the British Army,' Harry told them smoothly, as if her presence was perfectly normal. 'In the scramble yesterday, she was unable to get away.'

'Bloody hell.'

Georgina could see that these men were absolutely thrown by her presence. Not only was she a woman but an Englishwoman. They were probably bursting with questions, but they offered her tired smiles of sympathy and introduced themselves as 'Busker' McMahon, Dave Higgins and Joe Brownlie.

'We shouldn't stay here for long,' Joe Brownlie said. 'I know the missionaries are worried about Japanese reprisals if they're caught harbouring Aussie soldiers.'

Harry nodded. 'That's fair enough. We won't hang around.'

One of the missionaries, a tall, balding man of about fifty, appeared in the doorway with a tea tray. He looked distressed, as if he'd overheard Joe. 'We don't want to chase you away.'

'Don't give it another thought,' said Harry. 'We understand your position. You have a responsibility to look after your people. What do you plan to do?'

The missionary's pale blue eyes were bleak behind his rimless spectacles. 'We have no choice. We'll surrender and become prisoners.'

Georgina shivered, thinking of Cora and Teddy. She wondered again where they were now and decided that she had to imagine them safe and well. She would drive herself mad with negative thoughts.

'That's a hard call, but it's yours to make,' Harry told the missionary. 'My duty is to avoid capture at all cost.'

Over welcome second cups of tea and biscuits, the soldiers chatted quietly, tiredly – mostly about the best place to head to next. They all seemed to agree that to avoid the Japs they needed to withdraw further beyond the Keravat River.

'We should stick together,' Harry said. Georgina realised she was chewing her lip, thinking again about being a hindrance to these men. But she knew that if she offered to stay behind with the missionaries, Harry would be angry. He was committed to getting her out of here. And despite a few wary-eyed glances in her direction, the soldiers seemed very impressed by Harry. Perhaps they would forgive a woman's presence if it meant being in the company of a commando with jungle training, especially as he carried tinned food and medical supplies.

Unlike Harry, the other soldiers were dressed in short-sleeved shirts and shorts, and their skin was already dotted with red mosquito bites. Only one of them seemed to have a rifle.

'We need to set a clear goal,' Harry told them. 'I vote we head for Wide Bay. It's a safe anchorage.'

Joe looked surprised. 'You reckon we can get off the island by boat?'

'It's our best bet.'

'But the Japs are blowing up any vessels they can find,' warned Busker. 'Freighters, fishing trawlers, yachts. Anything that bloody floats.'

Harry nodded grimly. 'We'll just have to trust that someone from Moresby is organising an evacuation by sea.'

The men looked doubtful, but they were cheered when the missionaries gave them a bunch of bananas and a bag of rice as they bid them goodbye.

'God bless you and keep you safe.'

'And you,' Georgina said as she shook their hands.

One of the women pointed to Georgina's feet. 'Oh, my dear, you won't get far in those shoes. They'll fall to pieces in no time.' With that, she hurried away, only to reappear shortly with a pair of sturdy boots. 'See if these fit. They're much stronger.'

Georgina thanked her and she felt rather self-conscious with everyone watching her while she took off her muddy shoes and exposed her filthy stockinged feet. As she slipped her feet into the boots, they seemed a little big. She could wriggle her toes rather freely, but then she did up the laces and stood. 'They're surprisingly comfortable,' she said.

Harry was grinning. 'They're the cat's pyjamas.'

When they set off again, Harry scouted ahead. It was soon obvious that keeping to the track was the only real way to make any progress through the jungle. At the first patch of bamboo they stopped so Harry could help the other men cut walking sticks. They quickly realised how useful they were, particularly as they were heading up another mountain.

There was a tension in the other men that Georgina hadn't sensed in Harry. They kept looking back down the track, as if they expected the enemy to appear at any moment. She shared their tension, of course, but she was glad that the jungle canopy was thick overhead. It gave some sense of security against being spotted or attacked by the enemy aircraft that they could still hear high above them.

When they broke into an open ridge section, she could see deep, heavily timbered valleys below and then beyond them to more towering cloud-covered mountains. No sign of the sea. The terrain was so rugged, this was going to take days. But at least she was coping, so far. Apart from the incessant desire to scratch her red-raw insect-bitten tender parts, she felt she was holding her own.

It was hard, though, knowing that she couldn't show any sign of her relationship with Harry now. They hadn't discussed it, but she understood this was how it must be. Harry had taken responsibility for the group and she certainly didn't want to make any problems for him or cause any fuss, although she did ask for sticking plaster to cover the blisters the new boots caused.

Georgina was ploughing on, head down, watching where to place her feet on the broken, uneven ground when she suddenly bumped into Joe Brownlie, who was the man ahead of her. Then she realised everyone had frozen in their tracks.

Harry was stopped, about twenty yards ahead with one hand raised, signalling a halt, while he gripped his pistol in the other. Silently, carefully, he retraced his steps and when he reached them he spoke in a whisper. 'Jap sniper up a tree about eighty yards ahead.'

Fear, cold and immobilising, sliced through Georgina, but when Harry looked at her, his eyes seemed to glow with a silent message. Just for her.

Trust me. I love you. Just do what I say.

It was all the reassurance she needed.

He gestured for them to retreat, going carefully and quietly back down the track away from the danger.

At a safer distance, he spoke again, still in a low voice. 'A few more paces and I would have walked into his line of sight.'

'How did you spot him?' Busker whispered.

'He cut away some of the foliage to improve his line of fire and I saw small branches lying on the track with withered leaves. Didn't look right.'

'I want to know how these bastards got ahead of us,' demanded Dave. 'It doesn't seem possible. I've been expecting them to come from behind us ever since we started out.'

Harry gave a knowing shake of his head. 'We're not in the desert any more and I'm afraid we've got a lot of catching up to do. This mob are far better in the jungle than we are.'

'Well, thank Christ you've had jungle training,' said Dave.

Joe asked, 'So, what happens now?'

'I reckon there'll be more Japs manning a Nambu just a bit further up the track, waiting to ambush any parties coming through. We'll leave an obvious note pegged to the middle of this track, warning other stragglers there's a sniper ahead, and then we'll loop off upwind onto the high ground. Put some distance between them and us.'

With their note set carefully in place, they moved off.

'As quiet as you can,' Harry warned. 'No slashing at the scrub with your bayonet. No talking. I want to put us on an intersect with the track again, but at least a mile further along.'

Georgina had no idea in what direction they were travelling as they trudged on. For the next two days, the hot, sticky jungle, heavy with the smell of rotting vegetation, was their only shelter. They stumbled up an ever-ascending track, up a steep mountain and then, over equally treacherous terrain, they picked their way down the other side, only to face yet another mountain. In the mornings they packed up quickly and pushed on. At night they slept on wet ground, with hunger pangs gnawing at their bellies and insects biting their faces, arms and legs. Of course, she could no longer sleep snuggled close to Harry, but she was so weary it hardly mattered.

Filthy and mud-smeared, she thought about her parents and was grateful that her mother had no idea where she was. Her father would be horrified too, of course, even though he'd been a soldier in the last war and was proud that she'd joined the army. Apart from his years in the war, he'd embraced a life of privilege and elegant refinement.

Beneath a dripping tree, squashing yet another blood-filled mosquito, Georgina couldn't help recalling stories of her father's exclusive London Club, where men went to get away from their wives, to relax, and where the newspapers were reputedly ironed to remove surplus, messy ink and the coins were boiled to clean off any dirt. It all seemed so ridiculous now.

21

Georgina lost count of the days in the jungle.

Her sense of time faded alongside her dwindling energy, as she and the Aussie soldiers trudged on, following slick, muddy tracks, monotonously climbing up more mountains and slithering down the other side, tormented all the way by mosquitoes and leeches, by cut and torn hands and constantly wet clothes, plus the gnawing pangs of hunger.

Always, there were Zeroes zooming overhead. The Jap pilots obviously knew there were escapees in the jungle and they seemed to love taking pot shots, breaking the silence of the bush with the *rat-a-tat-tat* of their machine guns as they raked haphazardly across the heavily forested hillsides.

The greatest danger came when the soldiers reached the rushing rivers that filled the narrow valleys between the mountain ranges. The Zero pilots soon learned to circle there, waiting to gun down anyone who valiantly tried to cross. To Georgina's horror, there were bodies caught up in logs at several of the crossings.

Harry made their little group wait till nightfall to cross and they used guide ropes cut from lengths of sturdy vine spliced together.

From time to time the men offered to help Georgina, but she'd made a decision from the outset that she wouldn't be a hindrance so when someone tried to take her elbow to support her, she felt compelled to pull away.

'Thanks,' she would say politely. 'But I'm all right. I can manage.'

They quickly accepted that she was pulling her own weight, and Harry helped this by reminding them that a subaltern was equivalent to a second lieutenant.

Joe nudged Busker and winked. 'S'pose we should call her Ma'am.'

They didn't call her this, but they did end up nicknaming her Duchess because of her accent, which apparently sounded hilariously posh to Aussie ears – especially in the murky depths of a tropical jungle.

A duchess with infected sandfly bites, tropical sores and soggy, rotting boots, Georgina thought ruefully.

She noticed that the men also liked to call Harry 'Skipper'. It seemed Australian diggers choked on the word 'Sir', especially when they were all in danger together and far away from the pomp and ceremony of a parade ground.

They weren't in the least disrespectful, though. They knew they'd have perished without Harry. It wasn't just a matter of his jungle training and the fact that he could identify edible plants like kaukau or cassava, they also came to rely on his strength of character and leadership.

Through the really tough times, when their spirits were at rock bottom – when it was tempting to simply lie beside the track and refuse to move – it was Harry who cajoled and bullied them not to give in. Relentlessly, he pushed them on, somehow managing to mix encouragement with the harsh military orders his seniority required.

'Can't go one more step, Skipper,' Joe Brownlie said one night, when they'd been resting before a particularly ghastly river crossing. 'Leave me here. Please. I've had it.'

Harry knew Joe was in a bad way but as he stood beside him, a hand on his shoulder, his voice was sympathetic yet firm. 'You can't curl up and die, Private. Not until I bloody well give you the order.'

They got Joe across another river that night, but despite the quinine tablets that Harry rationed out for all of them, it soon became clear that Joe was suffering from malaria. Over the next few days, he sank into delirium and the men took it in turns to support or carry him.

Another night and another swift water crossing. Rain drizzled and no light penetrated the jungle. The only sound was the rushing river or an occasional grunt from an exhausted soldier. Everyone was focused on getting Joe safely across – Harry bearing the sick man over his shoulders, the others bringing up the rear – when Busker slipped on a muddy rock and fell.

Georgina, right behind him, let go of the vine rope and managed to grab the big man by his shirt collar, just in time. The water was only knee deep, but the force of the rushing river was fierce, threatening to sweep him from her grip.

Desperately, she braced herself, trying to hang on. Yells from the other men reached her through the darkness. Busker furiously tried to grab onto the slippery rocks, but he couldn't gain purchase and his rotted shirt began to tear apart in her aching hands.

Oh, help.

Miraculously, she managed to get a hand under his arm but she knew her strength was giving out. As the water rushed and eddied around them, her legs and feet were sore and weary, her back was straining and her arms felt almost pulled from their sockets.

Consumed by deadly weariness, she found herself thinking how easy it would be to simply slip into the water and let the current take her and Busker. It would be just like the summers in Cornwall when she and her friend Rob, the gamekeeper's son, used to hurl themselves into the brook that crossed their estate and float on their backs, letting the flow take them, drifting downstream.

She might have given in to this temptation if Harry hadn't suddenly appeared at her side, steadying her and dragging Busker to safety in one powerful movement.

The three of them stood together, feet braced, their clothes now completely saturated, gasping for breath.

'Have you got him?' called Dave through the darkness.

'Yes!' Georgina's cry was triumphant, her relief sweet.

Before long, without the need for any words, they continued their cautious crossing over the rocks.

They were all suffering from bone-deep exhaustion, and Georgina knew that none of them could last much longer.

Again Harry rallied them. 'We're all going to die someday, but not today. Call yourselves sons of Anzacs? We can't be more than a few miles from the coast now. So on your feet, soldiers.'

It was only beneath the thickest jungle canopies that they allowed themselves the luxury of a small fire to boil rice or kaukau. Once or twice they celebrated with brewed tea and stale biscuits. Bliss!

They also used boiled water to clean the worst of their cuts and bites and Georgina tore up the last of her half-slip to use as bandages.

These were the good nights.

But to Georgina's shame, there were times she genuinely wished she'd gone to the mission with Cora and Teddy. Surely a Japanese prison couldn't be as bad as this endless, muddy nightmare?

Just when she was at her worst, though, she would catch Harry watching her, see his grey eyes, fierce and worried, yet shining with a tenderness that speared straight to her heart.

Just remember I love you. Right?

It was enough to stir new hope in her breast, to believe in the possibility of a future when this war was over.

Days, weeks, it was all a blur.

The little party was on its last legs when they finally found themselves at the coast. One moment they were slogging along a jungle
pathway and the next their soggy feet were sinking into soft brown
sand and there before them lay a sparkling, palm-fringed bay.

At first, Georgina couldn't quite believe her eyes. She had to
blink several times to make sure it wasn't a mirage. And then she
couldn't see the bay at all, because her eyes were blinded by tears.
Tears of relief. And gratitude.

Harry, as cool as ever, kept them back under the cover of the
jungle trees while he studied the sweep of the bay for signs of the
enemy.

Busker's voice broke the silence. 'Skipper, take a look at this. It's
gotta be from our mob.'

He was pointing to words carved into the side of a large tree
trunk.

Circular Quay.

To Georgina's surprise, the other men grinned.

'What does it mean?' she asked.

'Circular Quay is a ferry terminal on Sydney Harbour,' Dave
explained. 'I reckon this must be a pick-up point.'

'Yes, there should be a boat near here,' Harry agreed. 'It's probably holed up in the mangroves, hidden during the day.' For the first
time in ages, his eyes were bright, almost excited, but then his gaze
narrowed as he scanned the dense scrub. 'Could be other Aussies
here. We need to take a look around.'

Georgina waited with Joe in the shade and they sat with their
backs against the smooth trunks of coconut palms, while the other
men, with renewed energy now, set off on a reconnoitre.

They returned with a party of five other Australians they'd
found sheltering at the far end of the little bay. Most of the men were
sick – they hadn't had the benefit of Harry's medical supplies – one

of them was suffering particularly with malaria and another was badly wounded.

And then the hoped-for miracle. A red-headed coast watcher with a thick Irish accent appeared out of the bush and introduced himself as Lieutenant Keith McCarthy.

'Part of a relief unit sent to extract stragglers after the fall of Rabaul,' he explained. 'I have an old pearling lugger hidden in a mangrove creek a mile or so away. We'll have you lot off here and on the way to Moresby tonight.'

It sounded unbelievable, too good to be true, but apparently, McCarthy had already rescued hundreds of Australian escapees from this side of the island.

'They were in worse shape than you lot,' he told them. 'You're damn lucky to have a commando in charge.'

Harry now produced quinine for the malaria victim, and they made the wounded soldier, Private John Cook, as comfortable as they could.

'The only thing that kept him going was the need to get the message out about the Toll massacre,' Lieutenant McCarthy told them grimly.

'A massacre at Toll?' Harry frowned. 'We were headed for there, but we saw Jap shipping in the bay and skirted it.'

'Just as bloody well.' McCarthy gave a sombre shake of his head. 'A couple of hundred of our boys surrendered at Toll and the bastards killed the lot. Jap marines took them into the jungle in groups and used them for bayonet practice.' His mouth skewered into a down-curling grimace. 'Burned some of them alive. And worse.'

Georgina flinched in horror, her imagination throwing up ghastly images of torture and the harrowing sound of men's screams.

McCarthy dropped his gaze to the wounded man in front of them, whose face was deathly pale. 'Johnny Cook feigned dead, but they still bayoneted him three times for good measure. He's in a bad way.'

'How did he make it this far?' Harry asked.

'These other men from Lark Force found him on the track. Carried him.'

The news of the massacre at Toll was sobering. Again Georgina thought of her aunt and uncle and found herself fighting off images of dreadful possibilities. She had to believe that nothing so dreadful had happened to them.

Her own safe arrival here at the coast and the promise of rescue felt somehow fragile now. They were so close to being rescued and yet she felt at her weakest, more nervous than ever. On a knife edge. How could she bear it if anything went wrong now, at the last minute?

Perhaps Lieutenant McCarthy noticed her tension. He smiled at her. 'So you've come all the way from Rabaul with this ugly lot?'

'Yes,' she said, struggling to keep her voice level. 'I'm so grateful to them.'

'She's been amazing,' said Joe, surprising her.

'There ought to be a better word than amazing,' chimed in Busker. 'She saved me on that bloody track. Me and the boys are planning to write to the postmaster-general. See if we can get this woman on our postage stamps.'

The circle of men chuckled, but their smiles were genuine.

Harry, squatting beside the fire, sent her a slow smile.

Just remember I love you. Right?

Once again, she felt reassured, and a great deal calmer. The afternoon would fly by and then it would be night-time. They would be gone from here. It was going to happen.

Clouds covered the moon. The boat pushed away from the shore and the sea and the sky merged into one vast inky blackness. On deck beside Harry, Georgina felt the salty breeze on her face, heard the slap of the sail and the splash of waves thumping against the bow. Within minutes the boat was through the breakers, then chugging smoothly out to sea.

The sick and wounded were tucked into bunks in the cabin below, an unbelievable luxury for these men.

On deck, a bottle of rum and tumblers were passed around. Georgina had never tasted rum before, but what the heck? She drank the spirit neat, feeling it spread like fire inside her, warming her, adding a pleasant wooziness to her state of exhaustion. She swayed a little on her feet and bumped against Harry.

Oh, the sweet temptation to stay there, leaning into his strength. Surely here in the darkness, no one would mind. Quite possibly none of the men would even notice.

'A penny for your thoughts?' she asked softly, close to Harry's ear.

'Only one thought.' She heard the smile in his voice. 'Can't you guess?'

She was smiling now, too. 'I'm hoping it's the same thought as mine.'

Throughout the long arduous weeks on New Britain, they had been so very professional and discreet, never once behaving like lovers. Yet during that time, each day had found Georgina falling more deeply in love with Harry. She loved his strength of character and his skills in the jungle, his calm courage and steadying leadership. All of this wrapped in a lean, suntanned and handsome man whose smile made her weak at the knees.

Now they had so little time left together. When they reached Port Moresby, they would have no choice but to go their separate ways. Harry would rejoin his unit and Georgina would be transported back to Canberra.

But here on this boat they were alone in the dark and standing close. So close now – almost touching – and Georgina was filled with an overwhelming yearning. If only they could steal a moment, just a *moment* from this bloody war.

Her hopes were dashed when Busker's voice came out of the darkness. Relaxed by rum, Busker was sitting in the bow with Dave and he probably had no idea that his words were blown towards Georgina and Harry.

'You reckon the Skipper and the Duchess are keen on each other?'

'Reckon?' Dave snorted. 'Well, of course they're flamin' keen. Blind Freddy can see that.'

Damn. Georgina almost groaned aloud. She'd had no idea that the men had noticed. The chemistry must have been far more obvious than she'd realised. To make matters worse, Harry was an officer, a commando with a position of status to uphold and now he would feel obliged to move away from her.

She closed her eyes, drenched in disappointment, waiting for Harry's polite excuse. He needed to check on Joe Brownlie below decks, needed to consult with Keith McCarthy about their arrival in Port Moresby.

And yet, perhaps this night wasn't destined to let her down on any level, for in the next breath, Harry slipped his arm around her shoulders and drew her in to him, till she was exactly where she needed to be. In his arms, with her head on his shoulder, his warm lips brushing her forehead.

'Remember I love you, George. Always.'

From below came the reassuring steady chug of the diesel motor – *thump-bang, thump-bang, thump-bang* – and the warm night closed around them. All else receded and it was just the two of them, holding each other close, whispering promises, while the boat rolled gently over a black and silver sea.

It was the most perfect night of her life.

22

Lucy, carrying a tin of shortbread and rugged up against the cold in a thick winter coat and gloves, sturdy boots and a woollen scarf, was in high spirits as she climbed a winding, muddy track to the home of Primrose Cavendish. At the top of the hill she found a wooden gate and a path of well-worn paving stones that led to an unpretentious whitewashed cottage with a front door painted in deep royal blue.

She felt a little breathless, not from the hill climb, but from eager anticipation. At last. She had finally discovered someone who was happy to talk to her about her mother and her grandparents. The elderly Miss Primrose Cavendish had once been Georgina's best friend.

It was Nick who'd suggested that the old lady could help Lucy. The idea had been hatched in his bed.

Instead of stealing back to the B&B after their truly amazing tryst, Lucy had found herself reclining against a luxurious mountain of black-and-cinnamon striped pillows in a gorgeous Englishman's bed and drinking his very fine single malt from a Scottish island with a name that was hard to pronounce. And to her further surprise, she and Nick had enjoyed rather a cosy chat.

Avoiding subjects like the off-the-planet chemistry they'd just discovered – it was too new and unexpected to be spoiled by comments – and unwilling to dissect their past relationships, they'd found it easiest to talk about their families. After all, it was the big thing they had in common.

Nick talked about his brother, Simon, and how especially close they'd been when they were young. Apparently, they'd shared a passion for a host of different outdoor activities – horse riding and hiking on the moors, sailing and swimming in the bay, playing cricket and rugby, shooting.

'It sounds like an idyllic childhood,' Lucy had told him.

'Yes. We were lucky. We were given plenty of freedom.'

'Did you have to go to boarding school though?' She knew this had been her mother's fate when she'd been sent to Cornwall.

'We did. We were sent to our father's old school. It wasn't too bad. Simon and I saw plenty of each other. We were close in age, and Simon was brilliant at sport so he often ended up in the same team as me, even though he was younger.'

'Did you mind?'

'Naturally. A dreadful blow to the ego.' Nick gave a shrugging smile. 'But I was a faster swimmer.'

For a dangerous moment, his eyes shone too brightly and his mouth twisted as he struggled with the memories. Lucy wondered if she should try to change the subject, but then he said more evenly, 'You know, I appreciate being able to talk about Simon. My parents won't. Or can't.'

Lucy reached for his hand, giving it a squeeze.

'After Simon died, my parents locked the door to his room,' Nick said. 'They left everything just as it was and now they never go in there. They've just tried to carry on as if – as if it never happened.' His mouth pulled into another grimace. 'I'm sure it's not healthy.'

'No, it can't be.' Lucy was remembering what Amelia had told her about Nick breaking up with his girlfriend soon after Simon's death, and then living like a Trappist monk. 'It must be hard for you.'

'Yeah.' He took another sip of his scotch and looked out through the open doorway to his lovely living area. 'To be honest, I'm not sure I can stay here much longer. I came back three and a half years ago, to save the family farm, so to speak. But it's up and running and paying for itself now. I could easily hand over to a good manager.'

'Where did you work before this?'

'London. In finance.'

Of course. Lucy could so easily picture Nicholas Myatt in London, a man of the city, juggling a high-flying finance career with an even higher-flying social life. Although she had to admit, Nick also seemed perfectly right in this setting. Perhaps he was a man-for-all-seasons, the kind of fellow who would fit in and do well just about anywhere.

Nick drained his glass and set it on the bedside table. 'Enough about me.' Beneath the sheet, he rubbed his foot playfully against Lucy's. 'I'd like to hear more about you.'

'Oh, well. How much time do you have?' She tried to match his playful tone, while hastily considering what she should tell him. She felt guilty that she still hadn't told him about the army, but there never seemed to be an appropriate moment. Perhaps it wouldn't be necessary to mention it at all, given the short time she would be here.

It made sense to choose the topic that was most on her mind – the fact that she knew so very little about her family's past.

'For starters, I don't have a brother or a sister. I'm an only child.'

'Because your parents had already achieved perfection with you.' He gave her a smiling wink.

'Yeah, something like that. More like, because my father took off when I was a baby. Or to be more accurate, my mum kicked him out.'

'Bad luck. But you've met him since, haven't you?'

Lucy shook her head. 'I was curious about him, of course, and I would have liked to meet him – even once, just to look him in the eye and say g'day. But when I was fifteen we got word that he'd died.'

She sent Nick a rueful smile. 'So that's one of the big black holes in my history. I've learned to live with that, but what bugs me is that both my mother and my grandfather do their level best to avoid talking about their past, too. I know practically zilch about my family.'

'That's rough.'

'Yes it is. It's weird. It's like living in a vacuum. Actually, it's really getting to me.'

'Which is why you came here.'

'Exactly.'

Nick leaned in and dropped a gentle kiss on the tip of her nose. 'Poor Lucy.'

It was nice to have his sympathy. Perhaps he understood. He might not know a great deal about his father's family, given he was adopted. 'At least you know all about the Myatt family's history, right back to when this Hall was built,' she said. 'I suppose you can probably trace their history back to the days of – oh, I don't know – Robin Hood.'

He smiled. 'We do have records of an ancestor who went to the Crusades.'

'My point, exactly.'

'But all that history can also be a burden.'

'You think?'

'It brings an added sense of responsibility.'

'But it must also give you a strong sense of identity.'

Now, for a long moment, Nick let his gaze rest on her and then his face broke into a slow, sexy smile. 'I find it hard to believe you don't have a strong sense of who you are, Lucy Hunter. I'd lay bets you're a woman who knows her own worth.'

Lucy considered this flattering remark as she drank the last of the delicious smoky scotch. She supposed she wouldn't have been so angry with Sam if she hadn't had reasonably high self-esteem. She needed a man who respected her achievements, not resented them.

'The difficulty,' she said slowly, 'when you don't know much about where you come from, is that it's hard to make decisions. About the future. I feel as if I need to know who I am before I can work out what I really want to do.'

'Do? As in?'

'With my life . . .'

At this, Nick's expression grew surprisingly serious.

'Don't worry.' She felt compelled to reassure him, adding a sweeping gesture that encompassed the bed and the king-size sheet that now covered them. 'I'm not talking about this. About you – and – and me. I know this is only a holiday thing.'

Nick was still frowning. 'So you have that worked out already? After one night?'

Now it was Lucy who tensed. 'Well . . .' She swallowed. Truth was, she didn't have anything worked out. From the moment Nick had taken her in his arms, her logical thinking had gone into shut down. She'd had no choice but to follow her instincts. 'I – I know I have to go home, Nick, and you have to stay here.'

He smiled, and perhaps it was her imagination but his smile seemed a little forced, not quite reaching his eyes.

'Of course,' he said and then, very smoothly, he changed the subject. 'Actually, if you want to know more about your grandmother, I think I might know someone who can help you. She's old, mind you. As old as my granny, but she's still in fine fettle. Her mind's sharp.'

'She's not like the old Dowager Countess in *Downton Abbey*, is she?'

'There's nothing ferocious about Primrose. I'm sure you'll like her. She's probably quite lonely, actually. Her nephew runs their main estate and she lives on her own in a little cottage that was once the gamekeeper's house. I'm sure she'd love a good chinwag about old times over a cup of tea.'

'And she knew Georgina?'

'I believe she was her best friend.'

'Then I'd love to meet her.'

Dipping his head, Nick gently nibbled at her shoulder. 'And now, as we have limited time, I believe we should make the most of this holiday thing.'

Lucy laughed and promptly rolled into his embrace. 'Yes, please.'

A man of his word, Nick had rung Primrose Cavendish the next day, and the visit was promptly arranged.

Now, here Lucy was. On the old lady's doorstep, waiting somewhat nervously for her to answer the knock.

Before too long, the door opened to reveal a stooped old lady with a cloud of soft white curls, a sweet round, softly lined face and twinkling brown eyes behind rimless glasses.

'Lucy!' she cried with a delighted smile and open arms. 'It is *so* good to meet you.'

Lucy accepted a gentle hug and kissed her papery cheek. 'And I'm very pleased to meet you, Miss Cavendish.'

'Please, call me Primrose. I was so excited when I got the phone call from Nick.' Primrose beamed at Lucy. 'After all this time – Rose's daughter.'

'Yes.' It was strange to hear her mother referred to as Rose. Ro had scorned the pretty name of her childhood, and had shortened it years before Lucy was born.

'You have her smile,' Primrose said.

'Have I really?'

'Yes, my dear.' The old lady narrowed her eyes as she studied Lucy. 'You take after Harry, I can see that, but you definitely have Rose's smile.'

How interesting. Lucy hadn't thought of her mum as a smiley sort of person. There'd been fun times, of course, but so much tension as well. Too often her mother had looked hassled and fretful with a distinct absence of smiles.

'I brought shortbread,' she said, holding out the tin.

'Oh, thank you, dear. Come in, come in. You can hang your coat here on one of these hooks by the door and then come and sit by the fire.'

Lucy found herself in a pleasant sitting room with faded Oriental rugs on an ancient stone floor, old wingback chairs upholstered in velvet, diamond-paned windows with a view of the garden and stone sills deep enough to sit in, a log fire crackling in the hearth. Through a doorway she caught a glimpse of a kitchen with pale custard-coloured walls, a heavy stone sink and pine cupboards.

Primrose's cottage had a charming, storybook quality, and it was, thought Lucy, the perfect setting for her.

In a lavender cardigan over a neat white blouse trimmed with delicate lace, a grey-and-lavender tartan skirt and well-polished, 'sensible' tan shoes, Primrose Cavendish reminded Lucy of an elderly Miss Marple. All she needed was some knitting.

'I'll put the kettle on in a moment when I catch my breath, but take a seat, Lucy.'

Primrose seated herself with some difficulty, and Lucy felt compelled to ask, 'Can I make the tea for you?'

'Well, thank you, dear. We'll see. I have a daily help, but I gave her the morning off so we can have a good chat in private. The cottage is so small, you see. But there's an electric jug, so the tea can be done in a flash. But first, tell me, how is your mother?'

'Oh.' Lucy had been so intent on the questions she would ask, she was slightly taken aback. She would have liked to say that Ro sent Primrose her love, but her strict sense of honesty prevailed. 'She's very well, thanks. She's just moved into a lovely inner-city apartment.'

'Oh, how nice for her. Does she live alone?'

'No, she has a partner, a new partner, actually. A very nice man.'

Primrose smiled. 'That's good to hear. I've often wondered how she was. I wrote to her a few times after she went back to Australia. Oh, it would be years and years ago now, but I only ever received brief replies. There was never much information.'

'I know what that's like,' said Lucy. 'Every time I've asked Mum about the time she spent here, she's clammed up.'

'That's probably because she was so unhappy here.' Primrose gave a sad shake of her head. 'The poor girl hated being taken away from her father and her home. She did everything she could to be sent back to Australia, or at least that's how it always appeared to me, looking in from the outside. She was smart enough to get herself into plenty of trouble.'

'Oh dear.' Lucy felt suddenly very sorry for her mum.

'Of course, her Aunt Alice never gave an inch to anyone,' Primrose added sourly. 'Alice foolishly tried to change Rosie, to turn her into an upper-class English girl. Hounded her about her table manners and was always inspecting her hair, her teeth, her fingernails; correcting the way Rosie spoke. She even tried to change her accent, for heaven's sake.'

Lucy's sympathy for her mother's plight deepened.

'Anyway, I have my breath back now and I should be serving you a cup of tea.'

'Please, let me do it.' Lucy didn't want the poor woman struggling to her feet again. 'You should stay there where you're comfortable.'

'Very well. Thank you, Lucy, dear. Everything's there on the kitchen table and there's a tray.'

Lucy was used to making tea with Harry, who often liked it in the old-fashioned way in a teapot, so she was quite at home, warming the pot and spooning in tea leaves. She set the delicate porcelain cups and saucers, milk jug and sugar bowl on the tray, as well as a plate with slices of bright golden cake laden with fruit that was standing ready under a rectangular glass cover. She brought an extra plate for the shortbread.

'Would you like napkins?' she called to Primrose.

'Yes, please. They're in the top right-hand drawer of the dresser.'

The napkins were beautiful cream linen with delicately crocheted edgings. *Mum would love all this now*, Lucy thought.

Primrose was on her feet when Lucy carried the tray back into the sitting room.

'Let's have the tea at the dining table,' she said. 'I don't manage juggling cups and plates on my lap very well these days.'

In the adjoining dining room there was a round table set into a deep bay window. A bowl of pink, white and yellow roses sat on the windowsill and another smaller fire burned in the grate.

'How lovely,' Lucy said as she set the tray down. She saw that Primrose was now carrying, with some difficulty, a thick book that looked like a photo album.

'It will be easier to look at photographs while we're at the table,' Primrose said.

'Perfect.' Lucy grinned at her. She couldn't wait to see what the album contained.

They settled to enjoy their tea. Lucy poured, which was just as well, as Primrose's hands were so shaky she needed both of them just to hold her cup steady.

'Make sure you try some of this cake,' Primrose said. 'Your mother used to love it whenever she visited me. It's traditional Cornish saffron cake.'

'Mmm, yum,' Lucy murmured as she sampled a bite. It was like a rich fruity bun with a hint of spice. 'Almost as good as a Cornish pasty,' she said.

'Oh, we Cornish like our food.'

But it wasn't long before the tea things were pushed aside so they could get down to the important business of examining the photo album.

'There are quite a few photos of Georgina,' Primrose said. 'All taken before the war, when she was still quite young.'

Eagerly, Lucy scanned a snap of a group of young people all mounted on horses, grinning and looking carefree. She found her grandmother in the group straight away, as well as a laughing girl with big dark eyes and flyaway curly hair. 'Is this you?' she asked.

'Yes.' Primrose smiled.

'You look lovely.'

'Well, thank you, dear. Such a long time ago. Can you pick out Georgina?'

'Here.' Lucy pointed to George, the slim girl with wavy, jaw-length hair and a more cautious smile. No, cautious wasn't quite the word. There was definite amusement lurking in her eyes, even though she looked more serious than the others.

'This is her, isn't it?'

'Yes, that's Georgina, and this is Alice, her sister.'

'And the young men?'

'This was my brother Michael. The others were neighbours. Arthur and Geoffrey Torrington.'

Over the page there were more photos of the same group of young people enjoying themselves in the outdoors – playing tennis, hiking on the moor in sturdy boots and with dogs in tow, horse riding, swimming. In each photograph Lucy sought out George and she was relieved to see that she was quite often smiling or laughing – although there was always *something* in her expression, a hint of gravity, perhaps.

It was a fanciful thought, but Lucy wondered if George had somehow sensed that these carefree days of youthful fun were numbered and that war was just around the corner.

'Oh, this looks like Kynance Cove,' she said as they turned the page to a photo of the group gathered on a sandy beach at the base of a tall cliff. They were all dressed in old-fashioned swimsuits.

'That's right,' said Primrose. 'We went down there for a picnic in Geoff Torrington's new car. It was such a beautiful summer's day and all so exciting.' The old lady gazed at the photo with a wistful smile, as if she could remember it clearly, almost as if she was back there in her mind, clambering down the rocky path to the sun-filled beach, carting picnic baskets, hats, bottles of ginger beer and towels. 'Have you been there, dear?'

'Yes,' Lucy said. 'Nick Myatt took me down there last week.'

'Did he now?' Primrose's eyes shone with noticeable interest and Lucy found herself struggling not to blush. She had no idea how the gossip chain worked in this part of the world. 'It's a beautiful stretch of coastline,' she said quickly, hoping she sounded quite calm and collected. 'So dramatic.'

Under Primrose's curious gaze she felt her cheeks grow hotter. Worried that she might give herself away to this rather perceptive old lady, she turned another page of the album. Now, the photos were suddenly indoors and all very formal.

'Oh, this is when we made our debut,' Primrose said, pointing to a photo of herself and George in long white gowns with tight gloves reaching up to their elbows and lovely corsages pinned to their shoulders.

'You both look so glamorous. Look at your hair, Primrose. You look like film stars.'

Primrose sighed. 'That wretched season was quite an ordeal. Such a fuss at the time, being presented to the King and Queen, and then the endless parties and dances.' She tapped the photo of George with a knobbly finger. 'I wouldn't have got through it without your grandmother.'

'Really?' This was an interesting revelation. 'But it sounds like so much fun. Weren't you supposed to enjoy yourselves?'

'Yes, of course we were, and a lot of girls had a jolly good time but, unfortunately, my mother was a very nervy type and I was her only daughter. I had three brothers, you see. No sisters. And Mummy fussed and worried over every tiny detail of my debut. And then after each party she used to hold a post mortem.' Primrose shuddered. 'Oh, I won't bore you with all that.' With a sudden smile for Lucy, she added, 'But I have to say Georgina was a wonderful help throughout the season. She was such a good friend.'

She turned the page and her expression softened. 'Everything was all right once I met Stephen, of course.'

Now there were photos of Primrose with a young man. In one photo that caught Lucy's eye especially, Primrose was wearing a very smart dark dress, beautifully tailored and fitted at the waist, then falling softly to just below her knees. She was also wearing a matching wide-brimmed hat that dipped rather elegantly at the front.

Her handsome male companion had thick, light-brown hair combed back and parted in the middle. His eyes were light coloured too, probably blue, his jaw square, his smile warm, and he looked dashing in a stylishly cut double-breasted suit.

'Wow, he looks hot,' Lucy remarked with a cheeky grin.

'Hot?' Primrose laughed.

'Handsome,' Lucy amended.

'Oh yes, Stephen was certainly handsome. I thought he was the most beautiful man alive. I met him at Georgina's coming out party in Belgravia. I was so in love with him.'

Seeing the unmistakable glow in Primrose's eyes, Lucy held her breath, guessing that there must have been a sad end to this story.

'He was killed in the early days of the war,' Primrose said softly. 'At Dunkirk.'

'Oh, Primrose, I'm so sorry.' Lucy felt a lump in her throat as she studied Stephen's handsome, laughing face. 'That must have been terrible. I can't really imagine.'

The old lady gave a little shrug, but Lucy could see that she was still very sad about her Stephen, after all these years.

'I thought I might die of grief, but somehow I got through it,' she said. 'During the war we were all very busy. There was so much to do. I threw myself into running this estate. My father wasn't well and my mother was a nervous wreck with all of my brothers away fighting, so really, it was up to me. I ran the farm with the help of a couple of girls from the Land Army. In those days we kept dairy cows and pigs and all kinds of vegetables, as well as the orchard.'

'That must have been a huge job to tackle on your own.'

'I enjoyed it,' Primrose said simply.

'Were you used to doing that kind of work?'

'No, but we all had to adjust and to take on new challenges.'

After a bit, Lucy ventured to ask, 'Forgive me for being nosy, but you never met anyone else?'

'Anyone else?' A wistful faraway look came into Primrose's eyes and Lucy feared she'd been impertinent, asking this question. But then Primrose flashed a smile that was almost saucy. 'Oh, I've been taken off the shelf and dusted a few times.' She gave another little shrug. 'But I never met anyone else I wanted to marry.'

Unexpectedly, Lucy thought of her mum again. She supposed Ro had been taken off the shelf and dusted a few times, too, but unlike Primrose, her mother had always convinced herself that each new man had to be *The One*.

'Mum told me she got into trouble while she was over here,' she said. 'I think her exact words were "blotted her copybook". But she's never given details.'

'That's fair enough, isn't it? Parents deserve to keep some secrets.'

'I guess you're right,' Lucy admitted, although she still believed her mum had taken this secrecy to an unfair extreme.

Watching her, Primrose said, 'You know you *are* very like Harry.'

Lucy accepted this not-so-subtle change of subject with a nod. 'I hadn't really noticed the resemblance until I saw a photo of Harry recently, taken when he was young, during the war.'

'Which was when George met him, of course.'

'Yes. I don't suppose you know how they met, do you?'

'Harry hasn't told you?'

'He's so touchy about it all, I haven't liked to ask.'

After a moment's consideration, Primrose said, 'Well, I wasn't on the scene. But the first time they met was in London, I believe, during the Blitz. I'm not quite sure of the exact circumstances, but George was in the army, in the Royal Army Service Corps, so perhaps they met at work.'

'The army? Really?' Fine hairs lifted on Lucy's arms and she felt a prickle in her throat. Why had Harry never told her that her grandmother was in the army? And working in the Service Corps would have been much like her own job, working in logistics. To Lucy it felt so significant, a precious and important link.

When she got home she would have to pin Harry down, *make* him tell her more.

'Did you meet him then, as well?' she asked, desperate for details, for anything really.

'Not then. I didn't meet Harry until after the war, when he came back to call on George.' Primrose gave an expressive roll of her eyes. 'The poor man got a terrible shock when he saw the size and grandeur of Penwall Hall. I think he was expecting a simple farm. And then, of course, George's parents were at their frostiest with him.'

'Yes, I believe the family could be quite snobbish.'

'My dear, the senior Lentons made snobbery into an art form.'

'But how romantic of Harry to come all this way to find George. What happened then? Was that when he asked her to marry him?'

Primrose frowned. 'The blasted man almost broke the poor girl's heart.'

23

Georgina, curled in an armchair in Penwall Hall's sitting room, was trying, rather futilely, to read *Brideshead Revisited*. The book had only been published the year before and it had caused quite a buzz in her circles. She knew she would enjoy it immensely if only she could concentrate on the page in front of her but today this was impossible.

Harry was on his way from Australia. In fact, he was due to arrive at the Hall within the hour. She would have gone to the station to meet him, but her father had needed the car to travel to Truro on a business matter, so Harry was getting a taxi and she had to wait at home. She was almost sick with excitement.

Such a long, punishing twelve months it had been since peace in the Pacific was finally declared. Georgina had been forced to strive for an almost intolerable level of patience.

First, there had been her own long journey home. There were no hastily arranged flights for her at the end of the war as there had been when she'd flown from London to Canberra with Major Duffy. She had to board a crowded troop ship, travelling back to England via Malaya and Ceylon.

She'd hated leaving Australia without having heard from Harry. At least she'd been able to track the movements of his unit while she'd been working in Canberra, and she knew that he'd fought in New Guinea at Kokoda and at Shaggy Ridge. This meant he'd been through some of the very worst and most desperate fighting of the war and she had no idea whether he'd survived.

Miraculously, by the time she finally arrived home, a letter had been waiting on the hall table, addressed to her in Harry's spiky script. Against all possible odds, he had not only survived, but was fit and well.

Georgina had taken herself to the boathouse by the lake, hugging his letter close to her chest, while she wept and wept with relief.

There was still more anxious waiting for her family, however, wondering fearfully about Cora and Teddy's fate. But at last a telegram had arrived from the Red Cross in Japan informing them of the sad news that Lord Edward Harlow had died in New Guinea in 1942, but that Lady Cora Harlow was safe and well and being shipped to England from Tokyo.

They were devastated to hear about Teddy, but at the same time it was an enormous relief to know that Cora had survived. And what a great moment of celebration it had been when at last her father had collected his sister from the Liverpool docks and brought her home to recuperate with them at the Hall.

The first sight of Cora had shocked them dreadfully, though. Georgina's formerly beautiful, elegant aunt had aged beyond recognition. Poor darling Cora was emaciated, her hair thin and snow white. Georgina and her mother had struggled to hide their emotions when they saw her.

Over afternoon tea in the very sitting room where George waited for Harry now, Cora had told them about Teddy's fate. Dry-eyed, straight-backed, she'd spoken quite bluntly.

'When it came to the moment of reckoning, Teddy remained a

true hero to the last. He refused to surrender, or even to bow to the Japanese, so they shot him. Right in front of me.'

Georgina had seen enough in New Britain to be able to imagine her aunt's ordeal in vivid detail. Poor Uncle Teddy. Poor Cora. She couldn't bear it.

'You might think Teddy was pigheaded or foolish,' Cora said. 'But he wasn't very well, you see, and I know he was worried about being a burden to me if we were captured, so I think he was incredibly brave.' Continuing in that same matter-of-fact, detached voice, she added, 'I was lucky. I was packed off to Japan with a group of missionaries.'

But what a terrible world it was, Georgina thought, when luck came down to being kept in a prison in Japan for three long years.

After Cora's return there had been difficult weeks of silence from Harry, and Georgina had been plagued by agonising uncertainty. She fretted that he'd forgotten her, that he'd never planned to make further contact, and there were times she felt certain she couldn't last another moment without knowing where he was or how he felt about her now.

When she'd sunk to her lowest ebb, another letter had arrived. Harry had written to say that he'd received all six of the letters that she'd sent to him, addressed simply to Kalkadoon Station, via Cloncurry, north Queensland.

He'd written to explain that his brother, Jack, who had joined the Australian air force, had been killed in Borneo near the end of the war and his aging parents had been almost completely flattened by their son's death. Understandably, there was a great deal for Harry to attend to at home. The cattle property had needed all kinds of attention and he'd been away in the bush, mustering and droving, for weeks on end.

But finally, Harry's parents were settled in a little cottage by the seaside somewhere in Queensland, he'd found a good manager to oversee Kalkadoon, and he could spare the time to make the journey back to England.

Now he was coming all this way to see Georgina. Not to London as she'd suggested, but down to Cornwall, to meet her parents.

She had barely slept this past week she was so excited. Surely Harry wouldn't come all this way unless he had a very special question to ask her.

After all, he'd crossed oceans, had come twelve thousand miles . . .

A sound at the sitting room door had her leaping up anxiously.

Stevens, the butler, appeared. 'Mr Harry Kemp has arrived, Miss Georgina.'

'Where is he?' She flew to the doorway. 'Oh heavens, Stevens, you didn't leave Harry waiting in the hall, did you?'

'I thought I —'

'You should have brought him straight in here.'

'I'm sorry, Miss Georgina. I'll —'

Without waiting to hear, Georgina rushed past Stevens and out of the room, flying down the passage to the hall.

Harry.

Standing by the walnut table at the foot of the staircase. Harry, out of uniform. In smart pale trousers, a dark jacket with a white shirt and tie. Tall, lean and suntanned. Looking rather stern.

And divine.

With a whoop of glee, Georgina rushed across the room and hurled herself at him like a small missile. Fortunately, she didn't knock him over and he caught her in his arms.

'Well, hello,' he said in that wonderful, smiley, sun-drenched voice of his and he wrapped his arms around her and kissed her in a warm hello filled with glorious promise.

At last. She was in heaven.

'Let me look at you, George.'

Keeping a firm grasp of her shoulders, Harry held her a little away from him and let his shimmering gaze run over her.

She had carefully chosen a simple dress of the palest blue georgette.

'So lovely,' he said softly.

Her heart gave a frolicking skip. 'I should think I'm rather different from when you saw me last, after all those weeks in the jungle.'

He smiled at her, his eyes burning brightly, as if he was drinking her in. 'You were beautiful then, too.'

'Oh, Harry.' Impulsively, she closed the gap between them again, flinging herself back into his arms. 'It's so good to see you. It's like a dream to have you here at last.'

She could feel the warmth of him beneath his shirt and she longed to bury her face into his chest. She might have done so, if Harry hadn't made a throat-clearing sound.

Lifting her head, she realised he was looking rather uncomfortably towards Stevens, who was standing by the door like a disapproving statue.

'I shall send tea to the sitting room, Miss Georgina.' Stevens spoke with excessive formality.

She gave an impatient nod. 'Thank you. And please tell William to take Mr Kemp's suitcase to the blue bedroom.'

'Of course.' Stevens bowed solemnly and withdrew, leaving them alone.

'He can be a stuffy old thing,' she said to Harry.

'You reckon?'

They shared a smile, but Harry looked a little shaken.

'This place,' he said, gazing about him and giving a low whistle. 'It's not exactly a farm.'

'Were you expecting a farm?'

'I thought that's what you said when we were in London. Your mother sent up eggs and homemade jam.'

'Oh yes.' But her mother hadn't collected the eggs or made the jam. Heaven forbid. That wasn't Lady Lavinia Lenton's way at all. 'Well, this is a sort of farm,' Georgina said. 'We do have farm*land*.'

'And you also have a butler.'

She took Harry's arm, pulling him towards the sitting room. 'Come on. Let's have tea. I want you to tell me everything. And then, when you're stuffed full of tea and cake, I'll take you on a tour. I'll show you our sheep and cows, the chickens, the orchard and the stables and you can decide for yourself if we're farmers or not.' She gave a dismissive wave of her hand. 'But you mustn't let any of this bother you.'

She could see, though, that Penwall Hall did bother him. He was still frowning as he looked about him at the huge high ceilings, the massive bank of windows with views all the way to the sea, the grand, climbing staircase. His frown was disconcerting, but Georgina refused to believe that her battle-hardened soldier hero, who had endured the worst war in history, could be unsettled by an old stone house and a few servants.

Just the same, she was rather pleased that her parents and Cora would not make an appearance until dinner.

Her parents were too well bred to refuse an unknown Australian their hospitality, but accepting him as a son-in-law would be a very different matter.

To Georgina's relief, Harry had brought a black dinner suit and bow tie with him and he looked absolutely splendid when he came down to dinner.

They met downstairs before her parents and Cora arrived. Although they were alone, Georgina refrained from throwing herself at him again. Their afternoon tour of the estate had been pleasant, but also somewhat disappointing. There had been plenty of private moments when Harry could easily have taken her in his arms and told her exactly why he'd come here to Cornwall but while he'd been lovely company, he'd behaved politely, like an interested guest rather than a lover.

Georgina reassured herself that he was doing the right thing and wouldn't speak of marriage until he'd met her parents. So now, she could only hope that her parents behaved.

'You've scrubbed up beautifully,' she told him, making no attempt to hide her admiration, as he accepted a drink from the tray that William offered.

'Thanks, but struth, George. You look —' Harry swallowed. 'Like a princess.'

Her dress *was* rather lovely, with thin shoulder straps that left a lot of her skin exposed. The slim-fitting bodice and floating skirt were made of ivory silk chiffon embroidered with white-and-silver-sequinned butterflies and ivory silk taffeta.

'I was hoping to impress you.'

'You succeeded.' He gave a quarter smile. 'Consider me *very* impressed.'

'Harry!' a delighted voice called from the doorway and they turned to see Cora gliding into the room, resplendent in emerald green, her arms outstretched in welcome.

Georgina had warned Harry to expect a change in her aunt and his smile didn't miss a beat.

'It's so good to see you, my dear man.' Cora embraced him and kissed his cheek warmly. 'We're all very grateful to you for looking after Georgina so beautifully.'

'Georgina was very good at looking after herself,' he said. After a beat of time, 'I was very sorry to hear about Lord Harlow. Please accept my condolences.'

'Thank you, Harry.' Cora pinned on the brave little smile that was customary for her now. 'It was inevitable, really. Teddy couldn't have countenanced surrender and being a prisoner of the Japanese.'

Harry gave a polite nod.

Then Georgina's parents arrived together, and Cora proved that she hadn't lost her gift for charm and diplomacy.

'Richard, Lavinia, isn't it wonderful to have Harry Kemp here at last?'

The warmth of Cora's question ensured that both Georgina's parents were smiling as they approached, although their smiles were decidedly careful. Even so, the atmosphere was all very pleasant as the introductions were made. Sipping their chilled sherry, the conversation was kept to boring but safe topics like the weather and the beauty of the Cornish countryside.

It wasn't until they were seated at the dinner table and starting on their watercress soup that Georgina's father began to quiz Harry.

'I believe you were here in England during the war?' he said.

Harry nodded. 'Yes, sir. I was based mostly on the Salisbury Plain.'

Georgina's mother gave a loud sniff. 'There were so many foreign soldiers here during the war. From America and the dominions. I hope they don't all plan to come back at once. We'll be overrun again.'

Georgina suppressed an urge to groan as Harry accepted this rebuff with a courteous nod. Fortunately, her father continued in a more positive tone.

'You were a captain, I believe?'

'Yes, sir.'

'It's always good to meet a fellow officer and a gentleman. I suppose you and your officer mates are all busy getting your former businesses and professions back in order.'

Harry attempted a smile, but he looked rather bemused.

'Richard,' chimed in Cora. 'You do realise it's different in Australia, don't you? Officers' commissions aren't based on a man's title or what school he went to. They're a recognition of merit and military competence.'

Georgina held her breath as, for a chilling moment, brother and sister stared at each other across the table. She knew her father hated being set straight, especially in front of a guest.

To her relief, he lifted his glass to Harry. 'I'd be fascinated to hear your story.'

Dutifully, Harry complied. 'I joined the army as a private, and I was commissioned as a lieutenant in Tobruk.'

'Tobruk, eh? And your captaincy?'

'That happened in New Guinea, sir.' A small smile flickered then disappeared. 'A case of finding myself in the wrong place at the right time. After a year of fighting Japs in the jungle, officers were in short supply.'

'I see.' Her father was frowning, still obviously not impressed.

'We all owe a huge debt of gratitude to Harry for keeping Georgina safe in that bloody jungle,' Cora commented.

'Your daughter is a remarkable young woman, sir.' Harry acknowledged Georgina with a smile that pierced straight to her heart. 'She more than pulled her weight in our little team.'

'And we are very grateful to have her home safely,' her father said with pleasing sincerity.

The huffing sound her mother made was much less sincere. 'She should never have been there in the first place.'

'That's water under the bridge, Lavinia,' said Cora.

Another huff. 'So what are your plans now, Mr Kemp? How long will you be staying in England? Will you be sightseeing? Drinking beer in the pubs you visited when you were here previously?'

Again Harry smiled politely. 'All of those things, I hope. I've booked my passage home for the end of the month.'

At this, his gaze flashed to Georgina and she was sure she read a special significance in his glance. Her heart took off at a gallop and she might have blushed if she hadn't also been aware of her mother's marked disapproval.

This wasn't going to be easy, but she'd always known that. At least her sister Alice and her titled husband weren't here to add to Harry's discomfort.

William appeared to remove their soup plates.

'How far outside Sydney is your estate?' her mother asked Harry, while Stevens served the fish.

'Lavinia, dear,' intervened Cora. 'Harry's property is nowhere near Sydney. Australia's huge. Kalkadoon in north Queensland is quite remote and probably about as far away from Sydney as Penzance is from Moscow.'

Georgina's mother's eyes widened in horror. 'Good God. You mean you live in the wilderness?'

'We call it the outback, Lady Lenton,' Harry said smoothly. 'And yes, I'll admit my property is remote, even by Australian standards.'

'You can't have any social life. What do you do? How do you fill in your days?'

'There's more than enough work on the property to keep me busy. After being away for so long, I've been especially busy since I was demobbed.'

Her mother frowned. 'With what kind of work?'

Patiently, Harry explained. 'Plenty of maintenance. The fences and windmills needed mending and many of the cattle had escaped, going wild in the hills and the scrub, so they had to be mustered and then driven overland to markets. There were cows with new calves that needed extra attention.'

Georgina's mother looked genuinely shocked. 'But you didn't do all this yourself?'

'Yes, with the help of a few stockmen.'

Her father's eyes narrowed as he studied Harry over his glass of riesling. 'So you're still pioneering?'

Harry's chest rose as he drew a quick breath. 'I suppose you could say that, sir.'

Georgina, dismayed by this grilling, felt compelled to come to Harry's defence. 'Don't you think we should let Harry enjoy his trout in peace, Father? He's spent five years fighting the King's enemies, surely he doesn't have to defend himself here at our dinner table.'

A chilling silence fell as her parents stared at her, nonplussed. Lady Lenton opened her mouth and then shut it again, as if she'd wanted to snap a retort, but thought the better of it.

Eventually, Georgina's father said, ever so politely, 'You must forgive us, Harry. I daresay our curiosity got the better of us. We know so very little about Australia, you see.'

'I understand that, sir.'

'I've bored Richard and Lavinia to tears with my stories about Rabaul and New Britain,' added Cora with a smile. 'So they need a new victim.'

It was time for a change of subject. 'Harry,' said Georgina. 'Perhaps now that the war's over, you might be able to visit the National Gallery and see your great-grandfather's painting. What was it called again? "The Dales at Dawn"?'

She knew this would impress her parents. They were friends with many of the highly skilled artists who chose to live in Cornwall, attracted by the milder climate and the quality of the light.

Indeed, her father proved more than happy to talk about his private art collection and, to her relief, over the next course of pheasant, followed by a dessert of cherry tart, the dinner conversation successfully stayed in safer waters.

Harry wasn't off the hook though, for, of course, her father invited him to withdraw to the library after dinner for port and cigars, and he couldn't very well refuse.

After the men disappeared, Georgina was sick with nerves. There was no way she could sit calmly chatting with her mother and Cora, while she wondered what was being said in the library.

Fortunately, the other women were quite happy to retire, so Georgina could escape. Even so, she paced restlessly in her room, leaving the door open so she could hear the first sound from downstairs that might suggest the men had finished.

She tried not to guess what they were talking about, but she couldn't help wondering. Surely her father had to be as curious as she was about why Harry had come all this way. Heaven knew, she wouldn't sleep a wink tonight without some kind of resolution.

At last there were footsteps on the tiles downstairs and deep male voices bidding each other goodnight. Breathlessly, she waited by the door. She had no choice but to ambush Harry as he passed by on his way to his room.

A soft footfall on the carpet outside, and she glided out of the shadows.

'Harry.'

'George, you're still up?'

'Of course I am. I had to see you. Will you come outside with me?'

He only hesitated for a second, looking back in the direction of her parents' rooms. 'Sure.'

She had a fur wrap ready and, pulling it around her shoulders, she led the way – back down the stairs, out through a side door and into the bright, starlit night. 'Let's go to the boathouse. We can talk there.'

She wondered if he could hear the pounding of her heartbeats as they made their way together, over the damp lawn, to the little wooden hut beside the lake.

'Was my father too awful?' She had to ask.

'No, he was perfectly reasonable.' Just the same, Harry sounded tense.

'But he demanded to know your intentions?'

After a beat, 'Yes.'

It was too dark to read his expression. 'And?'

'And I told him I needed to speak to you first.'

'Oh.' This sounded more promising. Georgina almost hugged him with relief.

It was dark and gloomy inside the boathouse and she opened the little cupboard where lamps and candles were stored.

'Here, let me,' Harry said, as she fumbled with the matches.

He struck a match firmly. Light flared and Georgina handed him a candle to light, and then another.

'That's better,' she said, as she set the candles in a pot of sand to cast their golden glow over the timber walls and floor and the cushion-lined benches. 'I can see you now.'

But what she saw frightened her. Harry was standing stiffly to attention, watching her sadly. Too sadly.

She felt a knife blade flash of panic. 'Harry, what is it? What's the matter?'

A sigh escaped him. 'I'm very afraid that I've made a regrettable mistake.'

'How do you mean?'

His mouth twisted unhappily and he looked away through the wide doorway to the black glassy surface of the lake and a solitary white swan, limned by starlight.

Georgina couldn't stand it, couldn't bear the suspense a moment longer. 'Harry, please don't play games.'

'That's the last thing I want.'

'You *are* going to ask me to marry you, aren't you?'

'That's what I'd planned.' He seemed to speak with difficulty, as if he was dragging the words out. 'But I realise now that I was fooling myself.'

'Why?' The single word was a cry, a howl of despair.

'George, I —'

'You love me.' Georgina didn't care that she sounded desperate.

Harry had told her that he loved her. So many times.

'The thing is, I have so little to offer you.'

So there it was. Just as she had feared. Harry had been overawed by her family, by the estate, the titles.

This was all going terribly wrong. Everything she held dearly was slipping out of her grasp.

'You've never seen where I live,' Harry said, confirming her fears. 'It's not a lush tropical plantation like your aunt and uncle's. It's way out in the outback. It's isolated and hot. We have drought for years at a stretch and then floods. And flies, damn it.'

With every word he uttered, Georgina's fear and frustration mounted. The one person she trusted to hold her world together was backing away, potentially walking out of her life.

In the candlelight his face reflected the same agony that was ripping through her insides.

'George, I've seen the way you lived in London. And now this —' He flung out his hand in an agitated gesture that indicated the Hall, the grounds, the lake. 'This estate is even grander and lovelier than your London house. And it's not just the house. There's the lifestyle – all your friends.' His jaw squared and his mouth was a tight, hard line. 'I'm sorry. Kalkadoon's no place for a lady.'

'Harry!' Her cry was close to a shriek. Silenced, Harry stared at her, his throat working with emotion. 'Will you shut up?'

Surprise flared in his eyes and Georgina drew a deep breath for courage.

'This cattle station of yours – Kalkadoon.' She was pleased that she could speak more calmly now. 'There's a – a house, isn't there?'

'Well, yes, there's a homestead. It's nothing flash, but there's —'

'And the homestead has a roof?'

'Of course.'

Feeling braver now, Georgina took a step towards him. 'A bed?'

Harry nodded.

She moved closer still. 'A mattress? Pillows?'

A sudden breeze made the candles flutter, but she could still see his handsome face and his slightly bewildered expression.

'Very well, then.' She was close enough now to touch him. 'If you'll also be there, then it sounds jolly perfect.'

Lifting a nervous hand she traced the satin lapel of his dinner jacket. She felt him tense beneath her touch.

'Harry, we had nothing but mud and mosquitoes and Japs trying to kill us in the jungle, and I fell deeply, irrevocably in love with you.'

'But George, you don't —'

She pressed her fingers to his lips, cutting off the words.

'The jungle confirmed things for me,' she said. 'It clarified the important things in life.' She offered him her bravest smile. 'And I now know with absolute certainty that every important thing that I want begins and ends with you.'

Then, without warning, her courage disintegrated, her mouth pulled out of shape, her eyes filled with tears and she couldn't see Harry any more.

But she felt his arms come around her, hauling her against his chest, and she felt his lips on her face, kissing her damp eyelids, her wet cheeks, her trembling lips.

'My darling brave girl,' he murmured against her cheek. 'I love you so much. I promise I'll do everything I can to make you happy, George. And . . .'

And anything else he might have said was lost as her lips parted beneath him and he kissed her.

Oh, what a kiss it was, filled with ocean-deep emotion and longing.

And passion. Soon, and with feverish impatience, Georgina wriggled out of her evening gown and draped it over a bench while Harry shed his jacket and tore at his bow tie so fiercely that buttons popped and bounced onto the wooden floor. The rest of their clothes came off between wild kisses and embraces, until they were at last together among the cushions and picnic rugs, deliciously, gloriously naked. In the candlelight.

Georgina wound her arms around Harry's neck. 'I'm going to be the perfect outback wife.'

He kissed a line from her jaw to her ear. 'I'll look after you, I promise.'

She wriggled her hips against his. 'I can already ride a horse, and I want —'

'George.'

'Yes?'

Now his hands were gliding over her skin. 'Shut up, so I can make love to you.'

Deliriously happy, Georgina obeyed.

24

    Dearest Primrose,
    *Finally, a photo of my darling little girl. Isn't she just the
most perfect baby you ever saw? Such a good, contented little
bundle, and look at that mass of dark curls! I think she's going
to be a beauty.*
    *I can't believe so many months have flown by already.
You've probably heard from my parents and know that I've
called her Rose Margaret. However, you might not know that
I was also thinking of you, my dear friend, when I called her
Rose – you and the poor struggling climbing rose I brought out
with me from England that is still, miraculously, alive here at
Kalkadoon. Margaret is for Harry's mother, who is the dearest
woman, and so thrilled to be a grandmother, at last, as is my
mother, of course. Rose is the first grandchild for both of them –
as you know, Harry's only brother perished in the war.*
    I think our little girl will probably end up being called

Rosie, though. Harry calls her that already, as do most of the others here. I don't mind.

I feel so blessed, Primrose. Not only have I had ten wonderful years here with my Harry, living the most amazing, happy and interesting life in the outback, but when I'd just about given up all hope of ever becoming a mother, I have this sweet, loving, little daughter. Shirleen, one of the Aboriginal women who live here on the station, gave birth to a baby boy just a few weeks before Rose was born and, given that both babies are already crawling and generally getting into mischief, we often put them in a playpen together while we get on with chores about the homestead. Such a sight – the little white and brown babies giggling and laughing together as they stand on chubby legs, clutching the side of the playpen, while they hurl all their toys out onto the verandah.

The mustering season has just finished, but it was a busy time. Shirleen and I fed the stockmen and it's hungry work rounding up cattle all day, so the men were constantly ravenous. I've lost count of the number of fruit cakes and steaks we cooked, plus enough corned beef sandwiches to feed several armies.

But last Sunday the men insisted I have the day off. It was Harry's idea, I'm sure. He stayed home, and we had the loveliest lazy day, just the three of us, picnicking by the river, and resting on tartan rugs in the shade of weeping paperbarks while Rose slept. Harry caught fish called barramundi and cooked them on a camp fire for our dinner and we remained by the water till the stars came out. It was perfect.

We might be remote here, Primrose, but as I'm sure I've told you many times, I'm never bored. There's always something happening on a big busy station, and then there are social events like picnic races and balls, or shopping trips to *one of the cities on the coast.*

    You must tear yourself away from your farm, so you can come out to visit us. You know you're always very welcome and I'm sure you'll find the Australian outback fascinating. The brilliant colours of red earth and blue sky are just the beginning.

    Anyway, when Rose is old enough, perhaps around five years old, Harry and I will bring her home to England so she can meet you all. That's something to look forward to, isn't it? I'd love to see you again and to have a really long chat about everything.

    Please write and tell me all about your family and the farm and the latest gossip from the village. And what about you, dear Primrose? Any new beaus?

    For the time being, Harry and I both send our love and we hope this finds you well.

    George xx

Lucy smiled as she carefully refolded her grandmother's letter along the well-worn crease lines. She'd read it many times already in the few hours since she'd returned from visiting Primrose, and each time, she loved it more. The images of life evoked in Georgina's lovely letter had given her an unexpected and precious window into her life with Harry at Kalkadoon and she was thrilled to know they'd been so happy.

Now, she turned her attention once more to the photo that George had sent with the letter. Primrose had insisted that Lucy take a couple of letters and the photo home with her.

'Rose might enjoy seeing them,' Primrose had said.

'Oh, she will,' Lucy had assured her. 'It will mean a great deal to her. Thank you.' She was remembering the way her mother's face had softened so noticeably when Rose spoke of Georgina, and Lucy knew her mum would be really touched.

The small black-and-white photo showed Georgina, looking a bit thinner and inevitably older than the other photos in Primrose's album of her teenage years, but still beautiful. She was squinting slightly in the bright outback sunlight as she held her sturdy infant in her arms. Both mother and baby were laughing and George looked so happy and proud. The baby had dark curly hair and she was reaching a chubby hand up to George's face as if she was trying to squeeze her nose.

Lucy loved the picture and found it very reassuring to see such clear evidence of their happiness. Not that George had been *un*happy in the other photos she'd seen, but there was something *more* to her smile in this photo. Yes, her grandmother had been very contented living in the outback with Harry.

Lucy felt this was important. It really mattered to her.

It was especially reassuring to know that her darling Harry had enjoyed a happy marriage. Lucy was sure he'd deserved this and, in ways she couldn't quite explain, the knowledge gave her fresh faith in her family. In her roots.

'You look pleased with yourself. Does that mean all went well with your visit to Primrose?'

Lucy grinned at Nick. 'The old darling was awesome. Look.' She drew the precious black-and-white photograph from her pocket. 'She's given me this snap of my grandmother and my mum.'

'Nice.' Nick leaned in to take a good look. 'Wow, check out those outback plains. Aren't they amazing? They seem to just go on forever.'

'Hey!' Lucy gave him a dig in the ribs with her elbow. 'You're supposed to be admiring the woman and the baby, not the land-scape in the background.'

'Well, the woman and baby are very attractive, too. Beautiful.

But of course, that's a given. They're related to you.'

This earned Nick another dig, but Lucy couldn't pretend that she wasn't a sucker for his flattery, and the smile that accompanied his comment made her as fluttery as she'd been on that first night in The Seaspray Arms.

She blamed his gorgeous brown eyes, sometimes wicked and, other times, surprisingly gentle. That wild, dark hair of his. Those cheekbones. The hint of a five o'clock shadow . . . his long, long legs in blue jeans.

Bottom line – Nicholas Myatt wasn't just deadset gorgeous to look at, he was a blissfully exciting lover.

And, amazingly, on top of his thoughtfulness in introducing her to Primrose, Nick was also cooking her dinner this evening.

A message had arrived on her phone mid-afternoon.

Dinner at my place? Smoked salmon spaghetti?

Naturally, Lucy had accepted. And now, judging by the large pot on the stove and the array of ingredients scattered on Nick's kitchen bench, he hadn't simply ordered a meal from Penwall Hall's kitchen, but was actually planning to cook it with his own fair hands.

This man was a keeper.

Or at least he would be a keeper for some lucky woman, who could stay in his company for more than a week. But if Lucy thought too much about saying goodbye, she'd end up droopy-mouthed and spoiling the pleasant, relaxed atmosphere.

'I had a lovely time with Primrose,' she said again, adding a deliberately bright smile. 'And I'm really grateful that you arranged for me to see her.'

'She's a good old stick. I'm glad she was able to help, especially as my mother phoned today to say that she and Dad want to stay on in London for another week.'

'Oh? Right.' Lucy knew she should probably feel more disappointed.

'But I can't imagine that my parents would be anywhere near as much help to you as Primrose has been.'

'She went out of her way to be helpful,' Lucy agreed. 'She said she felt she owed it to Georgina, given they were such close friends. She told me this story about losing an invitation or something when she was presented to the King, and Georgina finding it somehow, saving the day.'

Nick's eyebrows rose with interest, but he made no comment.

'Anyway, Primrose gave me a couple of letters as well as this photo. There's a letter from Georgina that I've read and it's lovely. She was all in raptures about her baby – Mum's going to adore it. And there's another letter from Harry, my grandfather, that he sent to Primrose at the same time he sent Mum back over here to Penwall Hall.'

'Wow. That might shed a little light.'

'Yes, I know. It's such a stroke of luck. I'm to take it home to Mum, though. I have no idea what it says. It's sealed.'

Nick's eyebrows rose again. 'Sounds intriguing.'

'It's not really cloak-and-dagger. Primrose went to great pains to explain that it wasn't sealed because she didn't trust me, but she *did* want to reassure my mother that she would be the first person to read it, apart from Primrose, of course.'

'It's been a successful day, then.' Nick slung his arm around Lucy's shoulders and dropped a warm kiss on her cheek. 'What say I open a bottle?'

'Brilliant idea.' She slipped the photo back into her pocket. Enough about her family. Nick had been incredibly tolerant, really. 'And let me help you with the cooking.'

'No need,' he said, as he drew a bottle of chilled wine from the fridge and used a corkscrew. 'This meal is dead simple. Once the spag is cooked, it's pretty much a matter of tossing in the salmon, some olive oil and a few capers.'

'Sounds like my kind of cooking.'

Nick handed her a glass. 'Why don't you choose us some dinner music?'

'What are you in the mood for?'

'Do you like jazz?'

'I don't really know much about jazz. I hardly ever listen to it, but I'd be happy to sample whatever you like.'

Moments later, with Oscar Peterson playing 'Georgia On My Mind' softly in the background, Lucy was perched on a stool at the black marble bench in Nick's snazzy kitchen, sipping his very nice wine, and chatting with him, while he set to work with an impressive chef's knife and a solid, man-size chopping block. He looked surprisingly at home, cutting slices of smoked salmon into thin strips, grating lemon rind and chopping dill.

And, sitting there, Lucy realised she was happy. Truly happy. All the way through to the soles of her feet.

Normally she wouldn't stop to measure her emotional state. Most days she just got on with her job, with her life, and took whatever came her way with resigned acceptance. This evening, however, she was very conscious of a heightened sense of wellbeing. She'd enjoyed an especially rewarding visit with Primrose, she'd read Georgina's uplifting letter and now, a handsome and charming man was cooking her dinner. His kitchen smelled deliciously of herbs and lemon. Piano music rippled seductively around her. The wine was crisp and cold and dry, just the way she liked it.

The whole scenario felt almost too good to be true and she was reminded again that it wasn't going to be easy to walk away from Nick without regrets.

She pictured herself leaving the Hall and driving her hire car to the station at Penzance, getting on the train and sitting through the long, scenic journey back to Paddington, a place that had been so exciting on the way down. After an overnight stay in London, she would be up early the next morning to catch the Heathrow Express. Inevitably, then, the long and tedious journey home: Townsville and going back to work and trying to sort out where she might live. Meanwhile Nick would be here and . . .

Lucy realised that he'd finished chopping. When she looked up from her glass, she found him watching her.

'You okay?' he asked.

'Yes, absolutely. I was just thinking about – about going back to work.' It was a shock to realise her mood had sunk so quickly from the heights of happiness, but perhaps she'd needed the reality check.

Nick was smiling. 'Take my advice. Don't think about work until you absolutely have to.'

'Yeah. I know – enjoy the moment.' Which, of course, was one of those philosophies that was much easier to say than to put into practice.

It was so hard to not think ahead, for here she was, spending another night in Nick's flat and they both knew that the night would end, almost certainly, in his bed.

Which was a damned delicious prospect.

So, in theory, she should simply enjoy the meal and the promise of the pleasures to come, but already her annoying conscience was questioning the wisdom of this plan.

Sad truth was, she was on the very brink of falling head over heels in love with Nick. Yes, it was incredibly short-sighted of her and yes, it was too soon, given the recent bust-up with Sam.

If she wasn't very careful, she would find herself setting out on the homeward journey feeling even more at a loss than when she left Townsville.

Added to this potential problem, there was Nick to consider. Lucy couldn't just ignore the no-girlfriends-Trappist-monk story that his friend Amelia had shared with her in the bar. Amelia had more or less inferred that Nick was emotionally vulnerable right now, and Lucy's conscience was suggesting that the wise choice would be to sort a few things out – have the awkward talk. Lay their expectations on the table before this lovely night rolled on to the point where they got too carried away.

Nick turned back to his cooking and, as he dropped a good fistful of dried spaghetti into the pot of boiling water, Lucy took a deep swig of her wine, for Dutch courage. She waited until he stirred the pasta to his satisfaction and set the wooden spoon aside.

'So, I was wondering . . .' she began carefully.

His eyes widened with mild amusement. 'Still musing?'

'I guess so.'

'And your question is?'

'It's just something your friend Amelia said at the pub the other night. She told me that you haven't dated since Simon died.'

'Did she?' Nick picked up the spoon again and gave the pasta a slow swirl. When he looked back at her his expression was wary. 'Does that bother you?'

'It doesn't bother me exactly. But it does make *this* —' Lucy gestured to the stove and then to the rest of his flat, including the doorway to the bedroom. 'Slightly more significant.'

His shoulders lifted in an easy shrug. 'Amelia has an over-developed mother-hen gene.' But he sent Lucy a quick, searching smile. 'You made it clear the other night this is just a holiday thing.'

Lucy swallowed. So she had. And apparently, the fact that she was leaving soon wasn't a problem for Nick. Despite his eight months' date drought, he was totally okay with having a fling, while she . . .

While she was beginning to care too much.

Actually, she wasn't just beginning to care. It had already happened. She cared a great deal.

Bloody hell.

'Lucy.'

Nick was watching her carefully and she probably looked miserable. Pinning on a smile, she said, brightly, 'So we're both on the same page?'

He frowned. 'Can I suggest you're over-thinking this?'

'I suppose that's quite likely.' She went to lift her glass and realised it was already empty.

Ever the perfect host, Nick retrieved the bottle from the fridge and poured wine into both their glasses. Then he set his glass aside.

'Amelia's right,' he said, leaning over the counter and locking his steady dark gaze with hers. 'You're the first woman in ages that I've wanted to take to bed.'

His words lit dangerous flashpoints all over her skin.

'I know you have a flight booked to Australia and you'll be leaving soon,' he said next. 'But that doesn't necessarily mean that we can't see each other again.'

Lucy swallowed. She hadn't really dreamed, hadn't dared to . . .

Leaning closer, Nick kissed her lightly. 'I really, really like you, Lucy Hunter, and I'm damned sorry you can't stay longer.' He brushed his lips over hers again in the sexiest of sweet teases. 'But we can take this one step at a time. Okay?'

Yeah, sure.

He was making perfect, fabulous sense, especially when he was this close.

'And at this stage,' Nick added, looking clear into her eyes. 'Let's not rule out any possibilities.'

'Sounds good to me.' She was already imagining the possibilities. After all, Australia was only a day's plane flight away.

Her unhelpful conscience nagged that perhaps she should clear up the tiny white lie about her army career and get everything out on the table, but before she could find the right words, Nick skirted around the counter to be closer, and he was drawing her into his arms.

'Have I told you exactly *why* you're the only woman I've wanted to make love to?'

Lucy's heart began to bang unevenly. 'Because I'm unquestionably the hottest thing on two legs?'

His dark eyes shone as he smiled at her. 'That's a very accurate start, although I'd like to go into more detail later, but for now —'

He drew her closer still and she lifted her arms around his neck. Their kiss was both intimate and stirring, turning quickly to fire, melting her worries.

One step at a time, she told her conscience.

25

A loud blast ripped through the morning stillness.

Lucy woke, her heart thumping, and her first thought was *hit the ground* – the order for any trained soldier in the face of a rocket attack.

In one fluid motion, she shoved the bed covers aside and rolled to the floor as another blast sounded. Then another.

She fumbled in the dark. *Where the hell is my weapon?* Panic strafed through her, white hot.

'Where's my pistol?' she cried, feeling on the floor for the holster. It should have been there. Right beside the bed.

'Lucy, what's the matter?'

'I can't find my pistol.'

'Your *what*?'

'My fucking pistol!'

'Lucy, for God's sake.'

She frowned. She was lying stock-still on the floor, her breath coming in fast pants, her body tingling with a familiar rush of adrenalin.

Something was wrong. Why hadn't she heard the sirens that

warned the base of incoming rockets?

Where were the shouted orders, the raised voices of her fellow soldiers?

A light came on.

Lucy blinked. On the wall in front of her hung a huge, gold-framed abstract painting that must have cost a fortune. Right beside her stood a king-size platform bed covered in black-and-cinnamon sheets. Nick Myatt's bed.

And there was Nick. In the bed. Sitting up, all wide shoulders and bare chest, his dark hair tousled and wild, and staring at her, shocked, as if she'd grown two heads.

Or perhaps he was staring at her as if she'd just hurled herself from his bed and dived to the floor in readiness for incoming rocket fire.

'It's only the local pheasant shooters,' he said.

'Pheasant shooters?'

'Yes, they're practising with clay targets at the moment, but they'll move off soon into the woods.'

Not Tarin Kowt, but Cornwall . . . and she was lying stark naked on the floor, her chest heaving as her panic subsided.

Small wonder Nick was looking at her so strangely.

The crack of another gunshot sounded, totally non-threatening now. It was obviously someone shooting nearby.

Out on the lawns.

A shooting party.

Friendly fire. Not the Taliban.

'Sorry about that,' she said, feeling all kinds of foolish as she hauled herself back onto the mattress. She rubbed at her knee. She'd banged it during her tumble to the floor and there would be a bruise for certain.

Nick was looking worried. 'Are you okay?'

'Sure.'

'Did you have a nightmare?'

'Sort of. I suppose I was still half asleep.' It *had* been a *very* late night.

'You were screaming about a pistol.'

'Yeah, I know. I'm sorry. I panicked when I thought I couldn't find it.'

'Couldn't find a *pistol*?'

Nick looked so shocked and bewildered, Lucy knew the time had come to explain. She gathered the sheet around her, pulling it over her breasts. It would be easier to talk if she wasn't quite so naked and exposed.

'For the past six months I've carried a weapon every day. It was part of my job, Nick. In the army.'

Horror joined the shock in his eyes. 'The army? You're a soldier?'

'Yes, I am.' She saw him flinch, saw his Adam's apple slide in his throat as he swallowed. 'I work in logistics.' There was no point in only telling him half the story. 'And I finished a deployment to Afghanistan just before Christmas. I'm on leave at the moment.'

Lucy had never heard Nick swear, but he swore now, colourfully and repeatedly and without restraint, as he leaped from the bed and strode across the room to snatch his jeans from the floor.

His movements were rough and angry as he pulled them on and, when he turned back to Lucy, his dark eyes held the torment she'd seen on the day he'd first told her about his brother. 'So, you're not just going back to Australia tomorrow.' He spoke coldly without any of his customary warmth. 'You're going back to the *army*.'

'Yes.'

'For God's sake.' He lifted his hand in a helpless, agitated gesture, ploughing tense fingers through his wild hair. 'You – you knew about Simon. I told you about him right at the start. Did you *never* think it worth mentioning that you'd served in Afghanistan?'

'I – I wasn't in the frontline.'

'That's splitting hairs. You were still a soldier in a war zone.'

'Yes, we were based in Tarin Kowt.'

For what felt like an uncomfortable age he stared at her, his expression both dismayed and puzzled, as he let this sink in.

'Why didn't you say something?' he said at last. 'Look at you. Look at what just happened. You're – suffering too. Shell shock. PTSD. What the hell are you doing here? You should be getting help.'

'Nick, I'm fine. I don't need a psychiatrist. We were assessed by a whole team of them in Dubai. And that was weeks ago. I know I'm fine. We were told to expect occasional uneasiness. What happened just now was a normal reaction.'

'You call that normal uneasiness? Screaming for a pistol?'

'I was sound asleep and there were gunshots outside and, for a moment or two, while I wasn't quite awake, I thought I was back in Afghanistan. That doesn't mean I have PTSD. Nick, you've been with me for most of this past week. I've been fine, haven't I?'

He dismissed this reasonable appeal with an angry shrug. 'God knows, I'm no judge. And I still don't understand how you could have kept this to yourself.'

With the benefit of hindsight, Lucy was asking herself the same question. It was clear her silence had really upset him and she couldn't have been sorrier. The very last thing she'd wanted was to cause him more pain. All she could do now was try to explain.

'I held off saying anything, *because* I knew you were very upset about your brother's death. I was trying to be sensitive. I didn't want to add to your distress.'

Nick's eyes narrowed. 'Were you ever going to tell me?'

'Yes, I was planning to.' Even to her ears this sounded weak now. 'I – I was waiting for the right moment.'

'And *this* is the right moment? *Now*? After —'

Nick didn't finish the sentence, but with another painful blast of clarity, Lucy knew what he was thinking.

After he'd taken her on tours of the region and wined and dined her. After he'd made beautiful, unforgettable love to her and talked about possibilities for the future . . .

'I'm so sorry, Nick.'

His grim, dark eyes locked with hers. 'Yes, so am I.' And with that, he left the room, striding off towards the kitchen without looking back, as if he wanted nothing more to do with her.

Aghast, Lucy watched him leave. She was sick with disappointment. With herself. With Nick. With the whole mess. Hell, Nick had a right be upset, but she didn't deserve outright *rejection*.

Surely he owed her a better hearing?

Immediately, she decided that of course he did. She couldn't just let him stomp off.

'Hey!' she called after him, and then, dragging a sheet free, she wrapped it around her, leaving it to trail like a train, as she hurried into the adjoining living space.

Nick was at the stove, setting an Italian coffee pot on the gas, and he turned stiffly, with clear reluctance, his expression bleak. He looked gorgeous, wearing nothing but jeans hanging low on his lean hips. The past few days and nights with him had been the happiest she'd ever known.

She had to put up a fight.

'Nick, can you at least give me a chance to try to explain?'

'I thought you had.'

It was true that Lucy didn't have a lot more to offer, but she had to try. She liked and respected this guy far too much to let things end this way.

'Okay,' she began, but her mouth was dry and she was forced to swallow and try again. 'I'm sorry I didn't tell you about the army right at the beginning. It's not something I normally hide. But when you told me about your brother's death, I could see how you felt about military types, and I guess – okay, maybe I was selfish – I wanted to stay in your good books.'

'You could have achieved that with a little honesty.'

'Yes. Obviously, I got it wrong. I've wanted to say something. I almost told you last night, but – but I left it too late.' To Lucy's horror, tears threatened.

She dragged in a deep breath, felt only slightly better, but knew she couldn't give up. Not yet. 'Just for the record,' she said. 'If we're talking about honesty, it took you a while to admit to the adoption business. And not long after that, you started kissing me senseless. It was a bit too late then for me to say, "Hey, by the way, I'm a soldier".'

His eyes flickered over her as she stood before him, wrapped in his bed sheet, but his expression remained scarily hard. 'That's where you're wrong, Lucy. That was exactly when you *should* have told me.'

'And what would have happened? Would you have stopped kissing me? Said a polite goodnight, and booted me out of your car?'

'Possibly.' Hands sunk into his jeans pockets, Nick looked away through the window and beyond, across the lawns, into the distance. He let out a heavy sigh. 'Probably.'

A chill skittered down Lucy's spine. It was so easy to see now that the army was a *huge* deal for him. If only she had spoken up before she made the crazy mistake of falling for him, but the falling had happened so quickly and so very completely.

Silence fell between them like a cold blanket of snow. She shivered.

Apparently, this was it. After everything she and Nick had shared this past week: after last night, which had been, without doubt, the best night of her life, Mr Perfect was dumping her, here in his kitchen.

Deja freaking vu.

Lucy couldn't hold back a groan. 'Damn you, Nick. I wasn't planning on falling for you. I've just been through a tough breakup. Seriously, I was all set to marry the guy.'

Her lips were trembling now and she felt her mouth pull out of shape, but she forced herself to go on. 'And here's the funny thing, *he* had a problem with my career choice, too. Different reasons from yours, but still —'

Suddenly it was too much. The fight was too hard. She had to stop before she broke down and made a blubbering fool of herself. But Nick was watching her with such pain in his eyes, she couldn't hold back her tears.

Embarrassed, she turned away and tugged a corner of the sheet free, so she could wipe her wet face.

'Lucy.'

She couldn't turn around. Didn't want to face him when she was such a mess.

His voice sounded close behind her. 'Lucy.'

'What?' she snapped, staring hard at her bare feet showing beneath the hem of the sheet.

'I do owe you an explanation for the way I've reacted. Why don't you get dressed? Have a shower, if you like. I'll make coffee and toast.' Reaching out, he gave her shoulder a tiny squeeze and perhaps it was pitiful of her, but she took it as a sign of encouragement.

In the bathroom, doubts crowded in once more. Despite the steady stream of hot water, Lucy felt as tense as a doctor's patient, expecting to hear potentially life-threatening news at any moment. She dressed quickly, pulling on her jeans, knee-high boots and cherry red sweater.

'That was quick,' Nick said when she reappeared. He was now wearing shoes and a rust-coloured shirt, but he wasn't smiling. 'I put everything on the coffee table.'

Lucy's nervousness deepened as they sat opposite each other. Nick leaned back in his chair and let his long legs relax, comfortably apart, but she sensed he was making a deliberate effort to appear at ease.

'The coffee's brewing, but it's almost ready to pour.' He offered her a plate of hot buttered raisin toast.

'Not just now, thanks.' She couldn't possibly eat. Her stomach was churning. She'd be sick.

Nick didn't take any toast either.

'So, my story,' he said carefully, letting his gaze link briefly with hers before fixing on the coffee pot that sat between them. 'I started dating this girl called Eleanor, while Simon was away in Afghanistan.'

Lucy remembered her name. It was the same woman Amelia Hartford had talked about. Eleanor from Truro.

'I really liked her and we got on very well,' Nick said. 'Things seemed to be getting serious and then, just before Simon was due home on leave, Eleanor told me she'd actually been out with my brother a few times before he was deployed. She'd slept with him.'

'Ouch,' said Lucy.

'Yes indeed,' Nick agreed. 'It threw me, I can tell you.' His expression was grim as he leaned forward and poured the coffee into two mugs – fancy matching mugs with a geometric design in black and green. Reaching over, he set a mug in front of Lucy. She murmured her thanks and he continued, grim-faced.

'Eleanor assured me that her liaison with Simon was casual and brief.' At this, Nick sighed. 'Anyway, soon after Simon got back from Afghanistan I took him aside and told him how things were, and he seemed perfectly cool about the whole thing.' His wide shoulders lifted in a shrug. 'So I continued to see her.'

There was a pause as he picked up his coffee cup and set it on the leather armrest of his chair and then he regarded Lucy steadily, without any of his usual warmth. 'It was only later that my parents and I realised how very badly disturbed Simon had been by the Afghanistan experience. And by then, while we were still trying to get him proper help, he – he had the fall.'

'I can't imagine how terrible that must have been,' she said softly.

'It's one of those unimaginable horrors that's impossible to describe.' Nick took a sip of his coffee, then held the mug in front of him, gripped it in two hands. 'He left no note, so we'll never know for sure, but Simon was well aware of the dangers of those particular cliffs so we could only assume it was suicide. It was a terrible time for us, and then, on top of my family's grief, Eleanor had a – a kind of breakdown.'

His jaw tightened as he struggled with the painful memories. 'Seemed she was overcome by guilt. Got it into her head that she had upset Simon and that she was a major part of the reason he died.' Another tense shrug. 'It became a huge issue between us and the only sensible thing, the only possible thing, was to break up. Eleanor moved away to Scotland.'

And Nick hadn't dated anyone else since, which meant the experience had shaken him very badly, Lucy thought glumly. Then she had come along and Nick had started to open up, to trust her with his emotions, until she'd revealed that she'd fudged the truth about her job. When that white lie was combined with the fact that her job involved the military – *whammo*. She'd hit some *very* raw nerves.

'I can see why you're so mad with me,' she admitted. 'I know honesty's important in any relationship, but after something like that you'd be . . .'

She let the sentence trail off. Couldn't think how to finish without shooting herself in the foot, and when Nick didn't respond, they both sat in uncomfortable silence, sipping at their coffee.

Far off in the distance, gunfire sounded.

'I wonder if they got a pheasant.' She needed to say something – *anything*.

'They'll have dozens already.' Nick made no attempt to elaborate.

Lucy drained her coffee mug and set it down, and wondered, sadly, if this was the end of their conversation. 'That was lovely, thank you.'

'Would you like any toast?'

'No, thanks.'

He nodded grimly.

Feeling tenser than ever, Lucy sat forward on the very edge of the sofa.

Nick squared his shoulders and looked as miserable as she felt. 'Lucy, I'm sure you understand that I'd rather say goodbye now. There's really not much point. I – I mean, I can't go on seeing you.'

'That —' She had to swallow a sudden and extremely painful lump in her throat. 'That sounds very final.'

'I'm afraid it needs to be.'

'Even —' She didn't want to sound pathetic, but she couldn't help it. She liked this guy so much, *too* much, and he was ripping out her heart with his bare hands. 'Even though I work in logistics?'

'It's still the army.' The flat finality of his tone chilled her to the bone. 'Simon wasn't in combat either. He was a medical officer, and I've been told that non-combat soldiers are actually more susceptible to PTSD than the men in the frontline.'

Lucy knew this was true. It was to do with the initial screening. On the whole, soldiers who were recruited and trained for combat were more emotionally resilient and better equipped to handle the inevitable trauma of the battlefield.

'I'm sorry, Lucy,' Nick went on grimly. 'It wouldn't really matter if you were deployed, or based at home. I just don't know that I could support you in the way that I'd want to. And whenever I thought about you and your job, I'd be thinking about Simon, too.

Reliving it all. The fact that you've kept silent —' He gave a weary shake of his head. 'The whole issue is too big. Too dark.'

Funny how she could sit there, calm on the outside, while her insides imploded.

'Well then,' she said as steadily as she could. 'I'm sorry, too.' There was no point in trying to argue her case any further and she certainly wouldn't plead. 'I – I guess I'd better clear off and leave you to it.'

It was only when she tried to stand that she ran into trouble. Her knees were so weak that she stumbled. Luckily, she managed to right herself without sending her mug or the coffee pot flying.

Nick was also on his feet, reminding her of how tall he was. Tall and dark and heartbreaking . . .

Oh God, she had to stop thinking like that.

Just get out of here, Lucy.

'Well, thanks anyway,' she said glumly. 'You've been an amazing host and, even though this hasn't turned out for *us* —' She had to stop to take a steadying breath, which resulted in an embarrassingly noisy hiccup. 'It's been truly fabulous. And – and thanks for fixing me up with Primrose and – and everything.'

She couldn't talk about the important things that had passed between them. She needed to get out of there fast.

'I'll just get my bag and my jacket.'

Nick cast a bleak glance around the flat. 'Is there anything else?'

Lucy shook her head. She hadn't brought pyjamas or a toothbrush.

'You've got Primrose's photograph?'

'Yes.'

He walked her down the hallway and she silently prayed that he didn't say anything crass like wishing her a good flight.

To her relief, he didn't, but what he did was probably worse. At the door, he kissed her cheek, and then he lifted his thumb and gently, *sadly*, rubbed the place on her cheek where his lips had been. 'I can't pretend that I don't have regrets about this.'

'That doesn't help,' she said tightly, fighting a welling tsunami of tears, and then she turned and hurried quickly away, down the side of Penwall Hall, around the corner to the front of the house. There, she ran the full length of the drive, only slowing as she reached the doorway to the B&B.

Somehow, she managed to walk sedately through the reception area and to manufacture a smile as she greeted Jane Nancarrow, who was watching her with undisguised curiosity. Then she fled up the carpeted stairs, fumbled with the key to her room and, at last, had the door shut behind her.

Collapsing onto the bed, she buried her face into a pillow and gave way to a storm of sobbing. Her heart was breaking and she was angry, too. Angry with herself, with Nick, with the Fates that had dealt such a horrible, bitter blow.

Now she knew she was as unfortunate in love as her mother had been, when she had desperately hoped that she would be lucky, like George.

26

Kalkadoon. At last.

Georgina knew Harry was nervous when they finally pulled up in front of the homestead. He had no need to be worried, though. She was as fascinated and excited about arriving here at his outback home as she'd been when they sailed into Sydney Harbour and when they'd docked at the stunningly beautiful Hayman Island during their voyage up the Queensland coast, stopping off for a luxurious honeymoon on a white beach with palm trees and exotic, cool drinks served in coconut shells.

Today, throughout the long and often rough car journey inland, she'd been spellbound by the new landscape opening up all around them. This was Harry's country. Her husband had been born and raised here and this red earth and wide blue sky had shaped him into the man she loved.

And now, here she was at Kalkadoon. Georgina saw the tall timber house, one of many scattered buildings, and the enormous trees along the creek, casting long shadowy fingers over pale paddocks. It was almost dusk and the buildings and the land were tinged with the bronze glow of the sinking sun. As she drew in a eucalypt-scented breath of outback air, she felt the quiet grandeur of the landscape seep into her spirit, almost as if this ancient land were welcoming her into its timeless embrace.

'So, here you are,' Harry said, taking her hand and linking his fingers with hers. His mouth tilted into the lazy, charming smile she so adored. 'Welcome to Kalkadoon, Mrs Kemp.'

'Your home is beautiful, Harry.' She might have said more, but her emotions were running high and she didn't want to cry, so she kissed him, because she was so very happy and, because these days, she grabbed any chance she could to kiss her husband.

'I warned you it's nothing like Penwall Hall,' he said.

'I didn't cross hemispheres to see Penwall Hall.'

She looked more closely at the house. Standing high on wooden stumps, it had walls of timber planks, painted white and the roof was unpainted corrugated iron. It wasn't a big house and it was quite simple in design, but it looked roomy enough, with deep, invitingly shady verandahs. 'Okay, I'll bite,' she said. 'Why is your house up on stilts?'

'To make it cooler,' Harry told her. 'Air circulates under the floorboards.' He swallowed. 'The high stumps also keep it out of the floods.'

Floods? This was something Georgina had never considered. It was hard to believe the small creek they'd crossed on several occasions could swell and rise to spread all the way to here. 'Does it often flood?'

Harry gave a careful shrug. 'Maybe twice in a decade.'

'Then a house on stilts is very sensible.' To Georgina's surprise, the thought of floodwaters swirling beneath her floorboards was more fascinating than scary.

She looked about her again at the enormous sky, now streaked with deep orange and pink, at the wide paddocks of champagne-toned grass topped by feathery pink seed heads, at the creamy trunked trees that lined the creek and at the distant purple hills. 'I can't wait to explore this country properly on horseback.'

Harry's tense shoulders relaxed. 'Have I told you lately how much I love you?'

'Not in the last half hour.'

Their smiling lips met in another kiss that might have lasted quite a long and lovely time if a strange cackling burst of laughter hadn't sounded in the distance. Georgina pulled away in delighted astonishment. 'Is that a kookaburra?'

'Sure is.' Her husband's grey eyes sparkled, just as they had on the night they'd met when he'd imitated this amazing bird. 'Perhaps he's singing you a welcome.'

A young Aboriginal woman appeared at the top of the homestead steps. She had a mass of dark curls and was wearing a blue cotton dress with bare feet. Her teeth flashed white as she smiled a welcome. 'Hello, Boss. Welcome home.'

They ascended the wide wooden steps and Harry introduced the girl as Shirleen. 'Shirleen looks after the house,' he told Georgina. 'Especially the kitchen and the laundry.'

Georgina held out her hand. 'How lovely to meet you, Shirleen.'

'Pleased to meet you, Missus.'

The girl's eyes were deep chocolate and shy, but there was also pride in her expression.

Later, though, after Shirleen had served tea and biscuits on the verandah and then left them to enjoy the last of the daylight alone, Georgina said to Harry, 'You know I'm expecting to cook for us.'

His eyes widened. 'You don't have to.'

'But I'd like to. I've been looking forward to it. Why do you think I've brought a big, fat recipe book with me?'

They both laughed. She knew he was still worried about how she'd take to his lifestyle but she was also quite confident they'd sort something out.

'Time to bring the suitcases in,' Harry said when they'd finished their tea.

He fetched the bags, plus the precious rose plant in a pot that Georgina had carefully nurtured throughout the long voyage from England. He set the pot on a small cane table and carried the luggage through to the bedroom. 'Let's hope they've set it up properly,' he said as Georgina followed him along a central passage.

In the doorway to the bedroom he paused and waited for her to join him. She knew he was as excited and curious as she was. In Sydney, soon after they'd disembarked, he'd taken her to a big city department store called David Jones.

'We're going to buy everything new for our bedroom,' he'd said. 'Furniture, mattress, sheets, curtains. Whatever takes your fancy.'

They'd had a wonderful time shopping and Harry had everything shipped and delivered all the way up to north Queensland.

'What do you reckon?' he asked Georgina now.

And there it was, everything they'd chosen together, looking even prettier than it had in the Sydney display room. The bed with its carved walnut ends and new thick mattress, the bright chintz spread. The pair of matching walnut wardrobes against the far wall and, between the windows, the lovely glass-topped dressing table with a big round mirror and a little matching stool with a padded cushion.

Floral curtains matched the bedspread and, through the windows, Georgina could see a moon-swept view of the paddocks beneath the evening sky. She even heard the distant lowing of cattle.

Beaming, she turned to Harry. 'It's perfect, isn't it?'

He smiled again, making the skin around his eyes crinkle as he pushed the bedroom door closed with a booted toe, slipped his hands around her waist and drew her to him. '*You're* perfect.'

Her insides danced as she saw their reflection, across the room, in the dressing table's mirror. 'Look at us. The Boss and the Missus.

That's who we are now.'

But she lost her fascination with this image as Harry's hands moved to undo the buttons at the back of her dress.

Pushing the fabric aside, he pressed a sweet string of kisses along her bared shoulder.

Shivering with delicious anticipation, she said, 'I have a premonition that I'm going to be very happy here.'

Harry kissed the back of her neck. 'Are you prone to having premonitions?'

Her thoughts flashed to the day they'd met. 'Absolutely.'

27

Ro waited anxiously near the baggage carousel as she watched the passengers from Lucy's flight ride down the escalators. Unlike the last time she'd been here, there were no troops today, just a typical collection of travellers arriving in Townsville. Retired couples in elegantly casual resort wear, businessmen madly checking their phones, Scandinavian tourists with deep suntans, young mothers with fractious infants. Several travellers, coming from Sydney or Melbourne, were dressed too warmly for the tropical heat.

An elderly woman, on reaching the ground floor, spied her family and hurried forward, to be embraced around the knees by an excited little girl in a glittery pink tutu over a purple T-shirt and shorts.

Watching their joyful reunion, Ro felt a stab of envy. Other people seemed to have such normal, happy lives, while for her, true happiness seemed always to float temptingly, just out of reach. Today she was nervous, too, so anxious about her daughter's return that she almost hadn't come to the airport at all.

She'd heard very little news from Lucy while she was away, just the occasional bland text or email from her mobile phone, enquiring after Harry, hoping that all was well and sending her love to every-one, while reporting that she was fine and having a great time. No details. But Ro knew that her daughter had spent an entire week in Cornwall at Penwall Hall and she shuddered to think of the stories Lucy must have heard.

Had they told her *everything*?

However, when Ro spied Lucy at last at the top of the escala-tor, it wasn't fear or envy, but a pang of pure motherly love that speared her chest. Her daughter looked so tall and slim and beauti-ful. Dressed in blue jeans and long boots and a soft fluttery blouse of blue and cream, with her dark hair rippling to her shoulders and framing her pale oval face, she might have been a model or a TV star. Ro noted with quiet maternal pride that several masculine gazes swung in her daughter's direction.

As Lucy reached the glass sliding doors, she saw Ro waiting on the other side and they both waved and smiled. In a matter of moments they were hugging and greeting each other.

'It's so good to see you.'

'It's wonderful to be home. You look well, Mum.'

'Yes, I'm fine, thanks.'

'And Keith?'

There was a slight hesitation, which Ro tried to cover. 'He's well, too.'

'And, most importantly, how's Harry?'

'Don't worry, love. Harry's okay. As well as can be expected.'

Briefly, this almost felt to Ro like a perfectly normal, trouble-free family reunion. It was only as she released her daughter that her nervousness returned. She hoped it didn't show.

'How was the flight?' she asked.

Lucy groaned. 'Long.' She gave a little shake. 'Oh, I shouldn't complain, really. There were a couple of decent movies, but I was so glad to finally land in Cairns this morning.'

'At least you weren't coming home from a war zone this time.'

Her daughter's mouth curved in a faint, almost bitter smile. 'No.'

'And you had a wonderful holiday?'

'Yes, it was fine.'

This flat response brought Ro a fresh spurt of concern. Something wasn't right. Now that she looked more closely, she could see that Lucy was too pale, with none of her usual sparkle, and she had called her holiday fine, when her vocabulary was normally peppered with words like fantastic or fabulous or awesome.

The uneasiness stayed with Ro as they turned to the empty baggage carousel to wait for the first signs of luggage.

'The country's looking a lot greener,' Lucy said. 'Has it been raining?'

'It's been bucketing down. The usual story for January. The highway was cut at Ingham for nearly a week.' Ro added a cautious question. 'What was the weather like in Cornwall?'

'Cold and overcast a lot of the time. A few wild storms and rare patches of sunshine.'

Lucy said this while staring hard at the carousel where the first pieces of luggage had begun to appear. It was difficult to read her expression, but Ro still had the sense that her daughter was unusually subdued. Normally, Lucy wouldn't talk about the weather unless there was a cyclone. Something was wrong.

She quailed a little at this prospect, worrying about the possible causes.

'There's my bag!' Lucy pointed, murmuring her excuses as she jostled her way to the front of the crowd and hefted free a smart, silver hard-shell suitcase. 'Lucky we didn't have to wait too long,' she said as she returned to Ro.

'Yes.' Ro fished for her car keys in a pocket of her handbag. 'Let's go, then.'

Halfway across the car park, she said, 'Would you like to stop for coffee on the way home? Maybe somewhere on the waterfront with a nice view?'

'Oh?' Lucy looked surprised. 'Okay. I'm still feeling a bit spaced out, so coffee might help.'

The idea of a detour had just occurred to Ro, but it would give her a little breathing space and a chance to ask the necessary questions in relative privacy. It would also give her an opportunity to explain the latest changes that had occurred in her life while Lucy was away.

'I used to miss this view when I was in Afghanistan,' Lucy said, as they found seats at a table right on the water's edge.

From here they could see the entire sweep of Cleveland Bay. Sand and palm trees fringed the still, blue waters that dazzled in the sunlight and Magnetic Island, looking lush and very tropical, sat just offshore.

'I guess it's easy to take the view for granted,' Ro agreed, as soon as they'd given a waiter their orders. And then, a small nudge, 'But did you like Cornwall?'

'I did,' Lucy said perhaps a little too carefully. 'It's very atmospheric with all those coves and cliffs and quaint little cottages. So easy to imagine the smuggling days.'

'And Penwall Hall?' Ro had to ask. 'I suppose it's as grand as ever?'

'Oh, sure. Very grand. The whole estate is looking really beautiful. They've done it up, mainly for tourists, so it can pay its way.'

Such cautious answers! So out of character.

Ro waited for Lucy to add details. In the years gone by, her daughter had been very chatty. As a schoolgirl Lucy would come home overflowing with stories about everything that had happened inside and outside the classroom. Even as a teenager in high school, when other children became withdrawn and uncommunicative, her Lucy would sit at the kitchen counter as they cooked dinner together, peeling potatoes or chopping onions, while regaling her with accounts of liaisons and bust-ups among her friends, of gossip about her teachers or post-mortems of sporting events.

Half the time, Ro hadn't really listened. She'd just let Lucy rattle on. Even after she'd joined the army, Lucy had loved to chatter, so it was a complete turnaround to have to prise information from her.

'So, you must have met people from the family?' Ro prodded.

There was a brief flicker in Lucy's eyes. It might have been pain or sadness, but it came and went so quickly, Ro wondered if she'd imagined it.

Just then, the waiter arrived with their coffees. They thanked him and Ro added sugar to her cappuccino and carefully stirred, wishing now that she'd ordered the carrot cake, as well, even though Lucy hadn't wanted any.

Her daughter took a tentative sip of her long black and then sat, staring out to sea with a pensive little frown. 'Actually, I couldn't meet your cousin or his wife,' she said, turning back to Ro as she put her cup down. 'They were away in London the whole time I was there.'

'Oh. That's a – a pity. And Alice?'

'She died a few years ago.'

'Really? I hadn't heard.' Ro knew she shouldn't sound quite so relieved, but she couldn't help it. She'd been so tense. 'Not that I've kept in touch.'

'But I did meet one of your mother's good friends,' Lucy said. 'An old lady called Primrose.'

Ro blinked. 'Primrose Cavendish? Goodness, I'd almost forgotten about her. She was lovely as I remember.'

'She's still lovely, Mum. So sweet and thoughtful and she has very fond memories of you. It's a pity you couldn't have been there, actually. I had morning tea with her and she showed me so many photographs of Georgina when they were young. Did you know that Georgina and Primrose went to London and were presented to the King and Queen when they made their debuts?'

'Oh yes. The family loved telling me about that sort of thing. They were very lah-di-dah.'

'So I gathered. Primrose confirmed everything you've said about Georgina's sister. That letter in Harry's tin showed Alice's personality to a tee. Snobby, cold and insensitive.'

Ro shuddered as the particular memory she was trying to suppress jumped into her consciousness like a burst of shrapnel.

To her surprise, Lucy reached across the little table and squeezed her hand. 'Mum, I felt for you, being sent there when you were so young.'

'Yes, well . . .' Ro was lost for words. Lucy's reaction was so different from what she'd feared. Perhaps her darkest secrets hadn't been revealed after all.

She could actually feel the knots in her shoulders and stomach beginning to relax.

Lucy smiled again. 'Primrose told me you used to escape to her place whenever you could and you stuffed yourself with her saffron cake.'

'Oh yes.'

'And look.' Picking up her shoulder bag, Lucy undid one of the zipped inner pockets. 'She gave me this photograph, too. It's for you, Mum. She wanted you to have it.'

Lucy pressed a small, aged, black-and-white snapshot into her hand and Ro gasped as she saw the dearly beloved, almost-forgotten face of her mother holding a gurgling infant. Such a fine, good-looking woman, with lovely smooth wavy hair and such a clear, intelligent gleam in her eyes, a hint of inner strength.

If only I could have known you, she thought.

And there, too, in the photograph's background was the long flat stretch of sun-bleached paddocks, complete with an iconic outback windmill. Kalkadoon. The childhood home that had become almost as mystical and perfect in Ro's imagination as the legendary Camelot.

'That baby must be me, I suppose,' she said in a choked voice.

'Of course it's you, Mum. Look at the eyes and the smile. That's *your* smile.'

'I guess.'

Ro looked at her tiny self. Such a happy, cheeky-looking baby she'd been. Perhaps, if her mother hadn't died when she was only five, she might have grown up feeling so much better about herself.

'Primrose thinks I have the same smile,' Lucy said.

'Does she?' Ro found herself touching her fingertips to her lips, testing their shape.

'It was the first thing she said when she saw me.'

'Goodness.' And suddenly Ro was awash with unexpected emotion. She'd been so braced for Lucy to return with her head filled with criticisms and horror stories about her.

'Primrose gave me a couple of letters, too,' Lucy said. 'Including one Georgina wrote when you were a baby that I know you're going to love. But I'll save them for when we're back at the apartment so you can read them in privacy.'

At the mention of the apartment, Ro was hit by a slam of panic. 'Actually, there's something I need to explain about the apartment.'

Lucy frowned. 'Oh?'

'I – I've moved out, love. I'm staying with your grandfather now.'

'Really?' Lucy couldn't have looked more shocked if Ro had announced that she'd moved in with George Clooney. She frowned. 'How come? I thought you said Harry was fine.'

'Well yes, he's pretty good, for the moment,' Ro hedged. 'But we know he's going to deteriorate.'

'Crikey.' Lucy let out her breath in a surprised huff. A beat later, her eyes narrowed shrewdly, as if she wasn't buying this news. 'It's – it's hard to imagine you living with Harry.'

'I know, but we're rubbing along okay.' Defensively, Ro added, 'He needs someone to cook and clean for him, and I didn't really like to leave him to Blue Care and Meals on Wheels.'

'Well, that's great, I guess, but you —'

Lucy gave a dazed shake of her head and Ro held her breath, hoping her daughter wasn't going to ply her with too many questions.

Unfortunately, Lucy's eyes narrowed again and another shrewd light flickered. 'How does Keith feel about this?'

Trying hard not to squirm, Ro picked up her coffee spoon. 'He's a bit disappointed, but he understands.' She concentrated on scraping foam from the sides of her cup, but she didn't miss her daughter's heavy sigh. 'You can still stay at the apartment, Lucy. I've spoken to Keith and he's expecting you.'

'But won't that be a bit weird? Just me and your boyfriend? Mum, *you* should move back with Keith. You love it there. I can move in with Harry. I'd be happy to.'

'But you have to go back to work soon.'

'Not for another week and, even then, I would have to cook and clean wherever I lived, so it wouldn't make much difference. And Blue Care can still check on Harry during the day.'

Ro's tension spiralled, making her chest burn. Trust Lucy to be so logical and willing.

Carefully, she slipped the precious photograph into her handbag and then felt among the jumble of pens and receipts at the bottom of the bag for a roll of antacids.

As Lucy watched her peel away the foil, she said, 'Mum, everything's okay with you and Keith, isn't it?'

It was another question Ro had been dreading. She waited till she'd chewed and swallowed before she replied. 'I – I'm not sure.'

'Oh no, Mum. God, no.' There was a shocking, almost despairing edge to Lucy's cry. 'Keith's the loveliest man. You can't have found something wrong with him already. I'm sure he's steady, a salt of the earth type.'

'I know.' *That's the problem.*

Ro pressed her lips together, trying to stop the tremble. It was too hard to explain this, especially to her daughter. 'I don't want to talk about it, Luce. Maybe later, but not now, when you've just got off the plane. You should at least use the apartment today. Keith's at work. You can have the place to yourself. He's fine with you using it. Catch up on some sleep and we'll sort the rest out later.'

Lucy didn't seem happy about this, but if she was moved to speak up, she must have thought better of it. Instead, with another anxious and searching glance in Ro's direction, she drained the last of her coffee.

Grateful for her daughter's silence, Ro hastily changed the subject. 'So, you haven't said whether you met anyone else from the Myatt family. Were either of the sons still living there?'

A fresh furrow formed between Lucy's eyebrows and, to Ro's surprise, she stared hard at her empty cup, almost as if she found this simple question extremely difficult to answer.

'One of the sons, Simon, died,' she said quietly. 'He was in the army, in Afghanistan, and he came home with PTSD. It – it was suicide. A complete tragedy for the family.'

'That's terrible. I'm so sorry to hear that.' Ro said this sincerely. Suicide was always so very distressing and she knew Lucy would be especially upset about the circumstances of this young man's death. But what a coincidence that he was in the army, too.

Lucy's face was still tight and for a long moment she continued to stare at her coffee cup, as if she was struggling with painful thoughts, but when she looked up again, she seemed quite composed.

'Did you know that your mother was also in the army?'

'Was she really?'

Lucy nodded. 'In the Second World War. In England. She was in the Royal Army Service Corps, so it was her job to help get supplies to the frontlines.'

Ro gasped. 'Just like you?'

'I know. It's a strange coincidence, isn't it? But then Georgina came out here and she was caught up in New Guinea when the Japanese were there.'

'Good heavens. Is that when she met Harry?' Ro felt a bit shame-faced, having to ask this.

'No. That happened in England beforehand. In London.'

There was so much about her parents that she didn't know. It was wrong, wasn't it? Ro had always blamed her father. Harry had claimed that he didn't like talking about the past, but Ro knew she was in part responsible. She'd been so caught up with her own prob-lems that she hadn't really taken enough interest.

Lucy finished her coffee and appeared restless now. She picked up her shoulder bag, as if she was ready to leave.

'So what about the other son?' Ro asked, as she pushed back her chair. Surely, Lucy must have met *someone* from the family to get all this news.

Lucy stood abruptly. 'The eldest son, Nick, was there,' she said as she concentrated on checking the contents of her bag. 'He showed me around the place and organised the contact with Primrose.'

'That was kind of him.'

'Yes.' Lucy's face was tight, her lips compressed.

Puzzled, Ro could only assume that something had gone wrong. She supposed Simon Myatt's death had cast a pall over everything. Perhaps it had really impacted on her daughter. After all, they had both served in Afghanistan.

The path back to the car took them beneath sea almond trees, where black cockatoos squabbled and squawked, and now it was the photo Lucy had brought that recaptured Ro's thoughts. She couldn't wait to take it out and look at it again.

She wanted to study her mother's face and her baby self and try hard to remember those precious, perfect few years at Kalkadoon, the best years of her life.

28

In Kalkadoon homestead's smallest bedroom, Georgina was day-dreaming, imagining the room repainted and decorated with new curtains. A soft buttercup would be nice. And lovely new furniture with perhaps a rocking chair, and a standard lamp in the corner.

They were very fortunate to have electricity in the outback. Harry had been anxious to make her life as comfortable as possible and, quite early on, he'd installed a special generator and a bank of big batteries to power lighting and the ultimate luxury, fans.

Now, as she pictured white dimity curtains fluttering at the window, footsteps sounded in the hall.

'So, this is where you've got to.'

Georgina turned, flashing a quick, happy smile as she hurried to greet her tall cattleman with a kiss. 'I didn't hear your horse.' Most evenings, if she hadn't joined Harry on horseback to help in the pad-docks, she would be on the front verandah, doing a little sewing or shelling peas, while keeping an ear out for his return. 'Has it been a long day?'

'A good day's mustering. I reckon we've cleared all the clean-skins out of the scrub at Redcliff.'

'Oh, that's wonderful then.' She knew the task wasn't finished yet. Harry and the ringers would still have to brand and dip the cattle they'd rounded up, and then separate the weaners from their mothers, as well as drafting off the animals to be sold. For now, though, the cattle were penned and that was the main thing. 'You must be ravenous. Dinner's ready in the oven.'

Harry's bright glance rested on the tape measure in her hand. 'What have you been plotting in here?'

'Oh . . .' She had promised herself she would wait till Harry was washed and fed before she shared her exciting secret, so she said, 'I was thinking that next time we're in the Isa I might buy a tin of paint and give this room a facelift.'

'But we hardly use this room.'

'That doesn't mean we should neglect it.'

He shrugged, gave her a fond smile and kissed the tip of her nose. 'I certainly won't argue. Not after the bonzer paint job you did in the kitchen.'

'Good.' Georgina was very proud of the fashionable cream and green kitchen she'd created. 'Now, wash up. There's a steak and kidney pie tonight.'

'I know. I could smell it as I was coming up the stairs.' Harry rubbed his stomach, still lean and taut after nearly a decade of marriage, thanks to the long days of hard physical work on the station. 'You couldn't have chosen a better night for it. I'm starving.'

Georgina smiled. This pie was Harry's favourite. 'I'll go and mash the potatoes.'

They would eat in the kitchen and she had already set the table, going to special trouble this evening with a freshly ironed tablecloth and a small vase of pink rosebuds from the precious plant she'd brought from England, having then nurtured it through the blazing hot summers and sometimes-frosty winters.

It had taken her a while to adjust to the seasons of northern

Australia. There were only two – the wet and the dry – but she'd soon learned that the rain brought relief from the hot steamy summer, either in a series of spectacular afternoon thunderstorms or with heavy, drenching monsoons.

And the dry seasons, the winters, were stunning with pretty white mists rising from the river in the mornings, followed by crisp, clear, cloudless days, while the frosty evenings brought endless skies that blazed with a million bright stars.

Georgina loved how life on the land revolved around the seasons – mustering in the autumn and winter and calving in the spring, hand-feeding when necessary, if the summer rains were late. She grew vegetables and raised chickens and did most of the cooking, but she was very grateful for Shirleen's help with the general cleaning and laundry and with catering on the occasions that she and Harry threw a party at Kalkadoon.

The social life in the outback had been a surprise. People thought nothing of travelling a hundred miles to attend a party or a ball, then sleeping overnight on stretchers lined along the homestead verandahs. These events were always so much fun, with plenty of dancing and laughter and a wonderfully playful sense of revelry. Graziers and their wives were hardworking, but they also really knew how to kick up their heels and celebrate.

The only true, and at times quite desperate, sadness for Georgina had been her inability to have children and, although Harry had never admitted it, she knew this lack weighed heavily on him as well. But there was always an upside, and for Georgina it was that, over the years, she and Harry had developed a strong sense of partnership. The Kalkadoon cattle station was a joint venture. Now that she understood the industry they made important decisions together and, when the mustering team took off to spend weeks at a time in the outer extremities of their vast property, Georgina usually joined them. Covered up, wearing a broadbrimmed hat tied on with a big cotton scarf, a man's long-sleeved shirt and cotton gloves, she'd loved riding on horseback, cooking on an open fire and camping out under the stars.

At first, Harry had been terribly anxious about her taking part in these musters, but it wasn't long before he'd realised she was completely at home and enjoyed the outdoor work almost as much as he did.

Even so, she didn't mind in the least that her involvement with this outdoor work would change now, after she told him her news.

The light in the kitchen was a mellow glow, while outside the bush was consumed by inky black night, and insects and moths buzzed and fluttered against the window screens. Harry ate two helpings of the steak and kidney pie, then Georgina made a pot of tea, which they drank while listening to the evening news on the wireless.

More Australian soldiers were being brought home from Korea. The test cricketers were having a tough time against the spin bowlers in England, while other Australian athletes were training hard for the Olympic Games to be held in Melbourne later in the year.

The news finished and Georgina turned off the wireless, but rather than taking their cups and saucers to the sink, she sat down again. The excitement she'd been holding in for days was rushing through every vein and close to bursting point now. She hadn't wanted to say anything until she was quite sure, but each day she'd been growing more confident, and now, she couldn't contain her news a moment longer.

Nevertheless, she spoke as calmly as she could. 'Harry, I was wondering when you're planning another trip into the Isa.'

'To buy paint?' he asked with an amused smile.

'Not just to buy paint. I'd like to see the doctor.'

His smile faded. 'Do you feel sick?'

'A little.' Beneath the table, her hands were so tightly clasped she could feel her nails digging into her palms.

Harry couldn't keep the worry from his eyes. 'Why didn't you tell me, George? What's the matter? What's going on?'

'Well, I missed my period last month and again this month, and my breasts have been very tender and I've lost my breakfast for the past three mornings in a row.'

Harry stared at her, his expression a complicated mix of concern, bewilderment and dawning hope.

'You don't think? Is – is it possible?'

'I think it might be,' she said. 'I mean, it's hard to believe after all this time, but —' She gave him her warmest, most encouraging smile – the poor man looked so desperately worried. 'It feels very real, Harry. I think it's happening this time. That's why I'd like to see a doctor.'

'Of course.' Harry was out of his chair. 'I'll get you there as soon as possible. We'll leave first thing in the morning.'

'Not until you've finished with the cattle.'

'Bugger the cattle.' Gently, he drew her from her chair and into his arms, holding her close against his chest.

She heard his heartbeats, as thumping and excited as her own.

'The stockmen can look after the cattle,' he said. 'I plan to take care of my wife.'

It was late in the afternoon.

Warm sunlight slanted through the blinds onto the neat white bed in the small, private hospital room where Georgina, propped by pillows, held her brand new baby in her arms.

Such a miracle, this tiny, perfect little girl with dark hair and neat little ears and the sweetest knowing face.

Already, the astonishing ordeal of giving birth was beginning to fade, rendered unimportant by the triumph of her baby's safe arrival. Georgina just wanted to stare and stare, and to cherish the warm weight of the little bundle wrapped in flannelette, now stirring in her arms.

A knock at the door and her heart leaped as Harry appeared, his damp hair neatly combed, clutching a bright bouquet.

'Hey there,' he said as he stepped cautiously into the room. 'They tell me I have a daughter.'

'Harry, come quickly. Come and look at her. She's *beautiful!*' Eagerly, Georgina patted the space beside her. Her heart stumbled when he neared the bed and she saw the silver sheen of tears in his eyes.

'Oh, darling.' Her voice cracked as she reached for his hand. 'I know, I know. It's just too good to be true, isn't it?'

Now tears were spilling down her cheeks, too, and for a moment, they could only sit there, their foreheads pressed together, gazing at their baby as they wept.

'What a pair we are.' George was smiling through her tears as Harry produced a clean handkerchief and she mopped at her eyes.

'I was so scared,' he said.

'Captain Harry Kemp was scared?'

'You bet. You have no idea what it was like to watch you disappear through those blasted doors and then to be left to pace the floor.'

'Poor darling.' Georgina could imagine how he'd hated the waiting. Harry was a man of action, a take-charge kind of fellow. To be so very worried and yet utterly helpless would have been agony for him. 'But look,' she said, unwrapping a layer of blanket so he could see their baby properly. 'Look at our little girl. Isn't she just the sweetest thing?'

'She's perfect,' he said, his face soft with awe. 'So tiny.'

'She's seven pounds. It's a good weight.'

Tentatively, he touched the baby's tiny hand and they both gasped with amazement as the little pink fingers opened like a flower and then curled and clung to his rough brown finger.

'Like a monkey on a tree branch,' he said.

'Isn't she clever?'

'As clever as paint.'

'And so pretty, like a perfect little rose.'

'Maybe we could call her Rose.'

It was one of the many names they'd talked about over the months of waiting, when they'd both declared fervently that they didn't mind in the least whether the baby was a boy or a girl.

'Yes, I think Rose might suit her.'

Just then, their daughter opened her eyes, blinked twice, then squirmed and gave a small squawk as she turned to nuzzle at Georgina's chest.

'Looks like she's hungry,' Harry said.

Georgina felt a flash of panic. 'Do you think so?'

'Have you fed her yet?'

'No. I was told to wait for the nurse to come back.'

Amusement shone in her husband's grey eyes. 'You don't need a nurse to show you what to do.'

Georgina supposed this was true, but from the minute she'd entered the hospital, people had started telling her how to breathe and what position to lie in and she'd become strangely compliant.

'Here,' said Harry. 'I'll hold her while you get yourself organised.'

'You think I should just go ahead and feed her?'

'Why not? You're her mother.'

It sounded so logical coming from Harry.

Their daughter looked tinier than ever in his arms as Georgina undid buttons on her nightgown and opened the nursing brassiere.

'I reckon, just hold her close and see if she knows what to do,' Harry said, when Georgina was ready.

Which was exactly what she tried and it was also how, within a matter of moments, their daughter latched onto her breast and began to suck lustily.

Georgina grinned. 'Isn't she clever? She knows just what to —'

'What are you doing, Mother?' a shocked voice demanded from the doorway.

The red-faced nursing sister was fuming as she stormed into the room. 'You were instructed to wait, to be shown how to feed your baby properly.'

'She seemed hungry.'

'That's for me to decide.' The sister scowled at Georgina over the top of her spectacles. 'Is Baby properly attached?'

'I believe so.'

Peering more closely, the nurse pursed her lips. 'You were lucky this time but, Mother, you can't feed your baby whenever you like. You have to follow a proper feeding regime and a very strict schedule.'

Georgina was feeling braver now and she merely smiled without replying.

With a harrumph, plus a glare for Harry and a warning that she would be back in ten minutes, the nurse sailed back out of the room, her veil flying stiffly behind her.

'I might have turned you into a rebel,' Harry said apologetically.

'I don't care,' Georgina told him. 'I can't wait to get home and to care for our little one without being bossed around.'

Several minutes later, she held out the blanketed bundle. 'Here, have another cuddle of your daughter, before they come back and boot you out.'

Harry's face was softened by instant tenderness as he gazed down at the baby. 'Hey there, Rosie,' he said gently. 'Did you know that your mum is a brave and beautiful headstrong rebel?'

With a cheeky grin, he sent Georgina a wink. 'And I won't mind in the least if you turn out just like her.'

29

The last thing Lucy needed was a day to herself, pacing about in an empty apartment. She'd had more than twenty hours on a plane with only her misery for company and throughout the flight, her thoughts had chased each other as fruitlessly as a puppy chasing its own tail. Of course her thoughts had been all about Nick.

Losing him had been the most unbearable experience of her life. She knew this didn't make sense given how brief their time together had been, but she was a mess. She longed to be back there in Cornwall with him, riding on horseback, or walking together and having her hair blown to bits on the windy cliffs at Kynance Cove. She wanted to be back in The Seaspray Arms with its low-beamed ceiling and crackling fire, enjoying a meal, just the two of them in a snug alcove.

She'd spent hours torturing herself by recalling every single one of Nick's special qualities, as well as those times when he'd looked deep into her eyes and she'd felt as if she could read his soul.

Now, just thinking about him, her heart soared and swooped like a kite in a gale.

But annoyingly, just when she really needed her mother's

company, Ro was abandoning her. She didn't even come into the apartment, but pulled up the car outside and handed her a key, leaving Lucy on the footpath. It didn't make sense. Just last month her mum had been so proud of her new apartment and proud of Keith.

What on earth could have gone wrong in such a short space of time? Lucy wanted to give her a shake. Shake some sense into her. How could she just walk away from everything she'd ever wanted?

Lucy vowed she would get to the bottom of this. Later. When the jetlag fog had lifted.

'I'll give you a call late this afternoon,' Ro said. 'But I'd better get back to your grandfather now to fix his lunch.'

'Give him my love.'

'Yes, of course.'

'Perhaps I'll come round later to see him.'

'All right. But give me a ring first.'

'Oh, before you go, here are those letters that Primrose wanted you to have.' Lucy extracted the precious envelopes carefully from her bag. 'There's one written by Georgina and another from Harry, so perhaps you should wait to read them when you have a little time on your own.'

'Okay. Thanks, love.' Her mum looked a little flushed as she set them on the seat beside her. Then, with a wave of silver bangles, she took off. Her purple Hyundai disappeared around a corner, and Lucy wheeled her suitcase to the huge glass doors that fronted the apartment block's foyer, found a swipe tag attached to the keys and used it, and the doors slid open. She rode the lift to the eighth floor and let herself in.

The apartment was as spotless as ever. Keith was clearly very neat and tidy, and the only thing out of place was a piece of paper left on the kitchen counter. When she looked at it more closely, Lucy realised it was a note that Keith had left for her.

Dear Lucy,

Welcome back and please make yourself at home. Sleep, watch TV, or use the pool on the roof. I'll be home about six and I'll bring something for dinner.

Till then, all the best,

Keith

Lucy read the note twice and frowned. It sounded so nice and normal, as if nothing was wrong. And on the surface, her mother's moving out might *not* be a problem. It wasn't entirely unbelievable that her mum might move into Harry's place, because his health was failing, especially as the sad reality was that her help might only be needed for a few months.

And yet, something about this still didn't gel. Lucy knew her mum. All her life she'd been aware of the tension that had plagued Ro's relationship with Harry, never boiling into outright warfare, but never allowing them the closeness that you might expect between a father and his only child.

But it was even more surprising that Ro had so willingly left her brand new apartment and her brand new man.

Every aspect of this new scenario was puzzling.

———

Kalkadoon Station
via Cloncurry
10 September 1966

Dear Primrose,

I am writing to you with an important request, but first I need to explain my situation. I have finally decided that I must send my darling little Rosie away from us here at Kalkadoon to live in England with Georgina's family.

I've had to make tough decisions in the past, especially during the war when men's lives were in my hands, but this decision has been the hardest. It breaks my heart to give her up, Primrose. Having lost my dearest George, I can't bear the thought of losing Rosie as well, but after five years of raising her on my own, I feel the time has come to put my own needs aside and to think of my daughter's future.

Rosie is ten now and growing fast. She is happy and healthy and loves the life here in the bush, but I know she's quite a tomboy, with few refined manners, and I'm sure she needs more guidance than I can offer as a single father in the outback. Within the next year or so, she will need a woman's wisdom and understanding.

I would like her to attend a good school, too. She's a bright little spark, but I have found it hard to keep governesses at Kalkadoon for long. These women are invariably very young and they find the life out here lonely. They usually leave after six months or so, and I'm sure there are glaring gaps in Rosie's education.

Of course, I could send her to boarding school in Australia. I attended quite a good school in Brisbane, but I can't overlook all the other opportunities that life at Penwall Hall can offer her.

I suffer from enough guilt already, knowing that I dragged Rosie's mother away from her family and from a life of comfort and privilege. Mind you, George always assured me that she was very happy here and, in my heart, I know that she was, which is some comfort. But my wife made the decision to come here as a fully informed adult. Little Rosie has had no choice but to live here, and she has no idea what the rest of the world has to offer or what might be best for her.

Here, the only adults to advise her are my housekeeper, Shirleen, and I – and I'm often away working on the extreme

*boundaries of the property. Rosie's best friend is Shirleen's son,
Dougie, a young boy, and while he's a fine little kid, she needs
girlfriends, too. In England she will have a grandmother and
an aunt, an uncle and cousins, who are all, I have been told
repeatedly, quite anxious to embrace her as their own. They
will also send her to a good girls' school where she'll be able to
make a host of girlfriends.*

*I love Rosie too much to deprive her of this chance to be
educated in England and to live with her mother's family, and
now that she's old enough to understand my motives, I can no
longer deny her this wonderful opportunity.*

*But Primrose, this decision breaks my heart. My little
girl means everything to me. She has such a sparkling, joyous
spirit. My life will be so dull without her – but at least my
conscience will be clear.*

*Which brings me to my request. I know our acquaintance
has been limited to those few memorable afternoons that
George and I spent with you in Cornwall, but I've never
forgotten your warmth and friendliness and I would really
appreciate it if you could manage to see my little girl from time
to time.*

*I know you are busy with your own farm, and I understand
that you can't intervene in the Myatt family's handling of
Rosie, but I also know from firsthand experience that they
can be rather stuffy. Rosie may find them oppressive at first,
and I think she might need a bolthole to escape to every now
and again. I hope you don't mind my asking this and I look
forward to hearing your thoughts.*

*In the meantime, I send my very warmest regards,
Harry Kemp*

Afternoon sunlight filtered through the kitchen windows, giving Ro just enough light to read by as she sat at Harry's ancient scrubbed pine table. From down the hallway she could hear his gentle snores. He was taking his afternoon nap, and the purring sound provided a surprisingly soothing background as she read the letters from her parents that Lucy had brought home.

Read them. And read them again, with tears streaming down her face.

Now there was a pile of damp tissues beside the letters on the table and Ro's emotions were overflowing, her eyes damp and blurry, her throat tight and raw.

She'd wept buckets while reading these letters, both beautiful outpourings of love from each of them.

She'd lingered over every word from her mother.

When I'd just about given up all hope of ever becoming a mother, I have this sweet, loving, little daughter.

And then, the heart-rending message from her father.

My darling little Rosie . . . It breaks my heart to give her up.

I suffer from enough guilt already, knowing that I dragged Rosie's mother away from her family.

Today it was Ro who felt guilty. During the many years since her father had written this letter, she'd brought him a truckload of worry and pain. And now, looking back, she knew very well that this wasn't the first time she'd encountered Harry's explanation for sending her to England.

He'd tried to talk to her about it on many occasions after she'd been sent home in disgrace at the age of seventeen, but she'd been so caught up in despair and her burning awareness that he'd broken his word to her by sending her away. She'd never really listened to Harry, had certainly never believed him, and now, too late, she could see the inescapable evidence – the love of *both* her parents here on the pages in front of her. In black and white. In their own precious handwriting.

My darling little Rosie.

This decision breaks my heart.

Ro's lips trembled again, her eyes welled with tears and she reached for yet another tissue.

'Ro, what's the matter?'

She hadn't heard her father's shambling footsteps coming down the hall and she was startled when he suddenly appeared at the kitchen doorway. Stoop-backed, he shuffled into the room, saw the letters and the old photograph on the table, saw the pile of sodden tissues and his daughter's face which was, no doubt, red and blotchy.

'What is that? Have you had bad news?'

'No, Dad, no.'

'What have you got there?' He pulled out a chair and sat down stiffly.

'Letters,' Ro said. 'Letters from you and from Mum. Lucy brought them back.'

'From Penwall Hall?'

'No, from Primrose Cavendish.'

'Really? Fancy Primrose keeping them all this time.'

Ro nodded. 'I'm so glad she did.'

He held out a brown, knobbly hand. 'Can I see them?'

'Yes, of course.' Ro pushed the thin pages across the table to him, then scooped up the tissues and took them to the rubbish bin. She felt emotionally exhausted and yet strangely cleansed, as if she could now see her life more clearly.

Looking at her elderly, frail father, she remembered how tall and broad shouldered he'd once been. When she was little he'd been her magnificent hero and she felt a fierce rush of love.

Quickly followed by shame.

Harry looked up from the letters, his long, thin face topped by snow-white hair and his grey eyes glittering damply behind his glasses. 'Your mother was so excited when you were born. We both were.'

'Yes, I could feel it just reading her letter.'

'You were the light of our lives.' With a fond smile, Harry picked up the photo Primrose had sent. 'Do you remember her?'

'Yes.' Ro breathed deeply to hold back a threatening sob. 'I remember the way she used to read me stories like *Winnie the Pooh* and tuck me into bed. And I know I used to love her perfume.'

Harry smiled. 'Moonlight Mist. I used to send away to Sydney for a bottle every year for her birthday.'

'Really? I loved that scent. I can't remember exactly how it smelled, but I know it was cool and flowery. And I remember how we used to sit together on the front steps and watch you come riding home on your horse.'

'And then you would practically break your neck rushing down the stairs to meet me.'

Ro nodded, her mind swirling with memories now. 'You'd lift me up to sit in the saddle and sometimes you'd put your hat on my head and it was so big it covered my eyes.' She tried to smile but it was a very shaky and tear-blurred attempt. Another tissue was necessary.

'Do you remember when we got you your own pony?' Harry asked. 'And the three of us went riding together?'

'I think so. Did we go down along the riverbank? Was there a track?'

'Yes, a cattle pad through the pandanus.'

Ro nodded. 'That's right. And the track took us under those big trees with low weeping branches.'

'River paperbarks.'

A small silence fell as they sat there in the shabby old kitchen, lost in the mists of their memories. Ro could hear the ticking of the clock on the dresser and the shrill sound of children's voices in a neighbour's backyard.

'Do you regret not staying out there at Kalkadoon, Dad? You loved it. You loved the bush.'

His bony shoulders lifted as he shrugged.

And then, because the guilt was nagging at her, 'I know you left because of me. You were worried sick about me when I came home from England.'

'Of course. You were so unsettled, and still so young.'

'And I refused to go back to Kalkadoon.'

She had been at her angriest and most rebellious when she came home from England and she hadn't wanted anything to do with her past life. So her father had moved to Townsville. 'You gave it all up for me.'

And there it was. An admission she'd never been able to voice was finally out in the open.

'It wasn't such a huge sacrifice, Ro. I was ready for a change after all those years in the bush. And then your little Lucy came along. I wouldn't have missed that time for quids. I've loved watching her grow. You've done such a good job with her.'

Genuinely shocked, Ro let out a gasp. 'You think so? Really?'

'Of course. Lucy's an amazing young woman. That didn't happen on its own.'

'But – but I always thought I was a hopeless mum. I thought Lucy just inherited a strong sense of herself from you, or maybe from Mum.'

'Lucy does remind me of George,' Harry admitted. 'But you put a huge effort into raising her, and it was mostly on your own. That can't count for nothing.'

Ro was so used to thinking of herself as a failure this new perspective was going to take a while to sink in.

Harry tapped the second letter, the one he'd written. 'This is my only regret,' he said sadly. 'I got it wrong, didn't I, love? When I sent you to England, I thought you were old enough to understand. But I was never very good at explaining myself, not in conversation.' He lifted a trembling hand to adjust his glasses. 'Your mother used to tease me about it. Called me her man of few words.' He blinked. 'But that's no excuse. I'm so sorry.'

'Oh, Dad.' Ro knew she couldn't let him shoulder the blame. She'd been letting him do that for too long. She'd convinced herself that she was unloved – unlovable – and, as a result, unsuccessful in her life and in her relationships. But now the truth she'd denied was reaching out and grabbing her by the throat. Of course her father loved her. He'd *always* loved her.

Deep down, she supposed she'd known this, but she'd never accepted it. It was easier to tell herself lies and it was hard to kill those wrong ideas once they'd made their home inside her.

Now, with the letters on the table in front of them, this was her chance, possibly her last chance, to finally set things right.

'I can't let you cop all that blame, Dad. I'm the one who has to apologise. I might not have understood your reasoning when I was ten, but I was perfectly old enough to listen to you later. I was too stubborn and selfish. And I blamed *you* for *my* mistakes.'

Grabbing another tissue from the box, she quickly dabbed at her nose. 'I've been so caught up with my own issues over the years, I didn't stop to think about how hurt and worried you must have been. I'm sorry about that.' Her mouth pulled out of shape as fresh tears threatened. 'I am truly sorry.'

Her father looked stunned, and Ro could hardly blame him.

She managed a rueful, slightly embarrassed smile. 'I've shocked you, haven't I? You never expected to hear me say that.'

'No, I don't think I did.'

It felt very awkward, talking so openly with him. Awkward but necessary. And right. 'Better late than never, huh?'

'Oh yes, love.' With tears in his eyes, Harry held out his arms. 'Come here and give an old man a hug.'

Her vision blurred again as she skirted the table and her father felt frail and bony in her plump arms, but so, so precious.

They clung together tightly, both of them trembling a little. It was quite some time before Ro eventually released him, and she still felt a bit embarrassed. But happy, too. 'I think we've earned a cup of tea.'

'Ro,' her father said gently, as she turned to fill the kettle. 'We still haven't talked about the other matter.'

She was standing at the sink with her back to him, but she felt her heart give a painful lurch.

'You've never talked about the baby,' he said.

'Dad, don't.' The panicked protest burst from her as she gripped the edge of the sink.

'Don't you think it might help to at least admit that it happened? I know it's a terrible wound that's never really healed for you.'

Oh God. She'd been feeling so good, so cleansed and now Harry had ruined everything by digging deeper, going down to the dark, buried heart of her pain.

The baby. The ghastly clinic they'd taken her to.

'Have you ever told Lucy about it?' he persisted.

'No, I can't, Dad. I don't want to.'

'You're strong enough, you know.'

'I'm not.' But she also knew that she wanted to be strong. All her life she'd wanted to be braver.

'You know Lucy went to England because she was looking for answers. And she brought you these letters.'

'Yes,' Ro admitted softly.

'If you finished the story, got it off your chest, you'd feel so much better.'

The really terrible thing was, she knew he was right. It wasn't just an old cliché about confession being good for the soul. Already, after a single, simple apology, she felt a huge emotional release.

She took a deep breath, switched the kettle on, then found mugs and teabags. 'All right,' she said quickly, before she chickened out. 'I'll tell Lucy tomorrow. She's jet-lagged today and there's stuff I need to talk to Keith about first.'

This last thought about Keith had only just occurred to her, but it was plain as day now that she'd cast him as another of her failures, when the poor man had done nothing wrong. She had decided that she wasn't worthy of him but that was just another excuse, wasn't it? Another avoidance tactic.

Enough. It really was time to get on top of her life, to be strong, just like her parents.

30

When Keith arrived home, Lucy was on the apartment's balcony, trying to shove a certain tall, dark Englishman out of her head and to focus on the beautiful view in front of her. It was dusk and the Townsville sky was a blushing shade of pink, the river a soft wash of gold and grey, and she could see the creaming wake of a Magnetic Island ferry as it chugged beyond the rocky walls of the river mouth and out across the bay.

At the sound of Keith's key in the lock and then his footsteps in the hall, she braced herself. This felt weird. Very awkward to be staying alone in the apartment with her mum's new boyfriend. If she hadn't been so jet-lagged, she would have found somewhere else. Tomorrow she would either swap places with her mother at Harry's, or most definitely begin flat-hunting.

'Hello there,' Keith called heartily as he set takeaway containers on the kitchen counter.

Lucy went inside and they kissed cheeks. 'Hello, Keith. Good to see you again.'

'I bought Indian,' he said. 'I hope you like it.'

'Absolutely. I love any kind of curry. But I'm sorry to be imposing on you like this. I hadn't realised Mum was so tied up with Harry.'

'Not at all.' Keith couldn't quite hide his frown. 'What sort of day have you had? Did you see my note?'

'Yes, thanks, and I took all of your good advice. I've slept, watched TV *and* used the pool.'

'Excellent.' Keith moved to the fridge. 'Would you like a drink? Glass of wine?'

'Um – yes, why not?' Lucy thought Keith looked tired, even a little haggard. There were definite dark shadows under his eyes. She hoped her mum hadn't done something stupid. 'I guess we'll eat on the balcony? Would you like me to fetch plates and cutlery?'

'That would be useful. Thanks.'

In a matter of moments, they were sitting at the glass table outside where a light, refreshing breeze wafted in from the sea.

'So, how are you, Keith?' Lucy asked as they raised their glasses.

'Very well, thanks.' He seemed surprised by her question and after a short sip of wine, he turned his attention, perhaps a tad too studiously, to lifting the lids from containers.

'Mmm. Smells fabulous.' But Lucy felt compelled to pursue the issue that bothered her. 'I must say I was pretty gobsmacked when Mum told me she'd moved into Harry's place.'

Keith's shoulders lifted in an uncomfortable shrug. 'I'm sure her father appreciates her company. Anyway,' he added a little too quickly, 'tell me about your holiday.'

She obliged, giving him a potted version of her travels, but it hurt to talk about Cornwall. She couldn't surgically remove Nick Myatt from her thoughts, and whenever she remembered him, she felt physical pain in her chest and her arms. Still, she told Keith about the Cornish scenery and the quaint little villages and she did her best to make it sound interesting. He listened with polite attention.

As they helped themselves to scoops of lamb korma, kadhai chicken and rice, night crept in. Keith lit the collection of pretty outdoor candles that Ro had bought. More lights came on in the buildings along the riverbank and their reflections shimmered softly on the water. A screeching flock of rainbow lorikeets swept overhead, flying to their night-time roosts. The setting was idyllic and yet Lucy had the distinct feeling that her companion was as sad and heartsore as she was.

Eventually, she had to say something. 'Keith, I hope you don't mind my asking, but is everything okay?'

'How do you mean?'

'Were you fine about Mum moving to Harry's? It all seemed a bit sudden to me.'

Carefully, Keith set his fork on his plate. In the candlelight his face was all planes and shadows but there was no mistaking his unhappiness.

'Lucy, to be honest no, I'm not okay. I'm at a loss. I don't know what went wrong. One minute we were so happy —'

To Lucy's dismay, Keith was clearly struggling for control. He drank a little wine, then set the glass down.

'Am I right in thinking there's more to this than Harry's illness?' she asked gently. 'Is it possible that Mum's using Harry as an excuse?'

'I'm sure of it,' Keith said with a sigh. 'Before she left, she was saying crazy things, like she wasn't good enough for me. She said she couldn't make our relationship work. And then she just took off.'

To Lucy, so familiar with the pattern of her mother's relationships, this made a crazy kind of sense. Her mum was so used to failure that she probably couldn't trust herself to make things work in a perfect set-up with a totally acceptable man. Sadly, her mum had probably been speaking the truth. She truly believed that she wasn't good enough for Keith.

'Sounds like she panicked,' she said.

'But why?' Keith lifted his hands in a gesture of helplessness. 'I keep asking myself what I did wrong.'

'I'm quite sure you did nothing wrong, Keith. I'm afraid Mum's —' Lucy sighed. 'She's complicated.'

'Well, I think she's wonderful.' His mouth twisted in a sad little smile. 'I couldn't believe my luck when I met her. After losing my wife, I had expected to spend the rest of my days as a lonely old man, and then I met Ro and she was so much fun, so easy to be with and so good with my daughters.'

His breath caught on a stifled gasp and tears shone in his eyes. 'I didn't expect to fall for another woman after Susan, but I fell for your mother like a stone.'

Lucy was fighting tears, too. The poor man looked so lost and bewildered, and she completely understood the pain he felt.

'I'm so sorry this has happened,' she said, reaching out to touch his arm. 'I'll try to talk to Mum tomorrow. You never know, between Harry and me, we might be able to knock some sense into —'

'Hello? Anyone home?' called a familiar voice.

Lucy's jaw dropped, and so did Keith's. It was Ro's voice coming from within the darkened apartment. A light snapped on and then they saw her in the hall. Her curly hair was damp, as if she'd just stepped out of the shower, and she was wearing slim-fitting white slacks and a flattering lime-green tunic top. Her make-up had been carefully applied.

Her high-heeled silver sandals tapped on the tiles as she came through the living room. At the open sliding doors, she stopped and smiled nervously at Keith.

'I was hoping you hadn't gone out.'

He made a flustered sound of denial. 'Lucy and I were just having takeaway curry. Would – would you like to join us?'

But Lucy was certain that her mother hadn't come here for a

meal and she was already rising from her seat. 'I've had plenty to eat,' she said. 'And I'm dead on my feet.'

Ro accepted this with a nod, but she hadn't taken her eyes from Keith. 'I was hoping to talk to you,' she told him.

Hastily, Lucy gathered up the remains of their dinner and took it through to the kitchen. If she'd seen what she thought she'd just seen – a shining and miraculous new confidence in her mother's eyes – she would happily spend a night locked away in her room.

Lucy and Ro travelled together to Harry's place the next morning. Lucy was feeling rather spaced out. The combination of jet lag and heartbreak had kept her awake for hours, but at least her mum and Keith seemed very happy this morning.

'I've promised him we'll make this work,' a bubbling Ro had told Lucy almost as soon as Keith had left for the office.

'That's fantastic, Mum.'

'I know. I'm so happy and relieved. I shudder to think how close I came to making a *really* drastic mistake.'

Lucy found herself embraced in a rare motherly hug.

'Thank you for bringing those letters home, Luce.'

'Did you enjoy them?'

'Enjoy them? I *adored* them. And I showed them to Dad and we had a really good talk about – well, about *everything*. It was actually very special for both of us.'

'That's wonderful.'

'Until I read those letters I never realised —' Her mum's mouth turned square as if she was struggling to smile, but needed to cry.

Lucy gave her another hug. 'Sounds like yesterday was a really big day for you.'

'Momentous.' Ro gave a snuffling laugh. 'A lot of bridge-building – with Dad *and* with Keith.'

'Well done, Mum.' Lucy resisted the urge to tell her she was proud of her, but it was the truth. The change she'd sensed in her mother last night was the kind of miracle she'd hoped for, but she'd never dared to believe it might actually happen.

'I'm guessing that Harry won't mind if you decide to move back in with Keith,' she said.

'Dad won't mind in the least. He practically booted me out the door last night when I told him I needed to talk to Keith.'

'Then I wonder how he'd feel about me moving in instead of you?'

'I guess we'd better find out.'

Harry's answer was emphatic.

'No, definitely not. You need to be with young people, Lucy, not nursing an old codger.'

'I wasn't planning to nurse you,' Lucy quipped lightly. 'I thought I'd freeload. Take over your spare room in return for a little bit of housekeeping.'

Harry's frown relaxed and he almost smiled. 'Delightful as that sounds, I have another proposition you should consider first.'

The three of them were sitting in his lounge room. Ro and Lucy were sunk deep in an ancient brown velvet sofa that had lost its springs a decade or more ago. Harry was in an armchair of similar decrepitude and now, with some difficulty, he edged himself forward and picked up a manila folder from the table before him.

Setting the folder on his knee, he let his serious grey gaze shift between his daughter and granddaughter. 'This is —'

'Hang on a sec, Dad,' Ro interrupted and she looked suddenly quite flushed and nervous. 'Sorry,' she added quickly. 'I don't mean to interrupt something important but, as you know, there's stuff I said I'd tell Lucy and – and I thought while we were all here together . . .'

Harry's eyes widened, but Lucy thought he looked pleased.

'Of course,' he said, setting the folder aside and Lucy wondered if there was some kind of conspiracy in the wind.

What on earth did they want to tell her?

Her mother looked tense and a bit sick now, sitting forward, arms folded, hugging herself. 'I know you've always had lots of questions, Luce – all the things I've never wanted to talk about. And I know I've driven you mad the way I always clammed up about England and Kalkadoon.'

Lucy's throat felt suddenly tight and sore. So many times she'd pestered her mum, but what was she about to hear? Now, when it seemed she was on the brink of getting answers, anxiety settled like a brick in her chest.

Be careful what you wish for.

'The thing is,' Ro said, staring at some spot on the carpet, 'Primrose was kind, not telling you the truth, but I was a little monster in England. I played up at school. I drove the Myatt family around the bend and in the summer I turned seventeen I ran away to London and fell in with a bunch of Aussies living in Earls Court. They had bought a Kombi van and were planning to drive back to Australia via the Middle East and Asia.'

Her mum paused and then hugged herself tighter. 'It was the start of a string of bad choices. They were a dodgy lot, but I was very naïve and desperate for a huge, grand adventure and I was so excited, until the Myatts caught up with me in Dover. We had planned on taking the ferry across to France.'

Lucy wondered if she was supposed to comment, but she couldn't think of anything. She was too enthralled.

Her mum sighed. 'Stupidly, I told them I was pregnant.'

'Were you?' The question just popped out. Already, Lucy's imagination was running wild, racing ahead and picturing a long-lost half-brother or sister.

Her mum nodded sadly. 'Yes, I was eight weeks pregnant, and

I told Alice because I thought she would let me stay with the baby's father. I thought she'd be relieved to offload me.'

'But you were in her care,' Lucy said. 'She probably felt responsible.'

Her mum nodded. 'Unfortunately, I've never been very good at seeing things from someone else's point of view. But of course, the Myatts' family honour was at stake.' Ro's lips trembled and her face looked on the verge of crumpling, until she caught Harry's eye.

Watching, it seemed to Lucy that Harry's mere presence in the room gave her mother fresh courage. Ro let her hands drop back into her lap and she sat a little straighter. 'The Myatts were very well connected,' she went on, in a calm, almost deadpan voice. 'There was an uncle in Harley Street, London, and Alice was able to bundle me off to the exclusive clinic that he worked at. It was all very hush-hush.'

'A clinic,' Lucy whispered, reaching to grip her mother's hand.

'I was so naïve and foolish,' her mum said next. 'I hadn't told my boyfriend I was pregnant and I had no real plans for how I was going to manage when I got back to Australia. Not that it mattered. My so-called mates dumped me as soon as the Myatts turned up and accused the Aussies of abducting me.'

'God, Mum.'

'I had no one on my side and there was so much pressure. I couldn't fight them.'

'How awful. You poor thing.'

Ro nodded and sat very still with her hand clasped in Lucy's and her lips tightly compressed, as if she didn't trust herself to say more without bursting into sobs.

Harry cleared his throat. 'It was unforgivable. The Myatts didn't consult me, either. They just terminated the pregnancy and packed poor Rose off home. All Alice cared about was avoiding a family disgrace.'

Lucy tried to imagine it – to be seventeen and lonely and scared and then pressured into ending a pregnancy whether she wanted to or not.

'I don't suppose you got counselling,' she said.

Ro shook her head.

'I can see now why you called Alice a bitch. You must have been so devastated and so bloody angry. Mum, you would never really get over something like that.'

As she said this, Lucy experienced a blinding light-bulb moment. In a blink, the answers to so many questions that had plagued her all her life were glaringly clear, and every answer sprang from the appalling fact that her mother had been forced to have an abortion at the age of seventeen.

No wonder Ro had never wanted to talk about England, and of course something like that would have stuffed up her later relationships with men. No doubt this issue was also at the root of her tension with Harry. After all, he'd sent her to England in the first place.

She would have come home in shame, with a huge sense of failure, with the feeling that she'd got her life wrong from the start and that she needed someone to blame.

'I can see why you didn't want to tell me,' Lucy said. 'And, for heaven's sake, you must have been so stressed when I took off for England.'

'Yeah,' said her mum softly.

'I'm afraid I talked Ro into telling you now,' Harry admitted.

A faint smile warmed Ro's face. 'And I'm amazed I've got through it without having a nervous breakdown.'

'See, you *are* stronger than you think,' he said.

'Either that, or there are no tears left in me after yesterday.' Her mum let out her breath with a soft huff, but she looked relieved and almost triumphant, as if she'd conquered a mountain. 'It's been a weekend for getting things off my chest.'

'Do you feel better for it?' Harry asked.

Her mother nodded. 'But I still feel ashamed that I blamed you, that I never really took responsibility for my own mistakes.'

'It's okay, love. We've sorted that.'

Lucy had never seen anything quite as satisfying as the warm smiles Harry and Ro exchanged. She wondered if Primrose's letters had been a catalyst. She liked to think that her journey to Cornwall had achieved some good for someone, even if it had left her feeling like debris thrown up on a beach after a shipwreck.

'Anyway, Dad, I stopped you from showing us your folder,' Ro said now, plumping up a cushion and then sitting straighter. 'No more interruptions, I promise. I'm all ears.'

'Ah, yes.' Harry picked up the folder again. 'This is my will,' he said, placing a large craggy hand on the document's cover. 'I daresay you will know its contents soon enough, but I've decided I also want you to hear about it now.'

Ro made a soft sound of dismay and looked as if she was about to protest, but she'd just promised not to interrupt and perhaps she caught the resolve in Harry's eyes. She shut her mouth firmly and sat back with her arms folded across her chest. But there was no mistaking her tension.

Lucy was also feeling nervous. Wills and death went together and she wasn't ready to face the reality of Harry's death. She certainly didn't want to hear him talk about it.

'As you might expect, I'm leaving everything I have to the two of you,' Harry said quietly.

Lucy's head spun. Her mother's news had been quite a shock, and yet somehow, strangely inevitable. But this sudden discussion about inheritance was *so* coming from left field.

'I know Ro has been worried about the responsibilities of Kalkadoon,' Harry continued. 'And Ro, I've fobbed you off, telling you it's all in hand, which is more or less true. As you know,

I've had managers out there for many years now and most years the profits have been ploughed back into the property. But whenever there was a little spare cash, I've invested it. Usually in the north-west in mining.'

Harry gave a casual shrug. 'The money's built up over the years. There are several hundred thousand there now, and I'm leaving this house and that money to you, Ro.'

Lucy heard her mother's gasp, saw her eyes widen with shock, but for once she seemed to have nothing to say.

This was understandable. Lucy was gripped by a similar numbing shock. Harry had always lived so modestly in his little worker's cottage. She'd never thought, never dreamed that he might have several hundred thousand spare dollars stashed away.

'As for you, Lucy.' Harry's face was still set in serious lines, but the faintest hint of a smile glimmered in his eyes. 'I'm leaving you Kalkadoon.'

Oh my God.

Lucy couldn't speak, couldn't *think*. She almost couldn't breathe.

'I know this will come as a shock,' Harry said with surprising gentleness. 'You've probably never given Kalkadoon any thought. You've never been out there, have you?'

'No. I – I'm afraid I've never been on *any* cattle property.'

Harry nodded. 'If you have time before you go back to work, I'd like you to travel out to Kalkadoon. For my sake, I'd like you to at least take a look at the place.'

Lucy's head was still reeling. She was trying to picture herself living way out west and running a cattle property, but it was like trying to imagine herself working in a lab in Antarctica or tackling brain surgery. She had absolutely no qualifications for working with cattle. She hardly even knew how to ride a horse.

Her mind flashed to Cornwall and the riding lessons that she'd so thoroughly enjoyed. Sadly, it was probably Nick's company that had made the experience so much fun.

To be in the outback on her own? It was such a different proposition.

'Just take a look is all I ask,' added Harry.

Lucy gave a bewildered shrug. 'I don't know what to say, Harry. Obviously, I'm still getting used to the idea, but sure, I'd be happy to take a look. I hope that doesn't sound ungrateful. I'm just so stunned.'

'I should warn you there's a proviso written into the will.' Harry was still watching her with a gentle smile. 'You won't be able to sell Kalkadoon for at least four years.'

Lucy gulped. The possibility of selling the place had already crossed her mind. Had her grandfather guessed? 'So you're definitely hoping that I'll give it a go,' she said.

He shook his head. 'Nothing definite about it. Last thing I want is for the property to be a millstone around your neck. All I'm asking for now is that you at least check the place out. If you decide you want to leave it to the manager, he'll happily take care of everything. It's entirely your call, Lucy, but you shouldn't make any decisions without seeing the property.'

'No.'

Ro spoke up. 'Well, I'm speechless. About all of this. I simply don't know what to say, Dad.'

'I haven't dropped off my perch just yet.' Some of the old twinkle shone in his eyes. 'So you'll both have a little time to get used to the idea.'

Lucy's thoughts were still racing. 'If I did decide to live at Kalkadoon, I'd have to leave the army.'

Her grandfather simply nodded.

'Is that what you want, Harry? You'd like me to give up the army?'

He didn't answer straight away.

'Don't tell me you're another one.' Lucy instantly regretted that she'd said this out loud. The words had spilled from her, frustration joining the bubbling cocktail of her emotions.

'Another one?' asked Harry. 'Who's telling you to leave the army?'

Lucy sighed. 'Mum would love me to and so would just about every guy I've fallen for.'

Both Harry and Ro looked surprised by this confession.

'It's a bit of a sore point,' Lucy said.

Harry was shaking his head. 'I'm not trying to push you one way or the other. As I said before, it's your call, Lucy, and I certainly don't want you to take on something that doesn't interest you.' He held her in his steady gaze. 'On the other hand, you never know – perhaps you're ready to take on a new challenge.'

As he said this, a tiny ping reverberated inside her. *A new challenge*. The words caused an unexpected, fragile stirring of excitement.

Rubbing at her forehead, she tried to calm her rushing thoughts. 'I really would like to get out there.' A new challenge could be just what she needed. 'But I don't have much time left. I'm due back at work at the beginning of next week.'

'Well, I'm free,' piped up her mum with surprising eagerness. She shot Harry a rather sheepish smile. 'It's high time I saw the old place again.'

'We'd have to get cracking, Mum. It will take a few days to get out there and have a good look around, then home again.' Lucy quickly calculated. 'Would you be prepared to leave tomorrow?'

Ro shrugged. 'Can't see why not.'

31

'Do you feel like Thelma and Louise?' Lucy asked soon after day-break the next morning, as the outskirts of Townsville flashed past them.

Ro laughed. 'I might if we were in a sports car with the sun roof down, not this great big thing.' She settled back comfortably into the well-padded passenger seat. 'But I do feel as if we're starting out on an adventure.'

'Yeah, me too.'

'I've spent a restless night,' Ro added. 'I'm feeling guilty that I never took you out there when you were younger.'

'Harry could have taken me.'

Ro shook her head. 'He was too diplomatic. He knew how I felt and he didn't want to upset me.'

'Oh well. I thought we established yesterday that you should stop feeling guilty.'

'It's not a habit you can break overnight.'

'Maybe you need to forgive yourself, Mum.'

This was met by a long silence before her mum said, 'When did you get to be so wise?'

Lucy laughed. 'It's easy to be wise about other people's problems.'

Truth was, very little would quell Lucy's chirpy spirits this morning. Zinging excitement had been building in her ever since Harry's amazing announcement yesterday. It was the same edgy, buoyant sense of anticipation she'd felt when she'd first set off on her deployment to Afghanistan. A journey into the unknown.

'I must admit I'm very grateful to Keith for insisting we take his Pajero,' she said. 'It has masses of grunt and I can really feel the tyres gripping the bitumen.'

'Yes, he's a sweet man.' Her mum's mouth curved into a fond, secret smile.

Lucy grinned again, confident now that Ro and Keith were quite securely 'Ro and Keith' – even though their new-found happiness highlighted her own misery.

Annoyingly, even with this new adventure ahead, the pain of losing Nick still held her in a sharp-taloned grip, which was another reason she was determined to enjoy their road trip. With any luck, the journey to Kalkadoon would provide the perfect distraction.

Lucy felt quite optimistic about this experience. She knew she had Harry's blessing, her mum was practically purring with contentment now, the Pajero was eating up the kilometres, and the country looked extra beautiful after the recent rains.

She tuned the car radio to a station that played country and western. 'To get us in the rural mood,' she said. And so it was to the accompaniment of crooning singers and soft, twanging guitars that they drove on to Charters Towers, then through the majestic White Mountains country to the west of the old mining town. Eventually they found themselves on vast, wide plains so flat they could see the curvature of the earth.

Here, paddocks of waving, champagne-coloured grass stretched as far as the eye could see, broken only by occasional clumps of low leafy trees or eroded black soil gullies. Big mobs of silvery Brahman cattle grazed, and telegraph poles tracked the straight line of the Flinders Highway into the shimmering distance till they looked like mere wisps of smoke.

'You can see why they call this Big Sky Country,' said Ro.

'And it just goes on and on.'

'It's not boring though, is it?'

'Not so far,' Lucy admitted. 'But I'll reserve judgement till we've been through Hughenden, Richmond, Julia Creek *and* Cloncurry.'

Her mum grinned. 'Sing out if you get tired of driving.'

'Sure. We can change after we stop for lunch.'

The radio crooned on, the landscape rolled out like a multicoloured carpet and Ro settled lower in her seat. Lucy was sure her mum was asleep and, dangerously, she allowed her thoughts to wander.

Unfortunately, they zeroed straight to Nick Myatt.

Major mistake. The mere thought of the man brought a raw stab to her heart. Valiantly, she tried to swing her mind elsewhere. A huge petrol tanker thundered past and she considered the logistics involved in running a cattle property so far west that everything had to be trucked in or out. Not so very different from her work in the army, really.

Then, fiendish things, thoughts of Nick slammed back again, and this time she couldn't halt the flood of memories. She was reliving that first night in The Seaspray Arms when she saw Nick at the far end of the bar. By now, those impressions were probably embedded in her DNA. Nick's height, his black sweater, those cheekbones and wild hair. His magnetic masculine intensity.

Oh God. How she ached for him.

She remembered the day he'd shown her over the Hall when she'd seen the photograph of Georgina with Alice and then another of him with Simon. Then there was the horse-riding morning and the dizzily happy day they'd spent on the Lizard Peninsula.

The blissful nights in his bed.

True, she'd only known Nick for a very short time, but in those few magical days, he'd lifted her feel-good factor to immeasurable heights.

It was hard not to make comparisons with Sam, but Nick hadn't been merely cute and sexy, he was an entertaining companion and a considerate and thoughtful host and Lucy suspected these were qualities Sam could never aspire to. He'd always been too self-centred.

Nick had shown her a glimpse of the way things should be. The way things could be.

If only . . .

'So these fellows you've fallen for . . .'

Her mother's voice, coming out of the blue, made Lucy jump.

'Sorry,' she said quickly. 'My mind was miles away.'

Ro sat straighter. 'I'm curious about these fellows you've dated. The ones who want you to leave the army. I knew about Sam, of course. I didn't realise there were others.'

Lucy's cheeks grew hot and she prayed she wasn't blushing. 'Just guys . . . guys I've met.'

'In Townsville?'

She knew her mother was watching her carefully from behind her sunglasses and she tried for an offhand shrug. 'It's no big deal, Mum. I'm not dating anyone now and if you don't mind, I'd rather not talk about it.'

'All right. Keep your hair on. I was only trying to show an interest.'

'I know.' In a bid to soothe, Lucy added, 'Sorry.'

'It's just that I've noticed you don't seem very happy, Luce. I knew you were upset when you left because of Sam, but I hoped you'd be over him by the time you came home from your holiday.'

'I *am* over him. Honest. Well and truly.'

She knew that her mother would almost certainly have had more questions about this, but a sign appeared providentially ahead, telling them they'd reached Richmond.

'Let's see if we can get a hamburger here,' Lucy suggested and, to her relief, her mum claimed to be starving. The subject of boyfriends was dropped.

Originally, they had planned to spend the night in a hotel in Cloncurry, but they made good time, arriving at the outback town by mid-afternoon.

Ro was behind the wheel. 'Would you like to push on?' she asked. 'We could make it to Kalkadoon before dark.'

'Yes.' Lucy could barely curb her impatience. 'Let's grab a cold drink and keep going. Harry told the manager at Kalkadoon to expect us either tonight or tomorrow morning.'

The country changed again after another hour or so, the black soil plains giving way to tree-studded red-dirt country with rocky limestone outcrops topped by scrub and vine. From the crest of one of these ridges, they spotted a line of trees winding across the landscape like a giant Dreamtime snake.

'That's the river,' Ro said, stopping the Pajero so they could take in the view. 'I'm pretty sure it forms part of Kalkadoon's boundary.'

'Wow. It's awesome country out here.' Lucy's voice was hushed and she leaned forward, staring intently through the windscreen.

'Hard to believe you'll own something like that, I guess?'

'Impossible,' Lucy whispered. After a bit, 'Is this how you remembered it?'

'Not really. Not yet. But I'm sure it'll all come back to me when we get closer to the homestead.'

'I wonder how Georgina felt when she first travelled out here.'

Ro smiled at her daughter. 'Probably very similar to the way you're feeling now.'

'Gobsmacked,' Lucy suggested.

Reaching over, Ro squeezed her hand. 'One step at a time, okay?'

To Ro's dismay, Lucy's face turned white and she looked as if she might cry.

'Lucy, don't stress about this.'

'No, I'm not. Sorry. It's okay. I'm okay.'

'I know the thought of owning a cattle station is a huge burden, love, and something you weren't expecting. To be honest, I'm relieved it's not my responsibility, but Keith and I will still be on hand to support you. Keith has a good head for business and he'd be happy to help with decisions.'

'I know. I'm fine, honestly. Just having a moment.'

Concerned, Ro watched as her daughter drew deep breaths. It wasn't at all like Lucy to be so fragile. Ro couldn't tell if she was truly worried about inheriting Kalkadoon, or if something else had upset her, something that had happened in England, perhaps. She hoped to get to the bottom of it over the next few days.

Lucy took over the driving again when they turned off the bitumen onto a rust-red track. An off-road driving course had been part of her army training and Ro was happy to hand over.

Ro wound down her window and took a deep breath, drawing in the scents of dust and grass and eucalyptus. They were the scents she remembered, just as she also remembered the bronze glow of the afternoon sun on the paddocks, the rocky red cliffs in the distance and the haze of soft, green bush along the riverbank.

They arrived at the river crossing – an ancient natural ford topped by slabs of concrete and rock and filled with three large concrete pipes to channel the water in the wet season. Halfway across the makeshift bridge Lucy stopped the car and wound her window down. 'What a beautiful river.'

The water was a refreshingly clear blue-green with brilliant white sandy banks lined with huge creamy-trunked paperbarks and backed by majestic cliffs. The limbs of the paperbarks hung low, trailing their fine, tapered leaves over the surface of the water like idle fingers. A low island of gravel and rocks in the middle of the river bend was home to a fallen tree trunk, scoured to a smooth ivory by floods and sunshine, and now the perfect perch for a flock of black cormorants.

'It's just stunning,' Lucy said softly. 'I wish Harry was well enough to have come with us.'

'Yes.' Ro was wishing she'd thought to bring her father out here before his health deteriorated.

Lucy picked up her mobile phone. 'How about I ring him?' As she pressed his number, her face fell. 'No network. Of course. Should have guessed.'

'You should be able to call him from the homestead.'

'Okay. That will have to do.'

They set off again, climbing away from the river over another rocky ridge, then along more twists and turns on a bumpy track. Then, suddenly, another turn, and the view Ro remembered.

Ahead lay a long stretch of paddocks and, in the distance, the house, a typical outback homestead, sprawling and high set, with a ripple iron roof and deep verandahs, set in an expanse of lawn and shaded by ancient trees.

'Wow, Mum,' Lucy said beside her. 'Welcome home.'

'Don't say that.' Ro's voice was already choked. 'Don't make me cry.'

'I reckon you're allowed to cry, coming back here after all this time.'

Ro managed to stay dry-eyed, however, and as they drove closer she could see the cluster of out-buildings beyond the homestead – the garages and big machinery sheds, the ringers' huts, a small cottage and a satellite dish, both of which were new, and a windmill or two.

A tall outback figure in jeans, a faded blue shirt and wide-brimmed Akubra, with a blue cattle dog at his heels, was hurrying in long-legged strides over the grass to open the front gate for them.

'You think he's the manager?' Lucy asked.

'More than likely.'

'G'day there,' he called as Lucy pulled up and he greeted them with a beaming smile.

Ro found herself staring at his smile, at his deep chocolate eyes and his white teeth, so bright against the dark brown of his face. *It couldn't be, could it?*

She and Lucy climbed out of the vehicle.

'Welcome to Kalkadoon,' he said and Lucy immediately offered her hand.

'Thanks. It's great to be here at last. I'm Lucy and this is my mum, Ro.'

Lucy and the manager shook hands and then he turned to Ro. 'Hello, Rose. Doug Prince.'

Ro gasped. 'Dougie? It *is* you?'

His bright grin split wider than ever. 'You remember me?'

'Oh my goodness!' She gripped his hand tightly. She and this man had been best mates till she was ten, riding horses together, fishing and swimming in the creek. 'Of course I remember, but it's been such a long time.'

'More than forty years.'

'I had no idea you were still here.'

'Never left the place. I've been manager for going on twenty years now.'

'Goodness. And I suppose you're married? Do you have a family?' How terrible that she knew none of these things.

'My wife June is here with me,' Doug told her. 'We've got two kids, a boy and a girl. Your dad helped us to send them to a good

school in Brisbane and they've done real well. Kathy's a nurse now
and Joey works in cattle. Into bloodlines and breeding. He's the
young gun down on a big cattle stud outside Rocky.'

'How wonderful!'

Doug nodded. 'He's a good bloke, your dad.'

'Yes.' Once again, Ro was incredibly relieved that she'd finally
made peace with her father. Doug was so right. Harry Kemp was a
very good bloke.

She looked about her now, studying the house and the big old
trees that shaded it. She turned to Lucy. 'When we were little, Doug
and I used to spend hours hanging out in a bottlebrush tree.'

'Hanging upside-down, more like,' laughed Doug.

'Yes. We were a pair of little monkeys. Is the tree still here?'

He shook his head. 'Died years ago in a drought. But I'll show
you somethin' that's survived.'

Beckoning for the women to follow him, he led them to a curved
ironwork archway separating two straggling garden beds.

'Your mother planted this climbing rose,' he told Ro. 'Story I
heard, she brought it with her from England, and we've kept it going
all these years. Harry used to care for it and then my mum, and later
my wife. Watered it by hand through the droughts. It's had a struggle at times, but it's managed to flower every year.'

'How amazing.'

'Awesome,' whispered Lucy, touching a reverent fingertip to a
dainty pink petal. 'This is the rose George named you after, Mum.'

Too emotional to speak, Ro nodded.

'Anyway,' said Doug. 'You're probably dying for a cuppa.' He
turned to Ro. 'I guessed you'd probably want to stay in the old
homestead?'

'But we don't want to put you out.'

He shook his head. 'June and I built our own smaller place a
few years back. A cabin, neat and easy to air-condition. The big old

house is a bit run down these days, but June's been in there, dusting and mopping and making up the beds.'

'Oh that's very kind of her.'

He grinned. 'Keeps her outta mischief.'

The homestead was old and shabby. Lucy was aware of the peeling paint and the tarnished brass knocker on the front door, the unpainted verandah floorboards worn to a silvery grey.

Inside, the furniture was rudimentary with a couple of camping chairs in the lounge room and an old TV propped on a wooden crate. The beds had metal ends and rather thin mattresses, but the sheets were snowy white and crisp and clean and there were soft cotton blankets neatly folded and ready if needed.

A big old-fashioned dresser dominated the kitchen and the stove looked ancient and battered, but it would do for heating up the food they'd brought in an esky. A great feature was the bank of windows on the far kitchen wall offering a view out across the paddocks and all the way to the creek.

'At least everything's very neat and tidy,' Ro commented after Doug had left them. 'A bit drab and spartan, but don't let that put you off.'

'Oh, it won't put me off,' Lucy insisted. 'I'm used to drab and spartan after Tarin Kowt. But I really like this house, Mum. It's a bit like Harry's place in Townsville, only bigger.'

Secretly, she was delighted with the big old house and she could easily imagine getting stuck into it with a paintbrush and scouring secondhand shops for the right kind of furniture.

She knew she mustn't get too carried away, though. Running a cattle property involved a hell of a lot more than playing house in the homestead.

32

Lucy was introduced to the business of running Kalkadoon the next morning when Doug conducted a tour of their immediate surroundings, starting at the machinery shed and taking in the cattle yards and various nearby paddocks with assorted water troughs, dams and windmills.

She learned that the property covered three thousand square kilometres and turned off four to five thousand head of Brahman and Brahman-cross cattle each year.

'Harry was happy with that number,' Doug told her. 'But I reckon, if you wanted to spend more money and effort to really muster out the cleanskins, you might pull as many as eight thousand off this place.'

Lucy stared at him in surprise. 'And I guess that would make a lot more money.'

He chuckled. 'A hell of a lot more.'

It was all rather mind-boggling. 'So how do you manage the mustering? Do you get help?'

'Too right. We hire a contract mustering team – it's pretty much the same mob every year. They're good. They know the country.

Mustering usually starts as soon as the wet season's over – late March or April.'

'And what happens now in January and February? General maintenance?'

'Yeah. I have to keep an eye on all the water troughs and the dams, and make sure the fences and yards are in good working order. Some seasons, if we haven't had enough rain, I take feed out to the cattle.'

He ducked his head towards the cluster of buildings that made Kalkadoon look almost like a small village. 'You saw the big machinery shed. This time of year, we put the vehicles up on a hoist. My off-sider, Bluey, is an ace mechanic, so he gives the vehicles a good overhaul.'

Lucy nodded at this. She'd been making a mental inventory and had counted a surprising number of vehicles – an excavator back-hoe, a cattle truck, two four-wheel drive utes and a LandCruiser. Not to mention a quad bike and two trail bikes.

Seemed there were more vehicles on Kalkadoon than horses.

She had to ask. 'Do you still use horses?'

'Yeah, of course.' With his hands resting on his skinny hips, Doug gave a shrug. 'We use the bikes a fair bit these days, and we get a chopper in to help with the mustering. But on a property like Kalkadoon there are so many gullies and scrubby hills you can only reach on horseback.' He shot Lucy a searching smile. 'How are you on horseback?'

'Oh, a very raw beginner.'

Ro gave a huffing little laugh. 'The only horse you've ridden is on a merry-go-round.'

Lucy tried to sound offhand. 'Actually, I had a couple of horse-riding lessons in Cornwall.'

Avoiding her mother's surprised look, she turned to Doug. 'I imagine you have to be very self-sufficient out here.'

'Too right. Only way you can survive.'

'And you'd have to order everything in. All the fuel and the food supplies, the spare parts for the vehicles and machinery.'

Ro piped up again at this point. 'That's Lucy's area of expertise, Doug. She works in logistics in the army.'

His eyes widened. 'Fair dinkum?'

Lucy laughed. 'Didn't you notice the fond pats I gave those big rolls of barbed wire and the bundles of star pickets? I feel at home seeing them, and those shipping containers and oil drums. I spend my days ordering and transporting gear, or managing construction projects for the army.'

Doug was grinning from ear to ear.

'Blow me down. Then you're tailor-made for this place, aren't you?'

Lucy couldn't help grinning back at him. 'Maybe.' Then more seriously, she said, 'But tell me the truth, Doug. This is your home, you've lived here all your life. How would you feel about someone like me owning this place and running it someday – with your help, of course?'

To her surprise he didn't hesitate. He looked her straight in the eye. 'I'm a Kalkadoon, so this place will always be my country. There's some native title that I can talk to you about, but your family has been good to my family for three generations now and I'd hate to see strangers or one of those big cattle corporations running it.' He smiled. 'I reckon it's time one of Harry's mob came back here.'

Lucy, needing headspace and the chance to let all the new info settle inside her, went for a long walk just before sunset. She followed a narrow track made by cattle, a deep sandy rut that led along the riverbank. In the shade of ancient paperbarks, she drank in the cool peace of the shadowy bush and the slow drifting water. She thought about Harry and George and she tried to imagine what their life must have been like when they lived here. Where were their favourite haunts?

She thought about her mother and Doug, playing here as kids, swimming and fishing and swinging in trees, and she wondered what it would have been like if her mum had stayed on and she'd grown up here, too, riding horses and canoeing on this river, helping with the mustering, cooking on a camp fire.

Surely, an outback cattle station provided the ultimate adventurous lifestyle? Lucy would have loved it, she had no doubts about that.

It was rather amazing to realise that she could still have that adventure if she chose to live here.

But what about the isolation? a small voice whispered. *Wouldn't you be lonely?*

Her counterarguments came with surprising speed. She would probably be too busy to be lonely. And she'd make friends with people on surrounding properties. Ro seemed to love the place, perhaps she and Keith would come to visit fairly often.

Today they'd enjoyed a jovial barbecue lunch with Doug and June and Bluey, dining at a long table set under a spreading tamarind tree. Her mum had recalled a raft of stories once she and Doug started reminiscing about the good old days. It was wonderful to listen to them, almost like discovering a new version of her mother.

June was still shy at the moment, but Lucy was sure that would change given enough time. Bluey, a red-headed Irishman, who'd come to Australia decades ago to work as a jackaroo, was an entertaining raconteur, a great teller of bush yarns, who kept them in stitches. Lunch had been fun.

Lucy knew there were bound to be all kinds of interesting characters out here and it wasn't as if she could never get back into town for a spot of social life. Anyway, she'd been surrounded by friends among her fellow soldiers, and while she'd enjoyed her job, she'd never felt a true calling in the army.

Here, she felt not a calling, exactly, but a sense of connection that was hard to ignore.

'Maybe I should just give it a go,' she said aloud, as the track took her beneath an archway of weeping bottlebrush. After all, she'd never had any trouble forming new friendships and if things didn't work out, she didn't have to stay here forever. If she was going to leave the army, she needed to replace it with something equally fulfilling.

But what really spoke to Lucy was the knowledge that this property brought her closer to her family. It was kind of ironic that she'd charged off to England in search of family connections, when they'd always been right here, waiting, and perhaps even more significant.

Harry, George and her mother had all lived here and, before that, Harry's parents, Lucy's great-grandparents. Of course, originally, the property had belonged to the Kalkadoon people and Lucy also liked the fact that Doug Prince was still here, sharing his people's heritage. She liked that he asserted his native title, too. Another owner might not appreciate or respect that.

Wrapped deep in these thoughts, Lucy had scarcely noticed that the track was veering steeply uphill until she found herself at the top of a cliff. From here, she had fabulous views up and down the majestic sweep of the river and beyond to another wall of even higher cliffs.

It was an amazing spot. So quiet and peaceful as she stood looking down at the clear green water and the smooth rocks beneath it, and then to the sky above, now purple and pink and streaked with orange.

Surely, this must be a favourite place for family picnics and celebrations. It would be the perfect setting for a wedding.

Damn. Hastily, Lucy scratched that last unsolicited thought, but not before it left painful scorch marks on her heart.

Annoyed, she whirled away from the view of the river and the sky. And that was when she saw it.

Over in the shade of a tall spreading tree, a headstone was surrounded by a pretty metal fence. With a soft cry she hurried across the grass and her eyes were already misty as she read the inscription.

> *In loving memory of*
> *Georgina Katherine Kemp*
> *19 June 1920 – 17 April 1962*
> *Cherished wife of Henry*
> *Beloved mother of Rose*
> *Remember me, won't you?*

Oh, George. Oh, Harry. Sudden swamping grief brought Lucy to her knees. How could Harry have borne to leave George here?

She thought of the photographs she'd seen of Georgina, so glamorous and ever so slightly unhappy in England and then so unmistakably happy here at Kalkadoon with her sweet chubby baby.

Kneeling in the short grass, wrapped in sadness, Lucy heard a high, keening call. Looking up, she saw a bird, quite possibly a falcon, a black shape against the bright sunset, circling high above the cliffs.

And in that moment she knew.

She had to come back here.

I want to be like them. I have to give it a go.

She owed it to Georgina, to Harry and to her mum. All of them, for different reasons, had to leave Kalkadoon before they were ready.

She, Lucy, had been offered a chance to reclaim the opportunities her forebears had lost – and she knew she couldn't refuse.

Ro was sitting under the poinciana, enjoying a sundowner with June and Doug in the last of the light, when Lucy came hurrying back.

One look at Lucy's face and Ro knew something had happened.

'Are you okay, love?' she asked, as her daughter flopped down into a spare chair after only the most cursory greeting.

'I found Georgina's grave.' Lucy's grey eyes glistened. 'It's on a high bank overlooking the river.'

'Oh.' Ro shivered as vague memories stirred. 'I'd like to see that.'

'I'll take you there tomorrow,' Lucy said. 'But it was so sad, Mum. You were still quite young when she died, weren't you?'

'Yes, I was five.'

'That's so sad,' Lucy said again.

A chill rippled down Ro's spine as she remembered the laughing woman in the photo Primrose sent, remembered the memories of her loving mother that she'd shared with Harry. She found herself struggling not to cry.

'It – it was quite sudden, wasn't it?' Lucy asked. 'An aneurysm?'

Ro nodded. 'I think so. I know it was a terrible shock foreveryone. Dad never really got over it and I've never had the heart to press him for details.'

'I was there,' Doug said suddenly.

A soft gasp broke from Ro and Lucy as they stared at him.

'I remember how it happened.' His habitually cheerful face was suddenly grave.

'Do you mind telling us?' Lucy's voice was little more than a whisper.

Doug nodded solemnly. 'I remember, cos it was Easter time and my mum and Missus George were in the homestead kitchen, making hot cross buns.'

'I wasn't there, was I?' asked Ro.

'No, you were away with the Boss. Those days, if you had half a chance, you used to follow him around like a puppy, so he'd take you out in the truck to hand feed the poddy calves.'

Doug grimaced, smiling awkwardly. 'I was hanging around the kitchen, cos there were so many good smells. I was always wanting to lick the bowl.'

Ro almost smiled as she imagined this.

'It was like the Missus just suddenly fainted,' Doug said. 'That's how it seemed. She just kinda slid to the floor. Mum was frantic. She tried to wake her, but she couldn't and she yelled at me to race down to the stockyards. "Tell your dad to fetch the Boss," she yelled.'

Doug's dark eyes gleamed with bright tears. 'By the time I did that and got back to the house, Mum and my auntie were gently lifting the Missus. They carried her into the bedroom and laid her on the bed, cos they didn't want the Boss to come back and see her collapsed on the floor.'

June reached over and patted her husband's hand, while Ro could only sit, mesmerised by Doug's story. She could hear the buzz of insects in the grass and the distant call of a lone crow, but her thoughts were winging back – back to the past.

She was seeing herself, a little girl with black curly hair and dressed in denim overalls, and she was helping her father to hold a metal bucket, while a calf greedily lapped up the powdered milk. She could see the calf's eager pink tongue and the milk sloshing, and when it splashed up her arm, she could smell it, sweet and creamy on her skin. She was trying to wipe her arm on the back of her overalls when Dougie's dad came charging up on his horse, making the dust fly. His eyes were wild, looking scarily big and round and white and he was yelling.

'Boss, you gotta come. Something bad happened to the Missus.'

Everything moved so fast. Her father abandoned the calves and the buckets, scooped her up in his arms and raced with her to the truck.

'What's happened?' she asked him as he climbed into the driver's seat, but he didn't answer, just started up the truck and stared grimly ahead as the vehicle rushed and bounced and juddered down the track, so fast that she banged her ear against the door handle, making it hurt.

At the homestead, the grown-ups wouldn't let her into her parents' bedroom. Her father disappeared inside and then the door was closed behind him. She was scared and hated it, hated the closed door and the house full of people.

No one would let her see her mother, and Shirleen and her sisters were wailing.

'Mum.' Lucy's voice came from far away. 'Mum,' she said softly.

Ro started as she felt her daughter's hand on her arm.

'Are you okay?' Lucy asked her gently.

It was only then that Ro realised she was crying. 'Yes, I'm okay, thanks.' She swiped at her eyes with the heel of her hand. 'It's just coming back to me, that's all. There's so much I'd forgotten.'

Doug was looking worried and Ro sent him a shaky smile. 'Thanks for sharing your story, Doug. It's important to remember.'

'It was such a sad time for all of us,' he said.

'Yes, I remember your aunties wailing and singing in language,' she said. 'Their songs were so sad.'

Doug nodded. 'Our women were devastated. They loved the Missus. The men attended the funeral when the minister came, but the women had their own mourning ceremony down by the river.'

Yes, Ro could remember now, seeing the women preparing for the ceremony, painting themselves with white stripes. The paint had looked quite startling on their dark faces and breasts. 'I think I was a bit frightened,' she admitted.

Doug nodded. 'Me too. It was so sad, such a very sad time.'

She could almost hear it again – the sounds drifting up from the creek – the low, melodic moaning of the women's voices as they swayed and danced to express their grief.

To her surprise, June got to her feet and circled the table to give her a hug.

'Thank you,' she said as she and Doug's wife, whom she'd only just met, exchanged watery smiles.

Silence fell over the little group. It was almost dark now.

Then Lucy's voice. 'From everything I've heard about my grand-mother, Georgina, she was quite an amazing woman. I'm very proud of her.'

'Yeah, you should be proud,' agreed Doug. 'My dad told me some of the stories Harry shared with him. Stories about the war in New Guinea. The Missus was up there, too. She was very brave.'

'A true heroine,' said Lucy softly.

And she was my mum, thought Ro. *My lovely, brave mum.* The knowledge gave her a warming glow inside and a new resolve to stay strong.

———

Back at the homestead, Lucy telephoned Harry. 'You knew, didn't you?' she accused, as soon as she'd checked that he was okay.

'What did I know?'

'That I'd fall in love with Kalkadoon.'

She heard his soft chuckle. 'So, you don't mind it out there, eh?'

'Mind? Harry, it's amazing, awesome. I've been blown away. I can tell you already, I want to give it a damn good go.'

After a pause he said, 'Are you sure about that, Lucy? Have you had enough time to think it through?'

'Well, obviously there are all kinds of details to be sorted. I'd have to give notice to the army and, for the time being, I'd still like to move in with you, if you'll have me. But I do feel like I'm fit for the challenges here. There's a heap of stuff I need to learn, Harry. I know next to nothing about cattle, but from a logistical standpoint

I'm well and truly qualified.'

Harry chuckled again. 'That's all good to hear, love.'

'And I *adore* the old homestead.'

After a beat, he said, 'Have you asked yourself whether you'll be lonely out there? There won't be much social life for you.'

'I know, but don't worry, I've given that plenty of thought and, at this point in time, it's not really an issue.' Her enthusiasm for dating was currently sub zero. She really needed a spell from that scene. 'Where boyfriends are concerned, I've been there, done that.'

'I don't believe you, my girl.'

'Well, let's just say that dating is not currently top of my priorities.'

'And you don't have to make a decision overnight. You should definitely give it more thought, but I'm certainly pleased to hear you like the place.'

'There's no doubt about that. Now, you take care, Harry, won't you? I can't wait to get back to have a good old chat about this.'

'I'll look forward to it.'

'Love you heaps.'

Ro was in the kitchen fiddling with knobs on the ancient oven, which was slowly heating up their dinner: a frozen lasagne they'd brought from Townsville. 'I give up. We'll just have to be patient,' she said.

'Harry sends his love,' Lucy told her.

'Oh, good. How is he?'

'He says he's fine, but I thought he sounded tired.'

Ro nodded. 'It's probably just as well we only have another day here.' She dropped frozen greens into a saucepan of water. 'And how did he react when you told him you're keen to take this place on?'

'He's warning me not to rush into it, but I know he's pleased.'

Her mum shot her a quick glance. 'And you're still feeling confident?'

'I don't know about confident, but I'm certainly determined. If Nick Bloody Myatt can take on Penwall Hall, I can take on this place.'

This brought her mother's raised eyebrows. 'Who's Nick Bloody Myatt? One of the sons?'

Already regretting that she'd opened her big mouth, Lucy knew she'd only make things worse if she didn't answer. 'He's the elder son. Word on the street in Portreath was he saved the Penwall Hall estate single-handedly.'

Ro looked more interested than Lucy would have liked. 'He must be capable then.'

'I guess.'

'Sounds like he didn't make a very good impression, though. Perhaps he inherited unpleasant genes from you-know-who.'

Lucy shook her head. 'He can't have inherited from Alice. She couldn't have children and Nick's father was adopted.' She frowned. 'Didn't you know your cousins were adopted?'

'I'm not sure. I might have been told.' Her mum turned down the heat under the saucepan and then she shot Lucy a searching glance. 'This Nick Bloody Myatt didn't hurt you, did he, love?'

'Hurt me?' Lucy echoed, stalling, because she couldn't think of an appropriate way to answer.

'I've wondered if something happened over there to upset you.'

In a sudden moment of weakness, Lucy almost told her mother everything. It was so tempting to simply offload the truth about Nick and her terrible disappointment, but then she remembered how unproductive it would be to drag all that into the open now, when she was trying so desperately to bury it and forget.

'No, Mum, Nick Bloody Myatt didn't hurt me. He was very charming.' In an effort to look as calm and unruffled as possible, Lucy leaned back against a tall cupboard and folded her arms. 'So, what colour paint do you think would go well in this kitchen?'

33

Keen to make the most of their last day at Kalkadoon, Lucy and Ro drove in the Pajero along a graded track to distant parts of the property, where they made billy tea beside a lagoon and took a host of photographs for Harry.

They photographed the reflection of trees in the reed-fringed lagoon, a flock of emus in a paddock and a mob of silvery cattle with white egrets on their backs. They took a few selfies of the two of them against a variety of scenic backdrops – a fallen log in a creek bed, at the foot of a bright red cliff, and leaning on a weathered timber gate.

On their return to the homestead, they had a quick sandwich and cuppa and then Lucy took Ro down the track along the riverbank that led to Georgina's clifftop grave. Ro knelt for ages, gazing at the headstone, and Lucy, respecting her mother's need for silence, could only guess what she was thinking and remembering and feeling.

'I love this,' Ro said at last, reading from the inscription. 'This last line: *Remember me, won't you?*'

'I know.' Lucy dropped to the grass beside her. 'It's gorgeous, isn't it? I think it's the same message George wrote to Harry on the back of her photograph.'

'Oh yes, of course, that's where I've seen it.' Her mother shivered and rubbed her arms. 'Gosh, that's so romantic. It's given me goosebumps.'

'I think theirs must have been a very special romance,' Lucy said quietly. 'When you think about how they met in England during the war, then they were in New Guinea together fleeing the Japanese, and afterwards how Harry went to England to brave Penwall Hall to ask George to marry him. And she came out here to Kalkadoon to such a different lifestyle.'

'Yes, it was all pretty amazing.' Tears glittered in her mum's eyes. 'I wish she'd lived longer.'

Lucy nodded, thinking how devastated Harry must have been to lose his precious George, thinking, too, how different her mother's life might have been if George had been there to guide her, if Harry hadn't been left, grief-stricken and alone, to struggle in the outback, a single father. 'If George had lived, I guess you wouldn't have had to go away to England.'

'That's true, but I can hardly blame her for that.' Ro pulled at a weed growing close to the headstone. 'I just would have liked to have known her. I know so little about her, really, but I – I never asked Dad. I was so angry with him, so damn selfish and pigheaded.' Dropping the weed, she pressed the back of her hand to her mouth, as the tears spilled.

'Hey.' Lucy slipped an arm around her mother's shoulders. 'I reckon you need to give yourself a break. You've been hard on yourself for too long.'

Her mum nodded, found a tissue and wiped her eyes and then together they diligently cleared away the grass and the weeds, and left a vase with half-a-dozen of Georgina's lovely pink roses. They also took more photographs for Harry.

Their work done, they stood for a few moments, looking at the neatly cleared site and the vase of roses, at the setting of the grassy headland and the river below. Lucy looked up at the sky, half-expecting to see another falcon, but today there were only soft white clouds.

Her mother let out a heavy sigh. 'So much we'll never know.'

'I guess every generation has its secrets,' Lucy said.

'That's true enough.' Her mother shot her a glance. 'Are you going to tell me yours?'

'Hardly.' Lucy managed to smile, but she wished she felt happier.

They left then and made their way back down along the track beside the river.

'I do feel as if we've achieved quite a lot in the last couple of days,' Ro said. 'Even though I still feel guilty about staying away from Kalkadoon for so long.'

'Well, we're here now and that's what counts. And Harry's happy.'

'Thank God I didn't leave it any longer. I'm so glad I came with you, Luce.'

As they emerged from the shady bush into bright sunlight, Lucy found herself squinting. The open paddock ahead was flooded with afternoon sunshine, and the sun caused a white flash as it hit a wind-screen up near the homestead.

'I didn't bother with my sunglasses,' she complained, lifting a hand to shield her eyes.

'Mine won't be any use to you. They're prescription.'

Lucy shrugged. They helped each other through the barbed-wire fence, placing a boot on the lower wire while holding up the one above, and then together they headed across the paddock.

'I wonder who that is,' her mum said.

'Who?'

'Whoever's arrived in that red four-wheel drive. I'm sure it just arrived.'

Lucy squinted in the vehicle's direction, but the sun was straight in her eyes, blinding her.

'It looks very bright and shiny, like a hire car,' her mum commented as they got closer.

'Might be tourists who've lost their way.'

'Wow,' Ro said, a few steps later. 'A pretty classy tourist.'

Curious, Lucy lifted both hands to shade her eyes and now she could see that a man was standing beside the vehicle. Tall, broad shouldered. Unruly black hair.

Her knees gave way. Literally. They simply unhinged, and she stumbled.

'Easy there, love.' Her mum caught her by the elbow.

Lucy was quite sure she couldn't walk another step. She felt faint. She must be hallucinating. Seeing a mirage. She'd spent too long in the sun.

'What's the matter, Luce? Are you okay?'

It seemed she'd also lost the power of speech.

'Lucy?'

The newcomer was walking towards them now. A long-legged figure in a milky blue, long-sleeved shirt and jeans.

Lucy's heart was banging hard, turning her chest into a punching bag. The thuds pounded in her ears.

She was aware of her mum's look of worried concern, but then her mother turned from her to the stranger. 'Hello,' she greeted him warmly.

'Hello.' The single word was enough to convey the high-class, deep resonance of his voice.

'Oh, you're English,' her mum said, ever so slightly gushing.

Lucy kept her eyes lowered, but she knew he was looking directly at her.

'How are you, Lucy?'

This wasn't real. It couldn't be real. How on earth had he got here?

Why had he come here?

'You know Lucy?' Her poor mum was, of course, now thoroughly confused.

With great effort, Lucy lifted her gaze. Just a glimpse of Nick Myatt's dark eyes caused a ridiculous zap, but a second glimpse showed that he also looked rather tense, as well he might.

She prayed that her trembling wasn't visible. 'Nick,' she said stiffly. 'This is unexpected.'

'I know. I do apologise for the lack of warning.'

'I'm Ro.' Her mother seemed very eager as she held out her hand. 'Lucy's mother.'

With a courteous dip of his head, Nick shook her proffered hand. 'Very pleased to meet you, Mrs Hunter. Nick Myatt.'

A gasp burst from her mum and her mouth formed an O, but no sound came out. Instead she took off her sunglasses and turned to Lucy, her eyes wide and questioning. A silent *what the fuck*?

But as the stunned cogs in Lucy's brain began to chug slowly back to life, she addressed Nick rather than her mother. 'How did you find us?'

'Your grandfather told me that you were out here.'

This still didn't make sense. 'I was talking to Harry last night and he didn't say a word about you.'

'I think he'd just finished speaking with you on the phone when I knocked on his front door. I called at the apartment first – that was the address you left with Jane Nancarrow at the B&B – and I spoke to Keith Hayes who was also very helpful.'

'Yes, Keith would be only too happy to help,' said Ro, all smiles.

'And then Mr Kemp kindly offered to accompany me out here,' Nick said.

'Accompany you?' Lucy frowned. 'You brought Harry with you?'

'Yes. I had reservations, but he claimed that he couldn't simply tell me where you were. He had to come and show me. I'm afraid he was quite insistent.'

In unison Ro and Lucy turned their attention to the parked car again.

The front passenger door was now open and there was Harry, waving to them.

'For heaven's sake.' Ro hurried forward.

Lucy followed, shaking her head. 'But I still don't understand.'

Harry was out of the car by the time they reached him, moving stiffly, but with a huge smile on his face. 'Hello there,' he called, grinning broadly. 'How's this for a surprise?'

'You can say that again, Dad.' Ro gave him a kiss. 'Are you sure you're all right?'

Lucy kissed Harry, too, and his grey eyes twinkled. He certainly didn't seem any worse for wear after the long car journey.

'What's this all about?' Ro demanded again. 'I thought you weren't up to coming all this way?'

'Yes, I know I told you that, Ro, but I wanted you and Lucy to look at the place on your own – without having to please me. But then I spoke to Lucy last night and you two were having such a good time out here, and I realised I'd really like to see the old place again.' Harry nodded towards Nick. 'Next thing you know, Nick came along and we got chatting, and well, here we are.'

'Chatting?' Lucy shot an anxious glance in Nick's direction.

Ro was eyeing Nick as well, and looking as puzzled as ever.

Of course, this was Nick's cue to give Ro one of his most charming smiles. 'I explained to Mr Kemp that I mismanaged Lucy's farewell in England. That I'd made a bloody mess of things, actually, and I wanted apologise.'

'Oh, I see.' In a matter of moments, Ro was beaming again, and she looked ridiculously excited as she turned and whispered to Lucy. 'Are you okay with this?'

'I guess,' Lucy whispered back, although her definition of okay was decidedly dicey at this point in time.

Apparently satisfied, her mother announced a tad smugly, 'Well, how about I help you upstairs, Dad. I'll make you a nice cup of tea. You're probably ready for a lie down as well.' She was clearly pleased with this brilliant idea and she was almost smirking at Lucy as she added, 'Then you and Nick can have a good chat.'

Nick gave an appreciative nod, while Lucy felt a wild desire to scurry after her mum and Harry to the safety of a cup of tea at the homestead but, of course, she was even more desperate to hear what Nick had to say. She knew she had to be careful, though. Her initial shock was receding, making way for dangerous emotions like excitement and hope, which she hastily quashed. This was no time for losing her head. She needed commonsense by the truckload to protect her vulnerable heart. And she had to remember that she'd made an important decision about Kalkadoon and she'd given her word to Harry, so even if Nick wanted her back, she wasn't available.

'Perhaps we should go back down to the river,' she told him, knowing that at least they would have privacy down there, but she covered this reason with a more practical excuse. 'You're not wearing a hat and there are shady trees.'

She felt exceedingly fragile as she and Nick walked side by side, their long shadows stretching ahead of them over the pale golden grass.

When they reached the trees, a welcome cool breeze swept up from the water. They stopped at a grassy bank with smooth rocks that were perfect for sitting. Lucy sat quickly and took off her hat, running her fingers through her hair and lifting the hot, damp tresses from her neck.

Nick's dark eyes watched every movement and the muscles in his throat worked.

'Why don't you take a seat,' Lucy said, sounding rather like a formal hostess as she pointed to a convenient boulder a few feet away.

Nick, however, remained standing as if he was too tense to sit. He already had an unfair height advantage, but now he towered over her and, despite her somersaulting emotions, she couldn't help noticing that he looked at home here in this alien landscape. In workmanlike blue jeans and with his long-sleeves rolled up to reveal naturally tanned, capable forearms, he looked ready for action and as in tune with the backdrop of melaleucas, bottlebrush trees and dazzling blue sky as he had amidst Cornwall's grey skies and cliffs and smashing waves.

Scrambling to her feet once more, she felt a need to state the obvious. 'You've come a long way.'

Nick nodded. 'As I told your mother, I've come to apologise, Lucy. I'm sorrier than you could ever imagine about sending you off the way I did. It was an unforgivable overreaction.'

She'd resolved to remain calm and aloof. Now a flame of hope stirred, but she quickly snuffed it. There was no point in getting excited. She had made her decision.

'I let the whole business of Simon and the army get in the way,' Nick said. 'When you arrived in Cornwall I was already in danger of letting it cripple me. But then, in those few days with you, I discovered that I wanted to get on with life and living.'

He tried for a smile but didn't quite manage it. 'You helped me to see what it was like to be happy again. And the reason I've come is simple, Lucy. I've missed you.'

Oh, help. She hadn't been prepared for such an honest admission. And Nick looked endearingly nervous. A shimmer in his gorgeous dark eyes suggested he was as vulnerable as she was and the thought almost brought her undone.

'I've missed your smile,' he said. 'Your warmth, your lively spirit. I missed you so much more than I could possibly have dreamed.'

Lucy wanted to tell him that she'd missed him, too, but she didn't dare. Somehow she had to find the strength to explain that she was no longer available – she had new commitments.

'But I haven't come here to make demands,' Nick said next and the sincerity in his dark gaze caused a new hitch in her breathing. 'I'm not asking you to leave the army. I came because I needed to talk to you face to face, to find out how you're feeling now, whether there's any chance – even though I don't deserve a chance – of sorting something out.'

Somehow, Lucy suppressed a whimper of despair. This had been her fantasy. Throughout the long journey on the plane back from England, she'd dreamed of an impossible scenario exactly like this, like something out of a romantic movie, where Nick chased after her to tell her he'd made a terrible mistake and he wanted another chance.

And she would have given him that other chance. So gladly.

Now, the impossible had actually happened and she wanted to hurl herself into his arms, to press her face into his massive chest. Desperately, she longed for him to hold her and to murmur gorgeous promises in his gorgeous English voice.

But she couldn't give Nick any sign of hope. Not now, not less than twenty-four hours after she'd committed herself to a future here. At Kalkadoon.

'Nick, I'm sorry.'

'I know I don't deserve —'

'It's not a matter of deserving,' she said quickly. 'It's just lousy timing.' Tears threatened and she blinked madly. 'I have another commitment, you see, and I've already given my word.'

To her dismay the colour leached from his face. 'What's happened?' Despite his pallor, his gaze was fierce. 'Have you gone back to your boyfriend? You're going to marry him?'

'No. God, no. It's not a guy, Nick.' She felt sick and dragged in a gulping breath, hoping it would steady her. 'It's this *place*,' she said. 'I'm committed to this property.' And then she hurried to explain.

'Well, not immediately. I want to spend as much time as I can with my grandfather. He might look well enough to you, but he's not at all well, really, and he's leaving me Kalkadoon in his will, and I —'

The enormity of it overwhelmed Lucy. She was trembling with the effort of holding back her tears, but she knew she had to get this over, make the cut quick and clean. Get it all out and crush Nick's hopes now before he said lovely things that would break her heart again.

'I'm sorry,' she said again and her voice was shaky and high pitched but she forced the words out. 'I've given Harry my word.'

Unable to bear the look on his face, she closed her eyes.

'Lucy.'

She opened her eyes but kept them fixed on the ground as she answered. 'Yes?'

'I think you're right.' Nick spoke with astonishing calm. 'We need to sit down to talk about this.'

'But there's nothing to —'

Fearfully, she looked towards him and he was already moving to the rock that she'd pointed out earlier.

Feeling sick and shaken and completely bewildered, she lowered herself to her rock. What on earth could they discuss? Everything was decided.

'I'd like to get this straight,' Nick said, sounding surprisingly composed now. 'You're returning to Townsville, to the army.'

'Yes. I want to apply for a discharge, but I have to give three months' notice.'

'And you plan to care for your grandfather?'

Lucy nodded. 'We have no idea how long he has.'

'Of course.' Looking at ease now, with the sun glinting on his black hair, Nick leaned forward with his elbows casually resting on his knees. 'But, in due course, you plan to return here to Kalkadoon.'

Lucy nodded. 'Under the terms of the will, I won't be able to sell the property for four years, and I've told Harry that I'll come here and have a darned good crack at running it.'

'I see.' To her surprise Nick still didn't look the slightest bit concerned.

'What do you see?'

'That if I decided to stay in Australia I'd be courting an heiress.'

She gasped. Had he really said those words *stay* and *courting*?

Keep your head, Lucy. Don't drop your bundle now. 'I'd be a very busy heiress with responsibility for several thousand head of cattle.'

Nick nodded rather solemnly. 'And I suppose this responsibility would involve living out here in this wonderfully wild country? Perhaps riding horses and camping out under the stars, or helping to muster all those thousands of cattle? Possibly wrestling the odd crocodile or two?'

'All of the above, I imagine.' She chanced a smile. 'Well, maybe not the crocs.'

Beside them, a dragonfly flitted across the water like a miniature bronze helicopter.

Nick sat a little straighter. 'Could you possibly see me fitting into that picture?'

The really crazy thing was that she could see Nick here, but she felt compelled to protect herself from yet another round of hurt and disappointment. 'But you're English,' she said. 'You're used to green fields and sea cliffs and bluebells – and London and everything – and this place is so remote. It's not looking too bad just now after the rain, but there could easily be another drought, or a cyclone and floods.'

'Your grandmother was English, but that didn't stop her from having a happy life out here.'

So true. A corner of Lucy's heart was overjoyed by Nick's persistence, but in the interests of her emotional security, she felt compelled to throw hurdles in his path. 'Don't you have to look after Penwall Hall?'

'I've done my bit for the Hall and, as I think I told you in Cornwall, with a good manager in place, it can look after itself now.'

'I – I see.'

The water in the creek was so still she could see their reflections. Dressed alike in jeans and sitting on their rocks with a backdrop of khaki bush and blue sky, they looked like a photograph in a glossy magazine. An ideal outback couple . . .

'I'm not proposing we rush into anything, Lucy. We both have things to sort out and you need to care for your grandfather. But I thought, perhaps – if you wanted – I could come back and spend some time here and help you.'

Lucy's heartbeats were racing, but she did her best to sound calm. 'You'd like to help me run Kalkadoon?'

'I'd like that very much.'

She knew he was speaking the truth. In England he'd dropped several hints about his fascination with the Aussie outback, and he was a man of enterprise. He would probably relish a new business challenge like Kalkadoon. There was every chance that he would love it here.

'Would it be a kind of trial run?'

'That's what I'm thinking.' His brown eyes now held a heady mix of tenderness and desire and hope. 'A trial run for both of us.'

For the first time since he'd arrived, Lucy felt the knots in her stomach and shoulders loosen. A trial run for both of them. She smiled. 'I think that might be a workable plan.'

'Good.' Nick was on his feet now and closing the gap between them. He reached for her hand and his fingers were warm and strong around hers. Their touch was all she needed. With a glad cry, she leaped into his arms.

'I've missed you so much.' Such a relief to tell him at last.

'I felt wretched when I sent you packing.'

'I've been miserable.'

'Poor Lucy. You know I'm in love with you.'

'Oh, Nick.' It was too soon to be talking of love. This was only a trial run, after all. They had both been burned and were cautious about second chances and yet she felt a wonderfully deep-rooted confidence in this new decision. It felt right. Gloriously perfect.

Winding her arms around his neck, she whispered, 'You know I'm mad about you.'

He pulled her close then and kissed her. Not the fast and hungry kiss she expected, but a slow and very thorough kiss, a deeply satisfying kiss that took a lovely long time.

When at last they drew apart, he was smiling.

'Not a bad start for a trial run,' she suggested.

'Not bad at all.' Then he gave her a cheeky grin. 'I can't wait for the real thing.'

———

Ro and Harry had finished their cups of tea, and Ro was sitting on the verandah while Harry rested inside when she saw her daughter and the delicious Englishman emerge from the line of trees that fringed the creek.

Instantly anxious to read their body language, she noted with relief that they both looked relaxed as they strolled across the paddock, dark heads close together, clearly deep in conversation. Every so often Lucy would give an animated wave of her hand as if to emphasise a point she was making. Then Nick must have said something that made her laugh.

They laughed together, almost doubling over, their faces alight and glowing with unmistakable happiness. A moment later, Nick slipped an arm around Lucy's shoulders and dipped his head to whisper in her ear. Quite possibly, he even nibbled at her ear. Her daughter looked radiant.

Ro almost hugged herself with delight. Just as she'd hoped from the moment she met him, Nick Bloody Myatt seemed to be fast becoming Nick Mr-Perfect Myatt.

When they reached the bottom of the homestead steps, they stood for a moment, looking back behind them at the flat stretch of paddocks and the trees that lined the creek. Ro decided there was something especially right about the picture of this tall dark-haired couple, both dressed in casual blue jeans and standing together. They reminded her of another couple who had stood right there on that same spot, looking just as happy as she'd toddled towards them on chubby little legs.

Ro felt a deep sense of satisfaction. It was so good to stop worrying about Lucy, or about her own relationship with her father, or about her and Keith. Her only problems this afternoon were practical ones. There were two more staying the night in the homestead and she would have to speak to Doug and June about extra bedding, but she wasn't sure what she could do about dinner. There was only a Lean Cuisine left in the esky and it couldn't possibly stretch to feed four. A strapping young man like Nick was sure to have a good appetite.

She was still pondering this hostessing dilemma as Lucy and Nick crossed the grass to the red hire car. She saw Nick open the back door and the two of them began to unpack the things stowed in there – rolled-up swags, a huge esky, carrier bags with bottles of wine.

'Oh my,' Ro said aloud. It seemed that Nick Bloody Myatt was not only impossibly handsome, he was also resourceful.

Grinning happily, Lucy turned back to her and waved. 'We've enough here for a party,' she called.

34

Harry was tired, so tired these days that the weariness seemed to have settled permanently into his bones. While the others were busy, he was pleased to be left reclining in a squatter's chair on the verandah, admiring his favourite view, of Kalkadoon's paddocks and the trees along the creek.

From here, he could hear Ro bustling about in the kitchen and washing their breakfast things. They'd had quite a feast, both this morning and last night, dining on the delicious food Nick had miraculously produced. Now, Lucy was taking Nick on a quick tour of the property, or as much of the property as she'd discovered in the past couple of days.

Harry thought about the two young people discovering Kalkadoon together and he liked the idea very much. He'd been feeling very pleased about that pair ever since yesterday afternoon, when Lucy had tiptoed into his room while he was resting.

'Hi, Harry,' she'd whispered and he'd seen immediately that her eyes were shining with happiness.

'Hello, love.'

'Are you okay? You look a bit pale.' Gently, she pressed her hand to his cheek. 'Are you sure it was a good idea to talk Nick into bringing you all the way out here?'

'I'm fine, Lucy, don't worry and don't blame Nick. This is exactly what I wanted. Where I wanted to be.'

'It's wonderful that you were able to come.'

And then, as she'd perched on the end of his bed, he'd asked, carefully, 'So you and your Englishman have had a good talk?'

'Yes, we have.' There was an immediate softening in her expression.

'He seems a likeable bloke.'

'You think so? Do you like Nick?'

Harry chuckled. 'I've always thought first impressions were important and I liked him straight off. I wouldn't have brought him out here if I didn't think he was up to scratch.'

'That's what I told myself. I'm so pleased you approve of him, Harry.'

She looked so very happy, as if her happiness was bubbling up and spilling over like a fountain.

I got it right, Harry thought with relief. The other bloke his granddaughter had almost married had never made her look like that.

'Thanks for bringing Nick out here,' Lucy said next. 'You know he's mad about this place, already. He loves it.'

''Course he does. Why wouldn't he?'

'Actually, he's interested in helping me to run Kalkadoon.'

'Is he now?' Harry wasn't at all surprised. During their day's journey from Townsville, Nick Myatt had asked all manner of pertinent and intelligent questions about the cattle business. 'And how do you feel about that?'

'Pretty damn happy,' Lucy admitted, blushing. 'Maybe over the moon.'

'Then I'm maybe over the moon, too.'

They had hugged then and Lucy had told him that they were planning a bit of a party – Nick had brought beautiful steaks and salad, as well as cheese and wine and Turkish delight for dessert.

'Do you think you're up for a small celebration?'

Harry chuckled. 'Try and stop me.'

And yes, it had been a feast to remember. The neglected homestead had limitations as a setting for a party, but Ro and Lucy had done their best to make the kitchen festive.

Lucy picked stems of bright-red bottlebrush, which she arranged in a wide-mouthed jar. And in the back of the pantry she found the candles that were used for blackouts. These candles, set in saucers and lit, transformed the old dresser, making the drab piece of furniture in need of a coat of paint look exceptionally pretty and romantic.

There were no wine glasses to be found, but Lucy washed out tumblers that had once been Vegemite jars and polished them with a tea towel until they shone.

Ro found a spare green-and-white striped sheet, which she spread as a tablecloth over the scarred and scratched table and then set about cutting and slicing ingredients for a salad, while Nick tackled the ancient stove and somehow produced very professionally seared steaks.

Harry, meanwhile, sat in an old rocking chair, in a corner of the roomy kitchen, out of the way, enjoying watching the proceedings with great satisfaction. It was such a pleasure to see Ro looking flushed and happy, setting the table or handing around plates of cheese and crackers, and to see the young couple, so clearly in love. Harry sensed a wonderful lightheartedness in the room, a newborn happiness that travelled like a current between all four of them – himself, his daughter, his granddaughter and her Englishman.

Nick uncorked and poured the wine, a good full-bodied red.

'Just a little for Harry,' Ro warned. And then, raising her glass,

'What should our toast be to?'

There was a momentary awkward pause as she sent a rather pointed glance Lucy's way.

'To Kalkadoon?' asked Nick diplomatically, and Harry decided he liked the man more than ever.

'Yes,' agreed Lucy, smiling and lifting her glass to salute them all. 'To Kalkadoon and to all who've ever sailed in her, or lived on her soil.'

This was met by laughter and a clinking of glasses and there was a general mood of jollity as they sat down to eat.

And now, this morning. Harry didn't blame last night's celebration for his weariness, although he had enjoyed the evening immensely. He was simply old – far too old . . .

This morning, Doug had called in and they'd had a good chinwag over a cuppa, discussing the hopes they shared for Kalkadoon's future. Doug hadn't been able to stay long, though, as he was expecting a phone call from a fuel supplier in Mt Isa. And now, as a flock of white cockatoos swept across the pristine outback sky and a magpie sang in the distance, Harry rested his head on the padded back of the squatter's chair and closed his eyes. It was warm in the sun and he drifted off pleasantly, picturing Lucy and her Englishman living and working here at Kalkadoon.

He remembered how he'd crossed hemispheres, just as Nick Myatt had done, to seek out the woman he loved. He thought about his dear Georgina and how very happy they'd been here together. And now another young couple, the *right* young couple, were starting over again.

Full circle.

Contented, he dozed, the drowsiness claiming him and soothing him, like the rhythm of a train. It wasn't long before he could actually hear the steady rattle of a carriage and the hum of wheels. And then, he felt the warm weight of a head resting on his shoulder, a neat nose burrowed against his neck.

A movement woke him. He opened his eyes and there, sitting on the homestead verandah right beside him, was the loveliest girl. She had honey-brown, wavy hair and hazel eyes and the softest white skin imaginable. She was dressed in a British army uniform.

She was George. *His* darling George.

At last.

He'd been waiting so long.

'Oh, hello,' she said and her cheeks went very pink, as if she was embarrassed that she'd been caught with her head on his shoulder, but her eyes were shining, as if she was also rather pleased.

Harry smiled at her. 'G'day.'

ACKNOWLEGDEMENTS

As always, there were many people who helped me to produce this book. I'm particularly grateful to the authors of the research books I used. It was more than a decade ago that I first read about the last London season in 1939 and, ever since, the idea of the debs whose lives were forever changed by World War Two has nagged to be in one of my stories. More recently, I was inspired by history books about the war in the Pacific, especially the fate of Lark Force in New Britain. I've tried to keep the history accurate, but in the interests of telling my particular story, some important details may not have been included.

I'd like to also extend a big thanks to those who helped with keeping the contemporary thread of this story true to life. Michelle Bird gave traditional owner cultural advice, John Andersen helped with cattle country background, and a patient Aussie soldier answered my questions about returning from deployment in Afghanistan. Thanks to all of you and thanks, too, to Louis Simon for additional proofreading help.

I am particularly grateful to the wonderful team at Penguin Australia, especially to Ali Watts for her invaluable and sensitive advice. Thanks also for the care and attention paid by Clementine Edwards, Fay Helfenbaum and Sonja Heijn, and to Louise Ryan for her enthusiasm and for making sure I took George into the palace.

Once again, the person who has earned my biggest vote of thanks is my amazing husband, Elliot, my brainstorming and research partner, my first reader and my unfailing cheer squad.

Read on for a sneak peek of

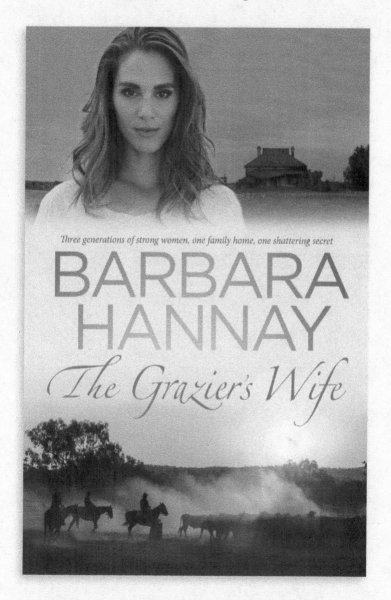

Three generations of strong women, one family home, one shattering secret

BARBARA HANNAY

The Grazier's Wife

Brought to you by Penguin Books

PROLOGUE

Ruthven Downs, Far North Queensland, 1970

Her husband was asleep at last.

Stella Drummond stood in the bedroom doorway, watching the steady rise and fall of Magnus's chest. He was sprawled on his back, fully clothed in stained moleskins, a checked flannel shirt and navy blue socks. She had managed to remove his elastic-sided boots when he'd collapsed on the bed, but she knew he was past caring about pyjamas.

His jaw was bristly white with at least two days' growth, his thick, grey-flecked hair a dishevelled coxcomb against the pillow, and his mouth hung open to reveal the gap where he'd lost a molar.

This was how Magnus always slept when he'd been drinking. Soon he would be snoring.

Stella was all too familiar with the pattern. After a day of uncommunicative moodiness, her husband would spend the evening drowning his sorrows in whisky. The drinking was accompanied by roaring outbursts of rage and crises of logic which were often directed towards her, and she had no choice but to endure the tirades until at last he was overcome by blessed sleep. Then she could breathe a sigh of relief. The ordeal was over.

This evening, however, Stella felt no sweet ripple of relief. She was shaking with a harrowing fear.

This latest rage had been by far Magnus's worst. Tonight there were consequences. Magnus hadn't merely given voice to his anger. He'd taken pen to paper and had written instructions for his lawyer, horrifying instructions that broke Stella's heart. And filled her with guilt.

Now, a snore erupted from the sleeping figure, a snore so loud she feared the noise would wake him. Swiping at her wretched tears, she turned out the light and swiftly left the room. Timber floorboards creaked as she made her way down the darkened passage to the study where a standard lamp cast a pool of yellow light over Magnus's desk and the dreaded white envelope.

Addressed in Magnus's thick, dark scrawl to Kenneth Woods, his lawyer, the envelope was sealed, but Stella already knew its contents. Magnus had made sure of that. He'd read his legal directive to her in his pompous, booming voice, taking sneering delight when he saw how badly it shocked her.

Naturally, he'd ignored her tearful pleas. 'Don't you bloody dare cry over spilt milk. You only have yourself to blame. You should have thought about the consequences before you snuck away with your fancy man.'

At least he hadn't been physically violent. Despite his increasingly drunken rages, Magnus had never raised a hand to Stella and she was grateful for that. She was grateful, too, that both their children were far away in Brisbane – Deb in her last year of art college and Hugh halfway through his university degree. She would have hated them to hear their father swearing at her as he had this evening, yelling and waving his fist as he hurled terrible accusations in her face. Accusations that were, sadly, true.

For Stella, however, the vile descriptions that still echoed in her head could never sully the beauty of the precious time she'd stolen to be with Tom Kearney. She could never regret going to Cairns to meet him. Those few, too brief, blissful days would be forever enshrined in her memory, bright and unsullied.

Deep within in her, she nursed a reassuring certainty that her memories of Tom would sustain her through whatever grim trials life, or her husband, chose to throw at her. Her only regret was that all these years later, Magnus had finally, mysteriously, found out about Tom.

Predictably, Magnus had overreacted and jumped to wild, irrational conclusions, with the result that he'd insisted on making these drastic changes to his will. Now he planned to drive to Burralea tomorrow to deliver his instructions to their lawyer.

This was to be her punishment, but the changes he'd ordered were totally unreasonable. Crazy. Fuelled by jealousy and based on wrong assumptions.

Unfortunately, Stella knew that her husband wouldn't listen to reason, especially not from her, and although Kenneth Woods was an old family friend as well as their lawyer she doubted that even he would be able to change Magnus's mind. Her husband's pig-headedness knew no bounds.

With a heavy sigh, Stella picked up the envelope, handling it cautiously between her thumb and forefinger, as if it were a bomb. She slipped it into the pocket of her apron, then made her way through the house to the verandah outside.

The night sky was filled with clouds, without a glimmer from moon or stars. Stella leaned forward, resting her forearms on the verandah railing, and looked out into a blackness so complete she felt smothered by it.

Down by the creek the mournful cry of a curlew drifted into the night in a soul-searing wail of despair.

I know how you feel, she told it silently and, despite the warm spring evening, she was swamped by a wave of hopelessness.

She shook the feeling aside. There was danger in indulging in maudlin thoughts and she turned her mind instead to memories of her arrival here at Ruthven Downs as a bride, remembering how she'd loved the homestead at first sight. She'd entered this marriage determined to be a good wife and mother and, for the most part, she'd succeeded. It had only been in recent years that Magnus's drinking had spoiled the delicate harmony she'd worked so hard to maintain.

Until now she'd managed to keep her marriage and her family on an even keel, and tonight she had to remain strong. Her son's future and the future of the Drummond family's vast cattle property now depended on her. She had to keep a cool head and to think this problem through.

Even the bleakest situations could be turned around. There was always a solution, and she was grateful for the crucial lesson she'd learned many years ago. Too late.

She must never, *never* give up hope.

1

Ruthven Downs, 2014

It had been a long day in the stockyards. As Seth Drummond drove his ute back down the winding, dusty track to the homestead, his thoughts were focused on creature comforts. A hot shower, a fried steak with onions, and beer. Not necessarily in that order.

Rounding the last bend, he dipped his Akubra against the setting sun and saw the familiar spread of the home paddocks and the horse yards, their timber fences weathered to silvery grey. Beyond the low, sprawling, iron-roofed homestead with its deep verandahs and hanging baskets of ferns, a huge old poinciana tree shaded the house from the western sun.

At the perimeter of the paddocks, a meandering line of paperbarks marked the course of the creek and, as the setting sun's rays lengthened, the distant hills became folds of rumpled velvet beneath an arching sky that deepened from pale blue to mauve.

Seth had lived here all his life, but he never tired of this view, especially at the end of the day when the landscape was dappled with shadows and light.

Today, however, a strange car was parked near the homestead's front steps. The small, bright-purple sedan looked out of place in this dusty rural setting.

Visitors.

On the passenger's seat at Seth's side, the blue cattle dog pricked up his ears and stiffened.

'Yeah, know how you feel, Ralph.' Seth gave the dog's neck a sympathetic scruff. 'I'm beat. Not in the mood for visitors.'

He edged the ute forward and as he did so, a figure rose from a squatter's chair on the verandah. A girl in slim blue jeans and a white T-shirt. She had a mane of thick, pale tawny hair, dead straight to her shoulders.

Recognising her, Seth let out a low whistle.

Joanna Dixon, the English backpacker, had scored a job as camp cook on last year's muster. She'd cooked a mean curry in the camp oven and she'd coped well on the job, giving as good as she got when the ringers labelled her the Pommy jillaroo and teased her about her toffy English accent.

Pretty in a slim, tomboyish way, with surprisingly cool, blue eyes, Joanna had also flirted with Seth rather blatantly. But his job had been to lead the mustering team, not to be sidetracked by the chance of a roll in the swag with the hired help.

He had no idea what Joanna was doing back here now, but his recollections were suddenly cut off. Joanna was bending down to lift something from a basket on the verandah.

A small bundle. *A baby.*

Seth cast a quick glance across the homestead and lawns, but there was no sign of another woman. Joanna was holding the baby against her shoulder now, patting it with a practised air.

Fine hairs lifted on the back of his neck. He went cold all over. *No, surely not.*

After the muster last year, Joanna had moved away from the district to pick bananas at a farm near Tully. Seth hadn't expected to see her again, and he'd been surprised when she'd turned up at the

Mareeba rodeo a couple of weeks later, all smiles and long legs in skinny white jeans. She'd greeted him like a long-lost friend and had mingled easily with his circle of friends.

They'd enjoyed a few laughs, a few drinks. Later that night, primed with rum and cokes, Joanna had knocked on his motel door. He hadn't turned her away that time.

Yanking a sharp rein on his galloping thoughts, Seth parked the ute next to her car. He drew several deep breaths and took his time killing the motor. There had to be a sensible explanation for this, an explanation that did not involve him.

Determined to show no sign of panic, he got out of the vehicle slowly. 'Stay here,' he told Ralph as the dog slipped out behind him.

Obedient as ever, the blue heeler sat in the red dust by the ute's front wheel, his eyes and ears alert. The girl on the verandah settled the baby in her arms. Seth removed his Akubra and ran a hand through his hair. After an afternoon in the stockyards, he was dusty and grimy: he'd been branding, ear-tagging and vaccinating a new mob of weaners, fresh from the Mareeba sales. He left his hat on the bonnet as he strolled towards the three low steps that led to the verandah.

'Hi, Joanna.'

'Hello, Seth.'

'Long time no see.'

'Yes.' She looked nervous, which was *not* a good sign. The girl Seth remembered had been brash and overconfident.

'How long have you been waiting here?' he asked.

'Oh.' She gave a shy shrug. 'An hour or so.'

'That's quite a wait. Sorry there was no one to meet you. I'm afraid I'm the only one home at the moment.' He forced a smile but it only reached half-mast.. 'I thought you'd be back in England by now.'

'I'll be flying home quite soon.'

Relief swept through Seth. He'd been stupidly worrying about nothing. This wasn't what he'd feared. Joanna was leaving, going back to England.

'That's why I needed to see you.' Joanna dropped her gaze to the baby in her arms, then looked at Seth again. He could see now that her eyes were too big and too wide, displaying an emotion very close to fear.

Alarmed, Seth swallowed. His mind was racing again, trying to recall important details from that night over a year ago. Hadn't Joanna said she was on the pill?

He found himself staring at the baby, searching for clues, but it just looked cute and tiny like any other baby. Its hair was downy and golden as a duckling, and it had pink cheeks and round blue eyes. It was wearing a grey-and-red striped jumpsuit and he couldn't even tell if it was a boy or a girl.

He swallowed again. 'How can I help you, Joanna?'

Her mouth twisted, and she looked apologetic. So not a good sign. 'I've come to introduce you to Charlie.'

Whack.

'A – a boy?'

'Yes.'

Seth couldn't think. He was too busy panicking. 'Is – is he yours?' A stupid question, no doubt, but it was the best he could manage.

'Yes.' Joanna gave her lower lip a quick nervous chew. 'And he's yours too, Seth.'

Slam. It was like being thrown from a horse and finding himself on the ground, winded. Seth struggled to breathe. 'I don't understand.'

'I'm sorry.'

Joanna truly looked sorry. Unfortunately for Seth, this only compounded the situation. She'd always been so cool and confident, and now, to see tears glittering in her eyes, an incredible impossibility seemed scarily believable and – *damn it* – feasible.

'Didn't you . . . Weren't you on the pill?'

'Yes, but I'd started the pill mid-cycle and things hadn't settled down. Obviously, I should have been been more careful. I should have warned you, but I never dreamed . . . It was an accident, of course.'

Again she looked down at the baby lying in her arms. She touched his soft, hair. 'I nearly didn't go through with it. I was so close to having an abortion. I had it all booked and everything. But I – I knew he was yours.'

She looked up at Seth with a sad smile. 'At the last minute I knew I had to keep him, Seth. I realised I had this little person inside me and I knew that one day he could inherit all this.' She gave a nod towards the wide, bronzed stretch of the Ruthven Downs paddocks.

Seth could only stare at her. He had no words. He was numb, dumbstruck. Trying to take in the horrifying news.

'Charlie's three months old. You can have a DNA test, if you like, but I swear you're the only guy I slept with around then.' Lifting her chin, she eyed him steadily. 'You're his father, Seth. Your name is on his birth certificate. He's Charles Drummond.'

Seth still couldn't think straight, but he forced his legs to move, to mount the steps. 'You'd better come inside.'

'Right, thanks.' With surprising speed, Joanna scooped up a bulging zipper bag and the basket, which Seth now realised was actually one of those capsules for putting babies into cars.

It was a lot to juggle when she had the baby as well. He wasn't keen to help her. It would be like admitting to a truth he didn't want to accept, but the good manners ingrained in him from birth were too strong. He held out his hand. 'I'll take those.'

'Thank you.'

The homestead door wasn't locked. Propping it ajar with one elbow, Seth nodded for Joanna to precede him into the central hallway. 'Lounge room's on the right,' he said, knowing she'd never been in the house before. When she'd been on Ruthven Downs previously, she'd only ever slept in the ringers' quarters or in a swag under the stars.

Now he followed her into the lounge room, still furnished with the same old-fashioned chintz and silky oak sofas and armchairs that had been in the house since his grandparents' day. The long room was divided by a timber archway and at the far end was the dining area, dominated by a rather grand, mirror-backed sideboard where a collection of photos depicted the history of Seth's family. The Drummonds of Ruthven Downs.

Seth's great-grandfather Hamish Drummond was there in faded sepia, looking serious and heroic in his World War I army uniform. In another frame, his grandparents stood together on their wedding day – his grandfather Magnus looking ever so slightly smug. Then, his father, Hugh, as a baby in a long, white Christening robe. His parents, rugged up in thick coats and scarves, on their honeymoon in the Blue Mountains. Seth was there too, aged around ten. He and his sister were both on horseback.

There were even photos of his aunt and cousin.

Now, as Seth set the baby capsule and bag in a corner next to a faded gold-and-cream oriental rug, he felt as if the four generations of family photographs were somehow watching him. Reproaching him for fathering a bastard.

'Take a seat, Joanna.'

'Thank you.' She seemed as edgy as he was and she sat with a very straight back.

'Would you like a drink? Water? A cuppa?'

'I'm fine, thanks. I have a water bottle. I can't stay long.'

Seth frowned. He supposed he should be relieved that this was only a brief call. She was going back to England, so at least she wasn't planning to move in with him.

But there were so many questions. He was too tense to sit. 'How come this has taken so long?' He tried not to glare at her, but he had no hope of smiling. 'You've known about – about *him* for a year. Why suddenly decide to turn up now out of the blue?'

The baby gave a little mewing cry and she settled him against her shoulder and began to pat his back again. She drew a deep breath. 'Look, I know I haven't handled this well. For ages I tried to carry on as if the pregnancy wasn't really happening.'

After only the briefest pause, she hurried on with her story. 'I had a job on a property just outside of Broome, doing a little cooking and helping the kids with School of the Air. I often thought about getting in touch with you, coming to see you, but I – I was worried. I was worried about your family's reaction.'

Giving a sheepish half-smile, she quickly dropped her gaze. 'Then I saw on Facebook that your parents were away on holiday in Spain . . .'

A nasty chill streaked down Seth's spine. Joanna was spying on his family? He felt instantly defensive about his parents, who were away on their first overseas holiday, a long overdue luxury that they both deserved so much.

'You mentioned that you'll be leaving for England soon.'

'Yes.'

'And you're taking Charlie.'

'No, Seth.'

Seth had been standing, but now, blindsided, his knees caved and he sank swiftly into the armchair opposite her. The truth was suddenly, painfully obvious. Joanna was dumping the kid on him. That was why she'd come. Now, while the baby's grandparents were safely out of the country. She didn't have the guts to face them as well.

'I'm getting married, you see,' she said matter-of-factly. With her chin high and sounding more like the cool and 'together' girl that

Seth remembered, Joanna added, 'It's been planned for ages. My fiancé is Nigel Fox-Richards.'

After an expectant pause during which Seth made no response, she continued less certainly. 'We didn't have a formal engagement, but it was all settled before I left England. Nigel's family has an estate in Northumberland. They're – they're quite well off.'

'How jolly,' Seth responded bitterly.

She had the grace to blush.

'So how does that work?' Distaste lent a hard edge to his voice, but he was too angry to care. 'Were you allowed your little adventure in the colonies before you settled down to married life in the castle?'

'Well, I suppose it was more or less like that. Nigel had this list of adventures, you see – trekking the Himalayas, sailing to the West Indies, hugging polar bears or whatever. He wanted to tick them off before he got too busy with the estate and our life together, so we agreed on eighteen months. Now Nigel's father's health is failing and it's time to take on all sorts of responsibilities.'

Bizarrely, Seth could already picture Joanna fitting into that scene. She certainly had the posh accent and he could imagine her in skin-tight cream jodhpurs and knee-high boots, a riding crop tucked under one arm, a string of pearls around her tanned throat.

'How does Nigel feel about Charlie?'

'He doesn't know about Charlie.' Her mouth tightened and her eyes were suddenly hard and determined. 'He's not going to know about him. He can't. He mustn't. That's the thing, you see.'

'No, I don't see.' Seth was on his feet again now, too angry to sit. 'You'd better explain. Preferably in words of one syllable, so everything's perfectly clear.'

Joanna sat even straighter, shoulders squared. 'I can't take Charlie back to England, Seth. There's no way that Nigel's family would accept him.'